D0851515

PLUM
ORCHARD

OTHER BOOKS BY JUNE HALL McCASH

Almost to Eden
2011 Georgia Author of the Year Award for First Novel

Jekyll Island's Early Years:
From Prehistory through Reconstruction

The Jekyll Island Cottage Colony

The Jekyll Island Club:
Southern Haven for America's Millionaires
(co-author William Barton McCash)

The Life of Saint Audrey,
a Text by Marie de France
(co-editor and translator Judith Clark Barban)

The Cultural Patronage of Medieval Women
(edited by June Hall McCash)

Love's Fool: Aucassin, Troilus, Calisto,
and the Parody of the Courtly Lover

PLUM ORCHARD

*a Novel
of Cumberland Island*

JUNE HALL McCASH

TWIN
OAKS
PRESS

ISBN 978-0-9844354-9-4

First Edition

Printed in The United States of America

Twin Oaks Press
twinoakspress@gmail.com
www.twinoakspress.com

Cover and Interior design
by GKS Creative
Cover photo by Ron Messier; Map by Art Growden

The poem "Wild Plums" is used with permission of the author.
Originally published in *NOTICING EDEN*, Poems by Marjory Heath
Wentworth, Hub City Writers Project, 2003.

To Ron and Emily, with love and fond memories
of all our happy times together,
as well as gratitude for your unfailing support
in not-so-happy times.

WILD PLUMS

I have walked this way before. Many times,
along these tangled paths to the sea,
I have seen the cardinals flashing
from the sweet myrtle, watched lizards
raise their heads to point the arrows
of their eyes. When I move my hands
through their world of wild beach flowers,
the yellow petals bleed a little at the center
each time they burst into flower.

Today there are hundreds of small plums descending
to the earth too soon. Like you, my friends,
they are wild, ripening, and fallen
to the ground which tears their skin
until it bleeds its thick sugary juice
across the sand. Flies are flocking.
But I can only gather handfuls of fruit
or flowers that were meant to die here,
and hold them for a little while.

—Marjory Heath Wentworth

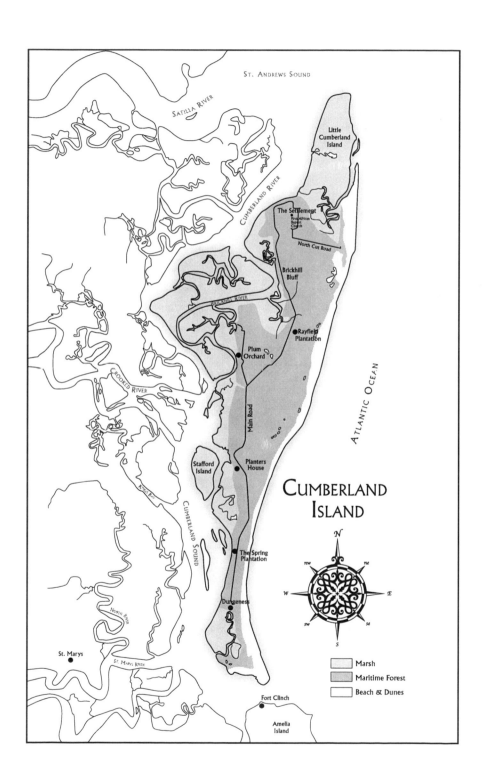

ST. ANDREWS SOUND

SATILLA RIVER

CUMBERLAND RIVER

Little
Cumberland
Island

The Settlement
First African
Baptist Church

North Cut Road

Brickhill
Bluff

BRICKHILL RIVER

Rayfield
Plantation

Plum
Orchard

CROOKED RIVER

ATLANTIC OCEAN

Main Road

Stafford
Island

Planters
House

CUMBERLAND
ISLAND

CUMBERLAND SOUND

N

nw   ne

W   E

sw   se

S

The Spring
Plantation

Dungeness

St. Marys

ST. MARYS RIVER

NORTH RIVER

Marsh

Maritime Forest

Beach & Dunes

Fort Clinch

Amelia
Island

Chapter One

A DISTANT ALLIGATOR BELLOWED IN THE DARKNESS, seeking a nocturnal tryst. Zabette heard his lusty roar, but like the steadier chirp of the crickets, it failed to distract from the comforting mahogany voice humming beside her, slow and easy. So unlike the crisp pace of the man she had lived with most of her life. *My old master*, she thought, crushing the myrtle leaves and rubbing them against her skin to keep the mosquitoes away. *My owner.* The word tasted bitter in her mouth.

She had never realized she was a slave until she learned that her grandmother had sold her to Robert Stafford when she was twenty-one. She'd thought he'd taken her away from Plum Orchard to live at Planters House because he loved her. And perhaps he had in his own peculiar way, at least at first. It didn't matter anymore, she decided, inhaling the pungent smell of the crushed myrtle. How naïve she had been. *I should have been wary. I should have expected it after what happened to Maman.* She had been only four years old at the time, but she would never forget that night as long as she lived. It was one of her earliest memories—though not her very first.

THE FIRST MEMORY SHE COULD RECALL was the afternoon her father had rushed through the front door of the clapboard Big House on Jekyl Island, his eyes lit up like it was his birthday.

"*Maman*," he yelled to Miz Marguerite, Zabette's grandmother—although she wasn't allowed to call her that, not then anyhow. He still spoke French to his mother sometimes, even though he was trying to get her to speak more English. But now he was excited, and he wanted to be sure she understood. "*Maman, je l'ai achetée.* I bought it. It's ours." His excitement was contagious. Zabette's face echoed his broad smile as she ran out the back door and across the dogtrot to the kitchen where her mother, the Bernardeys' cook, was fixing supper.

"*Maman*," she hollered, using the French word like her papa had, her eyes aglitter just like his. "*Maman*, he bought it." She had no idea what he had bought, but she knew it must be something wonderful.

Mas' Pierre, for that was her papa's name, had followed her to the kitchen and was laughing when he picked her up and put her on his shoulder. Then he kissed her mother on the cheek. "Marie-Jeanne," he said to her, and Zabette heard the joy in his voice. "We're moving. I bought it. We're moving to Cumberland Island. All of us."

What he'd bought, she would later learn, was a five-hundred acre plantation called Plum Orchard and another five hundred adjacent acres known as the Table of Pines—all on Cumberland. Zabette had lived her short life on Jekyl Island, where her father leased his cotton land from the du Bignons, who owned the island. She had been born there in 1820. It was her home, and she couldn't imagine living anywhere else.

But the next day her papa put her in front of him on his saddle and rode her to the south end of Jekyl, where he pointed across the waters of Saint Andrews Sound. "There it is, Zabette. That's your new home," he told her. She leaned forward and peered at the mass of trees on the next island. It didn't look very different from where they lived. But if her papa thought it was wonderful, then she guessed it must be.

SHE STILL HELD PICTURES IN HER MIND of the day they left Jekyl and floated across the water to Cumberland. She had never been on a real trip like that, never farther than the next house on the island, a mile away, and never across the water. It had been winter, she knew. Her *maman* had told her it was January, but Zabette remembered only warm sun on her back. People milled about the dock area while the child stood as quietly as she could, her mother holding her hand so she wouldn't get in the way. Marie-Jeanne had let Zabette help pack up the household goods that were being loaded onto the flat-bottomed barge—barrels of crockery and linens, along with oak dressers, brass beds, and stacks of tables and chairs. She remembered the livestock, all roped together, shuffling uneasily.

The du Bignon family had lined up near the dock waiting to say goodbye. All their children and several of their slaves were there. Even the old captain, who had first lured the Bernardeys to Georgia, had hobbled down to the landing and leaned against the railing of the dock to see them off. Some of the slaves were crying. Zabette saw tears in her mother's eyes as well.

"Why are you crying, *Maman*?"

Marie-Jeanne leaned down to kiss her daughter on top of her head. "We sayin' goodbye to people we might never see again." Zabette held her mother's hand even tighter. Her *maman* had told her about the day Mas' Pierre bought her to be his cook and how she'd had to leave her mother behind.

"You take good care of that young'un now," one of the older black women said to Marie-Jeanne, nodding in Zabette's direction. "She one of my babies." The old woman belonged to the du Bignons, and she was the midwife who had helped at Zabette's birth.

"I will, and I thank you, Berthe, for everything," said Marie-Jeanne.

"We gone miss you, chile" said Berthe. The Bernardeys and their people weren't moving very far, but the enslaved people, especially the women, had almost no chance to visit other places.

Marie-Jeanne led Zabette onto the barge as the other workers and their children boarded. The center of the barge was piled high with furniture, barrels, a few pieces of farm equipment, and crated pigs and chickens, while the cattle and horses at the far end of the vessel lowed and snorted. The figures on shore waved and shouted as they cast off, and those on board waved back. The child did not realize that she would never again set foot on Jekyl Island.

ZABETTE REMEMBERED HER PAPA'S FACE glowing with excitement as the barge drew near the Plum Orchard dock. They had turned up a waterway Pierre called the Brickhill River. He told her later it had originally been named for a brick kiln built on its banks by an early settler, but over time had become simply "Brickhill." She remembered the watery smell of the river. Her papa lifted her to his shoulders so that she could see above the handrail.

"There it is, *ma p'tite*," he said, pointing toward the shore. "Our new home."

Like all the dark-skinned children who were her playmates, she was eager to explore and squirmed restlessly in her father's arms. As soon as they tied up at the wharf, he put her down, and she raced off the barge with the other children. Her best friend among them was Adeline, who was about her age. Holding hands, the two little girls galloped toward the Big House like wild colts. They rambled through the empty rooms, laughing and playing hide and seek. The house, its wide veranda facing the river, was built of what the islanders called tabby—a mixture of sand, seashells, lime, and water. It looked immense to the children, larger and sturdier than the old frame house on Jekyl. The girls could only imagine what it must be like to actually live in such a place.

From an upstairs rear window, Zabette caught sight of the cook's cabin. She dashed back downstairs and into the sunshine. "There's our house, *Maman*," she shouted, pointing in the direction Marie-Jeanne was already heading, a big bundle in her arms.

The child raced inside ahead of her mother, Adeline following at her heels. It was only one big room, a little larger than their cabin at Jekyl, with three windows and a brick fireplace at one end, and there were wispy spiderwebs everywhere. Marie-Jeanne followed the girls in and set down her bundle to look around.

"This'll be fine, won't it, Zabette?"

OVER THE NEXT FEW DAYS, as the workers carried in all the furniture, hung pictures, and laid carpets, Marie-Jeanne helped Miz Marguerite arrange the Big House. The verandah soon became everybody's favorite spot. Marie-Jeanne served tea there to Pierre and his mother every afternoon, while Zabette chased butterflies in the yard and watched the silver porpoises play in the waters just offshore. Two live oak trees on the riverbank framed the view of the marshes on the other side of the river. Sometimes Miz Marguerite would let the child sit on her lap and nibble sugar cookies. At other times, Zabette sat on the front steps and played with the ragdoll her *maman* had made for her, while her father and grandmother drank their tea and watched the changing hues of the sunset that lit up the sky almost every afternoon.

Those were good times. But her best memory from those early days on Cumberland was the afternoon they had picnicked under the flowering plum trees that grew in the orchard for which the plantation had been named. The branches had begun to blossom early in their first spring there—that happiest of springs. Marie-Jeanne talked about the jellies and preserves and puddings she would make from the fruit. Her kitchen, like the one on Jekyl, was separated from the Big House by a dogtrot, but this one was larger. Zabette loved her mother's kitchen—the smell of yeast rolls and roasting meats and the sweet and tangy aromas of the desserts she created on a daily basis. She always felt safe and warm there.

On the Sunday of the picnic, Marie-Jeanne got up at *dayclean*, as the people in the quarters called the dawn, to fry a chicken, bake a pound cake, and devil some of the eggs Zabette had gathered that morning from the henhouse. That was one of the child's favorite duties. She always liked shooing the hens off the nest and picking up those warm, brown eggs nestled among the straw. They lay in her hand like a treasure, a perfect treasure, smooth as a river stone. Then she would watch while her mother transformed them, as if by magic, into something delicious.

By late morning, Marie-Jeanne had finished packing all the food into a large sweetgrass basket, tucking it in along with a tablecloth, napkins, plates, and silverware. Then, just before the sun was at its peak, she had sent Zabette to tell Mas' Pierre and Miz Marguerite that everything was ready.

Pierre was in an especially good mood that day. He gathered a folded blanket, a bottle of wine, and a wicker chair for his mother to use and headed out to the orchard, with Zabette trailing along behind, a chintz pillow for the chair in her arms. Miz Marguerite followed at a distance, carrying a little white parasol and a book from France that had recently arrived on a mail packet from the mainland. Just behind her Marie-Jeanne toted the heavy picnic basket.

Pierre spread the blanket in the very center of the orchard, where they were surrounded by a fragrant canopy of pale pink blossoms. Miz Marguerite settled into the wicker chair, while Zabette sprawled on the blanket beside her father to watch her mother arrange the tablecloth and set out the food.

From her entire childhood, that was the best day she could ever remember—with all of them together, the smell of her mother's wonderful dishes, plum petals dancing around them in the wind, and everyone laughing and talking just like a real family. Her *maman* even ate with them, though she fixed her plate after everyone else was served and went over to lean against a tree.

After they had consumed Marie-Jeanne's feast, Pierre unbuttoned his vest and lay back on his elbow on the blanket, his eyes warm and satisfied as he watched her put away the food. When her *maman* was done, Zabette talked her into racing to the edge of the orchard and back. They returned, laughing and breathless, Marie-Jeanne having let Zabette beat her by just a whisker, and both toppled, without thinking, onto the blanket beside Pierre. He cast an apprehensive glance toward his mother, but she, too, was laughing at their antics, so he'd allowed himself to relax and enjoy the afternoon.

When everyone settled down a bit and Marie-Jeanne had discreetly made her way back to her spot under the tree, Miz Marguerite opened her little book and began to read aloud some of the poems by a French poet whose name, Zabette would later learn, was Lamartine. She didn't understand all the big words. Her mother had taught her enough of her own Saint-Domingue French so that she could understand Miz Marguerite's commands. And she had learned more from listening to Miz Marguerite and her papa speak French sometimes to each other. But she would not have understood the poems no matter what tongue they were in. Nevertheless she listened—at least for a while—to the rhythms of the language that Miz Marguerite read so beautifully.

Ô temps, suspends ton vol! et vous, heures propices,
Suspendez votre cours!

Had she known then how fleeting such happiness could be, Zabette would have memorized those lines, asking time to stand still, to let her savor those happy hours. She would have made them part of her daily prayers.

As it was, despite the harmonies of the words, the little girl began to fidget long before the poem came to an end, wriggled out of her mother's arms, and was off chasing a squirrel. But during those moments while she had listened with both her parents to the mellifluous tones of her grandmother, she'd felt secure. Her *maman* was young and beautiful and looked as happy as Zabette had ever seen her. Her papa loved them both, she was sure. And Miz Marguerite—*Grand'mère*, as she would later call her—seemed to accept them all as her family.

But the world could change in the blink of an eye, as she would soon discover.

ZABETTE WOKE WITH A START from an unsettling dream in which a brown, furry bear had invaded the stuffy cabin and loomed menacingly over her mother, ready to attack. In fact, she had been awakened by a commotion on her mother's bed and Marie-Jeanne's voice, saying over and over, "Stop it, stop it! Now get on away. *Va-t-en*, William! You been drinkin'." She sounded as though she was about to cry, and the tone of her words had an urgency Zabette had never heard before.

Against the moonlight streaming through the small cabin window, the child could see the silhouette of a dark figure thrashing about on her mother's bed. The bear. There was no response, only a repetitious grunting sound that came from the moving shape over her mother.

"No, William, no! Stop it. Get away," her mother said.

Zabette slipped out of her own bed and ran toward her mother, trying to pull the dark shape away from her. She grabbed a piece of cloth and tugged at it, saying, "*Maman*, Let go of my *maman*!"

A foot kicked at her, and a gruff voice replied, "Get on outta here, young'n! You tell her, Marie. Or I'll . . ."

The movement on the bed stopped for a brief moment, and Zabette heard her mother say in a strained voice, "Go on, Zabette. Go outside."

The child didn't know what to do. She only knew that this bear, this man, whatever he was, was hurting her mother. She ran out of the cabin and straight to the Big House, banging on the door with all the might of her tiny fists and calling as loud as she could.

"Mas' Pierre! Mas' Pierre! *Papa*!" she shouted, forgetting she was not supposed to call him that, except when they were alone together, but she felt too upset to remember. "*Papa*, come quick!"

For a moment she thought that no one had heard. Then the soft glow of a lighted lamp filled the window of the upstairs bedroom. Pierre, tousled from sleep, leaned out over the sill. "What is it, Zabette?"

"Come quick, Mas' Pierre. That man is hurtin' my *maman*."

Pierre bounded down the stairs, barefoot and shirtless, buttoning his trousers before he opened the back door.

The sound of Zabette's voice had finally penetrated the bear-man's drunken stupor, and when Pierre flung open the door of the little cabin, the dark form had risen, stumbled away from the bed, and was tugging on his workpants and groping for the door.

"*Que fais-tu?* What are you doing here, William?" Pierre's voice was thick with anger.

Marie-Jeanne, sitting up in the bed with tears spilling from her eyes, clutched her torn nightgown tightly around her body. "*Je n'ai rien fait.* I didn't do anything, Mas' Pierre," she said. "*Ce n'est pas ma faute.* It's not my fault." At that moment the child slipped past the two men and rushed into her *maman*'s arms, frightened by the fury of her father's face and the anguish in her mother's voice.

Pierre quickly assessed the partially clothed body of his field hand William, the rumpled bed, and Marie's ripped gown, and he asked no more questions. Fury gave him strength to hold the small man's arms behind his back and drag him outside. By this time, Miz Marguerite, aroused by Zabette's frantic shouts and the banging on the back door, had come downstairs in her robe, holding high a kerosene lamp in her right hand, her long, gray hair hanging in a twisted braid down her back. When she saw her son scuffling with one of the young field hands, she began to ring the dinner bell by the back steps to call for help.

Zabette, not fully understanding what was happening and unable to comfort her mother who watched in horror, ran to her grandmother. Miz Marguerite too looked as though she was on the verge of tears. The child buried her face in a panel of her grandmother's robe.

Pierre had already found a piece of rope hanging on the side of the barn. He knocked William down, kicked him in the stomach, and tied his hands above his head. The young black man was clearly too drunk and frightened to put up any resistance. His eyes were wide with bewilderment and terror at what was happening. Now he lay on the ground, groaning and vomiting.

Several men were running up the dark road from the quarters, fearful that a fire had broken out. It was one of the terrors of plantation life, and they rarely heard the bell ring at night. But when they approached, they saw William lying in the dirt, his hands bound, and Mas' Pierre leaning over him with hatred in his eyes.

"*Viens.* Come here, and give me a hand," Pierre shouted to the nearest man— Zic. The old man's hair reflected white in the moonlight. He hesitated only a moment, but his bent figure stooped a little more at Pierre's words.

"Wha'd he do, Mas' Pierre?" Zic asked as he approached cautiously.

"*Peu importe.* Doesn't matter. He did what he shouldn't have done." Pierre's glance toward the cabin door where Marie-Jeanne was standing now, still clutching at her torn gown and sobbing, told Zic everything he needed to know.

Pierre was dragging William by his feet toward the back of the barn at the edge of the cotton field, where an old whipping post stood. Zic grabbed one of the young man's ankles, more in an effort to get beside Pierre and plead with him than to help.

"Mas' Pierre, he didn't know what he was doin'. He been drinkin' that muscadine wine Aunt Fanny brew up last summer. It's his first time. He ain't never been drunk before, and he ain't mean to do whatever he done. He jes' a boy."

But Pierre wasn't listening. He raised William roughly to his feet and began to tie his hands to the post. "*Va chercher mon fouet.* Go get my whip!" he said in quiet fury to Zic. The old man knew better than to ignore his orders, but as he moved slowly toward the barn, he said, loud enough for Pierre to hear, "Ha' mercy, Mas' Pierre. Ha' mercy."

"You want a whippin' too, Zic?" Pierre growled in a way they had not heard before.

"Naw, suh."

When Zic reluctantly placed the whip in his master's hands, Pierre sagged a bit, wearied by the exertion of getting William to the post. Although the slight young man was much smaller than his adversary, the effort had taken its toll on Pierre, who was not a strong man.

Others began to gather around. In the background, Pierre could see Marie-Jeanne, her cheeks smeared with tears and her eyes clouded with fear. Someone had draped a quilt around her shoulders. With that sight, a new surge of energy flowed into Pierre's arms. He ripped William's ragged shirt from his back and began with methodical rage to whip him with the biting edge of the leather strap.

To Zabette, who peered anxiously from behind her fingers at her father's action, he was like someone she had never seen before. He had always opposed such beatings, and it was the first time he had ever used the whipping post, which already stood behind the barn when they moved to Plum Orchard—a symbol of the master's authority. But tonight it was as though he enjoyed what he was doing, as though a cold cruelty fueled his body. He lashed William repeatedly, watching with icy calm as the tongue of leather cut into the young man's back and drew blood with every lick. Rage coursed through Pierre, giving him inhuman strength and vigor. The child trembled as she saw how he gritted his teeth and curled his lips. Large tears ran down her cheeks as she watched his fury. She squeezed her grandmother's hand and flinched with every blow of the lash, as though she were feeling it in her own small body.

Pierre ignored his mother's voice calling out to him, "*Arrête, mon fils! C'est assez!* Stop it, son! That's enough!"

Her pleading had no effect for two more strokes of the whip. Then he caught sight of Zabette, standing beside her grandmother, her face buried once more in the panel of the old woman's robe, her little shoulders shaking with sobs, and Marguerite's hand on the back of the child's head, holding Zabette close.

Pierre's hands fell to his side. He dropped the whip to the ground and turned away, as the energy drained from his body.

The dozen or so blacks, gathered in a distant semicircle, sensed that the ordeal was over and rushed to untie William and carry him back to the quarters. There they would do their best to comfort him, put salve on his wounds and bind them up with whatever clean rags they could find. No one could tell yet how bad it was, but everyone knew he would not be in the fields tomorrow. Their efforts were quiet and efficient, their movements calculated to attract as little attention as possible and not to send Pierre's wrath in any other direction. They moved as one, surrounded the beaten man, now unconscious, lifted him up, and started toward the road that led back to the quarters, cursing William's foolishness and Aunt Fanny's muscadine wine. They dared not curse the master.

It was suddenly quiet, and Zabette, thinking it had ended, opened her eyes and peeked cautiously around her grandmother's robe. Her father, his arms hanging limply by his side, was watching the men hurry away. Then a movement caught his eye, as Marie-Jeanne took a hesitant step forward, her hand outstretched, uncertain of his reaction.

"I just woke up, and he was there," she said, her voice was soft. "*Je n'ai rien fait.* I didn't do anything, Mas' Pierre. It ain't like you think." He made no reply. He was staring at her as though he did not know her.

Miz Marguerite suddenly reached for Zabette's hand and turned her toward the Big House. The child let herself be led up the back steps and into the house, but there she resisted, refusing to go any farther. She pulled free of her grandmother's grasp and ran to a window where she had a clear view of the back yard.

In later years she would relive this moment a thousand times, seeing in her mind the residue of anger in her father's eyes and hearing her mother's pleading voice speaking his name for the first time, "Pierre." She was free to say it now that all the slaves were beyond earshot.

Marie-Jeanne took another step forward, holding out her hand, seeking her lover's protection. Zabette did not breathe as she watched. "It wasn't what you think. Please, let me tell you," Marie-Jeanne said, touching his arm in a final plea.

He looked at her as though he didn't comprehend her words. Then he lifted his arm slowly, deliberately, and swung, hitting her full in the face with the back of his open hand. The blow caught her off-guard. She lost her footing and fell to the ground.

"*Putain,*" he whispered. "Whore." The word struck a blow sharper than his hand. He turned away, his shoulders sagging, to leave her alone on the gritty sand of the April night.

On her knees now, Marie-Jeanne was crying hard, blood trickling from the corner of her mouth. "Wait. My baby girl—Zabette," she choked out the name, her hand stretched out toward him. "Wait. Give me Zabette, please."

"*Maman,*" Zabette, her face and open hands pressed hard against the fogged window pane, called in a choked voice. She was barely able to breathe.

Pierre strode quickly into the house, closing the door firmly behind him.

"*Maman,*" Zabette said again, her voice weakened by sobs as she strained against the glass. Pierre moved toward the child and tried to pick her up, but she squirmed out of his arms, determined to keep her post at the window.

"Put her to bed, *Maman*," he commanded wearily. Then, his eyes red and unseeing, he climbed the steps to his own bedroom without looking back.

Zabette watched as suddenly Marie-Jeanne's knees gave way, she fell back to a sitting position on the ground, stunned by the finality of the closed door, and she wept. At last, still blinded by tears, she managed to get to her feet and stumble back into her unlit cabin. Zabette wanted to be with her, to help her bathe her face in the small tin basin on the table beside her bed, to wipe away the blood and tears. She wanted to climb in bed with her mother and not leave her to sleep alone, with the tiny cot next to hers empty. She wanted to throw her arms around her and hold her tight.

"You can sleep with me tonight, Zabette," Marguerite said softly, lifting the lantern and stretching out her hand to her granddaughter. "*Maman*," the child murmured once more, trying to catch her breath between sobs. Finally, unable to resist any further, she let herself be led up the stairs.

As they passed Pierre's bedroom door, which stood ajar, Zabette could see that her father had flung himself across the bed. Her grandmother quietly closed the door and led the child into her own bedroom, where the moving light of the lamp cast leaping shadows on the wall. Without speaking, Marguerite set the lamp on the nightstand, poured water from the pitcher on the dresser into the wash basin, and dampened a bath cloth so she could wash the clinging sand from the child's bare feet. Then, still silent, she tucked the little girl into bed, blew out the lamp, got in beside her, and reached out to hold her. Zabette felt hollow inside as she nestled in her grandmother's arms. In time, she let her swollen eyelids close, but even as she fell into a fitful sleep, she sensed that her world had changed forever.

Chapter Two

MEMORY CAN BE A FUNNY THING. Sometimes awful things happen that you think you'll never forget, but then they vanish in a flash, replaced by something wonderful. Other times, the awful things stay with you all your life. The pain Marie-Jeanne had felt the day Zabette was born was one of those terrible things she forgot the minute she looked on her daughter's face and counted her tiny fingers and toes. She was the most perfect thing the young mother had ever seen.

The birthing had been hard and dragged on a whole day. By late afternoon Berthe, the midwife, was hovering over Marie-Jeanne's cot, rubbing oil on her belly, and looking tense. But she was still crooning comforts like "You doin' good, chile. Now jes' relax." And finally Miz Marguerite, realizing the delivery was taking too long, came out to the cabin and sat by the cot and held Marie-Jeanne's hand through the hard contractions. The old woman and the midwife exchanged worried glances. Marie-Jeanne felt as though the searing pains were tearing her in half. She was screaming, though she would never recollect making a sound.

"One mo' time, chile, jes' one mo' time." The calm voice of Berthe seemed to ask the impossible. But Marie-Jeanne couldn't help herself. She tensed and pushed again, squeezing Miz Marguerite's hand till they both feared it would break. But then she felt a great gush and saw their worried faces relax all at once and break into smiles.

Berthe grinned big and wide and said with satisfaction, "We got ourselves a baby girl." She lifted the child by the feet and gave her a little whack on her bottom that made her cry. It was like she was announcing herself to the whole world with her wails. Marie-Jeanne laughed out loud, her ordeal over. Her baby was the most beautiful creature she'd ever seen. Her skin was light, almost as white as her papa's, and she had a headful of wet curls, more than ought to be on a newborn, her mother reckoned.

When Berthe laid the child in her arms and she peered into that perfect face, she completely forgot her birthing agony and the other dreadful things that had led to this moment. She forgot old man Scarritt selling her away from her *maman* and Mas' Pierre carrying her off, sobbing, tied to the side slats of the wagon as he drove away from the Darien plantation. For a time she even forgot the grief on her mother's face as she knelt in the dirt, clawing at the air and crying over and over, "Lord, ha' mercy."

Somehow her baby made up for it all—for that New Year's Eve when she had just turned thirteen and old man Scarritt, drunk as a loon, came staggering out to the cabin yelling her name—"Marie-Jeanne, come 'ere, girl. Yo' turn now." He already had his pants unbuttoned.

Her *maman* had shoved her out the window of the cabin and told her to hide in the bushes till he left. Then she opened the door and let the old man in to grope at her until he was satisfied and went back to his sour-faced wife. After it was over and she was back inside and out of the scratchy bushes, her *maman* had told her, "I won't be able to protect you always, chile. But when it happens, they ain't no need to fight it. He'll hurt you more if you do, whoever he be. Jes' close yo' eyes and make believe you somewhere else till it's over."

Marie-Jeanne had heard old man Scarritt say at breakfast the day he sold her away that two Frenchmen by the names of Henri du Bignon and Pierre Bernardey were coming that morning to look at the slaves he planned to sell. He mentioned their names, but she wasn't one of them. He always talked as though she wasn't even there or was too dumb to understand.

SHE WAS STILL WASHING THE DISHES when the Frenchmen drove up in a wagon. Peering out through the open window, she heard the younger and taller one say he'd come to look at the cook Mr. Scarritt had advertised for sale. He said their cook was too old to work anymore and had scalded herself real bad when she dropped a big pot of boiling water, so they were looking for a new cook. Ida Mae, who cooked for the Scarritts, was one of the five slaves the old man had lined up under the oak tree for the buyers to look over. Marie-Jeanne hated to see Ida Mae sold, even though she could be right hateful sometimes when the girl did something that caused old lady Scarritt to fuss at them both, but she never stayed mad long. She was a good cook, and she had a right good heart. The Scarritts would never be selling her if they hadn't fallen on hard times. Marie-Jeanne had heard them talk about how the spring floods and the summer drought had pretty much wiped out their cotton crop. She'd heard them say that they aimed for her to take over the cooking, a thought that terrified her, for she didn't have a notion about what to do. She'd watched Ida Mae and sometimes helped her make biscuits, but other than that, all she'd ever done was set the table, help serve and clear away the meals, and wash the dirty dishes.

Ida Mae's head was hanging low, but Tom, the fieldworker, held his chin up high and stared off in the distance with his mouth all tensed up like his mind was somewhere else and he was thinking hard, while the short Frenchman poked at the muscle in his arm.

"This here's Tom, Mr. du Bignon. He's a good worker, a little feisty," old man Scarritt said. "But ain't nothin' you can't handle, I reckon," he added with a laugh. Marie-Jeanne had seen the striped scars on Tom's back, after he had tried to run away and the pattyrollers had returned him to the plantation.

The other Frenchman, the younger one she took to be Pierre Bernardey, was looking over Ida Mae when Marie-Jeanne walked out the kitchen door to dump her dishwater.

"Who's that?" she heard him ask. Marie-Jeanne looked up. He was pointing at her.

"Her?" old man Scarritt said. "That's the kitchen girl, Ida Mae's helper."

"She can cook?" He was pensive for a second or two, and then he asked, "How much would you take for her?"

Old man Scarritt frowned and said, "I don't rightly know about her cookin'. But she ain't for sale. I plan to match her up with one o' my young bucks come fall, and I 'spect she might be good for five or six young'uns 'fore long."

Mas' Pierre was looking her up and down, and she felt her face grow hot.

Her *maman* was boiling bed linens in a black iron pot behind the kitchen. When Marie-Jeanne turned toward her, she saw fear in her mother's eyes.

"I sure do hate to have to sell Ida Mae. She's a real good cook and a good woman," old man Scarritt was saying.

"But how much would you take for *her*?" Mas' Pierre was pointing at Marie-Jeanne.

"I done told you, she ain't for sale."

"Well, if she *was* to be for sale, what would you take for her?"

"Don't plan to sell 'er, I done said." Old man Scarritt was getting mad now, until his wife stepped up and whispered something in his ear. Her sunbonnet covered most of her gray hair, and her thin lips ended in dark, deep-set creases at the corners of her mouth.

"All slaves can be bought. And I'd make you a right good price," the Frenchman said.

Old lady Scarritt watched her husband with narrowed eyes as he spoke.

"I reckon most nigger gals of childbearing age would bring 'bout three-fifty to four hundred dollars. But I couldn't let her go for that. She's right strong and smart. Real pretty too, I reckon. I've had 'er since she was a babe."

"Is that a fact?"

"Yep. Bought her and her mama from a French sugar planter still on the run a few years after that big uprisin' in Saint-Domingue down in the Caribbean." Marie-Jeanne's *maman* had told her about that uprising, how it had freed the slaves, but their master, Marie-Jeanne's own daddy, her *maman* said, wouldn't let them go. Instead, he fled the island and brought them to Georgia where he sold them both.

"Would you take five hundred?"

"I couldn't take less than seven hundred, I reckon." Old lady Scarritt, listening to every word, nodded in agreement.

It was a high price, Marie-Jeanne knew. Scarritt was only asking $350 for Ida Mae, who could cook rings around any kitchen helper. But it didn't seem to matter to Pierre. He stared at her for a minute and then turned back to the Scarritts.

"All right. I'll give you seven hundred dollars." The other Frenchman's mouth dropped open.

Old lady Scarritt shot her husband a smug glance and smiled big like she had won a prize.

Marie-Jeanne saw tears pooling up in her mother's eyes, and she was really scared all of a sudden. Scared that this strange white man was going to take her away from her *maman*, her only family, and scared of what the Frenchman expected of her, for she saw how he looked at her.

She rushed over to her mother and clung to her, as if to say anyone who took one had to take them both. But old man Scarritt pried them apart and handed Mas' Pierre a rope.

Marie-Jeanne was crying hard, but there was nothing she could do. He tied her to the wagon. She looked back at her *maman* who was kneeling in the dirt, crying over and over, "Lord, ha' mercy," and stretching her arms toward her daughter, who could see the tears streaming down her cheeks. Old Clem, the sailmaker Mr. du Bignon had just bought and whose hands were loose, put his arm around Marie-Jeanne and crooned a little comfort song that had no words. But she was still terrified of what was going to happen to her without her mother to protect her. She cried hard the whole way in the wagon back to the dock in Darien and in the boat to Jekyl Island until she thought she could cry no more.

She was not a pretty sight by the time Pierre Bernardey showed her to his mother. Her eyes were puffed up and red, her nose was running, and her dark curls had taken on a life of their own when her headscarf blew off as they crossed the water to the island. But she was still pretty enough for Miz Marguerite to know the real reason he'd bought her. When she questioned Marie-Jeanne and learned she couldn't cook a lick, that she didn't know a kettle from a saucepan, she tore into her son something awful.

"How could you waste our good money like that? I know Aunt Flora is getting old and can't manage those heavy pots and pans anymore. But this . . ." She hesitated, looking Marie-Jeanne up and down. "This is just an ignorant . . . " She sputtered, too angry to find the right word, but by then there wasn't much she could do about it. The girl was bought and paid for and she was here—on Jekyl Island.

"It's my money," Pierre said, "and I'll do with it whatever I want." Marie-Jeanne could hear anger in his voice. She could also see that his mother didn't like him sassing her like that, but he just shrugged and said, "She can learn."

He tried to placate his mother by pointing out to her that the girl could speak some French, that he'd heard her praying on the open water. It had always irritated old lady Scarritt when Marie-Jeanne and her mother talked to each other in French, since the Scarritts didn't know a word of what they were saying. The French of Saint-Domingue wasn't much like the French of France the Bernardeys knew. Marie-Jeanne could pretty well understand the commands, though she didn't always comprehend that fancified French the Bernardeys spoke to each other. But that was the least of her worries.

Her biggest fear was Pierre himself, Mas' Pierre, as she had been instructed to call him. She suspected he would come to her cabin at night and that he would hurt her, do to her what old man Scarritt used to do to her *maman*, the things that made her mother cry after he went away.

She waited that night, all rolled up in a ball on her cot. It was black outside, and she shook with anxiety in this awful, new place, this empty cook's cabin where she was all alone.

And then, just as she feared, he came. He came every night, and she dreaded his visits. It hurt, especially in the beginning. After a while it got so it wasn't as bad, and he started even to talk to her a little bit, telling her she was pretty and that he liked her little breasts. She hated it, but in time she got used to it.

And now, for a while at least, she could forget all that. She had this perfect child to show for all she had suffered.

She could even let herself remember the rest, how in time Pierre grew tired of coming to her cabin and would light a lantern at his bedroom window as a command for her to come up to his room in the Big House. She had no choice but to do as he said. Although she hated sneaking into the house and up the back steps like a thief, she liked the comfort of his bed. He would throw back the covers to let her in and then gather her into his arms. She had never slept in such a bed before. Her narrow cot had a mattress stuffed with cornhusks, but his big four-poster had a soft eiderdown. When she lay with him, he let her call him Pierre and made all sorts of promises about how he would always take care of her because she was his and his alone. Sometimes he even said he loved her. And little by little, she found herself starting to believe him.

PIERRE NAMED THEIR DAUGHTER ELISABETH after his grandmother. But from the very beginning, he always called her Zabette. He examined her from head to toe to make sure she was all right and pronounced her *"parfaite,"* perfect. He took to her from the very first. Her skin was almost as white as his, but she had her mother's dark curls and big brown eyes, except for the odd golden flecks like those in her father's gray eyes. And she had once heard Miz Marguerite say she had the straight nose and delicate chin of the Bernardey women.

Marie-Jeanne was aware that her mistress wanted her son to marry and have legitimate offspring. But he seemed content with the way things were, and he'd promised Marie-Jeanne when Zabette was born that he would never take a wife. She prayed it was true, and in fact she didn't see much chance of it. He was already in his mid-thirties and there were no unmarried white women on the island. Their closest neighbors on Jekyl, Henri du Bignon, son of the old captain, and his pretty wife Amelia, had three daughters, but the oldest, Louisa, was only twelve, Eliza ten, and little Sarah just a toddler. Pierre, who took almost no time from his planting and occasional medical duties, had little opportunity to meet young women and participate in the social life on the mainland and neighboring islands. She'd heard her mistress complain that the residents on Saint Simons Island to the north were of British and Scottish descent, and most were Protestants, not Catholics. And that she didn't want her son to marry someone "not of the True Faith."

Marie-Jeanne kept her baby with her most of the time, bundled up and snug in a kitchen drawer she had emptied and set on the counter top, where she could talk to her while she cooked, but sometimes Mas' Pierre would come fetch Zabette so his *maman,* who doted on the baby, could hold her and play with her. Marie-Jeanne missed her child on those occasions, but she had to smile whenever she saw the old woman rocking and singing to her baby, just as she would any white grandchild.

As Zabette learned to smile and coo, and then toddle and say a few words, Miz Marguerite would sometimes come fetch her in the morning after breakfast and take her to the Big House to spend part of the day. But at night Marie-Jeanne always brought her home. With Zabette at her side, she would kneel beside the bed to pray that the safety they knew would go on forever and that they would never be separated as she and her mother had been. Then the child would crawl into her mother's arms and sleep until dawn.

Those were the memories Marie-Jeanne wanted to hold onto. She was glad when Pierre said he loved her, but she didn't like the way he acted sometimes, jealous and sometimes downright mean, not to her, but to others. She remembered the time George, one of the field hands, walked off the road and came up to the door of the kitchen to ask her for a drink of water.

When Mas' Pierre caught sight of him out the back window of the Big House, he rushed outside.

"What're you doing here, boy?" he asked George in a rough voice.

"I ain't doin' nuthin', Massa, jes' gittin' a drink of water is all."

"Well, wait till you get to the quarters to get your water. You got no business here."

"Yessuh," George answered with a nod, handing the dipper back to Marie-Jeanne. "Much obliged, ma'am," he said, turning back toward the road that led to the slave quarters.

She nodded and wondered what had set Mas' Pierre off. But he went back inside and didn't say any more about it.

ZABETTE GREW LIKE A WEED and got prettier every day. She brightened everyone's life, and she was learning to speak the French her grandmother taught her and the Geechee plantation talk as well. She was like a little sponge soaking up everything that came her way. Marie-Jeanne was so proud of her that she could almost burst. Her child was the very center of her life.

Until that awful night—the night she would never forget as long as she lived. The night William came to her cabin and Mas' Pierre nearly beat that boy to death. He had never done anything like that before, and it put the fear of God in all the slaves. Then he hit her too and called her an ugly name. But worst of all, he took her little girl to the Big House. He never let Zabette live with her again. Anything else she could forgive, but not that.

The very next day he had some of the men move her belongings out of the cook's cabin and into an already crowded house down in the quarters. There wasn't much to move, except the presents he had given her over the years, a rocking chair when Zabette was born, an old trunk, a mirror, and a blue shawl. The folks that lived there, Lucy and George, weren't too happy about it, but they took her in and gave her a bed in the loft with their five children. The people in the quarters were always good that way. They made room for folks in need, and she did her best to help out wherever she could. Sometimes one of the children would even crawl up beside her and try to comfort her when they heard her crying in the night.

That same day Mas' Pierre sent her to the cotton fields, where she chopped cotton till her hands bled. She tied them up in rags torn from her petticoat so she could work the next day, chopping cotton from dawn to dusk. But she worried more about Zabette than about herself, until Zic told her that Pierre had brought in a new cook—a heavy, dark-skinned woman named Daisy. Marie-Jeanne knew her well, for Daisy, who usually worked in the cotton house as a seamstress, had sometimes helped out when the Bernardeys needed extra cleaning or food preparation at the Big House. She was a good woman with a broad open face and wide-set eyes. Although she was not as good a cook as Marie-Jeanne had become, she was a good-natured, intelligent woman who would no doubt learn as she had done. And she would follow Miz Marguerite's instructions without fail. But uppermost in Marie-Jeanne's mind was her daughter. She was glad to hear they had chosen Daisy, for she believed the new cook would be kind to Zabette. Tears filled her eyes as memories of all the dreadful things she had allowed herself to forget after Zabette was born flooded in once more. Her daughter had been torn from her arms just as she had been torn from her own mother's. What would become of her child now? And who was there to care?

BY THE END OF HER THIRD MONTH in the fields, Marie-Jeanne knew she was pregnant again. Her waist had thickened; her coarse cotton dress was tight; and she had missed her monthly flow twice now. But it made no difference. Like all the hands, she went to the field, sick or well. She would vomit between the furrows and then go on chopping. She didn't dare complain, since some of the women had been chopping cotton for thirty years or more and having babies sometimes right there in the fields among the cotton stalks. Certainly Mas' Pierre would never notice. He refused to look at her even when he rode his horse down to survey the fields. She was to him just another worker dressed in rough, dun-colored cotton. For him she was nothing.

Chapter Three

NIGHTTIMES WERE THE WORST FOR ZABETTE. She often awoke crying, and her sobs awakened her grandmother. Miz Marguerite had a small trundle bed built for her, but still the child whimpered and kept her grandmother awake. Finally Zabette's father moved her into a room of her own—the spare upstairs bedroom, where she slept every night clutching the tattered doll that Marie-Jeanne had fashioned out of old socks and rags. He bought her a new china doll at a store in St. Marys, but it sat stiffly on her dresser, its white face rigid and unfriendly, while Zabette cuddled and whispered to her rag doll. *Grand'mère*, as she was allowed to call Miz Marguerite now, read her stories and tried to teach her songs, but it did little good.

The child seemed lost. She had seen her father beat a boy and strike her mother. A few days later, she had watched from the back door as he'd hoisted William, like the carcass of a dead animal, into the back of his wagon. How could this be the papa she loved so much? The black man's hands and feet were tightly bound, though his wounds had only begun to heal. She could see tears streaking his dusty face. He looked so small and young compared to her father.

"He can't be more than sixteen," her grandmother said, as she came to stand beside Zabette. As soon as William could walk again after the beating, he'd come to the back door of the Big House to plead his case with his master. Zabette, listening from a hiding place she had found under the back stairs, heard him say, "I'se real sorry, Mas' Pierre. I was drunk outta my head. I ain't never gon' do nothin' like that again."

"Not here, you won't," Pierre growled, "I'm sellin' you into Alabama, boy. Now get out of my sight."

The child, wide-eyed, saw the tense cruelty on her father's face. She'd heard Zic tell her grandmother that it was the first time William had ever gotten drunk and would surely be the last. He hadn't known he would lose control like that. But when Miz Marguerite explained all that to Pierre, he just snarled. He didn't know Zabette was listening.

"I'd like to kill the bastard, but I paid $450 for him, and at least I'm gonna get my money out of him."

"But William has always been a good worker, Pierre," she tried again. "Maybe you could give him one more chance. He's never caused any trouble before." Her son just glared at her and turned away.

ZABETTE COULD SEE WILLIAM'S NOSE RUNNING, like hers did sometimes when she cried, but he had no way of wiping it. She saw the rough ropes that bound his wrists making sores where they rubbed. But he made no sound. He was looking upward toward the sky, his dark brows knit in pain and silent suffering. He flinched only once—when her father slammed shut the wooden tailgate.

She watched her papa climb onto the wagon seat and flick the reins at the horses to begin the slow pull toward the island's Main Road, which cut like a straight ribbon through the live oaks and palmetto undergrowth to nearby Rayfield Plantation, just north of Plum Orchard. The overseer there was going to take William, along with two slaves from Rayfield, to the coastal town of St. Marys to be sold.

Zabette stood beside her grandmother at the back door until the wagon turned onto the roadway and pulled out of sight behind the heavy undergrowth. Miz Marguerite crossed herself and said, "I hope he'll find a good master."

Zabette looked out at the empty yard. She wished her mother were here.

EVERY AFTERNOON AT DUSK the child sat on the wide windowsill of the upstairs hallway, watching the workers walk back from the cotton fields. The first time her grandmother found her there, she sat down beside her.

"What are you looking at, *ma p'tite*?" she asked.

"*Je cherche maman.* I'm looking for *maman*," she replied simply. But the distance of the road and the dim light made the women, their backs bent from hoeing throughout the day and sunbonnets hiding their faces, indistinguishable from one another, and Zabette never gave any sign that she saw or recognized her mother.

As a distraction, her grandmother let her help Daisy in the kitchen and show her where her mother had kept all the utensils. Her proudest moment had been showing Daisy where Marie-Jeanne hid the butter churn, tucked under a bench to keep it out of sight when it wasn't in use. It made her feel important, and she had watched her mother prepare so many meals that even at four, she felt she could help. Daisy was kind to her and patiently tried to teach her to set the table and cut biscuits from the dough she rolled out on the biscuit board. To Zabette it was a game. To Daisy it was training for an uncertain future.

Throughout the spring and summer, Zabette cried out from time to time in her sleep, but little by little the outlines of her mother's face became less distinct. As she succumbed to the affections of the present and protective figures of her grandmother and Daisy, her nighttime anguish began to subside.

Chapter Four

DESPITE HIS OUTWARD INDIFFERENCE, Marguerite knew that Pierre kept his thoughts away from Marie-Jeanne only by nursing his shield of anger and by staying away from the island as much as possible. She understood. She knew what it was like to miss someone you'd loved, and she had no doubt that her son had loved Marie-Jeanne. Marguerite had felt such anguish when her husband, Jacques, died. And she assumed her son's grief was not too different, for Marie-Jeanne was dead to him now.

At least they both still had Zabette. Before the child was born, Marguerite had not realized how lonely she had become. Coming to America to live on an island had never been her expectation when she married Pierre's father. She had planned to settle down in a simple house overlooking one of the quiet streets of Lamballe, France, where they had been married, and be the wife of a Breton doctor. But life took its own directions.

When the Revolution came, it did not at first have much impact on their lives. The Saturday markets and the neighborly gossip of the Lamballe burghers went on as usual. Most of the upheaval was in Paris. But it grew steadily worse, more intense, until poor peasants in the surrounding region, emboldened by the success of those in other parts of the country, began to burn and pillage some of the châteaux of Breton aristocrats. As the incidents of violence increased, even modest merchant noblemen began to worry. She and Jacques grew increasingly concerned.

She remembered vividly the night Captain du Bignon, retired from the sea, had come to their house. As shadows from the lantern danced against their walls, he'd painted for Jacques the picture of a magical island on the coast of Georgia.

"It's called Sapelo," the captain said, "and that's what we'll name our little colony—the Sapelo Company. It has rich soil, fresh water, warm weather, and plenty of game to hunt. And, *ah oui . . . des palmiers,* palm trees," he added as an afterthought.

"Are there many French people on the Georgia coast?" asked Jacques.

"Some, though most of the coastal planters are English and Scottish. *Mais très aimable.* Very friendly, I'm told. We'll plant rice and indigo and make a fortune in the New World."

They would be safe and prosperous there, he assured Jacques, and able to preserve their modest fortunes from revolutionary looters. Jacques listened intently, leaning forward as the older man described to him the role he would play if he decided to join them.

"We need a doctor since we'll be all alone on an island. And we're willing to provide passage for you and your family and a small retainer," he said persuasively. "You would have a place to live and security. You wouldn't have to buy a share unless you want to. All you would need to do is see to any medical emergencies and . . . *eh bien,* perhaps you could help with the planting and harvest."

How well she remembered that night that changed her life. Jacques told him he would think about it, and after the captain left, he talked it over with Marguerite.

"*Aller en Amérique?* Go to America? That God-forsaken place? Leave Lamballe and our home here? *Non, je ne veux pas,* I don't want to." That had been her first reaction, and their little boy had cried at the very thought of leaving all his friends. But Jacques was persuasive. He too painted vivid pictures—of the growing violence that was already threatening to destroy life as they knew it.

"Remember the food riots in Paris," he told her, "and the killings on the Champs de Mars last year. Even the king has tried to escape. Think of our son. We must keep him safe." It would get worse, he assured her, before it would ever get better.

And so they had come to Georgia. But nothing had worked out as they planned. Bickering, quarrels, and property disputes soon erupted in the little colony and persisted to the point that Sapelo became unbearable, with some shareholders not even speaking to others. Captain du Bignon, increasingly disgusted with the situation, finally traded his shares of Sapelo for those on another island farther south called Jekyl, which the group had purchased shortly after arriving in Georgia. It had not been difficult for him to persuade the Bernardeys to join them in their move, for they too were weary of the squabbling. Du Bignon moved his wife and sons, Joseph and Henri, into a red-roofed house on the north end of the island, abandoned after the death of the British major who had built it. And the Bernardeys constructed their own house a mile or so south at a site overlooking the marshes. Whatever hopes Marguerite had for Pierre to find a young, French Catholic woman to be his wife faded. The du Bignons had only sons, and not only had they severed ties with the Sapelo group, they had moved even farther from Savannah, where a majority of Georgia's French settlers lived. In the end, leaving Sapelo proved a wise decision, for one member of the company eventually killed another; one died of fever; and still another, fed up with the situation, returned to France and was guillotined, or so they heard. The entire company had quickly dissolved.

All that had been so long ago. Marguerite had been happy enough on Jekyl until her Jacques died. But she still had her son, and she had tried to console herself with the natural beauty around her, the ever-changing marshes that stretched between the island and the mainland, the pelicans and egrets that soared overhead, the soft-eyed deer that ate her flowers. Then once again, after many years, her life had been disrupted when Pierre had bought Plum Orchard. But by then she had Zabette to love, perhaps the only grandchild she would ever have. Marguerite smiled down at the little girl sitting on the tabby steps playing with her rag doll. *Things never turn out as you expect*, she thought, looking at the dark curls and the smooth face of her granddaughter. *But God knows what's best.*

Sometimes, weary of Daisy's cooking and seeing the sadness in Zabette's eyes, Marguerite would urge her son to bring Marie-Jeanne back. She had come to like the bright, pretty girl, who understood her French and who had learned to cook so well. Pierre had been like a different person when she was here, when he slipped out at night to the cook's cabin and later when he had set up his nocturnal signal to summon the girl. Marguerite had been aware of their nightly trysts. Through the doorway of her bedroom, left open to catch the evening breezes, she could see the lantern glow, moving back and forth, spilling through the wide crack beneath Pierre's closed door across the hallway. More nights than not, as she lay awake, she heard the soft footsteps that crept from the cabin and padded up the back stairs to Pierre's room.

Every morning, though, Marie-Jeanne would be in the kitchen by six o'clock, her crisp, white apron tied neatly around her waist, making biscuits and frying bacon for their breakfast.

"*Bonjour, Madame, bonjour, M'sieur,*" she would say, as she served their breakfast with well-honed efficiency. She never looked Pierre directly in the eye, at least when she knew Marguerite was watching.

No doubt the couple thought they fooled her with their pretense. Her eyesight might not be what it used to be, but her hearing was perfect. She'd listened many nights to the creaking of the stairs, and it came as no surprise when she noticed Marie-Jeanne's widening waistline and swollen breasts. Those days, she thought, were better than these.

"Pierre," she would say, "You know she didn't encourage William. He was drunk and forced himself on her."

"She could have screamed," he said stubbornly.

"I'm sure she thought she could fight him off."

"Then why didn't she?"

"How do you know she didn't? And what about Zabette? She misses her mother."

"She has her father and grandmother," he said, ending the conversation.

IN LATE JULY, ONE MORNING at the breakfast table, while Zabette was still in the kitchen helping Daisy, Pierre made an unexpected announcement.

"*Maman, je vais me marier.* I'm going to get married."

Marguerite set down her coffee cup so hard it almost shattered. She had said little these past few months when he often left the island to go into the town of St.

Marys, sometimes staying overnight. As a rule he went routinely once a month for supplies, but lately he had taken to having the slaves row him over once a week, sometimes twice, returning with a few supplies and almost always with little gifts for Zabette—the doll, a hair ribbon—new combs for Marguerite, and once even a tiny bottle of French perfume. Although Marguerite considered it wasteful of his time and effort, not to mention their money, the items were never expensive, and she suspected they were not the real purpose of his trips. He was entitled, she thought, to have a bit of time to himself to work out his feelings. But she was caught off guard by his announcement of his intent to wed.

Her stunned silence brought a rush of words from her son.

"Her name is Catherine Corb," he explained. "*Elle est d'origine française, comme nous.* She is French, like us," he told his mother. "Her father has a store in St. Marys, and he and I have already settled the terms of the marriage agreement."

"Well, this *is* a surprise!" His mother replied in a chilly tone, trying to regain her composure. "Do I at least get to meet her before the wedding?"

"*Bien sûr,*" he said. "Of course. I think it would be appropriate for us to invite her and her family to supper one night very soon."

"And when is the wedding?"

"The final banns announcing our intent to marry will be posted the second Sunday in August, so we have settled on a date of August 19."

"*Et alors?* Why am I the last to know?"

"To be truthful, *Maman,* I wasn't sure until . . . recently," he hesitated. "But I think it will be good for you and me both to have another woman here, someone to help you run the household, and someone to help me . . . " His voice tapered off, as though he did not know how to finish the sentence.

Marguerite knew he must have noticed Marie-Jeanne's swelling belly in spite of his efforts to avoid seeing her. Or he had heard about it. It must have infuriated him even more knowing that Marie-Jeanne was pregnant, most likely with William's child.

She recognized in him the obstinate streak of the Bernardeys. His father, God rest his soul, had been like that—the most gentle, loving man on earth, unless he was angry. Then the most unyielding. Even though Pierre must have known in his heart that Marie-Jeanne had not been intentionally unfaithful to him, he felt that in some way she must have acquiesced. Why hadn't she cried out? Why hadn't she fought William off? He had voiced these questions many times, and Marguerite understood. But she also knew from experience the power of a determined man filled with lust, particularly one under the influence of alcohol. In any case, it was too late now.

Perhaps this Catherine Corb would be good for him and could help him forget what had happened. She hoped so. While she was happy that at last he had found a good Catholic woman to give her legitimate grandchildren, she wished it had not been under such bitter circumstances.

"What about Zabette?" Marguerite asked him.

"What do you mean?"

"Will you send her back to her mother now?"

His face took on that granite look that she had come to know too well in recent months. "Certainly not! She will live here with us."

"But what if Mademoiselle Corb refuses to let her stay?"

"She won't refuse."

"But if she does?"

"I said she won't. We have already discussed it."

But men, Marguerite thought, *do not always understand the ways of women.*

A WEEK LATER MARGUERITE AND DAISY scurried about making last-minute adjustments to the table setting and parlor cushions. The Corbs were coming to supper and planned to spend the night since they could not return to St. Marys over the dark channel waters. Pierre went to the dock early to meet the guests who were expected at four o'clock.

The evening did not go well from the outset. Even though Marguerite had planned to be waiting on the front veranda when they arrived, their boat had docked almost half an hour earlier than expected, and she had just finished dressing when she heard Pierre's carriage pulling up in front of the house to deposit the guests. Marguerite hurried down the stairs, but it was Zabette who opened the door when the Corb family arrived. Marguerite, wanting her to make a good impression, had dressed her in her best blue, lightweight, lawn dress and added a little blue bow to her dark curls. Her skin glowed against the pale blue fabric, and she wore her most engaging and utterly guileless smile, her dark eyes shining with excitement to be the one to greet the guests.

"Ah," said Catherine to her mother as she stepped through the front door. "This must be the little darky Peter told me about."

She was speaking English. Marguerite, who was descending the hallway stairs as quickly as she could, overheard the comment. She froze at the tone of the word and at the pinched faces and wrinkled noses that Catherine and her mother were wearing as they looked at Zabette. Marguerite knew that the word was perfectly acceptable among whites, certainly more genteel than "nigger," equally common among the coastal planters, but it hardly described Zabette, whose skin was almost as light as that of Mademoiselle Corb herself.

"Va aider Daisy, ma p'tite," Marguerite said gently to the child even before she greeted her guests. "Go help Daisy, little one." Zabette nodded, oblivious to any tension caused by her presence, and slipped away silently. What Marguerite had expected of Pierre's fiancée she wasn't sure, but certainly not this stiff-corseted woman, her dark hair pulled tightly back in a chignon, who was peeling off her gloves in the parlor.

Marguerite tried for the rest of the evening to be an amiable hostess and even to like her future daughter-in-law. But from the very first moment, she found herself seeing only the worst. Catherine was, she supposed, attractive enough, but her features were sharp, a younger version of the elder Madame Corb's, which had softened a bit with age and too many rich desserts. Catherine bore little resemblance to her bespectacled father, Pierre Corb, a short, portly man with a thick moustache.

Marguerite's senses were heightened to the way the younger woman looked around the house, as though assessing the changes she planned to make. But perhaps it was only her imagination. She would try for her son's sake to embrace her new daughter-in-law, who, to Marguerite's irritation, always called him "Peter," even when she was speaking French. Throughout the evening, Marguerite did her best to be polite and friendly. Yet in spite of the efforts of all present, both women understood instinctively that they would never be friends.

As one of the terms of the marriage agreement that Pierre had worked out with his prospective father-in-law, he gave as a dower gift to Catherine a quarter of his land and property. What he did not tell either his bride-to-be or her father was that, at the same time he had papers drawn up for the marriage settlement, he also had his lawyer draft a legal document deeding half his land and property to his mother, reserving only one-fourth for himself, signing all documents as "Peter Bernardey." He knew that whatever belonged to his mother still belonged to him, and he had understood instinctively that he needed to provide for her, whatever happened. He was also sure that his mother would protect Zabette. Hence, he deeded half to Marguerite, but only a quarter to Catherine. Catherine was miffed when she found out about it. Her resentment of her mother-in-law deepened with the knowledge, for she no doubt understood that Marguerite, in spite of Catherine's position as wife, still had legal control of the household if she chose to exercise it. For the moment, however, Catherine merely set her lips firmly and said nothing.

PIERRE AND CATHERINE WED ON THE MORNING of August 19 in a small and simple ceremony in the parlor of her parents' home in the tiny coastal village of St. Marys. Marguerite attended, leaving Zabette at the plantation with Daisy. It would not do to have people speculating about her relationship with Pierre in this small town, where such offspring existed in abundance but were rarely acknowledged as family members.

A Catholic priest, as a special favor to Catherine's father, came down from Savannah to perform the ceremony, which was followed by chilled champagne, an unusual treat in St. Marys, and a luncheon on the wide porch of the Corb home, where they were sheltered from the August sun and could catch the breezes that drifted in from the marshes and the sea beyond. Monsieur Corb had well utilized his resources as a merchant to bring in *foie gras* and the best wines to celebrate the wedding of his only daughter. It was as fine a party as St. Marys had seen for some time.

PLUM ORCHARD, AUGUST 22, 1824

"Move the round table over here beside the sofa," said Catherine to Zic, who had been brought in to help. "And for heaven's sake, do dust underneath," she snapped at Daisy.

Marguerite, her mouth clamped tightly shut, hurried upstairs where she could not hear Catherine's commands. Although she was glad that Pierre no longer moped about the plantation, she had not been fully prepared for this daughter-in-law who felt that, as Pierre's wife, she ought to have complete charge of the household that Marguerite had prided herself on running so efficiently. The two clashed from the very first afternoon Catherine arrived.

"I have planned our meals for next week," the new wife announced proudly.

"They are already planned," replied Marguerite.

"Well, in that case, we'll just have to un-plan them. I've brought all the ingredients with me from Papa's store."

Daisy looked from one woman to the other and shrugged her shoulders in bewilderment as she watched Pierre and Zic carrying the packages into the house.

For the next several days, Catherine made her way through the house rearranging most of the furniture and complaining loudly about any dust or cobwebs she found. Marguerite, who had always supervised the cleaning with great care, was deeply offended by her constant complaints. Catherine grumbled loudly about the laziness of slaves in keeping a house clean, apparently unaware that she was upsetting her mother-in-law. The new Madame Bernardey criticized Daisy's recipes and Zabette's sometimes creative table settings.

"Look at this! She's done it again! Daisy, tell her one more time that the fork does not belong on the same side as the knife. For heaven's sake, will the child never learn?"

Her anger often made Zabette cry, for it was she who drew Catherine's greatest irritation and sharpest words. Daisy tried to shield the child and take responsibility herself, but Zabette seemed always to be in Catherine's way. She knew before she arrived that the little girl had a room in the Big House, and Pierre had made it perfectly clear that he intended for her to stay. Catherine assured him that she could tolerate the situation, but when she observed the affection that both Pierre and his mother lavished on the child, her heart changed. Thus far she'd said nothing about it to Pierre. But Marguerite watched her narrowed eyes and tight lips whenever she saw the child, and she suspected that Catherine was only biding her time.

Chapter Five

TUESDAY, SEPTEMBER 14, 1824

Before dawn, while the people in the quarters still slept, the winds began to howl. Then the rains commenced to fall in sheets and the gale grew stronger still. It was clear there'd be no fieldwork done that day. At first the people in the quarters clung together with a sense of relief, but by mid-morning what everyone hoped was only a bad autumn storm had whipped into a hurricane. Waves from the river lashed the shoreline, and wind tore at the trees.

Marie-Jeanne huddled with Lucy and her children in their tiny cabin, terrified that the furious gusts would sweep away their shelter. Some of them remembered the dreadful 1813 hurricane when they were still on Jekyl Island. It had laid flat the cotton stalks and pine barrens, while the slaves crouched on the upper level of the du Bignons' tabby barn or climbed trees to escape the flood. But this time, as the waters began to rise, there was no tabby barn, and Marie-Jeanne feared that in her condition, she might not even be able to climb a tree. George was out in the storm seeking a better shelter for them all.

"What you reckon we gone do?" asked Lucy, her eyes wide with fear for her children.

"I don't rightly know," Marie-Jeanne answered, wincing when a branch ripped from a nearby tree slammed against the side of the house.

"I'se scared, Mama," the oldest boy, Bartlette, spoke, and Lucy spread her arms to gather in all her children.

At that moment the door burst open. George stood there, wind whipping at his clothes. They could barely hear the bell ringing.

"Come on y'all. They's callin' us up to the Big House."

Walking against the wind was almost impossible. George carried the two smallest children, and they all bent forward holding hands, hurrying as fast as they could. It was risky to be out, with the debris flying about, but they knew it was perhaps their only chance. The Big House had strong foundations, and the main floor stood eight feet above the ground. It was large enough to hold everyone. By the time the little group reached the back steps, they were wading ankle deep.

Marie-Jeanne hoped against hope, as she entered the back door, that she would see Zabette. What she saw instead was a collection of wet, scared people, frightened not only of the winds and rising water, but of Miz Catherine, who was carrying on something awful. Mas' Pierre had let the slaves into her newly cleaned parlor and dining room to wait out the storm.

"How could you?" she complained. "Those filthy people—and Daisy's cleaned all week."

"Catherine, they could die out there. We have no choice. They're my property, and I can't afford to lose them. Now get on upstairs and sit in the hall with *Maman*." She flounced toward the stairwell, pausing for a moment to cast a disdainful look at the dark, anxious faces and downcast eyes of the people sitting quietly on the floor of her immaculate parlor.

Marie-Jeanne stiffened at the sight of Pierre, though he gave no sign of noticing her presence. She pulled her ragged shawl tighter around her shoulders. Her dress and hair were wet, and, like the others, she was chilled to the bone. She had not been in the house since the day he'd banished her. And were it not for her unborn child and the chance that she might see Zabette, she would rather have taken her chances in the tiny cabin or even up a tree for that matter.

But Daisy had met her at the back door when she first arrived.

"Come set with me," she urged, "and I'll tell you all Zabette's been learnin'."

Marie-Jeanne accepted the offer gratefully as they crept together into the hollow place under the back stairwell. Her swollen belly was obvious to everyone, and she didn't relish Pierre's seeing her, but he'd disappeared into another part of the house. She looked around hopefully for Zabette.

"Miz Marguerite's got her upstairs settin' in the hallway away from the windows," Daisy told her, understanding her anxious glances.

"She be all right? Are they lookin' after her?"

"She fine. Growin' like a weed. And let me tell you what all she can do now ... "

Marie-Jeanne listened hungrily to her daughter's new accomplishments.

The hours seemed endless, as the storm raged on for most of the afternoon. They sat mostly in silence, hearing only the furied gales and watching the water rise higher and higher. Finally toward evening the rains stopped and the wind died down. The water, which had almost reached the top step of the porch, began to recede.

"You reckon Miz Marguerite will let me see Zabette now?" Marie-Jeanne asked.

Daisy shook her head. "Ain't no need even to ask. Mas' Pierre won't 'low it. I'se sorry, honey. But he done made that clear." Disappointed, Marie-Jeanne rose heavily and followed the others outside to wade back to the quarters and see what damage the wind and rain had done there.

EVERYONE ON THE PLANTATION spent the next few days cleaning up from the storm. No one could work in the muddy fields. The hurricane's surge had ruined the cotton crop, Zic reported, but the barn had held and the livestock were safe. At least they would eat this winter. During the next few days, terrible news arrived from farther north. The storm had ravaged the area between Darien and Savannah. All the bridges were washed away, and more than a hundred people lay dead—drowned or struck by debris. Cumberland was lucky. They had not lost a single person and only the smallest animals had not survived.

MARIE-JEANNE'S BABY BOY WAS BORN on a Sunday morning in late December. It was the slaves' day off, so she was able to birth him in the quarters. She missed the quiet assurance and encouragement of Berthe, who still lived on the du Bignons' Jekyl plantation, but Lucy, who had taken her in, did a satisfactory job. And thank the Lord this time it went easier than before. It was hard having a newborn in this crowded household, but he was a balm that helped Marie-Jeanne fill the cavern in her soul left by the loss of Zabette. The baby even looked a bit like his sister, and his mother thought him beautiful.

Mas' Pierre refused to come and examine the child or give him a name like he usually did with newborns on the plantation, so Marie-Jeanne called him Jack, and the name stuck. Miz Marguerite, however, had Frederick drive her down to the quarters to have a look. The moment she entered the cabin door and caught sight of little Jack, Marie-Jeanne could see the shock on her face. Lucy and George had also noticed her expression and stepped outside to give her and Marie-Jeanne some privacy.

"I thought he'd look like William," Miz Marguerite said almost in a whisper. Marie-Jeanne watched as she touched the child's light-skinned face and smiled down at his irresistible beauty.

"No'm," Marie-Jeanne said softly, "he don't look like William. He look like his papa."

"Yes," the old woman said with a single nod, "he does." She picked the baby up and cradled him in her arms, rocking him back and forth as he started to cry. When she finally laid the child down again, Marie-Jeanne just watched as little Jack gazed up, with the wisdom only babies can have, into the eyes of his grandmother.

"What you gone tell Mas' Pierre, ma'am?" Marie-Jeanne asked quietly.

Miz Marguerite looked at her with steady and determined eyes. "I'm going to tell him he's got a fine-looking son."

"And will you tell Zabette she got a baby brother?" Marie-Jeanne asked hopefully.

Her mistress did not answer. She left the cabin and closed the door behind her.

Chapter Six

WHEN MARGUERITE URGED PIERRE TO GO to the quarters to see his new son, he muttered, "No son of mine."

"Pierre, there's absolutely no question about it. He looks just like you."

"No son of mine," he repeated, his mood darkening.

Although Catherine knew about Zabette, she had never learned all the circumstances of her husband's relationship with the child's mother. But when she overheard Marguerite's coaxing, she was furious with Pierre, accusing him of being unfaithful to her. He denied it, but the tensions between them were palpable. Her anger subsided only when she learned that she, too, was pregnant.

CATHERINE'S BABY WAS BORN on July 23. Marguerite stood on the front verandah and delivered the news to her son as he dismounted from his morning ride to inspect the cotton plants.

"*C'est une fille*, Pierre. Another girl," she said cheerfully.

He'd known Catherine was in labor when he left, but he'd expected it to go on for many hours. Given the July heat, Catherine had been blessed with an easy delivery, and the child arrived during the short time he had been absent.

Pierre managed to smile at the news. He had, of course, hoped for a son this time, but had learned by now that one does not always get what one wants from life.

He and Catherine had talked about names for either a boy or a girl. Catherine was determined to name the little girl Margaret Elizabeth—the latter being the last name Pierre would likely have chosen.

"*D'accord,* if you insist," he acquiesced. "But we'll call her Margaret after *Maman.*" The tone of his voice brooked no opposition.

In fairness, Marguerite thought, Catherine may not even have realized that Zabette's real name was *Elisabeth,* spelled the French way. Catherine had lived in America all her life and may not have been aware of the common French nickname. But even if she had, Marguerite doubted that it would have made any difference. The young Mrs. Bernardey was of the same stubborn nature as her husband, and if she had her way, Zabette and her mother would soon be a forgotten part of his past. But Marguerite wasn't so sure. At night sometimes she heard her son cough, and it sounded almost as though he were stifling a sob. She was probably imagining things, for he never mentioned Marie-Jeanne. But Marguerite suspected that he thought about the baby boy who looked like him— his son—and the child's mother far more than he cared to admit.

Marguerite led Pierre up to the bedroom, where Catherine, wearing a bed jacket embroidered with pink roses, lay propped against a white feather pillow. The new mother had combed her hair and pinched her cheeks to add color to her pale skin. And she held her newborn daughter, asleep in her arms. Marguerite watched Pierre, wondering if the little scene evoked for him, as it did for her, the memory of Zabette's birth.

When he entered the room, Catherine smiled brightly.

"Here is your daughter, Peter—Margaret Elizabeth Bernardey." She held the child up proudly for her father to see, and Marguerite watched his reaction. She knew he wanted to love Catherine as he should love a wife. And he obviously tried. But his mother suspected that the shadow of Marie-Jeanne's face always stood between them.

Catherine's next words caught Pierre off guard.

"You know, dear," she said, "little Margaret will soon need her own room. I thought this might be a good time to make other arrangements for Zabette."

Pierre's jaw tightened at her unexpected words. To Marguerite they came as no surprise. Although he had exacted from Catherine before their marriage the promise that Zabette could remain in the Big House, Marguerite knew that the girl's presence irked her and that she would do all in her power to get rid of the child.

"You know I'm right, Peter." Catherine adopted her most reasonable voice to persuade him with her logic. "After all, Zabette must learn who she is, and our daughter will need the room. She must come first."

Although Catherine said no more, Marguerite understood the implacable nature of her demand. Pierre pressed his lips together and gazed out the window, avoiding the determined eyes of his wife.

"I'll see what I can do, Catherine," he replied finally, though his voice held no warmth.

Despite his sudden distance, Catherine, empowered by the baby in her arms, smiled in a triumph she could barely conceal.

"Your own beautiful daughter," she said, holding up little Margaret, who briefly opened her eyes to look at her father. He bent over and kissed the child on the forehead, but not the mother.

"You need to get some rest now," Pierre replied. "*Maman* will see to the baby while you sleep."

Catherine let her body relax, as though she were suddenly aware of her own fatigue. She leaned back onto the pillows and closed her eyes, still smiling at her victory.

PIERRE COULD NOT BEAR TO CONFRONT ZABETTE with the news, and Marguerite suspected that the unpleasant task would fall to her. The child had been through so much, and she was no longer unaware of Catherine's antagonism. Already she had stopped taking meals with the family and had begun eating in the kitchen with Daisy. It had occurred so gradually that Pierre and Marguerite had not realized at first what was happening. Catherine had begun by insisting on what she called "adult time" at their evening meal, asking Daisy to change their suppertime to eight o'clock and to feed Zabette early so that she could get to bed "at an appropriate hour."

Breakfast had never been a problem. Zabette always arose with the sun, a habit she had learned from her mother, and Daisy fixed her something to eat and fed her in the kitchen long before the others came down to breakfast. Only the midday dinner, their largest meal, presented a dilemma, but Catherine took care of that by asking Zabette to help Daisy serve and then praising her lavishly for her help.

"It will be good training and help you learn what all grown-ups need to know about such things," she had told the child.

Zabette so wanted to please Catherine that she began to help serve at every noon meal, basking in the praise she received at the beginning. Soon it became routine, and the praise ceased. But by the time Pierre realized that he never saw his older daughter at mealtimes anymore, the new routine was well established.

While Marguerite spent more time with the child in the bedroom they had once shared, teaching her to read, Pierre tried to make up for it by taking Zabette riding with him in the mornings and teaching her everything he could about the plantation. In a curious way, it had brought them closer together, and they had not so much missed the mealtimes.

But this! Removing her from the household altogether, so that the new baby could have her room! Pierre had no idea how to handle the matter, when his own desires ran so counter to Catherine's demands. As always when he needed emotional support, he turned to his mother. Although Marguerite's outrage was equal to his, she knew that Catherine had been planning her strategy for some time and that she would not be moved. The older woman would willingly have taken the child back into her own room, but Catherine wanted her out of the house altogether.

"I don't know what to do, *Maman*," Pierre said.

"You might consider sending her back to her mother," Marguerite offered, though the thought of living without the child tore at her heart.

"*Non*," he said resolutely. "Then I would never see her. I want a better life for her, *Maman*."

Marguerite sighed. She wasn't sure that Zabette would ever feel at home in the quarters anyhow, having lived so long in the Big House. She agreed that they needed some other arrangement. She thought for a few minutes, then finally said, "I think we're going to need Daisy's help."

Chapter Seven

THE NEXT MORNING, WHEN ZABETTE CAME DOWN to the kitchen for her breakfast, Daisy smiled at her, as she always did. "My land, child, you is *really* growin' up."

Zabette grinned her widest grin and stood as tall as she could. Daisy always made her feel loved and needed. "I'm almost big as you," she replied, drawing herself up to the peak of her five-year-old stature and standing on tiptoes.

Daisy laughed heartily. "Well, you got a ways to go yet." She flipped the pancakes, Zabette's favorite, and turned the frying bacon. The child watched with rapt interest, enjoying the warm familiar smells of the kitchen.

Daisy took the skillet off the stove and removed the bacon from the pan, setting it aside to drain and crisp. She turned over the three pancakes she was making one more time before putting them on Zabette's plate and setting the sorghum and butter on the table. And she placed two thick slices of bacon on the plate beside them. Zabette sat down at her place as Daisy poured her a glass of the cold milk she had brought in that morning from the well house.

Daisy sat down beside her, smiling at the little girl. "Zabette," she began, "how would you like to spend the night with me tonight?"

Zabette, trying to cut up her sorghum-soaked pancakes, looked up at her with a sparkle in her eye. It would be fun to spend the night back in her old house, where she'd lived with her mother.

"That'd be fine, Daisy. I'd have to ask Miz Marguerite and Mas' Pierre." Even in front of Daisy, she never called them *Grand'mère* or *Papa*.

"I bet they say yes," Daisy said lightly." And it sho' will be quieter in my cabin, no squallin' baby to wake you up in the middle of the night." Zabette had not considered that, but it surely made sense to her. "Now finish those pancakes and run see if the folks be down for breakfast yet."

ZABETTE RACED ACROSS THE DOGTROT and into the dining room. Marguerite and Pierre were just seating themselves at the dining room table. They were the only ones who came down for breakfast as a rule. Since the birth of her baby, Catherine had begun taking her own breakfast on a tray in her bedroom. As soon as her grandmother sat down, Zabette ran with excitement over to the table.

"Daisy asked me to spend the night with her," she announced, bouncing on her toes. "Can I, please, *Grand'mère*, please, can I?"

"May I," Marguerite corrected. She had begun to practice her own English and was determined that Zabette should speak correctly.

"May I? Please," Zabette asked again.

"Well . . . " Marguerite hesitated, as she and Daisy, who had just entered the room with a pot of coffee in her hand, exchanged looks that the child could not decipher. All she noticed were their smiles. "I suppose it would be all right."

"She could even stay till that baby be sleepin' through the night, if you was a mind to let her," Daisy said.

"We'll see," Marguerite said noncommittally. "We'll see."

So Zabette moved back into the cook's cottage.

ON A FRESH MORNING THE FOLLOWING OCTOBER, Zabette's papa took her on one of their frequent rides together. She sat on the saddle in front of him, pensive, nestled against his warm body as they made their way up the road that stretched between Plum Orchard and Rayfield. Suddenly she turned to look up at him and said, "*Papa, Grand'mère* said that you cough a lot at night. I heard her tell Daisy. Are you all right?"

Pierre laughed at her frowning, worried face. "It's nothing, *ma p'tite*, just a little cold. I'm fine. You mustn't worry your little head about me."

But she had been upset by her grandmother's words. What would her life ever be like without her father? She didn't want her papa to be sick.

He said he was fine, and he did seem fine. The cough subsided after cotton picking, and she stopped worrying. He continued to go about his daily tasks and, when spring came, he supervised the planting himself. He never hired an overseer. Instead he used a black driver who got the slaves up and to the fields by sun-up. That allowed him to sleep a little later.

Zabette spent her mornings with Daisy in the kitchen until it was time to serve dinner. In the afternoon, after the slaves returned to the fields, she was allowed to wander into the quarters several hundred yards behind their house to find Adeline, who was not quite six and still too young to go to the fields. Aunt Flora, the former cook, now too old and crippled for any other kind of work, looked after the young children in the quarters during the day.

Adeline taught Zabette some of the hand-clapping games the slave children played: "Green Sally up, Green Sally down, Green Sally bake her possum brown."

The girls chanted, blending their sweet voices as they sat on the wooden step in front of Aunt Flora's cabin clapping the complicated ritual that accompanied the song. Zabette got tangled up so often that both girls dissolved in laughter.

In return Zabette taught Adeline the rhymes and counting games that her grandmother had taught her: "*Un, deux, trois, j'irai dans le bois; quatre, cinq, six, chercher des cérises . . .* " Adeline proved to be a good pupil, though her French pronunciation was a bit shaky.

ONE HOT SUMMER DAY, Zabette, who was learning to read at her grandmother's knee, brought her little picture book to the quarters. As Zabette read to Adeline from her perch on the step of Aunt Flora's cabin, the younger girl sat patiently on a nearby stool fashioned from a tree stump and listened attentively to the story of *Le petit chaperon rouge*, Little Red Riding Hood, as she tried to peer at the pictures upside down.

Aunt Flora, only half-listening as she sat nearby shelling peas for supper, did not approve. "Mighty dangerous things they be teachin' you at that Big House, Zabette. Slaves ain't s'posed to know how to read."

"But I'm not a slave, Aunt Flora."

"Yes, you is. Yo' mama was a slave, and that makes you a slave. "

Zabette was puzzled by her words. She didn't live in the quarters. She didn't work in the fields. She didn't wear the colorless cotton and wool garments the slaves wore. She didn't even talk like them. She couldn't be one of them.

"I'll ask Miz' Marguerite," Zabette said, sure it would settle the matter once and for all.

THAT NEXT MORNING, when her grandmother and father were in the dining room drinking their coffee and waiting for Daisy to bring in their breakfast, Zabette crept up to the large table and sat down in the chair beside her grandmother. She lifted her eyes to look earnestly at Miz Marguerite.

"Am I a slave, *Grand'mère*? Aunt Flora says I am."

She waited for her grandmother to answer, staring intently at her face, which had suddenly turned pale. The old woman was looking at her son at the other end of the table. The child's gaze went from one to the other. She was puzzled by their silence. She knew that life in the quarters was different from her own life and that most of the slaves had darker skin than she did, but she wasn't quite sure what it meant to be a slave—just that one had to work a lot and live in a small house.

"Well, am I?" Zabette persisted. "Am I a slave?"

"Well now, Zabette, that's an odd question," her grandmother answered. "Do we make you feel like a slave?"

"*Non, Grand'mère*," she answered, though she wasn't sure just how a slave should feel. Her voice was small and bewildered. "I told Aunt Flora I wasn't a slave, but she kept saying I had to be 'cause my mama was a slave."

Marguerite's eyes pleaded with Pierre for help. He cleared his throat. "Well, *ma p'tite*, your mother was our house servant." He could never use the word *slave* when he spoke of Marie-Jeanne, even now.

"Is that a slave?" the child persisted.

"Technically," he said, though she didn't understand the word, "but in our hearts, at the time you were born she was more like a member of the family."

Zabette was more confused than ever. "Am I a member of the family?"

"*Bien sûr*, absolutely," her father said. "You are my daughter."

"Then I can't be a slave," she said resolutely, satisfied with their answers, and raced back toward the kitchen to help Daisy bring in the eggs and bacon. She did not notice the painful glances Marguerite and Pierre exchanged, though neither said a word.

Chapter Eight

PIERRE BEGAN TO COUGH AGAIN as the days grew shorter. Zabette was only a child, but she fretted over him as much as his mother and Catherine did.

"Nothing to worry about," he assured them all. Fall and winter often brought these little indispositions, he argued. "Nothing to worry about."

On most days now Daisy lit the fires in all the fireplaces in the early morning to knock off the chill. By noon it usually warmed up enough to let them die down, and some days they weren't needed at all. Island weather was unpredictable this time of year. The Atlantic storms of early fall usually waned by late November, but tides were still high, and the morning winds often blew chilly off the ocean.

Although Zabette liked the smoky smell of the early morning fires, she didn't like the damp windy months. Even when the growing season ended, her father never rested. Once the cotton was picked, ginned, baled, and shipped off to the factor, his agent in Savannah, he oversaw the clearing of the fields and the hauling of mud from the marshes and manure from the pastures to fertilize the sandy soil and get it ready for the next spring planting.

The one break from the daily farm routine came when the weather turned cold, and her father brought the people from the quarters to take charge of butchering hogs and cattle. Most everyone on the plantation came together, and all were busy from sunup to sundown. Men in bloody aprons did the slaughtering, chopped the meat, and hauled the heavy chunks of ham and beef to the smokehouse to hang and cure for the winter's supply. Some of the women ground up the leftover parts and stuffed the pork intestines with seasoned meat to make sausages, setting aside some of the innards for chitlins. They also took charge of the beef maws, pigs' feet, and neck bones that would become meals for the slaves in the coming weeks. Others hovered over heavy iron pots, stirring the turgid brew of boiling water and lard that rendered up fat to make soap for the coming year. Usually Pierre would oversee it all, but this year he had given more responsibility to his most trusted hands, Frederick and Henry.

Even though Pierre's increasing weakness made it difficult for him to mount his horse, he still managed to ride his lands daily, sometimes with Zabette mounted before him. Together they would scout the fields to ensure that fences were intact and that none of the island's wild horses were feeding in the pastures.

Her father was as impatient for spring as she was, both eager for the earthy smell of freshly plowed fields and the new cotton plants peeking through the soil. Zabette loved the unexpected flashes of pink and the delicate scents of plum blossoms and purple wisteria. She looked forward to hearing the hungry new calves bawling to their mothers, the call of migrating birds moving north, and even the roars of alligators mating in nearby ponds—the sounds and smells of creation, of new life.

"WANT TO GO RIDING WITH ME, Zabette?" Pierre asked his daughter one morning after she and Daisy had finished clearing the breakfast table. It was an invitation that always made her feel special.

"*Oui, papa.*" She danced toward the back door to fetch her coat. These rides with her father were her favorite moments in the day. Perched on the saddle with her papa's arms around her made her feel safe. The woods were alive with bird calls as they rode. He showed her how the live oak trees near the beach bent away from the ocean winds, while near the river those same oaks stood upright to host the Spanish moss that hung from their branches. She loved the smell of the honeysuckle along the road and the gray moss that hung like old men's beards from the trees.

"See those dried-up ferns?" He pointed toward the brown, withered fronds that clung to the oak branches. "They're called Resurrection ferns, and when it rains they come back to life." Sure enough, after the next rainy day, there they would be, unfurled, lush, and bright green against the dark branches. It was as though he wanted to teach her everything he knew. And she felt growing within her a love of Cumberland that bound her to her father and to this island world.

Once he'd shown her how to clean and bandage a wound when Zic punctured his finger on a rusty nail from a broken fence. She turned away from the blood at first, but he encouraged her to look at the wound and taught her how to apply pressure and put the bandage on to stop the bleeding. He let her take his pulse. And he told her about some of the island's medicinal plants, stopping beside a prickly bush and breaking off a small branch.

"This is called a 'toothache tree,'" he said, "because if you crush the leaves and rub them on the gum, they can stop a toothache." She peered intently at the pointed green leaves so that she would be sure to recognize them. "But be careful of the prickly stems." He pulled off a leaf and crushed it against his hand. "Smell," he said, holding it to her nose. It smelled of lemon.

As they rode on, he pointed toward the woods. "See those thick vines over there." She nodded. "They're wild muscadines. They have grapes in the spring. Not much good for doctoring, I'm afraid," he laughed. The heavy drape of vines hung from sturdy branches and tangled their tendrils below in the sparkleberry bushes and yaupon hollies.

Winter light filtered through the palmetto fronds, and birdcalls pierced the silent woods. A woodpecker hammered on a distant tree, and an occasional lizard or snake scurried across the road in front of them, making the horse dance and Zabette squeal with delight. The child gobbled at the wild turkeys that fed along the edges of the forest, causing them to interrupt their quest for food and raise their heads. Best of all, she nestled against the familiar smell of her father's body.

Chapter Nine

As PIERRE RODE WITH ZABETTE, he found himself thinking more and more often about the child's mother. On days he rode alone, he sometimes indulged himself in remembering their time together and cursed himself for his obstinacy. Marie-Jeanne's face would appear before him unbidden, and he grew increasingly curious about the boy child that everyone said resembled him. He tried to concentrate his thoughts on Catherine and Margaret. But now, with Zabette leaning against his chest, he felt such love for this little girl, so bright and happy despite all that had happened to her, he felt his heart would burst. He knew that Catherine resented his rides with Zabette. He could not avoid the snapping anger in her eyes when he left the house on such mornings holding the child's hand. But he would not give in to their unspoken demands.

I've become an old married man, he thought, old before his time, snared in a marriage that was neither happy nor unhappy. *It's my own fault,* he told himself. He'd tried to be a good husband and show as much attention and affection to little Margaret as he did to Zabette. But the baby was still too young to interest him much. He was thankful that Catherine's preoccupation with little Margaret absorbed so much of her attention, for it helped assuage his guilt. Whatever its state, he knew, this marriage was a fact, a legal entity. He was determined to keep his vows, even though he bore them like a yoke—not with the wild sweetness he had tasted with Marie-Jeanne.

On his morning rides with Zabette, he felt his spirits lift as she asked him a million questions at every turn. He loved showing her the island, though he took care to keep her away from Cumberland's white families. The other planters knew he had a mulatto child, as many of them did, but the situation with Zabette was different. She had lived in his home like a family member. She could read as well as he could, which he certainly did not want other whites to know, since teaching slaves to read was against the law. She spoke fluent French and English. And she wore clothes that were as nice as those of other planters' legitimate offspring. There would have been too many quizzical looks and questions if he paraded her before them.

Except for these rides, she ventured no farther than the quarters to play with Adeline while the workers were in the fields. Adeline would soon be old enough to work alongside her parents and siblings, which might cause Zabette to raise new questions he didn't know how to explain beyond what he had already said. Now that she was helping Daisy in the kitchen, she was at least receiving training that would save her from the fields. But he was concerned about her future when he was no longer there to protect her.

To Zabette her kitchen duties were still only a game. She was learning where to place each silver fork when she set the table and how to squeeze fresh oranges for juice. She had even been trusted to shell peas and string beans. Best of all, she could cut biscuits from the dough that Daisy rolled out with her large rolling pin on the hard surface of the doughboy.

"I love making biscuits," she had once told her father. "I remember making biscuits with *Maman*. That was our most fun," she smiled. Then her eyes crinkled in pleasure as she recalled something even better. "But the best was our picnic in the orchard." Her mention of that perfect afternoon, still vivid in his memory as well, pierced Pierre's heart. His throat caught at the recollection of the sweet, smoky scent of Marie-Jeanne as she raced with their daughter among the falling blossoms and fell laughing beside him.

"Sometimes," said Zabette, her dark eyes suddenly solemn, "I can't remember *Maman* very well. Sometimes I can't remember her face."

I have the same problem, my child, he thought. He could feel Marie-Jeanne's presence, but the tender outlines of her face were no longer clear. When he caught a glimpse of her in the fields, she was like a stranger. She looked past him, but never at him. And he knew that he deserved it.

Zabette was his primary concern now. He would try with all his might to protect her, to make it up to her for what he had done to her mother. If he had his way, she would never be a servant at all. He was grateful for Daisy's attention and instructions to the child. At worst, Zabette would be a house servant. But Daisy fumed perpetually over what she considered the indulgence of "Mas' Pierre" and his mother, insisting that they spoiled Zabette terribly and created false expectations in her. "Wha's she ever gone be but a slave? Ain't nothin' ever gone change that," she insisted. "She might as well learn how to be one."

"Don't be ridiculous," he said. "I'll always look after her."

Daisy muttered under her breath as she flounced out of the dining room. It was clear that she didn't trust his promise. Why should she? Hadn't he also promised to protect Zabette's mother? *But I would never betray my daughter,* Pierre vowed. *Whatever happens I will always take care of her.*

PIERRE'S COUGH GREW WORSE in the winter months of 1827. By mid-January he was too weak to ride and his handkerchiefs were spotted with blood. Marguerite was beside herself. It was hard to make him see a doctor. He always thought he knew what was best.

"That Bernardey stubbornness again," she grumbled.

She talked to Pierre about moving inland, upcountry to a drier climate, but he would have nothing to do with the idea. Catherine too was worried and for once supported her mother-in-law.

"I'm needed here," he told them. "What would happen to the plantation without me?"

"That's exactly what I'm concerned about," Marguerite said.

He looked at her sharply, refusing to admit the thought. "Don't fret about me," he said repeatedly to them both. "I'll be fine by summer."

BUT HE WASN'T FINE. He grew weaker. Instead of mornings surveying his pastures or taking Zabette for early-morning rides, he just sat on the porch and gazed out at his land and the marshes beyond the river. He was dying, and he knew it. He worried daily for his family, especially his mother and Zabette. How would they manage without him? He had every faith in Catherine's strength to take care of her property and little Margaret. She would soon marry again, he felt sure. She was a fine-looking woman, despite her snappish ways, and her father was well off. Besides she would have her own land to bring to any new marriage. *She'd be a right choice young widow*, he thought.

But his mother was getting old. And Zabette would be at the mercy of too many forces if something should happen to Marguerite as well. Pierre knew that Georgia law did not permit Zabette to inherit from him or his mother. She would be penniless and in bondage. He wondered for the first time if Daisy was right. Had she had enough time to prepare Zabette for life as a house servant if it came to that? He couldn't bear the thought of her living in the quarters, chopping cotton, hauling the black marsh silt to the fields. His mother would take care of her, he knew. *But for how long?* What would happen to Zabette when Marguerite died? They would need an overseer for the plantation, and his mother would need help handling all the legal matters. Women who knew so little about business were easy to cheat. Uncertainties plagued him, and during the winter of his dying he gave the matter much thought. As his strength failed, Pierre finally decided on two things that he must do before he was gone.

For the first, he waited until Catherine went into St. Marys to spend a week with her mother to celebrate Madame Corb's fiftieth birthday. He sent his regrets, for as they all knew, he was not fit to travel.

Although he made every effort to get up each morning, by afternoon he was worn out and ready to rest. He would lie in his room with his eyes closed while his mother or Zabette read to him. More and more frequently, Marguerite would pass the book to Zabette to let her practice her reading. Sometimes they read in English from the travels of William Bartram, who had passed by Cumberland Island in 1794. And sometimes in French a work by Chateaubriand or Voltaire. Zabette stumbled over the hard words, but her grandmother patiently corrected her. Marguerite's French was much better than Pierre's. She had grown up speaking the purest French learned in the Touraine before her family moved to Brittany, while he often mingled English words with his own poor Breton French. He did not have the education or sense of literature that she had and was trying to pass on to Zabette.

On the afternoon of Catherine's departure for the mainland, Pierre said to Zabette, "*Ma p'tite*, can you go and fetch me a glass of cold water." She leapt to her feet to do what he asked.

As she bounded down the stairs, Pierre turned to his mother. "*Maman*, I need to speak with Marie-Jeanne. Can you bring her here tomorrow afternoon?" He spoke quickly, wanting to complete this conversation before Zabette returned.

"*Tu es certain*? Are you sure, Pierre?" she asked.

"I'm sure," he sighed deeply. "It's something I should've done a long time ago."

His mother nodded. "I'll bring her of course, *mon fils*," she said.

Zabette rushed back into the room with a brimming glass of water. "*Voici, Papa*," she said. "Here it is."

He took it gratefully. "You look so much like your *maman*," he said, touching her cheek. "So much."

Chapter Ten

WHEN THE SUMMONS TO COME TO THE BIG HOUSE reached Marie-Jeanne, she knew she had no choice but to go. But she hated the idea. What did he want of her? What further humiliation had he thought of?

As she stood with Miz Marguerite outside Pierre's room, she felt conscious of her bare feet, still dusty from the road. The old woman tapped on his door.

"*Entrez,*" Marie-Jeanne heard him call. As they entered the room, she hardly recognized him. He was thin and pale. His skin had taken on a sallow look, and his eyes were bright with fever. Could this be the same person she had known?

But she was aware of how much she too had changed. Her reflection in the mirror, broken during the move to the quarters, had long since made that clear. She had finally put the mirror away, stored it under her bed. But not before it had told her that she was no longer the pretty young woman she had been. Her skin was sun-darkened, lined, and rough, and her hair, once long and lustrous, was coarse and dry. Her hands were blistered. Her clothes were tattered, and dirty, for she had just come from the fields. A faded green bandana covered her head and was tied at the nape of her neck. Her eyes had grown dull and wary. Her face showed the bitterness of being forced to come here straight from her work and not even allowed to wash up.

Pierre had severed any connection between them forever, except for that of slave and master. It was their only bond—except for Zabette and Jack.

He gestured for her to come closer. She hesitated then took a single step toward the bed where he was half-reclining, half-sitting. He looked at her as though he had never seen her before. She stared at the floor, barely noticing when Miz Marguerite left the room.

Silence flooded the space between them. Finally Pierre whispered, "Can you ever forgive me?"

"You be the master. You can do what you want. I'se jus' yo slave," Marie-Jeanne replied in exaggerated dialect, her eyes fixed on a knothole on the floor.

"Marie-Jeanne, please look at me."

She forced her dark eyes to move slowly up from the heart of pine floor, across the bed and finally to his face. He was begging, not commanding, she realized. Despite her blinking to stop them, tears welled up and began to spill over her lower lids. The sight of him after such a long time weakened her resolve in spite of her determination to show nothing but indifference.

"I made a terrible mistake to send you away. I've missed you, Marie-Jeanne. So much." She said nothing, her hands kneading her crossed forearms.

"Please, talk with me. Forgive me," he pleaded. "I've treated you so badly."

Still she said nothing. How could she ever forgive his cruelty? What could she say? *What do you want of me,* her eyes asked, betraying her as tears ran unchecked down her cheeks. She saw only sadness when she looked at him, his face sallow and weak, dark circles around his eyes. They both knew he was dying.

"Marie-Jeanne, please, if you'll let me, I want to see your son, Jack. *Our* son," he corrected himself. "Will you bring him to see me? Soon? Tomorrow?"

She said nothing.

"Please," Pierre pleaded, "I need to see him at least once before . . . " His voice trailed off.

She looked at him again, surprised at his tone, and wiped her eyes with her fingers.

"I reckon," she replied without outward emotion, though she recognized the concession he was making in asking her for permission.

"I thought it was William made you pregnant," he said suddenly.

"Naw suh," she said. "I knew it couldn't be William."

"How?" he asked. "How did you know?"

"He ain't never succeed in what he try to do. He tore my gown and humped around, but he was too drunk for much else. I just kep' pushin' him off. He was jes' a boy."

"Oh, God, Marie-Jeanne, why didn't you tell me?" Pierre put his hand to his forehead, rubbing it as if to stop the pounding. She was surprised to see tears standing in his eyes, as he blinked them back.

She looked at him, a fragile smile of irony on her lips. "Don't seem like you ever give me a chance."

"*O Dieu, qu'est-ce que j'ai fait?*" he moaned. "What have I done?"

She had no answer. But she felt herself smile as she said, "Jack, he's a good boy, Massa. A good boy. He look like you."

"I was so wrong, Marie-Jeanne, so wrong. And now it's too late."

"Ain't never too late, Mas' Pierre. Ain't never too late to ask forgiveness from the Lord."

"I've already done that a million times, Marie-Jeanne. Now I'm asking forgiveness from you."

She made no move, no acknowledgment of his request, withholding what she knew he wanted most. It was the one thing she could not give. He asked too much.

"I'll bring him tomorrow, Massa," she said quietly as she slipped out of the room and closed the door behind her.

Marie-Jeanne watched Pierre's eyes widen when he saw two-year-old Jack in her arms. Miz Marguerite had ushered them into his room and stood behind them taking in her son's reaction. The boy was a tiny replica of himself— with dark sandy hair and a sweet rendition of his own thin face. The child's eyes were not dark brown like his mother's, but rather sea-gray like his own and with the same little flecks of gold. Pierre stared at him for a long moment, then reached out for the child's hand. Marie-Jeanne set him down, and with uncertainty the toddler let himself be drawn toward his father's bed.

Using every ounce of his strength, Pierre took the boy in his arms, "*Mon fils,* my son." He held him close and kissed the top of his head. The child squirmed in his embrace and with a whimper stretched toward his mother.

As she lifted the little boy up again, Marie-Jeanne noticed Pierre's moist eyes reflecting the light of the afternoon sun that streamed through the window.

"I can't undo what I've done to you and little Jack," he said in a low voice. "I'm married now, and it's too late to make things as they were." He tightened his jaw. "But I swear to you that the two of you will never be separated and you will never work another day in the fields. Find yourself a spot to your liking on my land, and I'll have a cabin built for the two of you. Mother will see to it." Miz Marguerite nodded in agreement. "I'll find something for you to do away from the fields."

He had not offered them real freedom, Marie-Jeanne noted, but something close. She knew, as he did, that it was illegal to free a slave in the state of Georgia. She knew, too, that freedom could be dangerous for a person of color. Unscrupulous planters could sometimes find ways to enslave free blacks. They could leave the state, perhaps, but in truth, they had nowhere to go, and even getting out of the state posed many risks.

She said nothing, but listened cautiously as he went on. "When I die, which will be soon, you will both belong to my mother. She'll see to your welfare. That I promise." Again Miz Marguerite nodded, as Pierre's voice broke into an uncontrollable cough.

Marie-Jeanne waited for the cough to pass. Then she asked softly, "What about Zabette?"

Startled by the question, he looked from her to his mother before he said finally, "You may see her if you like, but I think it's best for her to stay here. *Maman* needs her, and it's the only life she's known for a long time now."

Marie-Jeanne made no reply. So she was still a slave after all, in spite of his grand words. But at least she would have her own cabin and her son. She would no longer have to leave her boy to work in the fields. And at least she could see Zabette and sometimes hold her in her arms. It wasn't all she'd hoped for, but it was something—more, she knew, than most of her friends in the quarters could ever dream of.

She nodded, gazed at Pierre one last time, and with her son in her arms, left the room to seek her spot of land.

Chapter Eleven

WHEN MARIE-JEANNE AND JACK LEFT, Pierre felt cleansed, if not forgiven. She had smiled only once throughout the meeting, as she spoke of her son, but he thought he saw a softening in her eyes as he told her what he wanted to do. She no longer looked like the sweet, young girl he had taken to his bed so long ago, the girl he had loved, but he knew that she was today what he had made her. He hoped that what he planned to do would in part make amends for his foolishness. It was not enough. But it was all he could offer.

His second task was still before him. His body was giving out, and he knew he could not wait long. He was already having alternating fevers, chills, and night sweats that allowed little sleep. He brought a slave named John from the quarters to spend most of his days at the Big House attending to his master's needs and helping with his personal care. One morning when Pierre felt that he had strength enough to let John help him down the stairs, he sent word to his neighbor Robert Stafford, whose Planters House was just three miles south of Plum Orchard, inviting him for a quiet midday dinner—just the two of them.

His friendship with Stafford, the wealthiest man on the island, had been primarily as a hunting companion. Pierre had often gone quail hunting with both Stafford and Phineas Nightingale, the owner of Dungeness, the island's south end plantation. But he'd never hunted with the two of them together, for the two men despised one another, the consequence, he assumed, of a land transaction that had left them bitter enemies. He liked them both. Now, however, it was not hunting that he had in mind in calling Stafford to his home.

Pierre asked both his mother and Catherine, back from the mainland, to have their dinner served in their rooms. Curious but unquestioning, Marguerite, in an uncharacteristic gesture, invited Catherine and baby Margaret to her own room to dine. She asked Daisy and Zabette to bring dinner up before noon, and kept Zabette there to help with the baby. She turned it into an adventure—a ladies' dinner, she called it. No men allowed. Catherine accepted, touched by the rare invitation.

ROBERT STAFFORD ARRIVED SHORTLY AFTER NOON. Daisy answered the door. Standing on the threshold, his six-foot-three frame almost filling the doorway, he towered over the short, stout woman. His height and rigid bearing intimidated most people, Daisy included. But she ushered him into the parlor, where Pierre was seated in a carefully chosen stiff, upright chair. Without speaking or rising to greet his visitor, he motioned for Stafford to sit on the horsehair sofa nearby.

Robert was shocked by his neighbor's gaunt appearance. He had not seen him for a couple of months, despite the proximity of their plantations. Pierre seldom left the house now, and before this moment, Robert had had no idea he was so ill. He noticed a tiny spot of blood at the corner of Pierre's mouth.

Robert sat down awkwardly on the edge of the sofa, wondering how he could express concern without insulting Pierre.

Finally he asked, "What can I do for you, my friend?"

"Would you like a sherry? Over there—please, help yourself." Pierre waved once again toward a sideboard across the room. "And pour one for me, would you?"

A decanter containing an amber liquid and two small glasses sat on the sideboard. Neither man was accustomed to drink so early in the day, but Robert agreed that just now a little alcohol might benefit them both. He filled the glasses, handed one to Pierre, and sat down, facing his host once again.

Pierre took a sip from the glass and began to cough. He pulled out a linen handkerchief and held it to his lips until the coughing subsided.

"As you can see, Robert," he began tentatively, "I am a sick man."

"I didn't know, Peter," he said, using the English name for Pierre, as he always did. "I could have helped you out some this past fall."

"There is something you can do to help me now, if you're willing," began Pierre, pausing a moment and breathing heavily. "And I hope you will extend that courtesy to my mother when I'm gone."

Robert looked at him, searching for something to say. Finally, he managed to blurt out, "Oh, now Peter, I'm sure it's not as bad as all that. You'll be fine by Easter."

"No," Pierre said firmly. "I'll be lucky to make it till Easter. I'll probably be lying in that clearing east of the house before then."

Robert had never heard anyone proclaim his own coming death with such certainty before, and he was exceedingly restless in the presence of such resolute gloom. Even though he was a cynic about most things, he would deny his own mortality to the very devil if he had to. He could never imagine facing it with such conviction. Yet Pierre Bernardey sat here before him, the picture of one waiting to die. Robert took a large gulp of sherry. He was a man unaccustomed to feeling uncertain about anything, and yet he had no idea what was expected of him.

Pierre hesitated. Then he plunged into what Robert realized was the purpose of this invitation. "Robert, when I am gone, my mother will need help sorting things out. I'll do all I can to make arrangements before the 'event,' but I want to ask you if you will stand by her and help her. She and the plantation will be vulnerable."

Robert looked at him with a steady gaze as he took in what his friend was requesting of him. Peter was asking him to sacrifice his long-standing ambition to own all of Cumberland Island. He knew people considered him ruthless in the way he sometimes went about acquiring whatever land might come available. But he didn't care. He had a perfectly legal right to lend money to people and then, when they could not pay the debt in the allotted time, to seize the property they had offered for collateral. He didn't beg them to take his money, after all. They got themselves into their own messes, and he had little sympathy for people who couldn't manage their affairs. He thought with satisfaction of how he had taken advantage of a family dispute in 1813 to make a hasty purchase of six hundred prime acres that Cornelia Greene Littlefield had inherited from her father, the late revolutionary war general Nathanael Greene. Cornelia had sold her land to

Robert to spite the angry objections of her mother, Caty Greene Miller, now remarried but still the owner of Dungeness, the largest and most imposing house on Cumberland. He didn't care that the transaction had won him the family's perpetual animosity. He already had that. He didn't care that it deepened an ongoing feud between himself and especially the old general's grandson, Phineas Nightingale. He'd thumbed his nose at them all and built his home, Planters House, on that very piece of land.

What his friend was asking was something no one had ever asked before. He was aware that Peter was watching him intently as he considered the request. It was not easy to go against one's natural instincts and deepest desires. He fully understood what Peter wanted—to protect his mother from Robert's encroaching on the Bernardey land under any circumstances, from undermining Marguerite in order to get her to sell, and in fact even to help her hold on to her land—in short, to put aside his own personal goals to aid the mother of a friend. He was appealing to Robert's sense of honor. No one had ever done that before. Robert said nothing for a long moment. Then he raised his glass toward his friend.

"Peter, you need not worry," Robert said. "I'll look after your mother. You have my word." Robert Stafford never gave his word lightly. In spite of what everyone else thought, he considered himself a man of honor.

"But what about your wife and daughter?" Robert asked.

"I think that Catherine will do well on her own. She's a strong woman, and of course she has her father to help her in legal matters. She'll take care of little Margaret." He paused and coughed uncontrollably for a few moments, his handkerchief at his mouth to catch the blood.

When the spasm had passed, Pierre leaned forward. "But there is one more thing, Robert. One very important thing."

"What's that?"

"I have another daughter."

The existence of Elisabeth Bernardey was not news to Robert Stafford. In spite of Pierre's efforts to hide her from the white families of the island, news traveled through the slave grapevine. Everyone on Cumberland knew of her existence.

Nevertheless, he asked politely, "Another daughter?"

"A six-year-old girl, Elisabeth. Almost seven. We call her Zabette." Pierre paused, knowing that he had no choice but to confide in Robert. He would have to know everything in order to protect her. "She was born on Jekyl Island before we came to Cumberland. Her mother was our house servant at the time."

"A slave?" asked Robert, well knowing the answer.

"Legally a slave, but the child lives, or at least lived, with us until Margaret was born. Now she lives in the cook's cabin with Daisy, but her grandmother is seeing to her training." Robert noticed that he had not used the word "education," though rumors on the island said she could read. Robert wondered if he had avoided the word deliberately, for they both knew the law against teaching a slave to read. "She is bright and pretty and a joy to us both," Pierre added.

"Indeed," said Robert noncommittally.

"Her grandmother will look after her as long as she lives, but I want to be sure she's never sent to the fields or mistreated in any way. Can you help me?"

It was a tall order. Robert knew that even he could not guarantee for her entire lifetime that Zabette would never meet with those who would treat her as a common slave. But he could try. It was all Pierre seemed to be asking.

"I'll make every effort to protect her, Peter. But you know how the slave laws are. At least I think I can make sure she's never sold away from Cumberland or from Mrs. Bernardey during her lifetime or mine."

"I don't want her sold at all. Not ever. At least not to anyone who isn't pledged to protect her," Pierre said adamantly, gesturing with both hands. It set off another fit of coughing.

When the cough subsided, Robert said softly, "I'll do my best. We both know your mother won't live forever. But if necessary, I'll buy the child myself and keep her safe." It was the best he could do. The most he could promise. The most anyone could expect.

Chapter Twelve

MARCH 8, 1827

A light silver rain fell around the somber gathering of twenty-four mourners and a priest beside the grave that had been dug about fifty yards behind the Big House. Only the thick foliage of a live oak protected them from getting soaked as the priest said necessary words over the sturdy pine box. Then six slaves, one of them Pierre's personal servant, John, lowered the casket by ropes into the open grave.

Marguerite wept beside the coffin, her hand on the shoulder of her daughter-in-law who was holding little Margaret in her arms. They were flanked by Robert Stafford, his mother Lucy, and his widowed sister Susannah. On the other side of the grave stood Phineas Nightingale, grandson of the late Caty Greene Miller. He had become heir to Dungeness at the death of his aunt, Louisa Greene Shaw, who had no children of her own.

Nightingale had positioned himself as far away from Robert Stafford as possible, for as everyone knew, he had nothing but distrust and loathing for the man. Both had come to pay their respects to the memory of Pierre Bernardey, who had been a good friend and neighbor. The only other white man present was John Grey from The Spring Plantation, which lay to the south of Stafford's lands. Like Pierre, he had lived on Jekyl Island before buying land on Cumberland the same year Pierre purchased Plum Orchard.

Behind them at a respectful distance, but still sheltered by the giant oak, a small group of field hands had assembled and were humming an unidentifiable melody, adding a sense of beauty and solemnity to the service. Zabette, who could not imagine the finality of death or a world without her father, clung to Daisy's hand and watched her grandmother dab at the tears running in unstoppable rivulets like raindrops down her cheeks.

MARIE-JEANNE, HER SON JACK IN HER ARMS, stood on the far edge of the orchard watching the solemn ceremony. She had found what shelter she could beneath a plum tree, though its branches, just beginning to swell with new buds, offered little protection from the rain.

Despite the distance she recognized Zabette there beside Daisy and remembered her first awkward meeting with her daughter, once she finally had Pierre's permission to see her. She'd knocked on the back door of the Big House the very next day. They had both changed so much and Zabette had grown so that they hardly recognized each other. But they had hugged anyhow, and Miz Marguerite had let her take Zabette to see the spot overlooking the orchard where she would build her cabin. They felt almost like strangers, and Marie-Jeanne knew they would have to get to know one another again. She had seen her daughter only once more since then until today. Their reunion, they both discovered, would take time.

"Tha's your daddy they buryin'," she said to little Jack, holding him closer and pressing her wet face against his soft cheek.

AFTER THE SHORT SERVICE, Marguerite and Catherine invited the Staffords, Mr. Grey, and Mr. Nightingale to stop by the house. They would have come anyhow, she knew, for it was the custom on the island to pay respects to the grieving and to partake of whatever food had been supplied by friends and by the household. The dining room table lay heavy with it—ham biscuits and the pecan pie that Lucy Spalding had sent over, and bowls of sugared and salted nuts taken from the larder. Daisy had fried two chickens, baked a jam cake, and put out corn relish, deviled eggs, pickled peaches, and lemon tarts. Bowls of shrimp and oysters, crab cakes, and even a grilled trout sent over by Mr. Nightingale from Dungeness graced the table. She and Zabette made sure the plates were kept full.

It was more than the few people who came could ever eat, but it was important for the Bernardey women to show hospitality and plenty. Marguerite was fearful that the implication of plenty might be a lie, but it was customary nonetheless.

The gathering was somber, not only because of Pierre's death, but also because Robert Stafford and Phineas Nightingale spent the afternoon avoiding each other at opposite ends of the room. Marguerite and Lucy Spalding tried to fill the void in between with conversation, as did John Grey, but it was difficult, for they could sense the tension between the two men. Susannah, who had learned her social skills as the wife of a now-deceased English naval officer, moved systematically among the various gentlemen, trying to make conversation. And Marguerite made it a point, when she could break away from Lucy, to speak with each one of the men and thank them for their friendship with her son.

It was a difficult afternoon for Marguerite, already exhausted with grief. For once, she was grateful that Catherine was there to help as hostess. Marguerite had little patience with these two stubborn men, particularly at such a time. How Pierre had managed to be friends with both of them, she would never know. But she was well familiar with their obstinacy.

It was a relief when everyone finally left and she could retreat to her room. Zabette, tired of helping Daisy in the kitchen, was waiting there for her, reading to her little rag doll from one of the books her grandmother had given her. When Marguerite entered the room, she held her arms open for Zabette, who flew to her grandmother and embraced her around the waist. How comforting those small arms were. Marguerite bent forward to hold the child close.

"It's just you and me now, *ma p'tite*," Marguerite whispered to her. "We must take care of each other."

There was a light tap at the door.

"*Entrez*," said Marguerite.

It was Daisy. "I done put away the food, ma'am, and I wanted to know if you needs anything 'fore I leave."

"*Non, merci*, Daisy. Please, take some of the food for your supper, and fix a basket for the people in the quarters. The children will love your lemon tarts. Leave a few here for Zabette. I'd like her to stay here with me tonight."

"Thank you, ma'am." Daisy left her mistress and Zabette to share their grief.

ANTICIPATING MARGUERITE'S INSTRUCTIONS, Daisy had already loaded two large baskets of food to carry to the people in the quarters. They would eat well tonight and participate in their own way in the master's death. They would sit up much of the night, maybe sing a hymn or two, and talk about the deceased. Even though they all hated slavery, they had for the most part liked Master Pierre—except for the time he whipped William.

While most of them agreed that William had deserved some kind of punishment for his drunken foolishness, they despised the brutal lashing and Master Pierre's unexpected cruelty, and they had been sorry to see William sold away from the island and particularly to Alabama, which was known for its harsh conditions for slaves.

The rain had stopped, and a sliver of moon was rising over the horizon as they finished their supper and washed up their tin plates. The women put the children to bed, and people brought out stools and chairs or squatted around the fire John had built outside his cabin. They talked quietly among themselves for a while, and then as the fire blazed and sent its sparks into the darkness, conversation turned to their master's death.

"I reckon God done punish Mas' Pierre like the massa done punish William," the old woman they all called Aunt Flora observed once they had settled down to quiet talk. Some of the people nodded in agreement.

As slave-owners went, they all knew, Pierre Bernardey had not been one of the worst. But even so-called good masters were still masters. Frederick professed to know a slave who had belonged to John Couper over on Saint Simons Island, a man reputed to be the most benevolent of slave owners. "But when them Englishmen come in eighteen-fo'teen, I hear them Couper slaves done left in droves. Ain't come back neither," he said,

The War of 1812 and the English raids on Jekyl and Saint Simons and especially their occupation of Cumberland was still a vivid memory to the older slaves. Many of their bolder friends had escaped on British sailing ships, leaving some to wonder why they had not gone as well.

"You say folks call him a good massa?" Zic asked. "I say they ain't no such thing as a good massa."

"Tha's right," agreed John.

The other men and women nodded, some adding a staggered chorus of *Uh huhs* in affirmation. For all of them, freedom was only a dream, the beacon they wanted to follow. They had heard about others who'd escaped, even after the British left. But few had the nerve, and those who did often wound up dead, or crippled from the beatings they got, no matter who the master was. *Too risky*, they thought, though every now and then they heard about someone who got away and was never found. It gave them all hope.

Conversation turned away from old masters and toward the future. The people of the quarters were apprehensive now that Pierre had died. Their talk that night focused on what might become of Miz Marguerite and Miz Catherine. They feared that the two women might bring in a cruel overseer or, worse, sell off their field hands so that they could move inland.

"I reckon I know one thing tha's gone keep Miz Marguerite right here," said Daisy who had stayed to have supper with her friends in the quarters and who, because of her position in the Big House, spoke with special authority.

"Wha's that?" Frederick asked.

"Zabette." Some nodded thoughtfully. Others shook their heads.

"That chile's all she got now," she argued. "An' she sho' ain't gone take her to town."

"But she got Miz Catherine and her baby," said John.

"Yeh, but they don't get along too good," said Daisy.

"Tha's what I hear," Frederick nodded. "But I reckon anything could happen."

"Tha's right," Zic agreed, staring into the leaping brightness of the fire. "Tha's right," he said again, already lost in his thoughts.

Chapter Thirteen

R OBERT STAFFORD WAS AS GOOD AS HIS WORD. Less than a week after Pierre's burial, he rode to Plum Orchard in mid-afternoon, dismounted, and tied his horse to the hitching post in front of the house. He tapped on the front door, and Daisy rushed to let him in, leading him into the same parlor where he and Pierre had had their last conversation. He sat on the same horsehair sofa with apprehensions not unlike those he had felt that afternoon, and he waited.

MARGUERITE WAS RESTING IN HER ROOM, still unable to resume anything remotely resembling a routine since her son's death. The most energy she had mustered was to help Catherine decide on a tombstone for Pierre's grave. But Pierre's death had not brought them closer together, and they had disagreed even about the words that should be etched on the stone. Marguerite wanted it to include Pierre's birth name, but Catherine had insisted upon the Anglicized version, "Peter Bernardey." In addition to the date of his death, March 7, and his age, forty-three, they finally compromised on the inscription:

> *He knows his Saviour died*
> *And from the dead arose,*
> *He looks for victory o'er the grave*
> *And death the last of foes.*

Once the decision was made, Catherine took her daughter and went into St. Marys to place the tombstone order and spend a few days with her parents, leaving her mother-in-law alone with her grief.

Marguerite rose wearily when Daisy summoned her to the parlor. She smoothed her hair and dress with her hands. Leaning toward the mirror for a closer look at her puffy eyes, she splashed them with cold water and patted them dry. It was the best she could do. Robert Stafford stood up to greet her as she descended the steps,.

"How kind of you to call," she said, taking his outstretched hand.

"I just wanted to see how you were managing and to offer my services, Mrs. Bernardey," Robert said, with a slight stiff bow. "If I can be of help to you in any way, I want you to call on me. It's a promise I made to Peter and one I intend to fulfill."

"It's very thoughtful of you to come by, Mr. Stafford. At the moment, I'm not sure that I am ready even to consider what I may need in the way of help. Pierre was ... " she began to crumple.

Stafford put his arm awkwardly around her shoulder. "Perhaps I've come too soon," he said. But the time may arise when you may need a man's help, and I want you to feel free to call on me whenever that time comes."

Marguerite was grateful for his words, but she didn't know how to reply. She had always felt strong, but now that strength was failing her, and she thought she might indeed need help. All that came from her lips was "Thank you, Mr. Stafford. I'm much obliged."

He stepped back and bowed slightly from the waist once more. "I'm at your service," he said briskly and turned quickly to leave, even before she could offer him tea.

Marguerite watched through the lace curtains as he mounted his horse, trotted around the left corner of the house, past Pierre's grave, and back toward the road, his back ramrod straight as he sat in the saddle.

What a strange man, she thought. He was thirty-seven years old, she'd learned from his mother, but had never married. According to Lucy Spalding, he had shown interest in a woman only once, when he sought to court Phineas Nightingale's sister, Catherine. But she had spurned his suit, Lucy told her, and he never courted any woman again. Since then, his only drive had been for land and power. There was a natural aura of authority about him. And a curious magnetism that both attracted and repelled. Marguerite wasn't sure whether she liked him or not, but obviously Pierre had trusted him and asked him to see to her welfare. She had faith in her son's judgment, and when the time came, it was to Robert Stafford she would turn for help.

THAT TIME CAME SOONER THAN SHE'D ANTICIPATED. By the end of March, she mustered the energy to realize the fields were ready for spring planting, but she had no idea where to begin. Catherine knew even less about running a plantation, for she had grown up as a merchant's daughter on the mainland. The two slaves most knowledgeable about the plantation, Frederick and Henry, offered contradictory advice, one suggesting that the corn needed to be put in first, and the other telling her that the cotton seeds would mold if she waited too long. She had no idea what she should do. Finally, in desperation, she asked John to drive her to Planters House to talk with Robert Stafford.

Robert was not at home, but his mother greeted her at the door. "Marguerite, how wonderful to see you. Do come in, my dear. I hope you're doing well," Lucy welcomed her with genuine concern in her voice.

"I'm doing as well as can be expected. But I need your son's advice, Lucy," she said as she stepped into the cool, dark parlor.

"He should be along at any time. We can have tea while we're waiting," Lucy said, steering Marguerite to the floral sofa and seating herself in the green button-back chair beside it. She picked up a little bell and rang it to summon her cook, Amanda.

Marguerite accepted the tea with gratitude. She considered Lucy her only female friend on the island and one in whom she could confide. Like her, Lucy was hungry for female companionship. Although she had her widowed daughter, Susannah, at home, she longed to talk with someone of her own generation. Susannah was bitter over the loss of her husband and could talk of nothing else. He had whisked her away from Cumberland when the British troops left the island during the waning years of the War of 1812, promising her the moon. But she had found England cold and damp and the people disdainful of "backwoods Americans." She felt betrayed by her marriage and even more by her husband's death. Lucy was sick of hearing about it and tired of her daughter's self-pity.

But with Marguerite she could gossip a bit about news concerning other planters on Saint Simons or Jekyl Island. Amelia du Bignon on Jekyl, she said, had given birth recently to another boy—one they finally named for his father, Henry Charles.

"That makes eight living children now, can you imagine? And they lost little Louisa and the two others. Louisa was such a charming girl and the apple of her grandfather's eye, you know. It was no wonder that old Christophe didn't live very long after that. It was losing her that brought on his death, they say—not to mention that awful marriage of his son, Joseph, to his own niece! What was her name—Clémence? And remember how his father disowned him! A real scandal that was—even in Brunswick! Of course, that was several years ago, but nevertheless . . ." Lucy Spalding prattled on. Marguerite enjoyed her chattering at first but was beginning to grow weary. Nevertheless, she was determined to wait for Robert.

Finally, after nearly an hour, the front door opened, and he walked in, aware of her presence from the carriage and driver parked out front.

"My dear Mrs. Bernardey," he said. "How nice of you to drop by." He loomed awkwardly over her, his fingers worrying the brim of the hat in his hand.

Marguerite had little energy left for the niceties of social calls. "Thank you, Mr. Stafford. Your mother has been most gracious," she said, setting down the china teacup, which Lucy had filled twice already.

"Indeed." He smiled as amiably as his stony face allowed.

"Once you told me that if I needed your help, I had only to ask. Well, the time has come. It may seem a small matter to you, but I am receiving conflicting information from the men in the quarters. What should I plant first? Corn or cotton?"

Robert laughed heartily. "What a wonderful question! And one I can answer! Corn can be planted twice a year in this climate, if you get it in early enough, but cotton is a one-season crop. If I were you, I would have the corn put in at once, then move on to the cotton. In fact, it really doesn't matter too much, as long as you wait past any final freeze, and we're way past that already."

IT WAS THE FIRST OF MANY VISITS Marguerite would make to the Stafford household, and in return Robert visited her home frequently, helping her to prepare legal papers, suggesting ways of managing the slaves, offering ideas for crop rotation and planting schedules, and recommending the best Savannah factors to handle the cotton sales. He showed her how to keep accounts and even came over occasionally to help with ledger entries. He was a wealth of information, and Marguerite soaked in all the advice he could give her. Pierre had well understood how to bring out the best in Robert Stafford—to make him feel valued and needed. By giving him responsibility for her welfare, he had guaranteed that Robert would not try to take advantage of his mother. Instead, Robert became her most trusted friend. She wondered if the time would ever come when she could return the favor.

Chapter Fourteen

C ATHERINE, STILL IN MOURNING CLOTHES, was keenly aware of Robert's visits, of the land he owned at Cumberland, and of his unmarried status. He was, in fact, seven years younger than Pierre had been, much closer to her own age. But he paid her little attention when he came to visit, focusing his attentions solely on Marguerite, until finally Catherine stopped even coming down to greet him. She did not want or need his advice. She could always rely on her father, and she soon turned elsewhere for consolation as well.

Although Catherine still lived at Plum Orchard, she took to spending more and more of her time at her parents' home in St. Marys. Life was more active there, and she had the opportunity to interact with a variety of people, who came and went in her father's store. Compared to Cumberland, the dock at St. Marys virtually buzzed with activity, and seamen from various parts of the world sometimes stopped there to buy supplies and make deliveries. It was quite by chance or, as her mother would say, *bonne chance*, that she met her future husband. His vessel had just arrived in town, and he greeted her on the street as she was walking toward her father's store.

"Pardon me, madam, but I wonder if you could point me to a good general store." Several stores were clearly visible from where they were standing, and she would later wonder if it was just a ploy to capture her attention. If so, it had worked. She was quite taken by the curly, light-brown hair that peeked from beneath his jaunty captain's cap, and by the lilt in his voice. He was clearly

English. Before she answered his question, she asked him where he was from.

"I'm from Cornwall, ma'am, Cornwall, England. A little town called Penzance. You've probably never heard of it."

"Can't say that I have," replied Catherine. She was intrigued by the handsome captain. "My father's store is just over there. If you like, you can walk me there."

The seaman grinned and fell into step alongside the fetching widow.

"My name's Laen, William Laen," he offered. "And yours?"

"I'm Catherine Bernardey. What brings you to St. Marys?"

He was delivering a ship to Savannah that he had sailed from St. Kitts, he told her. "But beyond that, I have no special plans. Maybe I'll come back to St. Marys when I leave Savannah," he said.

"That would be nice," she replied just as they reached the door to her father's store.

William Laen stocked up on everything he needed, chatted a bit more with Catherine and her father, and said his goodbyes, to set out for Savannah. Within two weeks he was back, apparently intrigued by the young widow with her pretty little girl, a well-off father, a 250-acre plantation on Cumberland Island, and another 250 acres she expected to inherit from her late husband.

WITH MINIMAL COURTING AND LITTLE FANFARE, the couple was married, as they said in St. Marys, "almost by the time the captain had got his land legs." Captain Laen could hardly believe his good fortune so soon after arriving in America. Here he was, already a plantation owner with his own slaves, he boasted in his letters to friends in Cornwall. Pierre had left no will, or at least none could be found, and, thus far, no disposition had been made of the quarter of his lands and all the slaves he had reserved for himself when the property division was made at the time of his wedding. Catherine and William both assumed that Catherine, as his widow, was entitled to inherit his share of the property, which would make her land holdings equal to Marguerite's, but they had not counted on the interference of Robert Stafford.

STAFFORD INSISTED THAT MARGUERITE PETITION for a share of her son's inheritance, not so much for herself, he pointed out, as to ensure the future of Zabette. Catherine was furious, and her new husband did not make matters easier. Finally, after much legal bickering, in an effort to end the dispute, both Marguerite and Catherine agreed to let the matter be settled by arbitration.

While there had been little affection between the women when Pierre was alive, there was even less now. They faced each other, flanked by their lawyers, in the office of the Superior Court judge at the tiny courthouse in Jeffersonton. A scowling William Laen sat beside his wife. Marguerite had sought the advice of Robert Stafford, as she did in most things now, and he had recommended his friend Belton Copp, a lawyer and former postmaster in St. Marys, to represent her.

Copp was a round-faced man in his forties, originally from Connecticut, where Stafford had first met him as a boy. He was not much to look at, Marguerite thought, but he spoke with authority and she felt reassured by his presence. After much discussion between the two lawyers, most of which appeared only to complicate matters, the two women agreed to select one arbiter each and to have the court select the third. Binding themselves with a $10,000 bond, both women pledged to accept the decision of the arbiters.

Marguerite, at the advice of her lawyer and by her own preference, chose Robert Stafford as her arbiter, while Catherine selected a St. Marys man and her father's friend, Lewis Bachlott. The third arbiter, chosen by the court with a nudge from Robert, was Henri du Bignon of Jekyl Island, who knew the Bernardeys well, but who was reputed to be a fair-minded man.

For Marguerite it was important that Robert be a part of the group, for only he knew of Pierre's wishes concerning Zabette, Marie-Jeanne, and Jack. It was the division of the slaves that mattered most to her, for she was determined at all costs to honor her son's wishes. Catherine, on the other hand, encouraged by her husband, was far more interested in the land. Both women could only wait to see what the arbiters would decide.

ON THE FOLLOWING JANUARY 14, Marguerite and Catherine were summoned to appear once more before the Superior Court Judge in Jeffersonton to learn of the property division decided by the arbiters.

Marguerite dressed nervously. Although she was sure that Robert Stafford and Belton Copp had tried to take care of things as she would like, she couldn't be sure they had succeeded, and she would worry until the division was final.

The two-hour boat ride into St. Marys was brisk. The weather was chilly, though fortunately well above freezing, as it usually was in the islands this time of year. She had dressed warmly in a dark burgundy wool dress, a black wool coat, hat, and heavy gloves. The oarsmen kept warm with their rhythmic chants and the strenuous pull to the mainland. She always enjoyed their songs, which echoed up and down the river channels, though she failed to notice the blisters on their hands at the end of the two-hour trip to St. Marys.

By the time they arrived, Marguerite's nose and ears were icy, and she still had to suffer through the bumpy carriage ride to Jeffersonton, which had replaced St. Marys as the seat of Camden County in 1800. *Obviously*, she thought, *the people who made that decision didn't live on the islands.* It doubled the length of the trip from Cumberland and turned any dealings with the courthouse into an all-day affair. Her old bones just weren't up to this sort of thing anymore, and she always hated to leave the island. Relieved to reach the warm, but rather primitive courthouse, she braced herself for what was to come.

Once everyone was seated, the judge handed to each of the women a document that stated the decision of the arbiters. Marguerite glanced quickly over the land division and turned hurriedly to page two where the division of the slaves was listed. They had awarded Marguerite fifteen slaves and Catherine nine. As she scanned her list, her eyes fell gratefully on the names of Marie-Jeanne, Jack, Daisy (which they had misspelled as "Dassy"), Frederick, Henry, and John. She had gotten Aunt Flora and Zic and even Zabette's friend Adeline. Most of those awarded to Catherine had been the slaves most recently acquired and to whom Marguerite had the least attachment. Although she had to give up a hundred acres of Plum Orchard to Catherine, she was left with ample land to support her for the rest of her life.

With a sudden shock, she realized that one name was missing from either list—Zabette. She looked quizzically at Robert, who had been watching her reaction. He shook his head almost imperceptibly as a sign for her not to raise the issue.

The court session ended when the judge proclaimed the property division final and demanded a signature from both women. Once in the hallway away from the other people, Marguerite turned to Robert. "What about Zabette?" she asked.

"After a good deal of discussion, Belton and I decided that it would be best not to name her as a slave, not to make her status a matter of record in the document. We believed, quite rightly, that Catherine would be so engrossed in the land division that she would fail to notice. In the long run, I think it will be in everyone's best interest."

"But what will happen to Zabette? I don't understand. Is this legal?"

"Trust me, Marguerite. She will be looked after."

She did trust him. But still, she fretted over the uncertainty of her granddaughter's legal status. She could not help but wonder whether such vagaries might not have future consequences that neither of them could foresee. Zabette, she knew, was in God's hands.

Chapter Fifteen

NOVEMBER 3, 1835

The day was warm for November. The sun was shining festively and a wedding was planned in the quarters. Adeline and Solomon were going to jump the broom that afternoon, a custom that signified marriage among the slaves. The excitement of the children was rising, and the women had been cooking all morning to make ready. November was a wonderful time for a wedding; the harvest was in, so both Saturdays and Sundays were their own, a special treat Marguerite allowed her slaves for one month after the cotton was picked, ginned, shipped to Savannah, and by now, perhaps on its way to England.

Adeline, the fourteen-year-old bride, was nervous, but giddy with anticipation. She needed to get away from the quarters for a while and decided to go to the Big House to make sure that Zabette was coming to her wedding. She made her way down the lane past the smokehouse toward the back of Plum Orchard.

The house was quiet, but she knew Daisy must be in the kitchen getting things ready for supper early today so that she could attend the celebration. Timidly Adeline knocked on the door to the kitchen. Daisy opened it, brushing flour off her cheek. "What you doin' here, Adeline? You better get on back to the quarters and that man o' yours. Don't want to give 'im time to change his mind." She gave a hearty chuckle and rolled her eyes in innuendo.

"I jes' wants to see if you and Zabette is comin' to the weddin.'"

"Course we is. Zabette's done picked out her dress."

"Nothin' too fancy, I hope."

"Don't you worry, chile. Ain't nobody gonna outshine the bride on her weddin' day."

Adeline was not too sure. Zabette was fifteen now and had grown into a strikingly beautiful adolescent with light honey-colored skin. Her eyes were as soft as those of the doe that sometimes had to be chased from the cornfield—large, the color of strong coffee, and with those odd golden flecks. Adeline, though she was younger, looked older. Her hips were larger, her skin dark as molasses, and her breasts developed far beyond her years. Solomon said she was the prettiest gal on the plantation. She loved it when he said that. But she knew that Zabette was prettier, though in a different way. Although Adeline didn't have the words to describe her, she could sense Zabette's difference, her refined ways. Marguerite had even taught her to play simple songs on the piano. But she was a friend from childhood, and Adeline wanted her to come to the broom-jumping ceremony.

At that moment, Zabette, hearing Adeline's unmistakable voice, bounded down the back stairs and toward the kitchen. "Hey, Adeline, what you doin' here? You're supposed to be getting ready to get . . . marrrrrieed," she teased, laughing and singing the last word. She dipped her finger into the pot of jam Daisy was using to bind together the two layers of the cake she was making. Daisy frowned and whapped her hand playfully with the wooden spoon she was using.

"You gone come?" asked Adeline, watching as Zabette smiled sheepishly at Daisy and licked the jam off her finger.

"Course, I'm comin' with Daisy and maybe even Miz Marguerite."

Adeline's eyes widened. "Is she gone be there?"

"Only if you want her to be," said Zabette. She knew that her grandmother sometimes made a brief appearance at such celebrations in the quarters, as a show of support for what she called "her people." But Marguerite's arthritis was acting up, so Zabette wasn't sure whether she would make it or not, though she was sending a basket of oranges and a small ham that Daisy had baked the night before.

"Well . . . " Adeline hesitated. "I reckon it's all right."

"She's feelin' kind of poorly, so I don't know for sure," Zabette hedged, sensing that Adeline might have preferred not to have the mistress present. White people did sometimes put a damper on the jubilation of such events.

But she knew that, if Marguerite came, she would stay only a short time, watch the couple jump the broom, give them a present, maybe five dollars, and make her way back to the Big House. In fact, though she would not want to admit it openly, Zabette too would prefer her grandmother not go. She always felt more self-conscious around the slaves when Marguerite was present.

"What time you reckon we need to be there?" Zabette asked.

"'Fore the shadows get too long," Adeline answered. "At least a couple hours 'fore sunset."

Zabette nodded. She knew there were no clocks in the quarter, but from Adeline's description, she thought 3:30 by the grandfather clock in the hallway would be time enough. Her grandmother had taught her, along with Daisy, to tell time for her own convenience, so that she could request tea at 4:00 or supper at 7:00.

"We'll be there," Zabette said eagerly.

"Don't wear nothin' too fancy," she cautioned. Zabette understood. She didn't want to stand out in the quarters any more than Adeline wanted her to. She had grown self-conscious as her body developed and her awareness grew of the curiosity she aroused among the slaves. She liked the people in the quarters, but they tended to shy away from her and treat her with a certain deference. Daisy took her to the quarters sometimes and watched over her there, but she knew she was different from the others. She felt more accepted when she was with her *maman*, whom Miz Marguerite sometimes allowed her to visit. But her *maman* wouldn't be there today, she knew, because she was down with a cold.

When Adeline left, Zabette went back upstairs and hung up the white muslin dress with a touch of lace at the neck that she had planned to wear. She had only a few other choices, from which she selected a simple cotton dress that she had made herself with Daisy's help. It had a sprinkling of simple violets she had embroidered on the bodice against a background of pale blue and a solid blue skirt that tied with a sash in the back to make it fit. It was clean, not fancy, and, she thought, suitable for the occasion. She took it downstairs to show it to Daisy.

"I reckon that'll be fine, Zabette," Daisy approved, though they both knew that, even in such a simple dress, she would probably be better attired than the bride.

BY THREE O'CLOCK ZABETTE WAS READY. She looked at herself in the mirror and saw only her flaws. Her long curly hair looked unruly today, and her dress had a tiny stain on the right side of the bodice about two inches below the shoulder, where she had spilled a drop of gravy some time ago. It was dim since the dress had been washed and ironed a few times since, and likely no one else would notice, but she knew it was there. To hide the spot, she pinned a small ebony brooch that her grandmother had given her for Christmas the previous year.

Then she went into the hallway and tapped on her grandmother's closed door.

"*Entrez,*" Marguerite said wearily.

The drapes were partially closed against the afternoon light, and her grandmother, wearing her dressing gown, was resting on her bed, with three pillows behind her back, reading. A cup of tea sat on the night stand.

"*Grand'mère,* you're not dressed!" Zabette exclaimed.

"Oh, *ma p'tite,* you'll have to go without me. I'm feeling a little peaked this afternoon. I had a dizzy spell after midday and thought I'd better rest a while. I'm sure you can explain to Adeline for me. There's an envelope on my dresser for you to give her—a little wedding present."

Despite herself Zabette felt a small surge of relief.

She picked up the envelope and gave her grandmother a kiss on the forehead. "If you fall asleep, shall I wake you for supper?" she asked.

"Oh, yes, but not before six-thirty. I want Daisy to enjoy herself at the celebration."

"She has dinner all cooked. It will just need to be reheated," Zabette informed her.

"Then that should give her plenty of time." It never occurred to her that the wedding festivities might go on into the night.

BY THE TIME THEY GOT TO THE QUARTERS—a ten-minute walk past the smokehouse and down the road a way—the shadows were beginning to lengthen. As soon as they left the road and took the foot path twenty yards into the trees, they felt the bustle of activity. Solomon's daddy, Zic, was already making lively sounds with his hand-made fiddle, and a group of children were dancing in a ring to the rhythm.

Someone had set up a pair of rickety sawhorses that held up the boards where food was being laid out for a feast. A gaily colored tablecloth made of scraps of cloth—like a patchwork quilt without the batting—covered the boards. Zabette noticed that several of the squares were cut from a dress she had given to Adeline three or four years ago. It must have long since worn out, but it was still being put to good use. A jar filled with green leaves and purple and yellow wildflowers sat in the middle of the table. Not much was blooming this time of year, but whoever put together the arrangement managed to make it colorful.

The air buzzed with talk and laughter, and every once in a while, one of the men, inspired by Zic's fiddling, would break out into a little dance, sometimes grabbing a passing female figure to whirl around. She would oblige, giggling, until she could break the grip and get back to her chore of sweeping the yard or toting the food to the table. The weather was cool enough so that there were few flies and no gnats. Just in case, a young girl was posted at the end of the table waving a palmetto frond to fan away any insects that happened along.

Adeline ran out to meet them as soon as she saw them. Zabette handed her the basket of oranges she was carrying. She had buried the envelope beneath the top orange so that they would later find it as a surprise. Daisy went over to place the ham on the table with the other meats—a platter of fried chicken, a plate of possum, one of rabbit, and an empty bowl that would be used for the oysters roasting over the open hearth made from chunks of broken tabby.

As soon as Zic had spotted the two women, their arms loaded with oranges and the platter of ham, he struck up a lively and familiar tune, while his neighbor Harry joined in on his mouth organ. Solomon, sitting just outside the cabin door, started beating the rhythm on his thighs and singing, "Ham Bone, ham bone, pat 'im on the shoulder. If you get a pretty gal, I'll show you how to hold 'er . . . " His brother, seated beside him, leapt to his feet to dance. Zabette smiled at their lively performance and felt the desire to join in herself. But none of the other women were dancing. They were all working, though they kept the rhythm with their feet or their swaying hips.

One of the men, a new slave named Ben, recently purchased by Marguerite from Henri du Bignon on Jekyl Island, was watching Zabette, who was also beginning to sway to the rhythm. He sauntered over to her and said, "Hey, sugar, ain't seen you 'round here before. Wha's yo' name?"

"Zabette," she replied with a smile. "What's yours?"

"I'se Ben, the best Ben around," he said jovially, a little flirtatiously. He looked muscular and handsome, and Zabette was immediately drawn by his brown eyes, warm as melted chocolate. His teeth were pearl white, and his coffee-colored skin had a sheen like a new penny. He smelled of soap.

"Well, I'm glad to know you're around," Zabette said, returning his self-assured grin, feeling the color rise in her face.

He reached out to brush a stray hair back from her forehead, and an unfamiliar rush of warmth flowed from from his fingertips into her body.

"You get on away from her," said a curt voice at Zabette's elbow. She felt Daisy tugging at her arm, pulling her away from the conversation and this exciting man.

"Whatsa matter wit' you?" Ben asked peevishly.

One of the men by this time was at his side and began to pull him over toward the cabin door, talking to him earnestly. Zabette saw Ben look at her, his eyes widen, and his mouth open into an "oh." A shadow of disappointment, crossed his face, but he nodded at the other man and, with a final longing glance in her direction, turned away and back toward the other men. He did not speak to her for the rest of the afternoon.

Tears welled up in Zabette's eyes. "Daisy," she said to her grandmother's cook, "Why did you do that? He was very nice. I like him."

"'Cause I promised Miz Marguerite," was all she would say.

Zabette flushed again, this time with humiliation. She knew that she didn't belong here any more than she belonged at those fancy parties they gave at Dungeness, to which, of course, she was never invited. Sometimes she wondered if there was any place she did belong outside the Big House at Plum Orchard. And even there her status was peculiar. She loved her grandmother and felt safe with her, but when other white people came to visit, she was expected to go to her room or join Daisy in the kitchen, the only place she felt truly welcome.

Maybe she didn't fit in, but she was determined not to let anything spoil her afternoon. She was going to enjoy this party no matter what. She would join in the dancing even if she had to dance by herself. Adeline, when she saw her alone, came over and danced with her for a brief time, and then, one by one, the women took Zabette under their wing, though the men kept their distance. Zabette tried her best to take pleasure in this partial acceptance.

The rest of the afternoon passed without incident, with everyone clapping and squealing with delight when Adeline and Solomon jumped the broom. The men teased Solomon unmercifully, and Adeline was pulled by the women toward the cabin, where she and her new husband would spend the night. Zabette smiled once more at Ben across the yard. He nodded at her with a sad expression, not quite a smile, though almost, and looked away.

When the guests began the meal, Zabette watched as the ham, chicken, possum, and oysters were consumed first, along with the collard greens, green beans, squash, hoppin' john and a sort of stew made of corn, okra, and tomatoes put up after the harvest. There was Johnny cake and corn pone for bread and pitchers of buttermilk and potato wine, which the men had started drinking before the ceremony. She could smell the oranges, not the ones she'd brought, which had already been deposited in the cabin where the married couple would spend their first night together, but others brought from the orange grove at Dungeness. They were cut into slices, and the children sucked on them for dessert. There was even a flat, sweet honey-cake that one of the women had baked over her open hearth.

Zabette ate a crispy chicken wing, some of the green beans flavored with fatback, and a tiny piece of honey-cake. They were all delicious, but she didn't want to eat too much. Whatever she ate might mean that someone else would go without, if not today, then tomorrow. She knew that this was a feast for the people in the quarters, who mostly lived on the ration of corn and fatback they received from the storehouse and smokehouse.

Whatever they could raise in the little plots behind the cabins and the eggs from the chickens that wandered unconfined through the quarters were theirs to keep. They were also free to set snares for rabbits, possums, and raccoons and to fish or gather oysters in the sea or the river, which they called God's pantry. But they killed their chickens only on special days like this one, for they could sell their eggs on the island two for a penny and little by little set by enough to purchase something special for their children or themselves—a peppermint candy cane or a new pair of shoelaces.

The people in the quarters were all polite to Zabette, but when Daisy told her it was time for the two of them to leave and go fix supper, not a single one of them, in spite of their profuse goodbyes, said "Ya'll come back soon, y'hear," as they did with each other.

Zabette hurried with Daisy back toward the Big House, for they had stayed longer than they'd intended and the sun had already dropped beneath the horizon. It had been a fine afternoon, except that the moment she'd shared with Ben had been all too brief. She remembered vividly her rush of warmth at his touch, but tried to brush her feeling aside and think instead about the laughter and applause when Solomon and Adeline jumped the broom. It was an old custom that came all the way from Africa.

"But why a broom?" she asked Daisy as they walked together through the gathering dark.

"That ole broom clean away all the past sins and sweep off the evil spirits, they say," Daisy explained. Zabette thought it was a wonderful way to begin married life, cleansed of past sins, and she wondered if anyone would ever want to jump the broom with her.

Although she certainly did not envy the slaves their harsh lives, she did envy their easy camaraderie and their obvious affection for one another. She would give anything to have friends she could tease like that and who would tease back. Adeline had been the closest friend she'd ever had, and now that Adeline was a married woman, she sensed that their relationship had shifted somehow. A new emptiness welled up within her. It was harder to see the path ahead where the variegated shadows began to blend. As darkness gathered around her, she wondered if there was any real place for her in this world.

Chapter Sixteen

PLANTERS HOUSE, JULY 19, 1836
Robert Stafford was dining alone. His mother and sister were both upstairs, too ill to come down for meals. Robert had sent his most trusted slave, Peter, who had been with him since childhood, into St. Marys at first light to fetch Dr. Mitchell, but he had no idea when or if he might arrive. Both women were burning up with fever.

It had started with Susannah, who'd been exposed to yellow fever during a recent visit to Savannah where she'd found a raging epidemic at its peak. The symptoms had not shown themselves until her return to Cumberland. But only a few days after arriving back on the island, she started to complain of headaches and muscle aches. Then the fever began, alternating with chills. She would frequently vomit after meals. Lucy was constantly at her bedside, placing cool cloths on her daughter's burning forehead and trying to find food she could keep down. By the time Susannah began to show signs of jaundice, Lucy had also taken to her bed with a high fever and similar symptoms.

Robert had no idea what to do. He had sent for Marguerite Bernardey, but she herself was down with a bad cold and an attack of gout. Only then did he summon the doctor from St. Marys.

DR. MITCHELL, DUSTY FROM THE HASTY CARRIAGE RIDE from the dock, appeared that afternoon, his black medical bag in hand. He examined Susannah first and shook his head. The symptoms were all too familiar these days. By the time the body began to show signs of jaundice, it was usually too late. The kidneys were failing.

"Just keep her comfortable. Give her plenty to drink, and let her rest. Only God can cure her at this point. There's nothing I can do," said the doctor.

"What about Mother?" asked Robert. "Can you help her?"

Although Lucy Spalding's illness was less fully developed than her daughter's, there was no treatment known for her illness. "It's either yellow fever or malaria. There is nothing much I can do for her either, though she could still recover. She needs to drink plenty of fluids to wash out the sickness. And she needs to rest. We can only pray."

It was difficult to rest when one was constantly vomiting. Robert knew that he was on his own now, with only the servants to help out.

After Peter set out to take the good doctor back to Brunswick, there was a tap on the front door. Robert, who had been sitting in the parlor with his head in his hands, trying to think what he should do, got up to open it.

In the late afternoon shadow of the porch stood the most beautiful young woman he had ever seen. She was tall and slim, with dark curly hair tied at the nape of her neck. Her skin was bronze, her lips full, and her lowered eyes a warm deep brown. He thought she was familiar, but he could not quite place her. To him she looked like an angel in her white muslin dress.

"Mr. Stafford, Miz Marguerite sent me from Plum Orchard. She's sorry she couldn't come herself." Zabette had hesitated when Frederick drove her to the front door. Should she enter there or go to the back? The older she became and the more she learned, she was increasingly aware of her odd status—and never quite sure what was permitted to her. At age sixteen, she realized that she lived somewhere between Daisy's world and that of her grandmother, but on the fringes of both. And things, like knowing which door to use at a strange white person's house, could be troubling.

ROBERT GAZED AT HER INTENTLY. The mention of Marguerite Bernardey triggered a brief memory of the pretty child who had stood with the cook under the dripping live oak beside the grave of Peter Bernardey so many years ago. He had caught glimpses of her during his visits with Marguerite, but she usually disappeared into the kitchen before he could speak to her. He had even seen her gathering plums in the orchard one day. For the most part, however, Marguerite kept her out of sight from the island whites, even from him. It had been at least a year or more since he had seen her at all. Since then she had emerged from awkward adolescence to become a young woman. Robert knew now exactly who she was. "Zabette?" he asked.

She nodded. "Elisabeth Bernardey. Here to help with your mother and sister."

"Dr. Mitchell was just here. He says there is nothing that can be done." He felt awkward leaving the girl standing there and awkward about inviting her in. It was hard to accept the idea of a mulatto girl sitting in his parlor. But she was Marguerite's granddaughter. It was precisely the dilemma Marguerite had sought to spare both her neighbors and Zabette for so many years.

"We can at least make them comfortable," Zabette insisted. "Where are their rooms?" It was obvious that she did not intend to stop in the parlor, but to get to work immediately. Zabette had instinctively defused his awkwardness. She was sent here to serve, not socialize, she made it clear.

Robert led her up the stairs, showing her his mother's room on the left of the hallway and his sister's on the right. Zabette went first to Lucy Spalding's room.

"Can you have someone bring me a basin of cool water and a pitcher of tea?"

"Of course," he said, surprised by her apparent self-assurance.

IF ONLY HE HAD KNOWN how unsure of herself she was. This was new territory for Zabette, being in another planter's home. She didn't visit often in the quarters either because everyone there, except for her mother and her friend Adeline, who loved to show off her new baby, kept their distance from her. They weren't sure how to treat her, whether to act as though she were one of them, which she clearly wasn't, or whether to address her as "Miss Zabette," which she hated. Adeline, who was already pregnant again, had been working in the fields for many years now, and her hands had grown rough and her back a bit stooped. But she still welcomed Zabette to her family's cabin on rare occasions. They still shared secrets, though Zabette was careful never to reveal any of Miz Marguerite's business. The men in the quarters glanced at her discreetly, but never dared to approach her. She had seen Ben once more when she took an embroidered bonnet to Adeline's baby. Her heart leapt with pleasure, but he'd only nodded, acknowledging her smile, and passed on by, just as he had after the incident at the broom-jumping ceremony. Zabette lived in a world of her own. Her self-assurance was merely an imitation of her grandmother's demeanor. She felt none of it inside.

ROBERT WENT TO THE KITCHEN and gave Amanda instructions as Zabette had requested. The portly woman carried the basin and pitcher up the stairs, took one look at Zabette, plunked the basin and pitcher down on the bedside table, and returned to the kitchen with an annoyed look on her face. *Who do that prissy yellow gal think she be with such mighty airs?* Amanda knew perfectly well who Zabette was. She had heard about her from some of the people over at Plum Orchard. But she didn't appreciate her coming in here and taking over the care of Miz Lucy and Miz Susannah. What could she do that Amanda couldn't do? *What do she know anyhow?*

ZABETTE SIGHED, BUT SHE WAS NOT SURPRISED by Amanda's attitude. It was not hard to recognize the disdainful expression and the abruptness with which she had set down the basin and pitcher and marched out of the room. But it was obvious that Zabette was needed here, and she wouldn't be driven away. Amanda already had her hands full, and Robert Stafford didn't know what to do or even whether the disease was contagious. Zabette did not hesitate. Her grandmother had taught her well how to nurse those sick with fever, and as a doctor's daughter, she had learned quickly and showed a knack for it.

She sat beside Lucy Spalding's bed for more than an hour, putting cool cloths on her head to bring down the fever and trying to get her to drink the tea without success. Then she moved to Susannah's room. There she had even less success. Susannah's eyes were beginning to glaze over and look as though they were sinking into her yellowing skin. She was incapable of drinking at all, which Zabette knew was a bad sign. She applied the cool cloths to her patient's forehead. Once she thought she saw Susannah's eyes focus on her, but they almost immediately lost their attentive look and faded again as though lost in an uncomprehending haze. Zabette was not sure she could handle this all by herself, but she was determined to try.

It was her grandmother who had urged her to come and help Robert Stafford. Marguerite had felt bad that the one time Robert called on her for help, she was unable to go to him. Zabette, however, could be her representative. She knew as much now about tending the sick as Marguerite did. Zabette hated the idea of leaving her grandmother's bedside while she was sick and needed tending, though she knew her illness was not life threatening. Daisy, too, had urged her to go. She would look after Miz Marguerite, she assured her.

SEVERAL DAYS WENT BY. Zabette slept on a day bed against the window of Lucy Spalding's room, rising at night to check on the two sick women, fluff their pillows, and try to make them comfortable. She had sent Frederick home to get her a change of clothes, a bar of soap, and some personal items, not knowing how long she might be here. She was overjoyed when Miz Lucy's fever finally broke on the third day of Zabette's visit, and she rallied to the point that she could eat once more. But Zabette's tending did little good as far as Susannah was concerned. She grew worse every day, and Zabette feared for her life.

Robert peered into the sick room as often as he dared, without getting in the way. He visited his mother in the late afternoons. Although he spoke to her rarely, he was relieved to see that she looked so much better. On most days, however, he continued his usual activities on the plantation, riding over his fields, reviewing his accounts, and writing lengthy letters to his factor and banker in Savannah. He left the nursing to Zabette.

DURING THE SATURDAY NIGHT FOLLOWING, five days after Zabette's arrival, Susannah stopped breathing. Zabette found her lifeless body when she went in to bathe her in the morning. Her skin was cold. Robert was at his desk working on his accounts when Zabette crept down the stairs to tell him. Bringing such bad news was a terrible first-time experience for her. But she knew that Robert had been expecting it. Even so, his body slumped perceptibly when she informed him, as gently as she could, of his sister's death, but he only said, "Thank you for telling me, Zabette."

Seeing after the dead and dying, like birthing, was women's work on Cumberland plantations. Zabette and Amanda washed the body, while Robert went out to find the carpenter, a slave named Big George, to make a coffin. The funeral was set for Thursday morning because it wouldn't do to have the body linger too long in this heat. But there was a lot to do to get ready. Zabette and

Amanda clothed Susannah's body in her best dress, a moss green silk. When the casket was ready, with the help of Big George and Scipio, they lifted the frail corpse and laid it inside.

George got some of the other slave men to help him carry the wooden box down the broad staircase and lay the body out on two sawhorses in the front parlor, where people could come by for a final look. Robert notified a preacher in St. Marys, who would come out to the island and read the service, and sent messengers to the nearby plantations to let the planter families know.

Over the next day, a few people dropped by. Even Phineas Nightingale stopped in briefly to express his condolences. Although he detested Robert Stafford, he had liked Robert's sister Susannah and wanted to pay his final respects to her. On Sunday evening, Robert allowed the slaves who wished to do so to file by the coffin and say goodbye to Miz Susannah. Blacks from other plantations showed up, bringing food their mistress or master had sent over, and the ritual of mourning was carried out once again until, finally, on Monday, Susannah was laid to rest in the newly designated Stafford family cemetery.

STAFFORD PLANTATION, JULY 25, 1836

Marguerite, driven by Frederick, with Daisy sitting beside him in the driver's seat, insisted on coming to the graveside service. Although she was still weak and had to be assisted by Daisy and Zabette, one on each side, she wanted to be there for Robert. "*Grand'mère*, you should still be in bed," Zabette whispered to her as they helped her to a wicker chair that Robert had provided. Marguerite smiled wanly and squeezed her hand.

The service was short, and Frederick, aided by Scipio, carried Marguerite Bernardey, chair and all, up to Planters House for a bite to eat. Once inside the parlor, she leaned toward Robert, who was sitting in a stiff horsehair-stuffed chair, holding a plate of food that he did not touch. "I am so sorry about your sister, Robert. I know this has been very hard for you, to have both Lucy and Susannah so ill. But Susannah is in heaven with her dear late husband now. It would make her happy."

"That's one way to look at it, I suppose. Dr. Mitchell said it was yellow fever."

"So I've heard," she nodded. "It's a terrible illness."

"Did you know that my father died from yellow fever when I was ten?" said Robert.

"No, I had no idea. Of course, Mr. Spalding was your mother's second husband. I knew that, but not what had taken the life of Mr. Stafford."

"I'm worried for my mother, Marguerite." It was the first time he had called her by her first name, but they were friends now, and it was time. Marguerite scarcely noticed.

"But Zabette told me that she was much better."

"She was, until she heard about Susannah's death." Lucy Spalding had not been well enough to attend the funeral. She lay in her bed weeping, too weak to rise.

"May I go up to see her, Robert?"

"Well, it might do her good to see you. If you like, I can call in Scipio and Big George to carry you up."

She nodded. "Perhaps I am strong enough to walk."

"I wouldn't hear of it," Robert said firmly. "You've just risen from your own sick bed to come here to comfort me. I surely don't want you to take a turn for the worse because of overexertion on my account." He rose at once and went up the stairs to speak to his mother. Then he came back and went to the front door. Scipio, George, and Frederick were standing next to the carriage deep in conversation when Robert called out to his own two slaves. He held the front door open as they entered to carry Marguerite and her chair once again, this time up the oak staircase.

"Thank you, boys," she said, when they had put her down next to Lucy's bed. The two men exchanged glances. Frederick did not reply, but Scipio nodded, "You're welcome, ma'am."

Lucy was propped up on pillows, though her head was tilted back, resting, as though she did not have the strength to hold it up. Her eyes were red and swollen.

"Lucy, dear," said Marguerite, reaching for her hand. "I can't tell you how sorry I am about Susannah. I know how much you loved her."

"My daughter is dead," said Lucy softly, as though she were trying to convince herself it was true. "How can I go on? You know you've lived too long when you outlive your children."

"How well I know," said Marguerite softly, reliving her own grief at Pierre's death, but she shook it off. "Please tell me if there is anything I can do to help."

"You have sent us your Zabette. She has been a godsend. Thank you, Marguerite."

That statement made Marguerite's next sentence sound almost cruel, but she still had to say it. "I was hoping now that you are better that she would be able to come home," Marguerite broached the subject as gently as she could under the circumstances. "I miss her terribly. And I need her as well."

"Yes, I'm sure. Good servants are hard to find," said Lucy.

"You don't understand, Lucy," Marguerite said slowly, thoughtfully. "Zabette is much more than a servant . . . she's my granddaughter."

"Oh!" said Lucy, surprised at Marguerite's open acknowledgment of the relationship. They had known each other for years, and of course, she had known about Zabette, as had all the other people on the island. But she had never heard Marguerite make such an open statement about it. "Oh!" She could think of nothing else to say. She was too exhausted.

"I thought, perhaps, during your bereavement at least, it might be best for Zabette to come home and give you and Robert your privacy."

"I don't know how we could get along without her," said Lucy wearily. "But I suppose now that Susannah is gone . . . " The sudden memory brought a new flood of tears.

"Please don't take on so, Lucy. You'll be fine. Amanda is here to look after you, and Zabette can return later if you still need her. Just let her come home to me for a while."

"You've been ill too, I know," said Lucy.

"Not as ill as you, my dear. I'm so glad to see that you are better now." But looking at her friend, Marguerite was not so sure.

As ZABETTE CLIMBED INTO THE CARRIAGE to accompany her grandmother back to Plum Orchard, she noticed Robert Stafford standing at the front door, his hand raised in farewell. She nodded, as did her grandmother, both assuming that her duties at Planters House were at an end.

Chapter Seventeen

S carcely two weeks after Zabette returned to Plum Orchard, Scipio
appeared unexpectedly at the kitchen door. He handed a note to
Daisy, who took it directly to Marguerite as she sat on the front
porch cross-stitching a sampler. She glanced at it quickly.

"Oh, dear," she said to Zabette, who was sipping a cup of tea and shelling
peas for supper. "Lucy Spalding is desperately ill again. I must go there and help
Robert tend to her."

"I'm so sorry, *Grand'mère*. I thought she was doing much better."

Robert's tight script indicated that his mother had relapsed shortly after
Susannah's death. She had grieved until her fever had gone up again. Since then
she had grown weaker by the day. Amanda had done her best, but she could do
only so much. It was as though Lucy didn't want to live any longer. Robert needed
help, but whether it was for himself or his mother, Marguerite couldn't tell from
the note. Before she even finished reading it, she rose from her rocking chair.

"Can you help me pack a few things, Zabette?"

"Let me go instead, *Grand'mère*. You can't go up and down those Stafford
steps all the time. Miz Lucy liked my company. I can tend to her as well as you.
They know me now. They're used to me."

Marguerite looked gratefully at Zabette. She wasn't sure she could stand to be
at the house alone without Zabette again. But she knew that her granddaughter
was right. Her gnarled hands and knees hurt terribly when she climbed stairs,
and on some days she couldn't climb them at all. Zabette could perform nursing
duties as well as she, perhaps even better. But she was reluctant to let her go.

Marguerite picked up Robert's note again. This time she read to the end, where she found the last sentence: "Could you possibly spare Zabette for a short time to help with my mother? We miss her very much. Yours faithfully, Robert Stafford." It appeared that everything was conspiring against Marguerite. It was Zabette he was asking for, not her. How could she refuse? He had been so kind to her after Pierre's death. It was little enough to ask. Surely she could spare Zabette for another week or so, until Lucy was better. Just until then.

ROBERT'S FACE BRIGHTENED when the Bernardey carriage pulled up in front of Planters House, and he saw Zabette, clutching her small carpetbag, climbing down from beside the driver. He greeted her on the veranda, as she climbed the steep stairs that led up to it. He was smiling broadly, a rare expression, and she was glad to see it.

"Zabette, Miz Marguerite was so good to let you come."

"She's a good woman, and she's fond of Miz Lucy," Zabette replied. He opened the door for her as they entered the foyer. "Would you like a cup of tea?" he said, gesturing toward the parlor. Zabette glanced uncertainly toward the sofa and shook her head.

"Thank you, but I'd better get on up to see to Miz Lucy."

ZABETTE WAS SHOCKED BY THE CHANGE in Lucy Spalding since she had last seen her. She lay immobile, eyes closed, her face pinched and pale as death. She did not answer when Zabette spoke to her, though Zabette could see that she was not asleep by the tiny slit of eye that peeked when she heard the younger woman speak her name. Tears appeared at the outer corner of both eyes and slid slowly down her cheeks. Zabette wiped them away gently with a handkerchief she found on the nightstand beside the bed.

"Miz Lucy," she said softly. "You must try to get better. Mr. Robert needs you too." The tears, she knew, were for Susannah, tears that came unbidden and would not cease.

A weary furrow appeared on Lucy's forehead. Finally she whispered, "I can't. I can't."

"But you must try," Zabette whispered back, leaning closer, taking the woman's icy hands in her own and massaging them gently to get the blood flowing again.

She knew that her feet were probably just as cold and as she headed downstairs and out to the kitchen to get coals to prepare a bed warmer.

Amanda eyed her scornfully as she entered the kitchen. "Well, howdy-do, if it ain't Miss Priss back at Planters House," she said.

Zabette winced at her sarcasm, but she knew there was nothing she could do about it. The kitchen was Amanda's domain, and she would brook no intrusions. "Please, Amanda," she implored, "may I get some hot coals for Miz Lucy?"

"I'll take care of it," she said haughtily, reaching for the scuttle. "How many you need?"

"Just enough to fill the bed warmer."

"I reckon I can handle that," Amanda replied.

AMANDA WAS ALREADY BEGINNING TO REGRET her rudeness. She was not usually an ill-tempered woman. It was just that Zabette, with her fancy English and fine airs, even her clean, well-sewn clothes, was an affront, considering that she was just as much a slave as Amanda. She had just been luckier than most.

She had no idea how much Zabette longed for the laughter and music that rang in the quarters after dark, the fellowship that made their life bearable. She knew their suffering and often heard them singing out their trials and woes in the field. But they were bonded together by their sorrow. She longed to go to their Sunday preaching, maybe even sing in their choir. Sometimes on Sunday nights she sat in the orchard and listened to their spirituals, the deep voices of the men and the soaring tones and shouts of the women. But she did not belong to their church, to them, or even to her mother who, when she saw her from afar, looked like a different person from the one she remembered so long ago. Her brother Jack was handsome and much admired by the girls in the quarters, but she didn't feel she knew him at all.

ZABETTE SAT BESIDE LUCY SPALDING'S BED late into the night and listened to her whimper in her sleep, for even in her dreams she could not escape the grief. Zabette understood, for she'd felt that way for a long time when her mother was sent away from the Big House—a painful heaviness in her chest. But at least her mother was still alive, while Miz Susannah lay beneath the soil of the Stafford cemetery. It was, she supposed, more like the emptiness she felt at her father's death.

Athough she had learned how to tend a sick body, she was at a loss as to how to help an ailing spirit. Miz Lucy seemed to find comfort in her grief. Zabette could only offer up prayers for her recovery.

DAYS WENT BY, AND LITTLE CHANGED, except that Lucy grew weaker and slept more. Her fever was gone, but she showed no interest in anything. Zabette tried to get her patient involved in life again. She opened the windows and draperies to let in the sunlight and fresh air. She picked wildflowers to brighten the sick room. She talked with her, told her stories one might tell a child, and even sang some of the lively French tunes she had learned from her grandmother as a child. She served Miz Lucy her favorite foods and tried to entice her to take a few bites. But nothing worked. Finally, in frustration and despair, she spoke to Robert Stafford.

"Mr. Robert?" she approached him cautiously, tapping on the door of his study.

"Yes? Come in."

He was seated at a cluttered desk, account books spread out before him and others opened on a library table behind the sofa that faced a fireplace. "What is it, Zabette?" he asked apprehensively. "Is it Mother?"

"She's no better, Mr. Robert. Just gets a little weaker every day. I'm mighty afraid . . . " She hesitated, unsure how to phrase what she saw as an inevitability. "Unless you could . . . " How could she give him advice about his own mother?

"Tell me, Zabette."

"Mr. Robert, I just don't think she wants to live anymore. Maybe you could try to persuade her that you need her. You could talk with her, make her listen . . . " Her words trailed off.

ROBERT LOOKED AT HIS HANDS, rough from his daily rides, and thought for a moment. She wanted him to express a need for his mother, to pour out his heart to her so that she might be drawn back into this world. He understood what she wanted with perfect clarity, but he didn't know how to go about it or if he even felt it. He had never, to his recollection, openly expressed a need for anyone or anything. If he wanted something, he took it or bought it. If not, he let it go. Had he always been this way, he wondered? He prided himself on not being like other men. But there had been a time in his youth he could barely remember when he *had* been like them, when he too wanted love and a home and family.

He recalled with bitter irony the occasion when he had foolishly tried to court Phineas Nightingale's sister, Catherine. She was a pretty young thing in her early twenties, and Robert had been drawn to what he now perceived to be her silly and frivolous ways. He mistook them for femininity. But her Aunt Louisa at Dungeness made it clear that such a courtship was not suitable. And the one time when he defied her and came to call on Miss Caty, she and Phineas both laughed at him. His father had, after all, been one of their family's hired men in charge of the timbering of live oak trees on the island for sale to the U.S. Navy. Even Robert himself had worked for the Shaws for a time before he got together sufficient funds to buy his own land. But from the first moment he heard Caty Nightingale's laughter, he had determined to spurn the Shaws and the Nightingales as they spurned him, and he had hardened his heart against any kind of emotional need, putting a shell around his feelings.

When he had physical needs he couldn't satisfy himself, he simply took his pick of the women in the quarters, just like other planters in the region. But he permitted himself no emotional attachments. He needed no one, not even his mother.

And yet, he thought, how empty the house would be without her. He had to confess that he even missed Susannah, who had done nothing but mope once he brought her back from England after her husband died. It had irritated him immensely. But she was his blood kin, and when he'd received word of her husband's death, he had not hesitated. He took the first vessel he could book from Savannah and sailed to England to bring her back. It wasn't that he needed her, he thought. But she'd needed him. Well, he told himself, his mother needed him now.

After a long silence, he lifted his eyes to Zabette. "I'll talk with her this afternoon," he said. "I'll do my best."

THE LIGHT OF THE SETTING SUN STREAMED in through the open windows of his mother's room and splayed across her bed, though her head lay in shadow. Robert sat on a straight chair beside the bed with his back to the window.

"Mama?" he said in a tentative voice.

She opened her eyes only a slit, squinting against the light. Then she closed them again. "Hello, Robert," she said wearily.

"Mama, I want you to try to get well. I . . . ," he paused, almost choking as he said the words. "I need you, Mama." It was all wrong. He shouldn't just have blurted it out without any preamble, without anything leading up to it. It was too sudden, too crass. Cursing himself for his ineptitude with human relations, he sat, miserable, looking at the pale, shrunken face of his mother.

She was silent for a moment, and then she said, "Can you pour me a drink of water?"

He obliged, with a sense of relief to be able to do something. Cradling her back and lifting her to a near sitting position, he held the glass to her lips. Most of the water dribbled down her chin and onto her gown, though a few drops cooled her dry tongue. He cursed his clumsiness.

"A bit more," she said as he moved to set down the glass. She drank again. Then her head drooped back against the pillow.

"I suppose Zabette put you up to this," she said.

"To what, Mama?" he asked. He sensed feistiness in her questioning that he took as a good sign.

"To coming up here to tell me you need me." She was clearly unconvinced and unmoved by his words.

"But I do, Mama. What would I do without you?" And he suddenly realized that, in spite of himself and his obstinate pride, the words he spoke were true. He just didn't know how to make them sound true. What would his life be like without her? The solitude would be unbearable. Even though he talked very little, he was used to her chatter at dinnertime. Dining alone these recent weeks had not been pleasant. He was accustomed to the female voices of his mother and sister, the smells of their cologne and bath powder, and the rustling of their skirts. Now that the women had almost deserted his world for the kitchen or the upstairs sick room, the house was deafening in its silence.

"Robert," his mother said softly. "I love you, son. Please understand that. But you can do without me just fine." She paused to take a shallow, labored breath, then finished. "I'm of no use to anyone anymore."

"But you are, Mama. You are to me. I need you here, with me. Please . . . please try to get well."

She shook her head, as though his words made no sense to her. "You're strong, Robert. You don't need anyone." She hesitated. "Susannah needed me. Now she's gone." Tears welled up in her eyes and spilled down her cheeks. "I just don't want to live anymore, Robert. I'm too tired. Forgive me."

For the first time since he was a child, Robert felt the threatened sting of tears behind his own eyes. He fought them back. Suddenly aware of the stiffness of his back in the straight chair, he leaned forward and reached for her hand. It was cold. She let him hold it for a brief moment, then she withdrew it and weakly patted his arm. He had no words to say, though he was faintly aware that the shadows were gathering as the sun turned to a bright red ball almost touching the horizon. "It'll be all right, son. You'll be just fine. You'll see." She tried to smile, though her eyes remained closed.

Robert knew he had failed, but he didn't know what else to do. He sat silently beside her bed until the room was totally dark. Then he tiptoed out, closing the door softly behind him.

Chapter Eighteen

I t would take Lucy Spalding three more days to die. She did not speak or open her eyes again. It was as though she simply willed her life to end. During those final days, Robert sat beside her bed for hours at a time, gazing at her withered face and watching the sunlight crawl across the bed and the wooden floors of the room. He wanted to tell her how he felt as he watched her life slipping away, but he had no idea how to go about it. He felt eased only by the presence of Zabette sitting beside him.

At other times he rode across his lands to the edge of the sea and sat astride his horse, looking out over the Atlantic, wondering what had been the purpose of it all. His need for land and wealth. His determination to show himself equal to, if not better than, his Dungeness neighbors. Why had he been so obsessed? What did they matter? It was too late, he thought, to find a new direction for his life. He was already in his mid-forties. His father had been dead long before he reached that age. He could not imagine life without his mother and sister.

He remembered with a sense of shame the many times he had felt only irritation at their presence. Now, he realized, they had been his only comfort. His only family. He had no real friends, except perhaps Marguerite Bernardey, though there were many who owed him money. He knew he was not considered good enough for his "genteel" neighbors and that they viewed his money-lending activities with disdain. But their attitudes had not prevented them from coming to him whenever they needed loans. He had long ago told himself he didn't care, but deep within, he did. He alone had been responsible for isolating his mother and Susannah from the social life they craved. Marguerite had been an exception to the snobbery of people like the Nightingales. She had always been kind to his entire family.

After these rides Robert would return to Planters House, fearful that he would find his mother dead. He was always relieved to see Zabette sitting quietly in the room, cooling Lucy's forehead with a damp cloth or smoothing the covers on her bed.

At first he sat quietly when he joined her silent vigil. Then after the first day, as the shadows lengthened, he began to talk, to himself as much as to her, to fill the silence with his words. He spoke of his mother as a young woman, imbued with life and laughter. He described his childhood as the eldest of seven children. He told Zabette of his father, or what little he could remember of him since he had been only ten years old at Thomas Stafford's death. He recalled how he had been sent north by his stepfather, Isham Spalding, to school in Connecticut, how hard it had been to be away from his family, how the other boys had teased him because he was different, and how much he had tried to be like them, to talk like them and mimic their ways. It had been a difficult time in his life, but it had shaped the man he had become.

He described the loss of his brother and sisters, one-by-one—Clarissa, Elizabeth, Thomas, Harriott, Mary, and finally Susannah—how their deaths, each one, had bent low his mother's spirit. But she had shown amazing resilience. Once she had put away her grief, she always tried to approach life with renewed enthusiasm. But not this time.

In the darkening room, he described his trip to England in 1818 to fetch Susannah, who had been whisked away from the island in the wake of the War of 1812 by one of the English invaders, a handsome naval officer named George Hawkins, who became her husband. He told Zabette of the British invasion of Cumberland and how they had set up headquarters at Dungeness on the south end of the island. How the young officers had wooed the local girls. Susannah had been bedazzled by the splendid red uniform and the British ways of George Hawkins, whom Robert had barely known. Then how he had fetched her back to Cumberland when her husband died.

His voice softened as he told Zabette about the death of his stepfather in

1823 and how his mother, his sister Mary, and his half-sister, Jane, born from
Lucy Spalding's second marriage, had also come to live with him. All four of the
bedrooms on the second floor of Planters House had been occupied, and the
house had teemed with life.

All that had been more than a decade ago. Jane married a few years back,
he said, and now lived with her husband on the mainland. He remembered his
mother and Susannah sitting on the veranda, gossiping over needlework and
tea. How delighted his mother had been when Susannah came home to stay. He
recalled their planning meals together and tending the flowers in the garden.
Lucy had always been proud of her winter white camellias, which thrived, and
her red and yellow summer roses, which required constant attention to survive
the island's heat and insects. But even more than she worried over her flowers,
she worried over her daughter who had clung tenaciously to her role of distraught
widow. He reported how their mother had tried to lift her daughter's spirits. And
how little he'd helped in that process. God had at last given Lucy too much to bear
with the death of her last Stafford daughter, and she was so weakened by illness
that her will seemed irreparably broken.

"I failed them both," he said softly.

He talked of his mother without any particular order to his ramblings.
Spinning out her life and his own in the presence of Zabette was like giving
substance to their existence. They took on shape in the telling. His mother's
was a life of effort and repeated misfortunes, while he painted his own as one of
personal failure despite his financial success.

Robert could never remember talking to anyone like that before. It was as
though putting his thoughts into words liberated them. He needed to speak, to
tell all that had happened, if only to help himself understand it. Zabette listened,
nodding, smiling at his happiest memories, furrowing her brow with concern at
the sadder ones, letting occasional supportive murmurs slip past her lips.

To his surprise, Robert found himself even telling her about Catherine
Nightingale, of the rejection he had felt at Dungeness, and how he had vowed to
repay the unkindness of its residents.

"They laughed at me," he said in the semi-darkness. That, he realized, had
been the beginning of his hardened determination to succeed financially. "They
only laughed." He had never told anyone that before.

He was staring out the window at the final rays of the sun, sunk below the horizon now, spreading its fading hues of mauve and purple little by little across the evening sky. Then only a glow remained, coming from everywhere and nowhere. His deep voice trailed off in the rough beauty of the moment. Zabette too was watching the sunset, its color reflecting back onto her face. Robert caught his breath at her beauty.

After a time of silence, when no words were needed, Zabette finally asked, "Shall I light a lamp?" The room was bathed in gentle shadows. Had he really spoken out loud the story of his life or had he only imagined it?

"Forgive me," he said. "I have kept you too long. Surely it's past your suppertime." He knew that as a rule she and Amanda ate together in the kitchen well before he took his own meal. It was unusual, he supposed, for the servants to eat first, but as he preferred his own supper at eight, he had long ago suggested to Amanda that she need not wait to take her own evening meal until after he had eaten.

He hesitated for only a moment, and then he said, "I don't suppose you'd care to take supper with me this evening?" He was reluctant to end their conversation, for he feared that, once stopped, it might never be resumed. Zabette had listened so intently, so sympathetically, that it felt to him like a dialogue, not the monologue it truly was.

She smiled with uncertainty, though he could no longer see her well in the dark room. She appeared bemused by the question, and he could not read her reaction. It may not have sounded like an invitation exactly, couched in the tentative, even negative, way it was, though he had certainly intended it to be one. Then, after a moment of uncomfortable silence, she finally replied, "Perhaps I'd best stay with Miz Lucy while you have your supper. I can eat later, and I'm not hungry at all. But thank you."

Disappointed, Robert got up to light the lantern. "Well, then, I reckon I'll be goin' down. Perhaps I'll stop in a bit later to say good night to Mama, if it won't disturb you." He knew that Zabette slept on the daybed across the room in order to hear his mother if she called out in the night.

"That'll be fine," she said.

When the door closed behind him, Zabette felt his lingering warmth in the room. For her as well, it had been a remarkable afternoon. A strange sense of intimacy had bound them together for a time. She pondered the story he had told her and felt only sadness for Mr. Robert as she turned back to her vigil.

ROBERT HARDLY TASTED HIS SUPPER, though Amanda had fixed butter beans, his favorite vegetable, to go with her roasted chicken and sweet potatoes in bourbon sauce. For dessert she had made pound cake and topped it with some of the peaches she had put up during peach season. But he rushed through dessert, hardly tasting it, eager to return to his mother's room. As soon as he had finished supper, he climbed the stairs and tapped on the door. Zabette opened it at once, her cheeks wet with tears.

He was alarmed. "What is it, Zabette? Is it Mama?"

She nodded. "Just now, Mr. Robert. It was peaceful," she reassured him. "She just stopped breathing."

Zabette had already held a mirror to her lips for any sign of life and put her ear against Lucy Spalding's chest to listen for her heart as her papa had taught her to do, but there was only silence. She had grown fond of the old woman in the last weeks of her life, and she was disconsolate that she had been unable to revive the dying woman's spirits and prolong her life. She could see how much Mr. Robert depended on his mother. He hadn't realized it himself, she thought, until he acknowledged his feelings to her that afternoon. Now she stood before him, not knowing what to say.

Robert's tall frame crumpled unexpectedly into her arms. She heard him sobbing against her shoulder and felt his arms on her back. They had both known Lucy's death was inevitable, and yet it was so sudden. Without thinking, she put her arms around his waist to comfort him.

They clung together for a long moment, until finally he straightened up and took a step back. "I'm so sorry, Zabette. Forgive me."

"It's all right, Mr. Robert." She moved aside to let him kneel beside his mother's body. Miz Lucy looked as though she were sleeping. Even to Zabette, she appeared unchanged, and she could have sworn she saw the bedclothes rise and fall with her breathing. But the mirror did not lie. There was no breath left in her.

"Are you sure, Zabette?" She heard the anguish in his voice and nodded sadly.

He believed her, of course, but he needed to see for himself. He needed to be certain. He felt for his mother's pulse, as he had seen Dr. Mitchell do. Nothing. He could hear only the beating of his own heart. The thread between life and death was so thin it could break in an instant. How could she be gone? Just like that? One moment, when he went down to supper, she was breathing and the next moment, when he returned, she wasn't. So little had changed. And yet, everything had changed. He stayed on his knees, holding his mother's still-warm hand for a long time, reluctant to let go, for when he released her hand, it would mark the end of the longest relationship of his life with the only woman who had loved him as a boy, nurtured his dreams, and wept for him when he met with pain. Never, he knew, would there be another like her. As long as he held her hand, she was somehow still there. She could not be truly dead. If he could just hold on. He had never felt so numb and empty in his entire life.

After a while—he had no idea how long—Zabette, gentle as a shadow, touched his shoulder. "Mr. Robert, you need to get some rest now. Amanda and me—we'll wash Miz Lucy and lay her out in here till morning. I'll stay with her. Then you can decide on what needs to be done."

He rose, grateful that she had taken charge for the moment and freed him from thinking, from that feeling of incapacity that had invaded his being. He murmured his thanks and moved somehow toward his own room.

At dawn the next day Robert ordered Big George to make another coffin, the second in less than a month, and then wrote brief notices to be delivered to any neighbors he thought might attend. He set the funeral for ten o'clock the next morning. It stretched the limit in the August heat, but it was the best he could do.

Zabette assumed that she would stay at Planters House until after the funeral to help Amanda with food and preparations. She was also concerned about leaving Mr. Robert alone. He appeared for once almost helpless. When his man Peter brought his roan horse to the front steps mid-morning, he mounted, grim-faced, and raced the horse out the gate, across the pasture, and toward the sea. He returned shortly before noon. The horse had been ridden hard, and Mr. Robert was disheveled and wind-blown. Zabette suspected he had been riding on the wide sandy beach that bordered the island's eastern shore.

His hair stood in wild directions, and he looked like a man possessed of a demon. He stepped into the foyer and gazed toward the parlor where his mother's body lay. Then he mounted the stairs wearily, cleaned himself up, put on a fresh shirt, and came down for his mid-day dinner.

"Will you please eat dinner with me, Zabette?" he asked. This time there was nothing equivocal about the invitation. It was almost a command. "I need to talk with you about the burial." This time she did not refuse, though she felt self-conscious in face of Amanda's startled reaction and hostile stares at having to serve her. Zabette offered to help, but Robert insisted that "Amanda will take care of it." And she did, with obvious resentment Robert appeared not to notice, though Zabette felt it keenly. The chicken salad, made from leftovers of the previous night's roasted chicken, tasted like ashes in her mouth, but she said nothing.

Robert spoke little throughout the meal and chewed his food self-consciously. She waited patiently for him to discuss the funeral arrangements, but the only comment he made throughout the meal about the burial was that he hoped she would stay until after it was over. "It would be a help to me," he confessed as though such an admission were difficult for him.

"Of course, I'll stay, Mr. Robert." Frederick would drive her grandmother over for the burial, and most likely Daisy would come with her. She wasn't sure about the properness of his request, now that Miz Lucy was gone, but it didn't really matter. If he needed her, she would stay. Her grandmother would surely understand.

THAT NIGHT, AFTER SUPPER, which they also took together, the two sat stiffly in the matching rose-colored horsehair-stuffed chairs that had been placed beside the coffin in the parlor. Robert looked at her curiously and said, "How old are you now, Zabette? Seventeen? Eighteen?"

"Seventeen next April," she told him.

"Almost as old as my half-sister Jane was when she married Mr. Holzendorf and moved into St. Marys." He smiled grimly at the memory. "Mother thought her much too young." After a moment's hesitation, he asked. "What do you think?"

"I think age is in the heart and mind, Mr. Robert. Some of us are older at sixteen than others."

"I'm forty-five. An old man already," he said, looking at his knuckles.

"You don't seem old to me, Mr. Robert."

"You are good to be around, Zabette. Marguerite is lucky to have you, and I sure appreciate her letting you come over to look after Mama. I don't know what we would have done without you these past days."

"I tried to help a little, is all."

"I reckon you'll be goin' back to Plum Orchard after the burial."

"I reckon so."

"You wouldn't consider stayin' on here?"

She was a bit shocked at the suggestion. Stay on at Planters House? Whatever for? She liked it there and felt as much at home as she did anywhere, but it would not be proper for her to stay on past the funeral. He already had a cook, and Zabette was not a skilled cook anyhow. Perhaps he had a mind for her to move in with Amanda and help clean house, but she knew that would not set well with Amanda. In any case, the decision was not hers to make.

"That's not for me to say, Mr. Robert. But I 'spect Miz Marguerite will be needin' me back at Plum Orchard."

"We'll just have to see."

ZABETTE LAY AWAKE THAT NIGHT, tossing on the narrow day bed where she slept, alone for the first time in the bedroom she had shared with Lucy Spalding, and thought about Mr. Robert's words. The room was still, and she could see Miz Lucy's silver hairbrush and mirror on the dresser reflecting the moonlight. She could perhaps help Mr. Robert sort through Miz Lucy's things. He hadn't wanted to change anything at all in her room, and it lay just as she had left it. Zabette had changed the sheets and made the bed, but other than that, the water glass still stood on the night stand, dwarfed by the enameled pitcher beside it. Miz Lucy's spectacles lay on the Bible where she had marked her favorite passages, the ones that would be read at her funeral. It was as though she had only left for a moment and might return at any time.

Zabette knew that her grandmother wouldn't consider it at all suitable for her to stay on now that Miz Lucy was gone. But Zabette had been happy at Planters House, despite the circumstances. Over these past weeks and days, she had come to feel needed and wanted, and no one had ever poured out his heart to her the way Mr. Robert did in the days before his mother died. It put her in a mind to want to tell him about her own life, how her mother had been lost to her for so long, and then how her father had died. She thought he might understand why she didn't feel she really belonged anywhere and that she wasn't comfortable with anybody but her grandmother and Daisy. Except for him. The only two rooms where she ever felt happy were her grandmother's bedroom and Daisy's kitchen. She longed to tell him all those things. About her feelings at Adeline's broom-jumping ceremony and how the slaves had acted toward her, polite but distant. All except Adeline. She thought he might have listened.

But perhaps now that Miz Lucy was gone, all that would change. He might no longer feel the need to talk or have the will to listen. What did it matter? She would be going back to Plum Orchard in a day or two anyhow. No need to think about it.

Robert, too, lay awake, gazing at the branches of the live oak against the bright moon outside his window. He thought of Zabette asleep on the day bed in the room across the hall. It was strange to have her there now that his mother was gone, and yet, it felt right. He was reluctant to think of her leaving. Without her he knew that the silence would close in around him. Amanda went back to her own cabin after supper each night, and he would be completely alone in the house, alone with his memories and regrets. Forty-five years old, he thought, more than halfway toward death himself. And Zabette was there, so young, so vibrant, so alive. Yet when they sat together beside his mother's bed in the darkened room, their respective ages vanished. He felt at ease with her, as though she could somehow understand his needs, his failure to belong among the other island planters. Just her being there was a consolation to him. He'd never known a woman who listened more than she talked, whose very presence he found soothing.

With other women he never knew what to say, but with Zabette his words flowed out so easily. He wished she could stay on, but she was not like other slave women. He couldn't just buy her from Marguerite. He doubted she would sell her own granddaughter. His thoughts tumbled without direction or resolution.

Robert was tired, and as he finally let himself relax into sleep, the faces of his mother, Susannah, and Zabette, all looking like angels, drifted through his mind and into his dreams.

Chapter Nineteen

TOO MANY FUNERALS, THOUGHT ZABETTE, as she fastened the small carpetbag and replayed in her mind the burial of Miz Lucy. Before the sun had grown too hot, she had been laid to rest in a grave beside her daughter Susannah. Robert, dry-eyed and stoic, shook hands with the few islanders who had come. Phineas Nightingale was not among them, though his wife Mary attended the brief service. Marguerite Bernardey, driven to Planters House by Frederick, sat once again in the wicker chair Robert had provided for her. Zabette stood beside Amanda, as the same preacher who had conducted the funeral service for Susannah prayed over the body of Miz Lucy. Zabette hoped it would be the last funeral for a long, long time. She picked up her bag with an odd mixture of relief and reluctance and went down to join her grandmother for their trip back to Plum Orchard.

FREDERICK FLICKED THE REINS AND TIPPED HIS HAT politely to Mr. Stafford who stood on the front porch watching them drive away. He was completely alone now, except for Amanda, who was inside sweeping up the spilled crumbs from the dining room rug and the sand that had been tracked into the parlor. She would not need to cook for the rest of the day, as ample food remained from the contributions that island families had brought over. Robert didn't feel like eating in any case.

"Amanda, why don't you take the rest of the day off until suppertime," he said. In fact, he didn't want her around right now. He just wanted to be alone to think.

"I 'preciate that, Mas' Robert," she said, untying her apron before he could change his mind. She had stayed up late the night before and had been up since before dawn, preparing food and getting the downstairs ready for the mourners.

The house suddenly felt enormous, of unnecessary proportion. His bedroom, his study, and the dining room would have been enough for him. The other three bedrooms on the second floor had emptied out one by one, until no one was left. He had no family beyond nieces and nephews and a half-sister, all of whom lived on the mainland and whom he rarely saw. He felt a bit like the house himself, emptied of attachments.

In the ensuing days, he allowed routine to take over his life. Mounting his horse every morning, he rode beneath the late summer sun over his now-extensive property. He remembered the angry moment when he'd vowed to own all of Cumberland Island, to take over all the lands that belonged to Phineas Nightingale—especially his family home, Dungeness. While he had not yet succeeded in that goal, he was already the largest landowner on the island. Somehow all that was less important now, for he no longer had anyone to share his success. No mother or sisters. No sons. No wife. No one. And who would want to marry him anyhow? It was just too late.

BEFORE THE WEEK WAS OUT, during a late afternoon ride, Robert turned his horse, almost unwittingly, toward Plum Orchard. As he rode up the long driveway toward the Big House, he could see two women sitting on the porch. Marguerite was doing needlework, and in an adjacent rocking chair sat Zabette, shelling peas. The two women recognized his upright figure and wide-brimmed hat long before he reached the house. No one sat a saddle like Robert Stafford, his back rigid as a post and drawn up to his full height. Marguerite waved in welcome, and Zabette nodded and smiled.

"Howdy," said Robert, as he dismounted and tied his horse's reins to the newel post. He climbed the steps and removed his hat. "I hope you don't mind me bargin' in this way, but I wanted to stop by and thank you both for your help durin' these recent weeks. It meant a lot to Mama . . . and to me," he added. "I don't know how we could have got by without you, Zabette," he said speaking directly to her.

"I 'preciate it, Mr. Robert. And I'm sorry it didn't have a happier ending," she answered.

There was an awkward silence as Robert regarded Zabette with his penetrating blue eyes, while the young woman focused her attention furiously on her peas. But Marguerite noticed the slight flush that had come to the girl's cheeks.

"Well, Robert," said Marguerite, pointing to the porch swing. "Sit yourself down and visit a spell. I hope you can stay to supper. Daisy's fixing her Georgia pound cake, and you know how good that is, and she's churning ice cream from the last peaches of the season we're likely to get."

"It sounds mighty good, Miz Marguerite. But I don't want to put you out any."

"Nonsense, it'd be a privilege to have you. And company would do you good. I won't take no for an answer."

"Well, if you insist," he responded. Gratitude was awkward for Robert Stafford. He was more accustomed to people being beholden to him rather than the other way around, but he was grateful for the spontaneous kindness of these two women who were almost like replacements for the women he had so recently lost.

"Zabette," said Marguerite, "Go get Mr. Stafford a glass of sweet tea. He looks like he could use a cold drink."

Zabette leapt to her feet, her bowl of peas in her hand, eager to find an excuse to leave. She felt self-conscious sitting here with Marguerite and Robert together. Strange, she thought, how relaxed she could be with either one of them, but together was another matter. Her old uncertainties about what she was permitted to do in company swept over her again. Would she be expected to take supper with the two of them as she did most evenings with Marguerite? Or would Marguerite want her to eat with Daisy since she had a guest? Even though Zabette had eaten at Mr. Robert's table at Planters House, a fact she had not shared with her grandmother, she was unsure.

"Daisy," Zabette said, pouring a glassful of tea. "Miz Marguerite asked Mr. Stafford to stay for supper. I hope there'll be enough."

Daisy looked up from her biscuit-cutting and rolled her eyes in mock exasperation. There was always enough food at Daisy's table. She cooked as though company was always expected. The pork chops smothered in gravy were already in the warming oven, along with her squash casserole. She had chopped onions to add to the peas Zabette had shelled, and she gingerly touched the top of the stove to see if it was hot enough to put them on to cook or if she needed to add another stick of wood. Hot enough, she decided.

"What do you think, Daisy? Will Miz Marguerite want me to eat with them?" She'd already confided to Daisy that she had eaten supper with Mr. Robert alone, but this was new territory.

"I reckon Miz Marguerite will decide and let me know if I needs to set another plate, Zabette. Don't you worry yo' head about it."

When Daisy announced supper, only two places were still set at the dining room table. Zabette supposed that she was to eat in the kitchen with Daisy, and she felt a tiny jolt of disappointment.

But when he reached the table, Robert asked, "Marguerite, doesn't Zabette usually take her supper with you?"

"Well, as a matter of fact, she does, but tonight she won't mind eating with Daisy so we can talk."

"If you don't mind, Marguerite, I'd appreciate havin' her to supper with us. She's a mighty fine young lady, and I must confess I've missed her company."

Zabette's heart leapt at his words. He had missed her. It had only been a few days, and he had missed her.

Marguerite was astonished. It was the first time anyone of her acquaintance had ever asked about Zabette's dining arrangements and the first time any of her white friends had shown an inclination to sit at the same table with anyone colored. Of course, Robert knew that Zabette was her granddaughter and that her situation was rather irregular.

"Well, Robert, if you like."

Daisy, who had heard the exchange through the kitchen door, appeared almost at once with a dinner plate, a napkin, and all the appropriate silverware. She seated Zabette across the table from Robert's place, while Marguerite sat, as always, at the head of the table.

That was the first of many such evenings for the three of them. As the months passed and Robert recovered from his grief, he began to come to supper once a week and occasionally invited Marguerite and Zabette to Planters House, to the annoyance of Amanda, who still thought Zabette's presence entirely inappropriate at Mr. Stafford's table. But she kept her opinions to herself, at least in front of Mas' Robert and Miz Marguerite.

MARGUERITE HAD NEVER SEEN ROBERT ENJOY HIMSELF so much as he did on those evenings. And there was a thoughtfulness in him that he didn't show in his business dealings. She had once heard someone in her lawyer's office at St. Marys say that he talked like a triphammer. Working on a business deal or talking with Mr. Grey, who had served as her overseer since Pierre's death, his words came like water over rapids, unstoppable, forceful, sometimes rough. But alone with her and Zabette, she saw a side of him she had never seen before. He was far more likeable, and even his rigid posture relaxed a bit during their conversations.

Zabette spoke seldom when they were all together, and she had been trained not to look white people directly in the eye, but Robert encouraged her to talk, even soliciting her opinion about whether the pecans were as abundant this year as last or whether he ought to be thinking about entering the upcoming boat races at St. Marys. Marguerite was surprised by the vivacity with which Zabette offered her views. She assured him with what sounded like authority that the pecan trees were fuller with nuts this year than last. And she urged him most definitely to participate in the races, which were always lively and fun, especially for the men, black and white alike, who were always excited by the rowing competitions. Robert listened attentively to all her advice, nodding and smiling at all the right places. Zabette smiled back, her eyes shining.

During their most recent supper together he had sought her opinion once again.

"My people want me to build them a church," he announced. "They've always held their Sunday meetings in the clearing near the quarters. But some of 'em complain about the sun or the rain. You know, those meetings go on for hours and hours. I'd like to know what you think about it, Zabette. Should I build them a church?"

Zabette did not hesitate. "Well, Mr. Robert, if you can afford it, I think it would be a right Christian thing to do. They work hard during the week, and Sundays are a special day. Have you ever been to one of their meetings and listened to the singing? A church would be a fine thing to have on your plantation."

Marguerite watched Zabette's face brighten as she encouraged his generosity toward the slaves' religious needs and as she described their singing of the mournful yet hopeful spirituals. She knew that the child sometimes wandered down to the storehouse they used as a church in the quarters at Plum Orchard, but she didn't think Zabette had ever gone inside. She herself never went, of course, for their service was far too passionate for her Catholic upbringing. She had not realized how much Zabette had been affected by it. This was also a Zabette she did not know.

It took Robert more than a year and many such evenings to work up the nerve to broach the subject of Zabette with Marguerite. He thought about it a great deal. He hankered for the girl and found her incredibly beautiful, with her gentle eyes, raven curls, and light olive skin as smooth as the inside of the whelk shells that littered the beach. He had never desired a woman so much as he desired Zabette. He wanted her for his own, if she was willing to come and live with him, but he knew that he would have to persuade her grandmother first.

He thought of a dozen approaches to the issue and even held practice conversations with himself when he was on horseback and no one could see him, but none of them felt right. He couldn't offer to buy her outright like any other slave, for he knew that her grandmother would refuse without hesitation. He couldn't ask for her hand in marriage because it was against the laws of Georgia. He had tried to bring himself to open the conversation on several occasions, but opportunities were few. He wanted to do it when Zabette was not present, for he had decided that an approach based on logic rather than emotion might work best with Marguerite, and he knew he could handle it better. He expected she would want what was best for Zabette, and he thought he could provide assurance that he would always look after her. But finding the right occasion and the right words was not easy.

The opportunity finally presented itself when Zabette's mother came to the Bernardey house one Saturday afternoon to ask Marguerite's permission for Zabette to come to Sunday supper at the two-room cabin she shared with her son. It was Jack's twelfth birthday, or thereabout, as nearly as she could reckon with-

out a calendar, and she wanted to have a small celebration. Marguerite permitted, rather than encouraged, such visits, allowing Zabette to go "just this once,"
as she said every time. She didn't want Marie-Jeanne to get too presumptuous.

WHEN ROBERT ARRIVED, HE WAS SURPRISED to find Marguerite alone on
the porch.

"Zabette's visiting her mother and brother this evening," she told him, "and
taking her supper with them." Robert knew that Marguerite did not encourage
such visits, but he realized this was his chance to talk with her alone.

After supper he escorted Marguerite into the parlor, where, over brandy,
and in his usual abrupt manner, he brought up the issue without preamble.
"Marguerite, I've been wanting to talk with you about Zabette."

"Has she done something to displease you?"

"Not at all," he said. "On the contrary, she pleases me very much. In fact,
Marguerite," he hesitated only a moment. "I'd like to ask your permission for her
to come live with me."

Marguerite's shock showed in her face. "What on earth do you mean, Robert?
Live with you how? In what capacity? She's not really a house servant, you know."

"Yes, I know. That was not what I had in mind."

"Well, what *did* you have in mind?" He could see that she was annoyed by his
vagueness. He was pretty sure that she already knew the answer, but she wanted
to make him say it.

"The way you've raised Zabette here in your home you can't just marry her
off to one of your slaves. But no white man can marry her either, as you well know.
With all that in mind, what's her future going to be like, Marguerite?"

The old woman listened. He knew she must have gone over these questions
in her own mind a thousand times, wondering what would become of Zabette
after she died. She would will her property no doubt to Margaret Elizabeth, her
legitimate granddaughter, for Zabette could not inherit. But even if she could, she
would not be safe living at Plum Orchard on her own. The island was too small
for the white neighbors to accept that. And the colored probably wouldn't like it
any better. She would be at everyone's mercy. Marguerite would likely miss the
girl, but he would have to convince her that she had to stop thinking only about
herself and consider Zabette's future.

"I repeat, what did you have in mind, Robert?" she asked curtly.

"Well . . . ," he paused thoughtfully. "I . . . I fancy Zabette. She's been good to me and to my family. You know I can't marry her, Marguerite. You know the laws as well as I do. I would if I could. But I fancy her nonetheless. I had hoped that you could see your way clear to letting her come to be my . . . " He had thought hard about what word he should use. He didn't know much French, but he did know that the word *femme* meant both "wife" and "woman." He hoped she would understand it that way, ". . . my woman."

"Your mistress, you mean?"

Robert flushed, something he almost never did, but the word which sounded too crass for what he had in mind.

"Well, of course I'd treat her right and make sure that she was always taken care of. I guess neither of us will live forever, Marguerite, but I'm a mite younger than you, and I might live longer. I promise I wouldn't let her want for anything or mistreat her in any way."

She was silent for a moment. He was well aware of the thirty-year difference between his and Zabette's ages. Perhaps that's why she hesitated so, but she should know it was a good solution—perhaps the only one.

"I wouldn't want to force her to do anything like that against her will. Despite her color, she was brought up as a lady," she said.

He hastened to reassure her. "Nor would I. You know, Marguerite, I'm not a ladies' man. I don't fancy anyone else, and I'd be takin' her alone. I wouldn't ever marry. I'm too old and too ornery for that."

He hoped Marguerite did not find in his words any kind of judgment against her son for marrying Catherine Corb when he already had a slave mistress. He was just trying to instill confidence in her about his honorable intentions, as far as they could go.

"Well, Robert, let me think on it," she said, her voice a little softer now as she thoughtfully fingered the gold locket she always wore at her neck. "And I'll talk to Zabette."

"I'd rightly appreciate it, Marguerite. You won't regret it. I promise."

"I hope not," Marguerite replied. He felt her eyes looking at him as though she could see into his heart.

Chapter Twenty

ABETTE'S BROTHER, JACK, WALKED HER BACK to the gate of the Big House about nine o'clock. The night was bright, and the full October moon etched sharp, gray shadows on the ground. Her feet were light on the sandy road. She felt closer to her mother and brother than ever before, and she treasured the time she spent with them. Marie-Jeanne always welcomed her warmly, fed her well, and proudly showed her their half-acre garden with its neat rows of what remained of her sweet potatoes, bean stalks, cantaloupes, okra, and tomato plants, as well as their hen house and their sow and litter of squealing piglets. Zabette had loved getting to know her brother Jack, who bore an amazing resemblance to their father. She had grown fond of him in recent years. He was smart and handsome and, as an apprentice to Old John, the plantation cobbler, he had learned to make shoes as well as his teacher. The field hands on the plantation went barefoot most of the year, but in the really cold months they wore brogans made by Old John and Jack.

For a time Zabette had felt tentative with her mother and brother. The long-ago days she had lived with her mother in the cook's cabin were now distant childhood memories. But she still loved her mother and treasured the time they spent togeether in what they all called the "new cabin." Zabette was fascinated by her mother's handiwork, which kept her busy now that she no longer had to work in the cotton fields—the sweetgrass baskets she made for the plantation and the fabrics she wove from cotton threads dyed with blackberry juice, sassafras leaves, or dandelion roots. She saw the other women on Sundays wearing kerchiefs or shawls made from the colorful fabrics her mother had woven. Zabette begged Marie-Jeanne to teach her how to make the baskets and dye the threads. And she had learned to love the feel of the pliable sweetgrass beneath her fingers as she tried to duplicate her mother's work.

Sometimes they all sat quietly on the front porch of the cabin and listened to the night sounds of the hoot owl in the nearby pine forest and the rustle of palmetto fronds as the deer and racoons made their nightly rounds. At other times, Marie-Jeanne would sing to them the old songs from Saint-Domingue she had learned from her mother, and if Zabette and Jack begged long enough, she would tell them the tales she had learned from her own mother during her childhood—tales of Anansi the Spider, whom they called Aunt Nancy, or of wickedly clever rabbits and foxes, who always outsmarted other critters who thought they were superior. These were good evenings, never meant to last, but good and heart-warming all the same.

Zabette gave Jack a hug, as he left her at the gate and turned back toward his mother's cabin. She knew that she would go up to her comfortable room, her soft bed with its chenille counterpane and feather pillows, but she was aware that her mother and brother would sleep tonight on mattresses stuffed with smoked Spanish moss and corn husks. She didn't envy their discomfort, but she admired the loving home that her mother had made for Jack, two rooms brightened by colorful quilts sewn from pieces of cloth Marie-Jeanne had woven herself and hand-me-down scraps from Marguerite's cast-offs. They had few possessions, but the cabin was homey with its brick fireplace that gave off the smell of burned pine. And they had plenty of food—the usual ration of corn and bacon, along with the fish and crabs that Jack had become adept at catching in the marshes or along the shore. It was more than many people had, Zabette thought. And they didn't have to work in the fields like the other slaves. Their life was better than Marie-Jeanne had ever thought it would be after that long-ago incident with William.

Toward the end of the evening, Zabette had finally found the courage to ask her mother about her relationship with Pierre. At first Marie-Jeanne sat silent, staring out into the gathering dark. Then after a few moments, she began to speak.

"I been done cry my last tears 'bout that," she said. "I'se sad that yo' papa is gone. He made a heap o' mistakes, I reckon, but he done try to make up for 'em.

And I 'spect he raised you up the best he knew how. I'se jes' sorry he didn't get to know Jack better 'fore he died."

"So am I," whispered Zabette. It was the most her mother had ever talked to her about her father. Her words stretched like a bridge joining the two halves of Zabette's life.

SHE CLIMBED THE TABBY STEPS of Plum Orchard, drawn toward the light inside and feeling better about herself than she had in a long time.

When she entered the house, her grandmother was sitting alone in the lamp-lit parlor. Robert was gone. He had left before dark as he always did, and Daisy had finished cleaning the kitchen and returned to her cabin for the night.

"Did you enjoy your visit?" Marguerite asked.

"Oh, I did, *Grand'mère*! We had such fun. *Maman* tried to teach me how to weave a basket, but I was dreadfully clumsy. And Jack has learned to play a mouth organ that Old John gave him. *Maman* told the most wonderful stories. Thank you for letting me go. I hope you enjoyed yourself with Mr. Robert." It was the most Zabette had said in one breath for a very long time. "I thought you'd already be in bed."

"I've just been sitting here reading my Bible and thought I'd wait up for you."

"Well, that was mighty nice of you."

"Do you remember this passage of Scripture, Zabette? From the book of Ruth." She read the passage in French: "... *où tu iras, j' iras* ... whither thou goest, I will go; and where thou lodgest, I will lodge: thy people shall be my people, and thy God my God."

Zabette nodded at hearing the familiar passage.

"Ruth was talking to her mother-in-law," Marguerite said. "In a way, it's been like that with you and me. And I treasure you. You're all I have left. But you know, Zabette, I'm getting old, and we need to think about your future. I won't live forever."

Where was this leading? Zabette wondered. Was her grandmother ill? Was she thinking of letting her go to live with her mother? Had she selected a husband for her in the quarters? Her mind raced with possibilities.

"Oh, but *Grand'mère*," she protested, "you have many years left."

"Not so many, child. Not so many. And an opportunity has presented itself that I think will ensure that you are taken care of when I am gone."

Zabette was alarmed now. It wasn't merely the musings of an old woman concerned about a distant future, she realized, but rather a plan her grandmother had already devised. Any change in her life, the thought of being sent away from Plum Orchard, terrified her. At least here she had her grandmother and her mother and brother not far away. But she said nothing, for she expected that she had no real choice in the matter.

"Zabette," Marguerite said softly, "Mr. Stafford has asked for you to come and live with him . . . ," she paused, searching for the right words, "to manage his household and live with him as a wife might live with a husband, only . . . well, you know there can't be a legal marriage because of the state law against such things between white and colored. But he promises that he would look after you just as he would a wife and that you wouldn't want for anything."

Zabette was staring at her grandmother, open-mouthed with astonishment. "As you know, child," Marguerite went on. "Mr. Stafford is a wealthy man, and this could be a fine opportunity for you. And for any children you might have."

Her words took away Zabette's breath. Her grandmother would permit this? She sat silent, her hands clutched tightly in her lap, and let the words sink in. Living at the Stafford house had not been disagreeable to Zabette, and she had appreciated the way Mr. Stafford had talked with her, almost as though she were an equal. But he was thirty years older than she. She liked him well enough, and he was still tall and manly and not unattractive. But the part about living like a wife frightened her. She had little direct knowledge of such things. She understood that Marguerite meant that he wanted to bed her and that she might have babies. She had seen the dogs mate and occasionally the cattle, and she knew the acts led to puppies or calves. But she would have no idea of what people do or what would be expected of her.

"What do you think of Mr. Stafford, Zabette? And how do you feel about all this?" her grandmother asked.

She thought for a moment. "He's been kind to me, and I like him. But I hate the idea of leaving you, *Grand'mère*. If I went there, could you come to live with us?"

"Oh, no! I would visit, of course, and you could come back to Plum Orchard to see me any time you wanted. You'd be close by. But the invitation was for you alone. Mr. Stafford said he fancies you and misses having you at his house. Do you think you would like to live there?"

Zabette was flattered that a man like Robert Stafford would want her, but she hadn't thought about him in such a way. "There is so much I don't know, *Grand'mère*. How would I behave? What would I do when he . . . if he wanted to . . . ?" She didn't even know the right words to ask the question.

Her grandmother laughed softly at her anxiety. "You needn't worry about all that, child. I can explain things to you, and I assure you, matters will take care of themselves when the time comes."

"If . . . if you think it's best, I suppose . . . it would be all right." *But would it really?* she wondered. She did not believe that her grandmother would knowingly send her into a situation that would hurt her. But leaving Plum Orchard, the only place she had ever known since she was a young child, was a frightening prospect. She was filled with uncertainty.

"Well, then, it's settled. I'll talk with Mr. Stafford next week to set the terms."

THE FOLLOWING WEEK when Robert was to come to supper, Marguerite asked Zabette to eat early and go to her room so that she and Mr. Stafford could talk privately. She had Daisy put all the food on the table at once—they could serve themselves—and sent her to her cabin. Thus, over their quiet meal Marguerite set forth the circumstances under which she was willing to let Zabette come to live with him. He was to understand that it was a conditional arrangement for the first year, and then, if Zabette were happy enough, Marguerite would consider signing the necessary papers to make it permanent.

She could not simply free Zabette. The slave laws of Georgia had made such manumission illegal in 1835, and even before that it had been dangerous. But Robert was willing to take her on any terms Marguerite required. He agreed to give her another week to get Zabette ready, and he would return the following Sunday for their regular supper and take the girl home with him.

Zabette sat at the top of the stairs, trying to listen to their conversation and learn her fate. Its tone sounded to her more like a cattle trade than anything else. She could only hear snatches of words and phrases and hoped it was not all as impersonal and businesslike as it sounded. She felt as though she were being left out of something vitally important to her own life. Perhaps even white girls felt that way when their parents were working out the terms of a marriage agreement with their suitors, but somehow she felt more like a heifer than a bride. Of course she wasn't a bride, as Marguerite had made perfectly clear to her. But her grandmother had also pointed out that there wasn't much choice if she wanted children. She couldn't just jump the broom like Adeline even if she wanted to, her grandmother told her, for she had been brought up like a white girl.

Zabette had heard of free colored men, but she had never actually met one, nor was she likely to. It was difficult for free blacks to live in Georgia, and their freedom was always threatened. Zabette had heard from Daisy that old Capt. du Bignon over on Jekyl freed his slave mistress and her daughter in his will when he died and before it was illegal. But once they were free, they'd had no place to live. Daisy didn't know whether they'd managed to leave Georgia safely or what had become of them.

In the end Zabette's grandmother persuaded her that she was fortunate to have a man like Robert Stafford, who wanted her for his companion, his "woman," as he had put it. *Sa femme, sa compagne.* Somehow it all sounded less ominous in French.

Her grandmother tried to prepare her for her first night in Robert's bed. She was to submit to whatever he demanded of her but to be modest, at least the first time, and eventually to pretend to desire his advances, but not wantonly, if she wanted to make him happy. Men always like to feel that they please a woman, though they must first conquer her and overcome her modesty, her grandmother said. She explained to Zabette what the male organs were like, and that he would touch her in ways and places where she had never been touched before. It might hurt a bit the first time, but she would get used to it, Marguerite assured her.

As for her household duties, she was to plan the meals and oversee Amanda's work in cooking and cleaning. Occasionally she would probably need to get additional help for the deep cleaning in the spring. As much as Zabette dreaded her first night with Robert, she dreaded Amanda's reaction even more. She knew the Stafford cook would not take kindly to Zabette's having any kind of authority over her, and she began to steel herself for Amanda's contempt and hoped someday to earn her friendship. In spite of her grandmother's efforts and advice, Zabette was terrified. But the decision had been made, and, no matter what she thought about the matter, she would become Robert's "woman" the following Sunday.

HE ARRIVED AT FOUR O'CLOCK, not on his horse, but in a carriage, pulled by a team of horses, which he drove himself. Dressed in his best dark blue suit, his hair slicked back with macassar oil, he appeared as nervous as Zabette felt, as they sat before the fire blazing in the parlor grate. Then throughout the evening meal, she could feel his eyes on her. Everyone tried to act festive, but the tension in the room was palpable. Robert was eager to leave before dark, and the days were getting shorter now. He even declined his customary brandy. Zabette's grandmother had helped her pack her things that morning, tucking a sachet among her clothes and including her own finest nightgown, worked with little white roses around the neckline, as a gift. She'd reassured Zabette that everything would be fine and that she could always return to Plum Orchard if the arrangement didn't suit her.

Robert carried Zabette's valise down the stairs to store it securely behind the carriage seat, while she slipped out to the kitchen to say goodbye to Daisy. The older woman hugged her tightly and whispered in her ear, "That man better be good to you, or he'll hear from Daisy."

Zabette gave her another hug and wiped away a tear as she left the warm, comforting kitchen. Her grandmother was waiting on the front porch. She took Zabette's arm, and they walked down to the foot of the tabby front steps where the carriage waited. There the two women turned to face each other, and Marguerite kissed her granddaughter on both cheeks, while Zabette squeezed her grandmother's hand and inhaled for one last time her familiar smell of lavender.

"J'ai peur, Grand'mère," she confided. "I'm afraid."

"You'll be fine," her grandmother whispered. "And you can always come home as long as I'm here."

Robert offered his hand to help Zabette onto the seat, then rounded the carriage to climb up on the other side. He gave a brisk wave to Marguerite, flicked his whip at the horses, and they were off. At the end of the driveway, the carriage moved onto the road that led south toward the Stafford plantation. Zabette's heart thumped as she looked back and waved to her grandmother, silhouetted against the orange brightness of the setting sun. But when the pine trees on the roadside blocked her view, she gripped the carriage handrail and turned to face the darker road that lay ahead.

Chapter Twenty-One

WHEN ZABETTE AWOKE, IT TOOK HER A MOMENT to remember where she was—in the large bed made especially for Robert Stafford's oversized frame. He was no longer beside her. She warded off the October chill by pulling the heavy quilt up to her chin. *What time is it?* she wondered. The sun was well off the horizon, so about eight-thirty. she guessed. She had not slept much the night before, and she was still drowsy.

She remembered her first moments alone with Robert. The unexpected sweetness of his words, words she had not expected to hear. She was trembling when he took her in his arms. He was gentle at first, kissing her and slipping the nightgown from her shoulder to touch his lips to the little mole at the nape of her neck and then to her nipples, which to her surprise became suddenly erect.

He laid her down with the ease of a child and caressed her—her hips, her breasts, her buttocks, her hair—exploring her body with his large hands, pausing, as Marguerite had said he would, at places where she had never been touched before. She lay still, shivering with uncertainty. Then he lifted her nightgown and thrust himself inside her. She felt a sharp pain and alarm at the urgency and relentlessness of his movements. It was as though he had forgotten she was there. She tried to hold in her mind Marguerite's words telling her that she must endure it, that it would soon be over, and that it would hurt less as time went on.

When it was over, he kissed her lips once more, then rolled onto his back and after a few moments began to snore, lightly at first and then more loudly. That had been perhaps the hardest part—getting used to the rumbling sounds that came from his throat and threatened to keep her awake all night. She turned her back to him and put the pillow over her head, until fatigue finally took its course, and she too slept.

Now she lay in the morning light, trying to remember only the sweetness of his words and realizing that she would have to get used to the rest. But he had appeared satisfied, and that was what mattered. She allowed her eyes to close for a few moments before she must get up and face whatever the day might bring.

As ROBERT GALLOPED HIS ROAN-COLORED STALLION toward the beach, he cursed himself for his clumsiness the night before. It had been so long since he had been with a woman—too long, and he feared he had rushed her too much. He ached as he remembered her fragrant, musky smell, her young, sweet flesh, her soft skin, and her willingness to welcome him. He should have taken more time to give her pleasure, but he wanted her so much that he couldn't help himself.

At least before he took her to his bed, he had remembered his intent. Tilting her chin toward his face and gazing down at her large eyes, her full lips, and smooth skin, he said to her, "I take thee, Zabette, to be my wedded wife, forsaking all others, to love and to cherish, till death do us part." He didn't know if he got the words just right, but she smiled and murmured back, "Till death do us part." Though there was no wedding contract, no preacher or priest, no ring, no registration at the courthouse, no invited guests, at least he could give her that. A vow. "If not before a man of God, then before God himself," he said.

The morning sun burnished the live oaks that bent away from the sea. The ocean was rough, and he sensed a coming storm. It was the season for storms. But rather than dreading it as he usually did, he thought of Zabette and the fact that they could huddle together at Planters House and listen to the howling wind. Although he rarely spoke of it, Robert loved the island fiercely, even the fury of its hurricanes and steamy summers. There was an elemental nature about it that excited him and made him feel alive. He knew that with Zabette, he would experience it in a new and textured way, sweet as summer strawberries. They would face everything together, even the terrors of raging winds and pounding rains that threatened to submerge the island.

He desired Zabette and perhaps even loved her. Caty Nightingale, who had poisoned his life for so long with her rejection, had caused him to build walls around himself so he was not sure he could even feel love anymore. Now Caty dwelt in the oblivion of his heart, while Zabette was at its forefront. The walls had crumbled, and his determination for revenge against the Nightingales had almost ceased. What did they matter? He had everything he wanted. For the first time in his life, he felt like a lucky man.

LIFE AT PLANTERS HOUSE took Zabette some getting used to. Sleeping with Robert proved to be the easy part, and she came to look forward to the private moments they spent together. He told her so much about his boyhood, his years in Connecticut, where he had lived with the family of his St. Marys lawyer, Belton Copp. The adult responsibilities thrust upon him when he was only ten years old had delayed his plans and dreams for the future. But like other men, he had wanted a family. He no longer seemed a man decades older than Zabette, but instead like one just getting started in life.

Only occasionally did the nagging remembrance of what had happened to her mother cross Zabette's mind, but she refused to let herself dwell on it. She lived in Planters House after all, not in some tabby outbuilding as her mother had. For the sake of appearances, Robert had built a rather large tabby cottage next to his own house and furnished it simply. He called it "Zabette's cottage" to his white friends, though the only person who lived there was Amanda, who made clear to Zabette her disdain of the new arrangement. Zabette could understand Amanda's resistance to her, for Amanda was compelled to serve her. Zabette hated the situation, but she didn't know what to do about it. She always praised the cook's delicious meals, but it had no effect.

It was obvious from the beginning that Zabette's life at Planters House was not to be one of leisure. She must learn her duties. Robert expected her to oversee the running of the Big House, to make sure it was stocked with provisions, to plan the meals and supervise the cleaning, polishing, mending, and sewing necessary to plantation life. Her first task was to undertake a thorough cleaning of Planters House, which had not been done since his mother's death. Mattresses had to be turned, carpets beat, and furniture moved to uncover the dust of many months of negligence. Zabette remembered that her stepmother Catherine had started her days at Plum Orchard in exactly the same way. Small as she had been at the time, Zabette remembered her grandmother's umbrage at every speck of dust Catherine wiped up with her fingertips, scowling and mumbling under her breath. But Lucy Spalding was not there to be offended. Amanda grumbled at the extra work, though Zabette helped and even brought in two other women to assist them. And soon the house sparkled from their care. The silver coffee service gleamed once again on the sideboard, the carpets looked brighter, the doilies and the antimacassars were all freshly laundered, starched, and ironed.

Zabette's duties also included overseeing food distribution, clothing allowance, and health care for Robert's slaves. She didn't mind so much going to the quarters to check on the sick when the workers were in the fields, but she felt uncomfortable there when the cabins were full of people. They were uncertain how they should treat her. She suspected that, like Amanda, they resented her privileged position, though they never said anything. Only Amanda, secure in her unsurpassed culinary skills, dared comment to her face. Zabette preferred that to the silent stares and whispers as she passed through the quarters. Still, she was determined to do her best. Over one of Amanda's delicious suppers one night, she raised the subject to Robert.

"It would be so much easier," she began cautiously, "to tend the sick if they were all in one building—a kind of hospital."

Robert was immediately intrigued by the idea. The workers' cabins stood about a quarter of a mile to the east of Planters House. Large oak trees at the site shaded three rows of log houses, with large brick fireplaces where the families did their cooking. The spacing of the cabins left room for each family to have a small garden, chicken coop, or pigpen.

"It wouldn't have to be a large hospital," she said. "Maybe two stories with six or seven beds on each floor. That way we could keep the contagious folks away from others who might just be injured," she suggested.

"Makes sense to me," he replied obligingly. Nothing seemed impossible to him anymore. "I'll look into it. In the meantime, why don't you sketch out a plan you think would work."

THE NEXT DAY ZABETTE INVADED Amanda's *sancta sanctorum*—her kitchen—a red brick building separated from the Big House by a well-worn path. As a rule, only Amanda was allowed inside, except when Zabette came to give her instructions. Amanda eyed her with suspicion as she crossed the threshold. She was surprised by Zabette's first words: "Amanda, I need your advice."

"You needs *my* advice?" the dark-faced woman asked incredulously. Zabette could imagine what she must be thinking—*She don't be askin' my advice when she move in to Planters House. I got some advice for that yella gal all right.*

Zabette doggedly ignored her reaction and persisted. "What do you think of the idea of building a plantation hospital, a small building where we could isolate the sick and take better care of them?"

Amanda paused, considering her words. "This ain't jes some high an' mighty idea you done cooked up? You really means it?" she asked. After a moment or two to think it over, Zabette could see that she had decided to take it seriously and embrace the idea. "If we'd a had that hospital a few years back, all those slaves what died of fever might still be 'live. An' so many of our slave chillun die. I done lost two of my own."

"I didn't know. I'm so sorry, Amanda," Zabette answered, touching her arm. After a pause, she said, "Maybe you can help me come up with some ideas about how to build it."

"I don't know nothin' 'bout buildin', but I reckon it oughta be plenty warm. It can git right damp and cold out here in the wintertime."

"That's true, Amanda. Maybe we should have a fireplace at each end. What do you think?"

"I reckon so. Got to have big hearths tho', to keep them sparks from settin' fire to it. Don't wanna burn up no sick folks."

"Big hearths to keep the cinders from popping out onto the floor. That's a good suggestion."

"Oughta have big windows too. In spring and summer, sick folks needs plenty o' fresh air."

"Big windows. Absolutely. With shutters that could be closed to keep out the rain and cold in winter." Amanda beamed at Zabette's acceptance of her suggestions.

Zabette thanked her for her advice and went back into the Big House, careful not to overstay her welcome in Amanda's domain, but the infirmary became a project that they would discuss many times in that kitchen, with each stay a bit longer than the one before. Zabette loved the smells of Amanda's kitchen, which reminded her so much of her childhood with her mother and of her days with Daisy. The aroma of roasting oysters and baking bread, of fruit pies and wild turkey, gave her a sense of well-being as did nothing else. Zabette discussed the infirmary individually with Amanda and Robert, though never the two together, until finally, when she and Amanda were both satisfied with her rough sketches, she presented them to Robert.

IN FEBRUARY ROBERT SET OUT to make the infirmary a reality. He was gone much of every day, supervising the construction and tending to his regular plantation duties—having fences mended, withered cornstalks and cotton plants cleared away or plowed under, and manure and marsh mud hauled to the fields to renew the soil before spring planting. He spent several days with his men rounding up some of the island's wild horses to break and sell on the mainland. They weren't worth much, but Robert was never able to bring himself to shoot them. The ponies, marsh tackies as some called them, had run wild on Cumberland for centuries, ever since the days of the Spanish missions. They could be a nuisance, for they sometimes liked to feed on the pasturelands set aside for Stafford cattle or on the tender new corn in the spring. The slaves were also permitted to tame some of the ponies for their personal needs. It kept them from grazing on Stafford land, and Robert knew that he could always call on them when he needed extra horses to haul lumber or pull the wagons loaded with cotton bales to the dock. The rest he sold in St. Marys.

The hospital, while it was being constructed, brought Robert and Zabette together in their common effort. In the early mornings after the slaves were in the fields, they sometimes walked to the site to check the progress of the work. It took several months to build. Robert didn't want to spare good field hands to help, so the two plantation carpenters had to do most of the work themselves. But once it was done—just as Zabette and Amanda had imagined it—with large windows and chimneys at each end, Zabette had it whitewashed inside and out to make it more cheerful. She always saw that there was a vase of wildflowers in the center of the room. She believed one needed to make the sick want to get well, and nothing did that better than nature. Or love willingly expressed. She remembered poor Miz Lucy and how she had just given up on life. Zabette didn't want to see that ever happen again to anyone under her care.

The result was splendid. The patients came quickly to depend on Zabette and crave her gentle touch as she bound their wounds and applied whatever remedies she had learned from her father and from trial and error. They began to call her "Miss Zabette" and showed her all the deference the slaves at Plum Orchard had showed her grandmother. All but Amanda, who still called her simply "Zabette."

Including Amanda in the planning and discussion of the infirmary had worked wonders in their relationship. Despite her gruff exterior, Amanda had a big heart and a keen intelligence that allowed her to understand better than anyone else the uncertainties and complexities Zabette confronted as she tried to weave her way along a difficult path. And Zabette knew that something important had changed when the cook said to her one evening as they talked in the warmth of the kitchen: "You want to cut out them biscuits, chile, while I baste this here roast fo' supper."

Rewarding Amanda with a grateful smile, Zabette picked up the biscuit cutter and set to work. Amanda's letting Zabette have even a tiny role in her kitchen was like giving her a badge of trust. Ever since she was a little girl, the kitchen had been the place where she felt the greatest bond with the women in her life—all except her grandmother. She understood that Amanda had just granted her a place in her heart as well.

AS SOON AS THE WINTER CHILL WAS PAST, Zabette and Amanda planted a new kitchen garden that would include green beans, radishes, peas, okra, squash, pumpkins, sweet potatoes, and tomatoes. Two orange trees, a fig bush, and a lemon tree within the tabby walls would provide fresh fruit. At the same time, Zabette turned her attentions toward restoring Lucy Spalding's flower garden, especially the roses, camellias, and gardenias, which had suffered neglect since her death. Modeling it after her grandmother's flower garden at Plum Orchard, she also planted jasmine, daisies, black-eyed Susans, larkspur, and azaleas to ensure fragrance and cut flowers throughout the spring and summer. She enjoyed gardening and found these efforts more pleasure than work.

In the evenings after supper, she and Robert sat in the porch swing to admire her gardening efforts and to watch the sun set over the marshes. She loved to smell the fresh-turned soil as he told her about his day. Occasionally he even asked about hers. On evenings when he held her hand and nuzzled her neck, she learned to anticipate their lovemaking and his nocturnal exploration of her body. And she had decided to interpret his inevitable snoring as a sign of contentment.

AS THE SEEDLINGS OF HER GARDEN began to sprout, Zabette noticed that her body was beginning to change as well. Her breasts were swollen and sore. She felt nauseous in the mornings and was often unable to keep her breakfast down. She suspected she was pregnant but secretly feared that she might be coming down with something she had picked up at the infirmary. Amanda would surely know, she thought, and was always happy to give her advice. Zabette sat on a kitchen stool nibbling on one of the oatmeal cookies Amanda set out for her and described her symptoms.

"When you have yo' last monthly flow?" Amanda asked.

"About two months ago, I guess," Zabette replied.

"Lawd, ha' mercy, chile. Ain't nothin' to worry 'bout." Amanda's face spread in a big, warm smile. "You gone have a baby sho' nuf. And tha's mighty fine news."

"A baby!" Zabette exclaimed, relieved to have her own diagnosis confirmed. "I thought maybe that was it, but I wasn't sure. Oh, thank you, Amanda," she said, hugging the portly woman tightly. Amanda hugged her back, feeling like a privileged insider who knew the news even before Mas' Robert did.

ZABETTE TOLD ROBERT THAT NIGHT in bed when he reached for her. She had hugged the secret to herself all day, waiting for this moment.

He sat bolt upright in bed. "What did you say?"

"You're going to be a father."

She couldn't see the blue of his eyes in the darkened room, but the white of his teeth was evident in the smile that broke across his face. He let out a small whoop, pulled Zabette toward him, and kissed her enthusiastically again and again.

"You are a wonderful woman," he said between kisses. But after that night he treated her with gentleness as though he was afraid to touch her, until Zabette assured him that she was not made of porcelain.

She did not tell her grandmother about the baby until she felt sure that she was not going to miscarry. Zabette had seen too many miscarriages among the island women, but little wonder since most of them worked in the fields until the day they delivered. She knew of at least one baby at Plum Orchard born between the cotton furrows two Octobers ago. It survived, but she had no idea how many others lived or died under such circumstances. Childbirth was risky in the best of circumstances. She would have to request that in the future pregnant women be assigned duties less strenuous than chopping cotton. Perhaps she could persuade Robert by pointing out the property he was losing each time a newborn died.

WHEN THE TIME CAME FOR HER CONFINEMENT, Zabette, apprehensive about giving birth, asked Marguerite to spend a few weeks at Planters House. She remembered Catherine's screams while Margaret Elizabeth was being born, though everyone had said it was an easy delivery. Amanda assured her that she would forget the pain once she held the child in her arms. Still, she was afraid. The midwife for the Stafford plantation was one of the slaves that Robert had bought as part of the Rayfield property in 1834. They called her Maum Bella. Amanda assured Zabette that she was very good at bringing babies.

"She know all they is to know 'bout birthin', Zabette. She be mighty good at it. She done bring a passel of chillun in the quarters—and two of 'em was mine." Zabette was reassured, but still she wanted her grandmother there for emotional support.

MARGUERITE SEEMED PLEASED to have been asked. Frederick drove her to Planters House on Saturday, October 12. She came prepared for a two-week stay and longer if needed, leaving John Grey still serving as her overseer at Plum Orchard. One had no idea when babies might come, but from the looks of Zabette it would not be long. Her whole body was swollen, and she was clearly uncomfortable, even sitting in the parlor. Marguerite made sure that Maum Bella was always close by and requested that she stay for a few nights in Amanda's cabin.

On the following Tuesday morning, October 15, before first light, Zabette got up to use the chamberpot. Suddenly she realized to her horror that water was running down her legs. She got a towel to clean up the mess before Robert saw it, but as she bent down, she was struck by a sharp pain in her abdomen. She stifled a cry, not wanting to awaken Robert. Despite her pain, she managed to wipe the floor clean. She wouldn't want him to slip and fall because of her negligence. Unable to get back to her feet, she crawled into the hallway and to the door of her grandmother's room, where she tapped on the door since she could not reach the knob.

Her grandmother replied, "*Entrez.*"

But Zabette could only call to her. "*Grand'mère, j'ai besoin de toi.* I need you." Marguerite flung back her covers and padded barefoot to the door.

"Zabette! What's happened?" She helped the girl to her feet and called, "Robert!"

"Don't wake him, *Grand'mère.* He needs his rest."

"Nonsense," said Marguerite and called again, even louder, "Robert!!"

Robert had leapt up the first time he heard his name called and rushed to the doorway when he didn't see Zabette in bed beside him. "Good heavens! What's wrong?"

"You're about to become a father," Marguerite said. "Now help me get her back to bed. Then go fetch Maum Bella."

Marguerite spread a soft cotton blanket across the bed, and together they laid Zabette down. She felt the pain in her belly subside as she stretched out on the bed.

"I feel better now," she said.

"The pain will come back, my dear, though maybe not for a while, and it will get worse. Now make yourself as comfortable as you can, and when you feel it returning, breathe as fast as you can. I'm going to make sure Robert found Maum Bella and that Amanda puts on some water to boil. Now you just relax. Everything's going to be fine." She patted Zabette's hand and then her cheek, smiling down at her dishevelment. Already there were voices outside, and it was clear that Robert had delivered the message.

He bounded back up the stairs, his eyes frantic. "What should I do now?" he asked.

"Just go downstairs and ask Amanda to make you some breakfast. All this is going to take a while, Robert," Marguerite said.

"You mean I can't stay with her?"

"Well, for a short time perhaps, but then I want you to go downstairs. A birthing room is no place for a man," Marguerite assured him.

He rushed into the bedroom and sat down beside Zabette to hold her hand. "What can I get you?" he asked her, trying to plump up the pillows Marguerite had put behind her head.

She leaned back, feeling better than she had in months, but knowing it was only temporary. "I'm fine," she told him. "Don't worry." He poured her a glass of water from the pitcher beside the bed and held it to her lips. "Thank you, Robert. Now go on. They'll call you when it's over."

As Maum Bella and Marguerite came into the room, he stood up to leave. "You'll let me know, won't you, if she needs anything."

"Absolutely, Robert," Marguerite assured him as she shoved him out the door. "Now get!"

THE BABY, A TINY GIRL WITH LIGHT SKIN and a head of damp hair the color of midnight, arrived before noon. Once he heard her cries, there was no keeping Robert out of the room. He was momentarily shocked by the scene when he burst into the bedroom, but Maum Bella quickly covered Zabette's legs with a quilt and shooed Robert back into the hallway. They knew they couldn't keep him out for long, and Maum Bella hurriedly wrapped the afterbirth in heavy canvas and put it in a croker sack, while Marguerite sponged off the baby and wrapped her in the little blue blanket she had saved from Zabette's own birth.

Robert was waiting anxiously beside the door when Maum Bella opened it again. "I reckon you can come on in now, Mas' Robert," she said with a grin. He crossed the threshold and in two large steps was kneeling beside the bed. Zabette's hair was still damp from the effort of giving birth. He wiped the sweat from her brow and looked into her eyes, searching for signs of pain and weakness. He had seen so much blood that he was sure she must be bleeding to death. But her color looked good, and her eyes were shining.

"She gone be fine, Mas' Robert. It were an easy birth," Maum Bella reassured him.

"Are you sure?" he asked.

"It's a girl, they tell me, Robert," Zabette said softly. "I hope you don't mind too much."

"Mind? Of course not! A girl is what I wanted all along," he said enthusiastically, though he had not yet looked at the baby. He was far too elated to see her mother smiling and out of pain. "What shall we call her? Elisabeth for her mother, I think," he said, finally looking around for the child.

Marguerite gently handed the baby, wrapped snuggly, into Zabette's arms. Robert looked at the newborn with disbelief. She was incredible, with perfect little eyes, a nose, and lips the color of plum blossoms. Her skin was as white as his own. Only the full head of black curls suggested the mixed blood of her birth.

"I've thought about it, Robert, and I wondered if we could also call her Marie for my mother or perhaps the English equivalent Mary. You had a sister named Mary, so she could be named for her as well. And for the blessed Virgin," she added for the benefit of her Catholic grandmother, who smiled broadly and nodded.

"Elizabeth Mary," he said. "That's a fine name."

"Or Mary Elizabeth?" she suggested softly.

"An even better name!" he roared. He would have agreed to anything she wanted at that moment. Robert Stafford had never in his life felt so elated. He was a father! There would be lots of life in Planters House now, he thought. This was only the beginning.

Chapter Twenty-Two

CUMBERLAND ISLAND, 1841

Everyone who knew Robert Stafford was amazed at the change that had come over him during the past few years. They were surprised to find an affable, almost handsome, man behind the stern mask he had worn for so long. Where he had been taciturn, he was now talkative. Where he had been dour, he now sometimes showed a smiling face.

He had always found it to his advantage to maintain an impassive façade outwardly, showing no enthusiasm for anything that might interest him for fear that someone would snatch it away. His was a nature that required control of all situations. Robert had always found it easy to dominate men but hard to ask them for favors. His steel-blue eyes could fix upon a man and refuse to let him go, while his stature and his brisk, booming voice, when he chose to use it, would cow most men into submission. Instead of a Georgia drawl, he had affected in all his business dealings the more rapid speech he had learned in Connecticut during his boyhood days. It convinced most of his adversaries that he was a quick-thinking man determined to have his own way.

Only a few, like Phineas Nightingale, saw it for the pretense it was and found it more irritating than commanding. Whenever the two men confronted one another in public, Nightingale exaggerated his aristocratic Georgia speech patterns, drawling his vowels and dropping his *r*'s in a way that made Robert feel mocked. Even that wouldn't bother him now. These feelings, he thought, were relegated to the past. In his acceptance of the vulnerability of love, he became an engaging man who drew people to him rather than pushing them away, as he had always done before. His eyes softened, and a frequent smile played around the corners of his mouth.

Other planters noticed, as did the St. Marys' tradesmen and even the slaves. Amanda had commented to Zabette as she rolled out her biscuit dough, "Mas' Robert don't come down here to my kitchen no more like a ol' bulldog a-shoutin' orders an' a-fussin' at me. 'Them biscuits be too hard! Them beans be too salty! Where's my pie you was gone make from them peaches I brung ya?'" she bellowed in imitation. Zabette had to laugh at the accuracy of her imitation.

"He be mighty differ'nt these days. Why, he even say 'thank you, Amanda' to me last night when I brung him dessert. You done sweetened 'im up, I reckon, Zabette."

Zabette smiled at the tribute. Amanda was still the only plantation worker who didn't call her "Miss Zabette," an appellation that always made her feel uncomfortable. She loved the cook's candor with her. She always felt safe with Amanda, now that the woman had finally accepted her as a part of the household. It was like sharing the kitchen of her childhood with Daisy or her mother.

Though Zabette had rarely seen the blustery face of Robert that Amanda described, she'd heard about it from others. But she knew better than anyone else that he had not always been that way. So many things had toughened him against the world. Even though he sometimes publicly boasted his "right smart Yankee education," she knew that his experience at the New London Grammar School had been a painful time that hardened his heart against the taunts of older boys who were different from him. He had learned he was safer if the world saw only his tough facade and that he must never reveal any vulnerability.

It was a miracle, Zabette thought, that he had ever emerged from behind that mask long enough even to consider trying to court Caty Nightingale those many years ago when he was twenty-seven, and she was six years his junior. It also explained his businesslike approach to her grandmother when he unveiled his desire to bring Zabette into his life. Although at the time she had felt like a horse being traded, she knew now it was just Robert's way. She rejoiced at his new enthusiasm for life and his lowered guard, not just with her, but with others as well. She prayed to God that it would last.

DURING ONE OF THEIR WEEKLY VISITS to Plum Orchard, Zabette and Robert both watched in rapt attention as Marguerite played patty-cake on the veranda of the house with Mary Elizabeth, while Robert drained the last of his brandy from the snifter. It reminded Zabette of her own childhood, when it was she who played patty-cake with her grandmother.

Suddenly the little girl, weary of the game, crawled into her mother's lap and leaned back to watch the fireflies begin their evening performance in the garden. They sat in comfortable silence, listening to the crickets and frogs and the occasional splash of a fish in the nearby river. Mary Elizabeth yawned, and nestled sleepily into her mother's arms.

"We need to be leaving soon," Zabette remarked. "The light's fading, and we need to get Mary Elizabeth in bed before too late." Robert nodded in acquiescence, though he appeared to be enjoying himself.

Zabette rose to take Mary Elizabeth inside to change her before they started their carriage ride back to Planters House. As she closed the screen door behind her, she noticed her grandmother lean toward Robert. Then she heard her soft voice, "Robert could you come by sometime later this week. We need to talk about a matter concerning Zabette." Zabette paused in the doorway, curious, but her grandmother said no more.

ROBERT WAS STARTLED BY HER WORDS. He had almost forgotten that legally Zabette still belonged to Marguerite. He no longer thought of her as Marguerite's slave granddaughter, for they seemed as natural together as any family.

For a moment, his heart sank and his mind whirled. Surely Marguerite was not going to make her come back to Plum Orchard. Technically, Mary Elizabeth belonged to her as well, since the offspring of slave mothers were the property of the mother's owner. Surely Marguerite would not do that, he thought. She must see how he depended on Zabette, how much he loved her and the child.

After a long pause, he said, "Shall I come tomorrow—around 4:00?"

"That would be fine, Robert. I'll expect you. Come for tea, but please come alone."

HE DID NOT SLEEP WELL THAT NIGHT, tossing so much that Zabette finally reached out to him and shifted her body closer to his. Her touch always calmed him. He drifted finally to sleep, but his dreams were uneasy.

WHEN ROBERT TROTTED DOWN THE DRIVE to Plum Orchard the next day, Marguerite Bernardey was sipping tea on her veranda. She had been waiting for him. Daisy had put out an extra cup and saucer; cucumber sandwiches and lemon wafers lay on a plate beside the silver tea service. Marguerite's embroidery hoop, with its half-completed sampler of hummingbirds, red flowers, and green leaves, lay on her lap.

"I had almost given you out," Marguerite said gaily in mock accusation.

"I meant to come earlier, but there was a problem with the gin that I had to see to." The cotton had been picked and piles of it were waiting to be ginned and baled before it could be shipped to the factor, who handled his sales in Savannah. "I hope I'm not too late for a cup of that tea," knowing full well that she was already pouring it.

Robert and Marguerite seldom saw each other any more without Zabette and Mary Elizabeth present. And while they both enjoyed the presence of the young woman and her child, they also appreciated each other's company. Robert knew he was the one man that Marguerite felt she could be completely honest with, as he was with her. They valued that quality in one another. He had kept his promise to Peter, and it was a good feeling. If it hadn't been for him, he knew Marguerite's life would have been more difficult since her son died. And although they sometimes disagreed with vigor and forthrightness, they trusted one another. Robert had come to value her opinion and to deal with her more or less as an equal, even though she was a woman. A lot of Georgia men would take him for a fool, he suspected, but he had learned to respect her ideas more than those of a lot of men he knew. And he looked after Zabette and the child better than most men would have done. Still he was apprehensive.

Robert settled in a wicker rocking chair and accepted the cup of tea that she held out to him. The afternoon was warm, and the light was gilded by the low arc of the sun as it cut across the southern sky. The view of the river and the marshes beyond was soothing. Yet in spite of the calm, Robert felt tense.

Marguerite had greeted him cheerfully, but he knew that she would greet him that way no matter what. He talked more than usual in clipped sentences to allay his nervousness.

They discussed the cotton crop, which was a little better this year than last since no storms had come to flood the fields just before picking time. That was a good thing, too, since prices had been falling ever since the cotton crash of '39. In an effort to make conversation, Robert began a tirade, one that Marguerite had heard months ago at one of their suppers, about that "fool President Harrison," who back in March had delivered an inaugural address that had lasted nearly two hours in a Washington snowstorm.

"Served thirty-two days," Robert snorted to display his intolerance for fools. "Caught pneumonia and died of his own ego. Served him right. Longest speech, shortest term. Let's hope Tyler's got more sense," he muttered. But he doubted it. Robert didn't have much patience with states rights' politicians like John Tyler, even though it was the popular Southern position. Strength, he had always declared, lay with the Union.

Marguerite tolerated Robert's pronouncements, even those she was hearing for a second or even a third time, but they both knew that they were only dancing around the true topic. What happened in Washington rarely affected life at Cumberland, except for cotton prices. She understood that Robert was trying to stay on familiar territory, and she listened for a while before steering the conversation toward his unsanctioned relationship with Zabette.

"Robert," she said finally, during a brief pause in his harangue. "Let's talk about my granddaughter."

He fell silent, waiting for her to begin.

"You know I care about Zabette very much," she said. "I want her to be happy and protected from ever being sold away from Cumberland after I'm gone."

"Not much chance of that, Marguerite, not while she's with me."

"But she's not your property," Marguerite reminded him.

He nodded grimly, "Yes, I know."

"Anything could happen. You know how uncertain life can be for someone like Zabette." They both remembered that she had not been listed as property in the settlement between Marguerite and her daughter-in-law. Robert had thought it best at the time, but still it placed Zabette in an awkward category as neither an acknowledged slave nor a free person of color. He knew that her grandmother might be fearful of raising the issue in any legal document, but now that Catherine was out of the picture, it might be in Zabette's best interest for it to be clarified.

"I take good care of her, Marguerite," he reminded her. "And Mary Elizabeth too."

"I know you do, Robert," she assured him. "And that's why I want to settle her situation. I am willing now to make her your property." She paused as his heart leapt. Then she continued, "I won't take money for her, but I want to have my lawyer draw up a deed of gift or sale or whatever is needed, so that there's never any question about your legal ownership of her."

"And Mary Elizabeth?" he asked, nervous in spite of his elation.

"The child too, of course, and any future children you might have together."

"Marguerite, I don't know what to say."

"There's one condition, Robert," she stated firmly. "If you ever mistreat her in any way, I will reserve the right to bring her back to Plum Orchard to live with me. There is nothing I can do after I die, but I will always protect her during my lifetime."

He nodded. "I understand, though I don't think you need to worry about that."

"I hope not, but I will have some type of clause in the agreement, however strange it might be in a property transfer, that gives me the right to have her with me at Plum Orchard should the need arise. Do you find that condition acceptable?"

Of course he did. Anything to make Zabette legally his. It wasn't marriage, but from his perspective it was the next best thing. She would finally belong to him by law. "I accept your condition, Marguerite. When shall we draw up the papers?"

"I'll contact my lawyer to take care of it the next time I'm in St. Marys. In the meantime, please don't mention any of this to Zabette. She need not know that anything has changed."

ON TUESDAY, DECEMBER 28, 1841, Marguerite braved the winter tides and had herself rowed to St. Marys to sign the legal papers. She read over the document Belton Copp had drawn up, cringing a bit at some of the wording, but understanding its necessity:

> I, Margaret Bernardy of Camden County, in Consideration of the Good Will and affection as well as for services rendered in the management of my negroes and plantation, and business generally, for the last eight or ten years by Robert Stafford, of the same place, have sold . . . to Robert Stafford . . . the following property viz My Mulatto Girl Elizabeth and her child Mary about two years old. . . . With this proviso the said Robert Stafford agrees that the said Mulatto girl Elizabeth shall remain in the property of the said Margaret Bernardy during her natural life. . . .

It was this last sentence she was looking for, to make sure that she still had the legal right to bring Zabette home if Robert ever broke his word.

Marguerite signed the document without insisting that it be redrawn to correct her misspelled name. She was eager to get it over with, and all legal documents, she knew, were full of such errors. Her neighbor and overseer John Grey served as witness, without fully understanding the nature of the document. All he had to attest to was that she had signed it. Zabette and her daughter would now belong to Robert, but only after her death. No one else could make a legal claim to them, and Marguerite still had the right to bring them back to Plum Orchard should the need ever arise.

Chapter Twenty-Three

BY THE FOLLOWING SPRING Zabette realized that she was pregnant again. The baby was not born until early December, and this time the labor was hard. The child's head was large and seemed to lodge in the birth canal. Maum Bella was clearly worried, begging Zabette to push until the young woman was weeping and exhausted. Her strength was giving out. Maum Bella massaged her abdomen with oil and gave her some terrible tasting tea to help her to relax. Finally, after a long and painful labor, the child was born—a boy—to Robert's joy. This time there was no question about the name. As the firstborn son, he was to be named Robert Stafford, Jr., for his father, though they would call him Bobby.

Although he was physically large like his father, the baby did not develop as quickly as Mary Elizabeth had. His responses were slow, and Zabette feared that he would not please his father. But Robert loved the boy tenderly and did not seem to care that he was different from his sister. Boys were naturally different from girls, he reasoned. A son and a daughter! What more could a father want?

Never before had Robert's life been so full. What stupidity, he thought, that he could not show off his family to the other white residents of the island. He couldn't believe that they wouldn't share his happiness. His children were as white as theirs, and far more beautiful. But Zabette didn't want him to take them anywhere they might be subject to the scrutiny of other planters. He knew she was right, so he attended festive gatherings and funerals alone. But he insisted on private outings with them—frequent carriage rides around the island and occasional picnics on the deserted beach.

On a Sunday morning in late April, when the weather was perfect and pleasantly warm after a good rainstorm the night before, Amanda packed a lunch so the family could picnic on the beach. Mary Elizabeth loved chasing gulls and watching pelicans dive for their food. Zabette brought a small basket to help her daughter collect some of the whelk shells that littered the beach after a spring storm. Robert pointed out to her all the holes where ghost crabs lived and held up for her scrutiny abandoned shells of horseshoe crabs and dried casings of whelk eggs. Zabette and Robert watched with contentment as their daughter dug in the sand and waded in the surf. Zabette held Bobby in her arms, pointing out the laughing gulls and terns that stalked the seashore's edge.

Amanda had packed a wonderful basket of deviled eggs, fried chicken, pickled okra, and candied sweet potatoes, her best yeast rolls, and a whole pecan pie. Robert spread a quilt on the sand and held the baby while Zabette set out the sumptuous picnic. Bobby had not yet learned to sit up, though his big sister coaxed and teased him constantly to do so. Zabette propped him up against a pillow to feed him, as he hungrily watched every bite of food that went into the mouth of his sister, whom he adored.

After they had eaten, Bobby was almost asleep, and Mary Elizabeth, ready for a nap herself, was getting tired and cranky. Zabette packed up the remnants of their feast while Robert shook the sand off the quilt and folded it. Content with the day, they headed to the carriage for their drive back to Planters House.

Bobby snuggled in his mother's arms and was asleep before his father had even turned the horses around and climbed into his own seat. Mary Elizabeth leaned against her mother's body, and Zabette shifted the sleeping baby to support him with one arm, while she put the other around the little girl, whose tight dark curls were unruly in the ocean's breeze.

Robert had decided to come without a driver so that they would have more privacy. Peter, who had served as his driver, companion, and most trusted servant since they were boys, was relieved. He thought the beach an utter waste of time unless one needed to catch fish, and he had been happy to stay in the stables, groom the horses, and take a nap for part of the day.

Robert turned the carriage south toward his plantation, letting the horses choose their own slow pace, in no hurry to get home. The day had been perfect, and he longed to have it last forever. Mary Elizabeth's eyes were beginning to droop, and Bobby slept peacefully in his mother's lap. Robert loved to watch Zabette in her role of mother and had been delighted when she had told him several days earlier that they were already going to have another child. As they meandered toward the plantation, Robert contemplated his sense of well-being. He did not recall ever being so completely aware of the harmony of his surroundings. He had always taken the island's beauty for granted, but now it had become a place of sheer wonder. Had the oak trees always been so magnificent? Were the resurrection ferns always so green and lush after a good rain? He drove contentedly toward Planters House and his own domain.

Suddenly Robert noticed another carriage moving briskly in their direction. Recognizing the rig and horses as those of Phineas Nightingale, he was surprised because he had thought the Nightingales were away from the island at the moment. As they drew closer, Robert could see the driver in the high front seat, while Phineas and his wife, Mary, wearing a large dark blue sunbonnet, sat side-by-side in the passenger seat. He wondered if they were merely out for an afternoon ride or if they were headed to Plum Orchard to call on Marguerite or maybe on their way to visit someone at High Point at the north end.

As the two vehicles approached one another, Robert smiled affably and tipped his hat to Mrs. Nightingale, who turned her head sharply in the other direction. Phineas leaned forward and spoke to the driver who cracked his whip to urge his horses on as quickly as possible past the Stafford rig.

Robert was visibly stung by their snub, but he brushed it aside as best he could, consciously deciding that not even Phineas Nightingale and his prissy wife would spoil his day. He looked over at Zabette to see her reaction. She was staring straight ahead, holding Bobby and Mary Elizabeth a little closer to her breast. But despite her best efforts to control it, for she had no spare hand to wipe it away, a single tear slid down her cheek. If he could have read her thoughts, he would have understood that she cared not so much for herself, but for him. She had noticed Robert's stiffening as the Nightingale carriage passed by, and just for a moment she saw his old darkness return.

THE FOLLOWING DAY, ROBERT WAS KNEELING BESIDE A POST, checking a break in the fence line, when he caught sight of Phineas Nightingale on his white gelding riding toward him. He looked up, wary as Nightingale approached, but prepared to be friendly despite yesterday's snub. The rider stopped about ten feet away from the fence and, without dismounting, raised his voice.

"Curse you, Stafford," Phineas said. "Don't you ever greet my wife that way again when you're with that mulatto whore and those bastards of yours. My wife is a good, Christian woman, and I won't have her insulted in such a way. You do it ever again, and I'll see you on the beach at Amelia Island with pistols at dawn."

Robert was dumbfounded. He stood up to confront Nightingale, staring at him in disbelief. Before he could speak the bitter words rising within him, the rider spat on the ground near his feet and turned his horse toward the Main Road again, trotting away without giving him time to respond. If he could have reached him, Robert would have knocked Nightingale to the ground and beat his face to a pulp. He knew that wasn't the gentlemen's way in coastal Georgia, but he didn't give a damn. Many's the time he had witnessed the kind of duel Nightingale proposed. The north shore of adjacent Amelia Island was a favorite place for such armed confrontations. Old Henri du Bignon had shot Doc Holland in the thigh in a rifle duel there some years ago. But Robert couldn't imagine himself doing such a thing, drawing on a man in such a calculated way. Beating him in a fit of anger, however, was quite another matter, and his blood was boiling for just such a fight. But Nightingale was gone, already vanished among the palmettos and pines.

Robert's anger seethed, demanding some kind of physical action. He raged at the sky, bellowing out his fury in sounds that weren't even words. He lashed out with his fist at the fence post, ripping his knuckles open as they struck the hard wood. He battered it down with his foot, kicking it again and again until the toe of his boot was badly scarred. His jaw clenched and his eyes filled with tears of rage, he picked up the fallen post, smashed it viciously to the ground again and again, trying to break it to smithereens. But when he couldn't, in his frustration and with a loud grunt and a roar of anger, he threw it as far as he could across the field.

Finally, his fury spent, he sank to the ground again and sat there for a long time, feeling as he had the day when Phineas's sister, Caty, had turned her mocking laughter toward him, when her brother whispered something in her ear as Robert rode up. Humiliation and anger blinded him, and he had ridden away in hot fury and shame, beating his horse to make it go faster and faster until the lathered horse was almost on the point of collapse.

It was that same fury that possessed him now. He felt his old bitterness flow like bile into his body, polluting it with its blackness. His fists and jaw tightly clenched, he raised one arm to the heavens and renewed his vow under God to take over all of Nightingale's land, impoverish him, and make him eat dirt. He sat for a long time, waiting for his fury to abate and watching his knuckles bleed.

What a fool I've been, he thought, *ever to think these island snobs could be human. What a goddamn fool I've been.* He was determined he wouldn't make that mistake again. Only vaguely recalling the joy he'd felt the day before, he knew he would never again let down his guard.

SUPPER THAT NIGHT WAS A DISMAL AFFAIR. Robert, his right hand bandaged from what he had explained as an "accident" that resulted from mending the fence, was sullen and silent. Zabette, not feeling well herself, made little effort to talk since Robert showed no interest. She put the children to bed early and went upstairs to lie down. When Robert finally came up, he undressed, blew out the lamp, and sank wearily between the sheets. He did not reach for her as he usually did, but lay awake, rigid, staring into the darkness. She too lay awake for a long time, wondering what had happened to put him in such a mood.

WHEN SHE AWOKE THE NEXT MORNING he was gone, and Mary Elizabeth was tugging at the sleeve of her gown.

"*Maman, Maman,* I'm hungry. And Bobby is crying."

Zabette roused herself to check on her son, whimpering in his crib. He was wet and hungry. After she changed him, she called Amanda to give the children their breakfast. As a rule, they took breakfast with their parents, but today Robert was gone. And Zabette was feeling a pain in her abdomen that she recognized all too well, a pain she did not welcome for she knew it was far too soon.

Chapter Twenty-Four

ROBERT LEFT AT FIRST LIGHT FOR THE MAINLAND village of St. Marys, urging the boatmen to row as rapidly as possible. Once there, he rented a horse to ride to the Camden County courthouse in Jeffersonton to check on Phineas Nightingale's land records. It was a damn nuisance to have the county seat way over there rather than in St. Marys where it used to be. It was a full day's trip, and he knew that he had to leave early to get his work done at the courthouse before the county clerk closed for lunch. Although he hadn't mentioned it to Zabette, he had told Amanda that he would not be home for dinner and might be late for supper.

WHEN HE RETURNED TO PLANTERS HOUSE late in the day, the sun was already low on the horizon. Maum Bella was anxiously waiting for him by the front steps. "Mas' Robert, Miss Zabette, she fine. I hope you ain't mad wit' Maum Bella. I done the best I could, but she done lost the baby."

Robert steadied himself on the bannister, but said nothing. Was this part of Nightingale's curse? Could anything else go wrong? He felt his entire world crumbling. Finally he whispered angrily, "Where is she, Bella?"

"She lyin' down now. But she be fine, long as she get some rest. She be pretty upset. I's her first miscarriage. That do upset a woman."

"What was the baby, Bella?" he asked before climbing the stairs.

"'Nother li'l boy." She hesitated, then added, "But you done got one son, Mas' Robert. An' two fine chillun'. And she'll have more." Her false cheerfulness was intended to make him feel better.

Robert mounted the steps heavily, climbed to the second floor, and opened the door to the bedroom. Zabette was lying down with her eyes closed and a damp cloth across her forehead. He thought at first she was asleep, but when the door creaked, she opened her eyes.

"Oh, Robert." She looked at him and tried to sit up. Her eyes were puffy from crying, and her face was still wet with tears. He had no idea what to say to her and stood there in silence.

She said in a tone of anxious apology, "I'm so sorry, Robert. I don't know what happened. He looked so perfect. Tiny, but . . . perfect." She began to cry again.

"Don't be upset. Can't be helped," he muttered.

"But I know how happy you were about this baby," she held her hand out to comfort him.

"Lots of folks lose babies. I'm sure there'll be others," he said, patting her outstretched hand distractedly. He would not let himself feel this loss or be penetrated by Zabette's sorrow. He had already let himself feel too much, and look where it had gotten him. Feelings weren't for men, he reflected. His world called for actions, not feelings. What was one baby more or less? One more mouth to feed. And there *would* be others. Maum Bella said so.

"Robert . . . ," she pleaded, stretching an arm toward him. He knew that she wanted him to take her in his arms, to share her tears, to comfort her and let her comfort him, but he could not. It was as though some dark form stood between them that had not been there before. He felt it pulling him away from her grief.

"You get some rest like Maum Bella said. You'll feel better tomorrow." He turned and left the bedroom, closing the door behind him, and went downstairs to his study.

He took out the tax records he had copied in Jeffersonton and his own account books. Then he spread out his frayed map of Cumberland Island and sat down to plan the downfall of Phineas Nightingale.

PLANTERS HOUSE, JUNE 14, 1843

Just as he had the day before and the day before that, Robert Stafford sat frowning at his desk, poring over the tattered map of Cumberland Island that the county surveyor, John McKinnon, had drawn up in 1802. It was the map Robert had used for years, as had his stepfather before him. Robert had studied it many times, spreading it out like a sacred scroll, occasionally redrawing boundaries and altering names as properties changed hands. What delighted him most was being able to scratch out a name and write "Robert Stafford" in its place as the new owner. Each time he made such a change he dreamed of the day when he might own the entirety of Cumberland Island.

He realized now that he had been excessively distracted by Zabette and the children. He had let himself become complacent and focused on trivia—like a child's getting a new tooth or learning to walk. He had grown too damned contented, he told himself with annoyance. But the recent incident with Phineas Nightingale had revived his impassioned desire to banish the likes of the Shaws and the Nightingales from the face of what would otherwise be his paradise.

Some nights Robert was tempted to relax in Zabette's arms and try to tell her about his feelings as he used to do, but such nights were increasingly rare. On one such occasion, he blurted out the recent taunt and curse of Phineas Nightingale, leaving out the most offensive language about her and the children. Most nights he simply took her body roughly, as though it were his right. And as far as he was concerned, it was.

Robert's bitterness toward Nightingale had begun to etch itself in the lines of his face, in the scowling corners of his mouth. Zabette tried to make him smile. She would bring the children to sit on his knee or reach out for his hand when they sat on the verandah together. But nothing could make him forget the morning Nightingale had insulted him to his face—not just him but his children and Zabette as well. *It was the last straw.* The desire to destroy Phineas Nightingale had taken over his life, and he would show no quarter. Seizing Dungeness, which had been in Nightingale's family for three generations, had become his obsession.

Robert thought about the showy ostentation of the house built by Nightingale's grandmother, the widow of Revolutionary war general Nathanael Greene, Caty Greene Miller, and her second husband Phineas Miller. Robert had been twelve or thirteen when it was completed. It was the most magnificent house he had ever seen. Some said it was the only four-story tabby house in the country. Its imposing facade rose up more than seventy feet, and sailors approaching from the sea could see it towering over the live oaks from miles away. Its walls were said to be six feet thick at the base, built to withstand any hurricane that might threaten the island.

Robert had long coveted the house and its south end location, the best site on the island as far as he was concerned. He had watched the splendor of the grounds evolve to include magnificent gardens, with magnolias, olive, orange, and peach trees, date palms, and an extravagant variety of shrubs and flowers. Ironically, its first owner, Phineas Miller, had pricked his finger on a thorn in the garden and died of infection in 1803 only months after they moved into the new mansion. But his widow, Caty, lived on at Dungeness until her death. He recalled her as a magnificent woman, strong and determined, with bright snapping eyes, a woman with clever ideas who had encouraged her friend Eli Whitney to create his cotton gin, helping Sea Island cotton become even more profitable for coastal planters.

Caty Miller was also the kind of woman who would put up with no shenanigans from her children. Her first husband, General Greene, had left enough good land on Cumberland for all his children to own large plantations, land he had received for his services in the American Revolution. But his widow had refused to divide up the property. In her mind, the land symbolized the unity of the family. It was family land and should remain undivided and under her control. Her children had different ideas. They simply wanted to get their share of the inheritance and go their separate ways.

One of those children had been Phineas Nightingale's mother, Martha Washington Greene, who lived with her husband John Nightingale at The Spring Plantation, the tract of land now owned by John Grey. After Nightingale's death in '06, Martha had married a Rhode Island doctor named Henry Edward Turner, and moved north. Her new husband, according to the local grapevine, badgered her to demand her legal share of her father's Cumberland land. Martha's sister Cornelia and her husband, Ned Littlefield, were equally impatient to have the matter settled. Finally in 1810 the two sisters joined forces to compel their mother to divide the land and property that went with it. They persuaded her to let them have their land, but Caty stubbornly hung on to all the slaves claiming that she still needed them as collateral to satisfy any outstanding debts against the estate of her first husband, though he had been dead for almost a quarter of a century. It was obvious to her children that she had no intention of ever declaring the estate closed.

Cornelia and Martha finally confronted their mother one sunny afternoon in the parlor at Dungeness to demand that she relinquish their share of slave property and General Greene's personal belongings, including his military honors from the Revolution. Their mother was furious and dismissed them from her sight, calling them "ungrateful wretches." In the end, she would disown them both, leaving them only one insulting dollar each in her will, while she bequeathed Dungeness and its lands to her one loyal daughter, Louisa Greene Shaw.

Robert was only twenty-three at the time, but it was this feud he had taken advantage of to acquire his first piece of their land. Cornelia took revenge on her mother by selling him her Cumberland tract known as Littlefield Plantation. To add insult to injury, Cornelia and her husband made away with Caty's seven best slaves and fled to Tennessee. Caty was furious, but there was nothing she could do. Most of her children had never loved the island as she did and had no qualms about selling pieces of their father's land grant.

Some years later Robert had managed to purchase the Rayfield Plantation that belonged to Caty's son, Nathanael Ray Greene. Nat preferred to live in Rhode Island, and his children finally sold Rayfield, along with its fifty-three slaves, to Robert in 1834. Phineas Nightingale's mother, Martha, sold her land as well, but not to Robert, who could not at the time afford to buy all the property he coveted. It was John Grey in 1825 who purchased The Spring Plantation.

With the sale of his mother's lands, Phineas should by rights have inherited nothing on the island. But as Robert saw it, he had, with clever calculation, buttered up his Aunt Louisa, who had no children of her own. And at her death in 1831, she had obligingly left both the Dungeness property and her Oakland Plantation to her "favorite" nephew, Phineas Nightingale, making him a wealthy man overnight—an effortless fortune simply handed to him on a platter, which Robert found particularly galling.

He fidgeted with the map, remembering the moment he had learned of that inheritance. His man Peter, returning from the docks where he had picked up the month's supplies for the plantation, told him, "I done heared Mr. Phineas be the new owner at Dungeness," he had reported to Robert.

"What?" asked Robert in disbelief.

"Miss Louisa done lef' it to him in her will is what I heared."

Robert could feel his face growing red as his blood pressure mounted. He himself had intended to buy the property from the Shaw estate. Since Louisa Shaw had no children, he had wrongly assumed that her nieces and nephews would sell her land and divide the profits. It had never occurred to him that she would play favorites. He cursed under his breath.

"You reckon Mr. Phineas and his missus will be movin' to Cumberland?" Peter asked.

"I have no idea," Robert said curtly, as he turned on his heel and walked up the stone steps to Planters House. *How could Louisa Shaw have been such a fool?* he wondered.

Nightingale had handled the entire estate like an idiot, he thought bitterly. It took him less than a decade to fritter away most of his undeserved inheritance with bad management. Yet in spite of his incompetence, he hung on tenaciously, even though his financial future always seemed to dangle at the end of a very thin thread.

Robert thought him an imbecile for some of his decisions. Instead of relying on cotton as his main crop, like most island planters with good sense, he had turned his interests increasingly to citriculture, with groves of orange and lemon trees and even olives, all of which were subject to even more possible setbacks than cotton at this latitude, and cotton was risky enough. Louisa Shaw had planted citrus orchards that thrived, but she had never been foolish enough to depend on them as her primary crop.

Unfortunately for Nightingale, both his timing and luck had been bad. Robert smiled at the memory. Phineas's financial problems had begun with the big freeze of January 1835, when he'd lost many of his orange trees. Even worse had been the invasion two years later of tiny insects known as purple mites. Adding to his troubles, the country's worst depression in memory proved to be the *coup de grâce* to Nightingale's financial woes.

Considering all that had happened, Robert thought with a cynical smile—or what passed for a smile these days—Nightingale must have felt like Job, as he sat inside Dungeness watching the ten days of heavy rain that poured on the island in late August of 1841, ruining what little remained of his crops. His debts mounted, and he appeared on the verge of total collapse.

Robert reviewed the entire unfolding of events with malevolent delight, considering it God's judgment against the man who had treated him as an inferior all his life. By 1839 Nightingale was already virtually penniless, and the following year he advertised his Cumberland lands for sale.

All this had happened, Robert recalled bitterly, during the time he had been most besotted by Zabette and charmed by the children. He now cursed himself for wasting his time and energies with such a lack of focus. By the time the advertisement drew his attention, Nightingale had withdrawn it. His father-in-law, John Alsop King, governor of New York, as well as some of his other relatives had propped him up financially, and to Robert's fury, they kept Nightingale from going under completely, preventing Robert from snapping up the land he had coveted for so long. He felt like a starving Tantalus, whose grapes were always snatched away by the wind just as he reached out to grasp them.

During those years, when Phineas had been most vulnerable, Robert's desire to take over the entire island, while still a distant goal, had diminished in importance, as love and family had become his focal point. Until the moment when Nightingale, from the height of his horse, had spat on the ground at his feet, Robert had almost lost sight of the true purpose of his life. But at that moment, all the bitterness of the past had boiled up in him once again, the snobbery of Louisa Shaw and her nephew, Phineas, who had never seen fit to invite him to the parties and dances they held at Dungeness, and Caty, who had driven him from their doorway laughing at him the one time he had come uninvited. He remembered with stark clarity and bitterness what he had almost forgotten. He would never be such a fool again.

He'd once thought that, when his fortunes as a young man had improved and he had acquired enough land and wealth to think himself worthy of courting Caty Nightingale, the Shaws and Nightingales might even think him a potential asset to their family. But their mockery had reminded him that he was nothing more to them than the son of one of their workers, utterly unworthy to darken the doors of Dungeness on their social level.

He felt only scorn and disgust for their preference to live in genteel poverty while they turned up their noses at his methods for making money, which they considered crass. They scoffed at his money-lending and at the perfectly honest interest rates he imposed, though that did not stop them from borrowing from him when they were in need. They rebuked him for foreclosing on unpaid loans and seizing the lands that had secured them. But to his satisfaction, he grew wealthier while they grew poorer. In the end, he intended to be the one in a position to scoff.

Now, as he studied his map, he was preparing for his biggest coup of all— the takeover of both plantations Nighingale had inherited from his Aunt Louisa, Oakland and Dungeness. Despite his high-handed airs, Phineas, as usual beset by debts and lawsuits, had not paid his taxes on either property for some time, a fact that Robert had learned during his review of the tax records that day in Jeffersonton.

He had discreetly pointed out this "oversight" to the clerk in the small courthouse office shared by the Camden County court clerk and tax assessor, and he was waiting for matters to take their course and for the lands to be sold on the courthouse steps to pay the taxes. But many weeks had passed and so far nothing had been done.

Perhaps he had been too subtle for that idiot clerk, he thought, and he planned to return the next day to Jeffersonton to press the matter further. He was annoyed at having to make the trip a second time, but it appeared to be necessary.

Robert also had his eye on John Grey's Spring Plantation, which Grey had recently taken to calling "Spring Garden," a romantic name Stafford thought rather silly. But whatever Grey wanted to call it, it was one of several tracts that stood between Planters House and Dungeness on the southern tip of the island. Robert knew Grey was also having a hard time financially and was further crippled by the economic depression. As early as 1831 he had come begging for a loan.

Then, to boost his income, Grey had taken on the job as Marguerite's overseer, in addition to trying to manage his own lands. But his debts kept mounting. Stafford had renewed his loan in 1842 and offered him an even more sizeable loan. Grey accepted gratefully, but there was a condition. This time Stafford required him to secure the loan with his 500 acres and to agree that if he were unable to pay the note, he would turn over his land and his thirty slaves to Robert Stafford.

Robert liked John Grey and would help him as long as he could. He was a good neighbor, and Stafford felt sympathy for his plight, but he had no doubt that in the end Grey would forfeit on the loan and be forced to give up his land. As Stafford well knew, not only had Grey been unable to pay off his loans in the past, but he was also not in the best of health. Robert would not push Grey hard, but if his friend were forced into bankruptcy, he would be there, waiting to take advantage of the opportunity.

Perhaps the most desirable aspect of The Spring was that Phineas Nightingale's father was buried on the property. Nothing would give Robert greater pleasure than for Nightingale to have to ask his permission to visit his father's grave. He smiled at the thought, rolling up his map and putting it back in its case. He savored the moment like a chess master who already foresaw the endgame but was prepared to toy a bit with his opponent.

Chapter Twenty-Five

CAMDEN COUNTY, GEORGIA, JUNE 15, 1843

Robert started the following day already in a bad mood at having to make a second trip into Jeffersonton to find out why the tax collector had not acted on his request. This time he would make it a demand. It was absurd, he thought, that something hadn't been done long before, for like most of Nightingale's other debts, his property taxes to Camden County had not been paid for several years.

Hot, dusty, and in a fouler humor by the time he reached the Tax Assessor's officer, Robert was not prepared to soften his demand or waste time with any preamble or niceties. This time he wanted answers. He walked straight up to the counter, behind which the county clerk, Perceval Cohen, sat shuffling papers.

Robert banged his fist on the counter and spoke in his loudest, most domineering voice. "Cohen," he demanded, "how long do you plan to put up with this delinquency of Phineas Nightingale? Here's the evidence, in case you've overlooked it," he said sarcastically. "He owes three years' back taxes!"

He shoved the tax records he had copied in his cramped handwriting toward the face of the nonplussed clerk.

"Mr. Stafford, we are making every effort to collect," Cohen answered, peering over his glasses at Robert Stafford, clearly trying to look as stern as possible, but Robert's years of practice at staring men down with his flinty eyes made it difficult for anyone to maintain confidence in the face of such scrutiny.

"As a taxpayer I *demand* that you either collect those taxes or put these lands up for auction, and I *demand* to be notified when this is to take place."

"I can assure you that the matter will be taken care of as soon as possible," the clerk replied noncommittally to Stafford's rapid-fire demands, trying not to look at the steel-blue eyes that peered so intently at him.

"See that it is. If not, I'll be back," said Stafford, pounding his fist once more before he turned abruptly and left, slamming the door behind him.

As ROBERT STAFFORD LEFT HIS OFFICE, Percy Cohen knew that he had probably sounded irritated, though he had tried to keep his voice official and authoritative. He was not surprised to see Stafford back again, for he had both expected and dreaded his return.

Stafford probably thought him a friend of Nightingale who was trying to let the matter ride for as long as possible, knowing that times were hard for many people just now. But there were things that Stafford did not know and that Cohen had no obligation to reveal. In fact, the matter was already under litigation. Nightingale was in debt to more than the County. Phineas's other numerous creditors were also at his door, demanding that his lands be sold to meet his obligations. The case now in the courts had been brought by some of Nightingale's own family members to whom Louisa Greene Shaw had left generous annuities in her will.

As heir and administrator of her estate, it had been up to Phineas to see that these obligations were met. But like so many other of his commitments in recent years, the annuities had gone unpaid. Louisa Shaw's niece, Margaret Greene, and Phineas's four half-sisters—Martha, Julia, Emily, and Louisa Turner—all of whom depended on the annuities for their livelihood, were fed up. Nightingale still had resources in the form of his land and slaves, and these women were determined to have their due. But they all knew how much Dungeness had meant to their benefactor, Louisa Shaw, and to her mother, Caty Miller, and they did not want to see it alienated from the family. Thus, the women had banded together to buy the land themselves once the court ruling had been made in their favor. They were perfectly willing to sell it back to Nightingale once he got his finances straightened out, but until then, it would remain safe in the hands of his cousin, Margaret.

ON THE AFTERNOON OF AUGUST 2, from a passing boatman, Stafford learned to his consternation and fury of the "sale" of Dungeness that had taken place the day before. The clerk had neglected to notify him, and he had seen no notice of it in the newspaper, *The Republican*, to which he subscribed and carefully read. He was so angry that he left the next morning before dawn, even taking one of the oars himself for a time to speed him toward St. Marys. He felt that he could have outrun the broken-down horse the liveryman had rented him to get him the twenty-five or so miles to Jeffersonton in time to berate Percy Cohen before he could possibly think of locking up for lunch. The county clerk had fully expected him to show up. And he was ready.

"Mr. Stafford, I'm sorry that you failed to see any notice about the selling of the Dungeness tract," he responded to Stafford's fulminations. "But I'm sure you can understand the emotional attachment these ladies have to that particular piece of land. They wanted it to stay within the family, and we tried to oblige. I would have done the same for you under similar circumstances."

Stafford was livid. The piece of land he wanted more than any other had slipped through his fingers once again. He would have paid anything to get it. Anything. He was almost speechless with rage at the clerk's apparent stupidity.

"Mr. Stafford," Cohen went on. "I'm happy to inform you that two more pieces of Mr. Nightingale's land will be sold on August 5. Both of these are adjacent to property you already own and would surely be more appropriate in terms of your cultivation."

The clerk had no idea of the personal issues involved, and he had apparently expected Stafford to be pleased by the news. But the planter was not placated. "You are a fool, Cohen, a simpering idiot and a damned fool, and you don't know anything at all about my needs."

"Mr. Stafford, there's no need for such language. I'm sure . . . "

"Obviously you're not sure about anything. You're nothing but a milksop, kow-towing to the Greenes and Nightingales like everybody else in this God-forsaken backwater."

"Mr. Stafford," the clerk was trying to adopt a reasonable tone, in contrast to that of Robert Stafford. "General Greene *was* a hero to our country."

"Goddamit, man, General Greene's been dead for more than fifty years now.

His family doesn't deserve any more consideration than yours or mine. You're a perfect ass for this action, and I'll have your job if you ever cross me again."

Robert stomped out of the office, slamming the door so hard that the glass bearing the title of both County Clerk and Tax Assessor's Office rattled as though it would break. Livid with rage, he rode his horse back to St. Marys so hard that the owner of the livery stable refused to rent him another in the future at the regular rate. He was compelled either to pay double or to stable one of his own horses for his use in the town. He chose the latter. If there was one thing he did not lack for at Cumberland, it was horses.

STAFFORD RETURNED TO JEFFERSONTON in a cloud of hot dust on the afternoon of August 4, prepared to spend the night in the little town's only boardinghouse and be on the courthouse steps at ten the next morning when the additional Nightingale lands were to be sold. He endured the cramped bed, too short for his six-foot-three frame, and the breakfast of fried eggs nestled in a pool of bacon grease and garnished with a pile of dried grits. Usually when he had to put up with such wretched food, he thanked God for Amanda. She wasn't much to look at, but she could cook like an angel. For once, however, he barely noticed and ate the food without comment.

He was on the steps of the courthouse at nine a.m., determined that the sheriff, the tax collector, and the clerk weren't going to conspire against him this time and try to sell the land out from under him. The morning sun was already broiling the pavement, and the humidity was making him sweat into his dark suit and high collar as he waited. By ten it was even hotter, and Robert felt that he was waiting in one of the inner circles of hell.

Little by little people gathered, eight of them in all, to bid on the land, hoping to pick up a bargain. He was not the only one who had learned of the so-called "public" sale that had taken place without anyone knowing about it, nor the only one who was annoyed. At ten on the dot, the burly sheriff showed up with an auctioneer. The first tract to be sold was the 1200-acre Oakland tract. Robert had hoped that Nightingale would be there to watch him take it off his hands. But he was nowhere to be seen. As a part of the land package, eleven slaves were being sold, four of them too old or too young to be of much use to Stafford. *Just more mouths to feed and useless slaves to drive up the price,* he thought. But he didn't care.

He would have bought dead livestock if they had come with the sale and hurt Nightingale in some way. He did a quick mental calculation. The land was good and worth at least a dollar an acre. The slaves at most should be worth an average of $500 apiece. But he was willing to go even higher if he had to.

The bidding was lively at first, until it became obvious that there were two determined buyers, Robert Stafford and James Clubb, who quickly outbid everyone else on the courthouse steps. As badly as he wanted this prime land, Clubb's resources were no match for Robert's, particularly with the slaves thrown into the deal, and the auctioneer finally banged down his gavel when, after Robert's bid of $6,000, nothing more was heard from Clubb.

The second piece of land was adjacent to the Rayfield tract Robert had bought in 1834. It was a valuable piece of land to him because it would allow all his lands to adjoin one another, even though on the surface it wasn't worth as much as Oakland. It was a 3,000-acre tract, though some of the land was swampy and useless. Even so, Robert was willing to pay a high price because of its location. Once again Clubb bid against him, thinking that this time he might have a chance without the slaves thrown into the deal, but Robert simply eliminated him from the bidding by jumping the bid to "Three thousand dollars!!"

Everyone stared at him in disbelief. It was a lot to pay for such poor land that would yield little in terms of income, but Robert had lost patience with the nickel-and-dime bidding. The cost did not matter. He would have the land, for with that day's purchases he would have the satisfaction of replacing Phineas Nightingale as the largest landowner on Cumberland Island.

He knew that one day he would also inherit at least a part of Marguerite Bernardey's Plum Orchard. Only the year before, Marguerite, with his encouragement, had had a will drawn up. With the understanding that he would use the proceeds to take care of Zabette and her children, as well as Marie-Jeanne and Jack, whom she planned to bequeath to him as well, she willed to Robert one-half of all her property plus the five-acre home place which was to be "set apart." He knew that the extra five acres included the piece of land where Marie-Jeanne and Jack now lived, though not the regular slave quarters. She wanted to be sure that all her son's children were looked after, and the extra five acres would be more than ample for their needs. He would have discretion about what would happen with the tabby house where Marguerite now lived and the grave plot where her son was buried and where she intended to be buried beside him.

Marguerite had recently brought Jack into her household by day to train him as a house servant so that there would never be any question of his being sent to the fields, should he find himself on a plantation that already had a good cobbler. This training would provide him with two skills for his future protection, and having Jack in her home during the day was almost like having her own son with her again, he looked so much like Pierre. Sometimes she would even forget and call him "Pierre."

She willed the other half of her property to her legitimate granddaughter Margaret Elizabeth, whom she loved dearly but saw rarely. The girl was being ardently courted by a boy named James Downes, whose family held a small parcel of land on the north end of Cumberland. Robert liked the Downes boy and hoped that the two young people would marry. Margaret had always been as friendly to Zabette as she dared, though she could never publicly acknowledge her as a half-sister. If Robert, who had been named executor of Marguerite's estate, had to work with someone else in settling the property division, he would just as soon it be young Downes as anyone else. He was a reasonable sort, even malleable, Robert thought, and he wouldn't give much trouble. He knew that the estate would likely be a significant one by Georgia standards. While Marguerite would never be a rich woman, she managed her lands well enough with the help of Robert and John Grey, and if all went well in the interim, she could leave an estate of up to ten thousand dollars.

Even more important to Robert, a legacy of that size would be the final fulfillment of Robert's promise to Peter Bernardey. He had never taken advantage of Peter's mother, though he might certainly have done so since she had known so little about business, but he had faithfully looked after her interests. In a sense her interests were Zabette's interests, as well. He thought it only right that, in the end, at least a portion of Marguerite's land would be his. He could perhaps use it to benefit his children—her great-grandchildren—if need be. The rest he would find a way to acquire.

As he returned to Cumberland that afternoon, after a heavy dinner of gristly beef, boiled potatoes, and fried okra at his boardinghouse, Robert felt infinitely better than he had two days earlier. He even made it back to Planters House in time for supper. Zabette and Mary Elizabeth sat on the front verandah where, to his annoyance, the child was playing with the tattered rag doll Zabette treasured above all her other possessions, even though he had bought his daughter two beautiful porcelain dolls imported from France.

"She's much too young to play with them, Robert," Zabette had said, placing them gently on the either side of the dresser of her room. "She'll break them. Let's give them to her when she's older." Mary Elizabeth had shown no interest in the dolls, which she could not cuddle as she did the rag doll. Robert grumbled that he hated to see his daughter playing with such trash, no better than the homemade toys one might find in the quarters.

"Did you have a successful day?" Zabette asked, as Robert mounted the stone steps that led up to the verandah.

"Quite successful." He picked up Mary Elizabeth and gave her a kiss on the cheek. "I bought the Oakland tract and that piece of land that joins your grandmother's property. That should allow us to expand our fields considerably come fall."

"I'm glad," said Zabette. And she *was* glad because it seemed to make him happy. When Robert was happy, everyone relaxed. But when he was unhappy, which was most of the time of late, the tensions within the household increased. The very air vibrated with his anger or discontent. Tonight, she felt, he was telling the truth. It *had* been a good day. Although she knew it did not make up for what he saw as the betrayal earlier in the week, it would do for the moment.

Zabette did not share Robert's hatred of the Nightingales. They had not embraced her relationship with Robert, but she had never expected them to. Marguerite had made it clear to her throughout her life that she would never be accepted as an equal by white people on the island. But Phineas Nightingale had always been kind to her grandmother and to her as well when she was a little girl. He'd always brought her an orange, when they were in season, and occasionally given her pieces of candy when he'd come to see Marguerite. Although she had always been scooted off to the kitchen when he arrived, he had once winked at her in a conspiratorial way as if to say, "I know you're here even if they send you away." She didn't believe he meant to be cruel that day of the picnic. And she knew that his insult was not aimed at her personally, despite the unkindness of his later words, but rather at the unsanctioned relationship between her and Robert.

His wife might have been a different matter, but Zabette did not really know Mary Nightingale, though she thought her to be a fine-looking woman. Rumors about her and her supposedly distinguished family circulated about the island. Zabette had heard that she came from a northern family of ardent abolitionists. Then how could she be married to a slave owner? Evidently her love for Mr. Nightingale outweighed her moral principles. Zabette had also heard that her father was governor of New York, but that may just have been a story that went around the plantations, aggrandizing the status of all involved. She knew stories sometimes got bigger as they passed from lip to lip. But to her it didn't matter. Zabette had no reason to hate either of the Nightingales. Their one-time snub of Robert and her as a couple hardly seemed worth carrying a grudge as Robert did.

Such grudges, she thought, were like drinking poison and waiting for the other person to die. For Zabette there were many people to forgive, herself included for her failures toward her mother and brother. She saw them so seldom, and the few visits she did manage were all too brief. There was never enough time to do all she felt she needed to do, and the bitterness of a life-long antipathy would have weighed her down. She couldn't understand how Robert could nurse such ill feelings for so long, but they had become part of who he was. Without his hatreds, she wondered if he could even identify his life's purpose.

Perhaps she had not loved him enough to help him overcome his darkness. The thirty years between their ages was never the problem. He still desired her. That was evident, she thought, gazing wistfully at her once-again pregnant belly, but she found that she desired him less when he simply reached out for her in the night and took her, without those moments of communication that had been so important in their early months together. For the first time in her life, he had made her feel that she was needed for who she was and for what she alone could give. But all that had vanished. Now he made her feel as though any female body would do. If there was darkness in her heart to match his, this was it—the gaping hole between them, like an open wound. *Would it ever heal*, she wondered? She could only wait and hope.

Chapter Twenty-Six

P LANTERS HOUSE, MARCH 26, 1846
Zabette and Robert sat on the porch in the sunset's afterglow watching their children chase fireflies in the garden. Although Robert remained taciturn and unenthusiastic about almost every aspect of life, the one thing that could still bring him sporadic pleasure was the children. Mary Elizabeth at almost seven was becoming a talkative and captivating young lady. Zabette watched her trying to instruct her brothers on how to catch the slow-moving insects. She was tall for her age and resembled her father, except for the dark color of her eyes and her raven curls that were difficult to control but softened the chiseled Stafford contours of her face.

Her little brothers, Bobby and Armand, tumbled about the yard like playful puppies. Even through their babyish features, the imprint of their Stafford lineage was already evident. Zabette worried often about Bobby's slowness. Although he was more than three years old, it was only along with Armand, his two-year-old brother, that he was learning to talk in simple but complete sentences. He was bigger, though far less agile, than his little brother. But his father adored him, carrying him whenever he fell behind the others and showing him special favoritism.

For Zabette, there was no such thing as a favorite child, though she had fretted most over the birth of Armand. She had gotten pregnant again almost immediately after her miscarriage, and she worried that her body had not had adequate time to recover. But the delivery, two weeks early, had gone well, and Armand was a happy, bright child. Their mother adored them all and wrapped her entire life around them, to the extent household duties would allow.

Sometimes those duties seemed overwhelming, but even with all her responsibilities, spring was a time when Zabette felt her spirits lift, a time of new life when there was the garden to plant and the house to make ready for the coming season. Soil had to be prepared, seedlings set out, mattresses turned, carpets beat and aired, and furniture moved to clean the winter's dust from behind and underneath in preparation for the warmer months. Even though there was no social season to prepare for at Planters House since there were few guests, Zabette always insisted on a good spring cleaning. Sometimes John Grey or one of the planters from High Point would drop by, but the only female visitor was Marguerite, who came to see her granddaughter and great-grandchildren or to talk business with Robert, which she did less frequently of late.

Zabette was concerned about her grandmother's health, for Marguerite now left her chair infrequently. But in spring Zabette had less time to visit her, with so much to be done on the plantation. Her most onerous task was supervising the making of clothing for Robert's more than three hundred slaves.

"I won't have my slaves in rags," he told Zabette. "It would reflect on me. I want those Nightingales to see my slaves better dressed than theirs."

She tried to persuade him to buy some of the garments ready-made in northern factories, but he refused. "I want them made right here on the plantation. Not like those shoddy things Phineas buys for his slaves."

She sighed, knowing it would make unnecessary extra work for many people. She would need to spend a lot of time away from the children, checking seams, helping cut cloth, and encouraging workers. The one consolation was the company of the garment workers in the cotton house, where six women worked, spinning, weaving, and sewing. In winter, she enjoyed sitting among them by the fire and listening to their gossip and songs to the rhythm of the looms. In spring the cotton house was cramped and stuffy as the wool jackets and pants and osnaburg shirts took shape. But the women did not complain. At least they could work sitting down, and almost anything was preferable to chopping cotton.

On Sunday mornings, Robert would conduct an inspection of the quarters, making sure that everything was tidy and that "his people" were dressed in clean, well-mended clothes before they went off to worship at the little church just beyond the bridge, the one he had built for them with Zabette's encouragement almost ten years ago now.

Zabette took pride in the church. Although Robert would not permit her to attend services there, she made sure that the clapboard structure got a coat of whitewash each spring. She would sit on the verandah and watch with envy as the men, women, and children passed by on the Main Road on their way to church, where they would spend most of the day.

On Sunday evenings she sometimes took Mary Elizabeth by the hand and walked with her to a nearby grove to listen to the singing, which pierced her heart with longing. She and Robert did not go to any Sunday service, and this was her closest contact with the God Marguerite had taught her about when she was a little girl. The slaves' God seemed less distant, more human, than the Catholic God Marguerite talked about. Her grandmother never spoke of God's "tender loving care" or how he might "gather his chillun in his arms," as Reverend Lockett did on Sunday nights, when Zabette and Mary Elizabeth listened in the darkness outside. She wished Robert would come with them. Perhaps the singing might touch his heart too. But she knew it was useless to ask.

SPRING ALWAYS BROUGHT A SPATE OF INJURIES and sickness, so Zabette spent more time than usual in the infirmary, though Robert had lost interest in it. She made willowbark tea for fever victims and kept rags dipped in cool water on their foreheads. And when young Cato was bitten by a rattlesnake, his brother Sampson had tied a rag around his leg above the wound and raced to Planters House to get "Miss Zabette." She rushed to the boy still lying in the field, quickly cut a cross over the fang marks, and sucked out at least some of the poison. His leg swelled painfully, but he lived.

A few days later Big Tom stumbled in the ditch that separated two fields and broke his leg. The workers fashioned a crude litter and dragged him back to the infirmary. Zabette put the leg in a temporary splint of sorts and had Dr. Mitchell summoned from St. Marys. She didn't trust herself to set the leg on her own.

Fortunately, she felt better prepared to handle the most recent emergency.

A young seamstress named Patty had gone into labor while Maum Bella was at High Point for the birth of one of the Bunkley babies. With help from Amanda, Zabette had delivered the child herself. She'd seen Maum Bella deliver so many babies over the years that she felt that she could handle any normal birth herself. Fortunately, Patty already had given birth to three children and it was an easy delivery. Zabette and Amanda laughed gleefully at their accomplishment, and Patty shyly asked if Zabette minded if she named the baby girl for her. Zabette didn't mind at all. She was honored.

"If we get too many 'Zabettes' runnin' round this island," Amanda joked on the way back to the Big House, "we ain't gone be able to tell one of 'em from another."

"I guess we could have worse problems, Amanda," Zabette laughed. As she would learn all too soon, she was absolutely right.

THE FOLLOWING SATURDAY ROBERT RODE TO THE SOUTH-END WHARF, accompanied by his man Peter, to meet the mail boat, as he did every week. They thought they were arriving early, but the boat was already pulling up to the dock as they dismounted.

To Robert's amazement a familiar figure stepped down the gangplank—his old friend and lawyer, Belton Copp.

"Belton, what a wonderful surprise!" Robert said warmly. "It's been way too long."

"What do you mean—surprise? I wrote you weeks ago."

Both men laughed when the boat captain handed Robert a small pile of letters, the one on top postmarked March 2 from Belton Copp, who said, "My God, you'd think it had come from Europe."

Robert and Belton had seen one another rarely since 1833, when Belton had married a Connecticut woman named Betsey Barber and moved his law practice, or most of it at least, to his hometown of Groton, Connecticut. He had accepted a post as director at the newly established Whaling Bank in New London, just across the river from Groton. But he still had a few clients in St. Marys and a fair amount of unfinished legal business that occasionally brought him back to Camden County. This time he had planned to include a visit to Cumberland and his old friend Robert Stafford, who had repeatedly urged him to come.

"I hope you intend to spend a long time with us at Planters House," Robert said, "if you can stand the bedlam of three children."

"I love children," Copp replied, "and I have a houseful of my own."

"Really? But you haven't met my two rowdy boys," he said, slapping Belton on the back. "Mary Elizabeth is an angel compared to them."

"I'm sure I'll enjoy them all." Copp smiled warmly. He had been eager to see his boyhood friend again and to look in on his erstwhile client Marguerite Bernardey.

The two men had known one another since Robert was twelve, attending the New London Grammar School, just across the river from the Copps' home in Groton. Belton's family had taken Robert in as a boarder and embraced him like another son, which had helped to mitigate the harsh discipline of the school's headmaster, who believed that only the cruelest punishments turned boys into men. Belton's friendship softened the schoolmaster's blows and the taunting of Robert's schoolmates, who spoke differently from him and who had been reared to scorn slave owners. Even though Belton was six years younger than Robert, he had sympathized with the older boy's misery in an unfamiliar world, and the two had become unlikely, lifelong friends.

Those years had toughened Robert considerably, and when, at sixteen, it was time for him to return home again, he did so with mixed feelings. Cumberland was his birthplace, and it was in his blood, but he had learned a lot about survival in Connecticut. Belton's father, Daniel Copp, took a special interest in the boy after his own father and brothers had died of yellow fever. And when it was time for Robert to go back to Cumberland, Mr. Copp had accompanied him, using the trip as an opportunity to learn about the area, which he thought held great promise. As a result, he decided to invest in his own plantation on Point Peter in the St. Marys area and move his family there to try the planter's life for a time.

The Copps eventually moved back to Connecticut, all except Belton, who stayed on, serving for a few years as postmaster in St. Marys, until he decided to become a lawyer. He'd found a distinguished lawyer in Savannah named John McPherson Berrien, a state senator and a northerner like himself, who took him in to read law. Once he'd completed his training, Belton had run for public office and been elected Camden County's representative to the state legislature in 1824.

Thus, over time what had begun as a boyhood friendship had ample opportunity to ripen into deep mutual respect between the two men. Belton planted deep roots in coastal Georgia, but he was still a New Englander at heart. Robert had not been surprised by his decision to settle in Connecticut after his marriage, but he missed him a great deal. Friends were one thing of which Robert Stafford had no surplus.

Robert ordered his manservant to give his horse to Belton, leaving Peter to walk the three miles back to Planters House, carrying Copp's valise and briefcase. The two white men rode the lands together, talking endlessly about plantation matters, politics, and the recovering economy, and reminiscing about their childhood, and their adversities, which had softened into fond though bittersweet memories. They arrived at Planters House, rested and animated. An exhausted Peter reached the house half an hour later to deliver Mr. Copp's baggage.

AMANDA PREPARED FOR THE UNEXPECTED GUEST a sumptuous supper of cucumber salad, her best okra and shrimp gumbo, and yeast rolls, ending it all with bread pudding and whiskey sauce. Robert instructed Zabette to feed the children early and send them to bed. She was to take her own meal in the kitchen with Amanda. She wondered at Robert's not wanting her at his table—whether he wanted to talk with Mr. Copp in complete privacy or whether it was because he thought his friend would not approve of her presence. Certainly Belton knew of her existence and of her relationship with Robert as a consequence of his legal work for both Robert and her grandmother.

Although she always enjoyed the time she was able to spend alone with Amanda and she would have offered to let the two men dine alone, she was hurt by Robert's request. It reminded her of the old days when her grandmother used to send her to the kitchen when white folks came to dinner.

"Reckon them menfolks has plenty to talk about," Amanda said, trying to console the feelings Zabette thought she was hiding so well. But Amanda had a keen sensitivity. She understood the other woman's unspoken pain, having experienced enough of it in her own life.

"I reckon so," answered Zabette. "They haven't seen each other for more than three years."

"I sho' feel sorry for Mr. Copp havin' to go back up north when he leave this here island."

"Lots of people like it up there, Amanda."

"I reckon so, but it be way too cold for me. Least tha's what I hear."

"Me too. I think I prefer Cumberland Island to anyplace on earth."

"Why, chile, you ain't never been nowhere. How you gone know?"

"I just can't imagine anyplace better, can you?"

"My mammy used to tell me 'bout her home in Africa. It sounded mighty nice. And she weren't no slave back there. Her pap was a prince, she tell me."

"My mama came from Saint-Domingue in the Caribbean Ocean, but she was still a baby when she came to Georgia. I think her papa was a planter, but she never knew him. Her mama was a slave like she was." The old question rose up in her mind. What was she? "Sometimes I wonder about my own situation. I'm not slave or free."

Amanda laughed. "Honey, you don' know what it's like to be no slave. You live like white folks."

"Not really, Amanda," Zabette replied. "You of all people should know that. Am I any freer than you to go where I want and do what I want? In a way, I'm less free." She sat silent for a moment. Then she added thoughtfully, "They don't even want me over in the quarters." She had never talked like this with anyone before, not even Daisy. And though she had wanted to share these feelings with Robert, he no longer seemed interested.

"What you talkin' 'bout, gal? They loves you over there."

"Not like they love you, Amanda. You're one of them. They like what I can do for them. They like my nursing. But they don't feel at ease around me. It's not the same thing."

"They respects you. Tha's even better than love."

"No it's not. They have to respect their master too, but I don't want to be respected like that. Not because they think they have to or because they're dependent on me in some way." The words were tumbling out with feelings she had bottled up for so long.

"Even my own mother and brother don't act completely natural around me. I know they love me, but *Maman* doesn't ever just fix collard greens and black-eyed peas and possum pie. When I go see Mama and Jack, they make it a big occasion. They put on their best clothes, and Mama fries a chicken and gives me the best dishes in the cabin. I'd just like to be able to visit, to sit in front of her door and help shell butter beans while we talk. But it's just not like that." Zabette fought back the tears welling up in her eyes.

"Well," said Amanda, "tha's the way it is wit' you and me in my kitchen, ain't it, chile?"

"Oh, Amanda, of course it is. What would I do without you?" She hugged the older woman's ample body, and Amanda hugged her back. They ate their meal in thoughtful silence, watching the sun set over the marshes through the large western window of the kitchen.

THE TWO MEN TALKED FOR MANY HOURS AFTER SUPPER, drinking brandy, obviously enjoying one another's company immensely and discussing what they considered serious and complicated matters. Zabette was almost asleep by the time Robert came to bed. As was his frequent habit, he reached out for her and put his hands on her breasts, indifferent to the fact that she had been on the verge of sleep. She smelled the brandy on his breath and wanted to turn away, but as usual she acquiesced to his demands, chiding herself for the resentment that welled up within her. She had made him a promise their first night together, and it was a promise she intended to keep, however difficult it might be. But Robert was only four years away from being sixty, while Zabette was only twenty-six. All he wanted was physical relief, while her body still longed to be caressed, desired, and needed, not just used. She'd tried to make him understand, but she'd finally given up, for her efforts were useless. It was over more quickly if she just let him have his way. But afterwards, she wept in the silent dark for the young woman she could feel dying inside her.

Chapter Twenty-Seven

P LANTERS HOUSE, MARCH 31, 1846
Three mornings later, after two more nights of earnest conversations and many glasses of brandy, Belton Copp arose before dawn to take his breakfast, as Amanda grumpily reported when she brought a platter of fluffy scrambled eggs and crisp bacon to the table for Zabette, Robert, and the children. She was the one who had to get up and fix him something to eat before he left.

"He done knocked on my cabin door 'fore the sun come up. I thought at first it was one o' them *fulafafas* wakin' me up," she complained, using the Geechee word for the woodpeckers that sometimes started hammering before dawn.

"Thank you for taking care of him, Amanda. It was good of you." Zabette said. Robert nodded, his mind obviously on other things.

Zabette filled the children's plates. Armand was growing too big for his highchair, but he was still messy, and half the food ended up on the floor or in his lap. "Just watch your sister," she said to both boys. "She's a tidy eater, not like you rascals."

Robert studied all three children, but his eyes rested more thoughtfully on Mary Elizabeth. After Bobby turned over his usual glass of milk and the children had finished eating, Robert watched Zabette wipe the boys' faces and hands. Then he said suddenly to his daughter, "Mary Elizabeth, why don't you take your little brothers outside to play in the yard. It's a fine day." The children knew that the tabby wall around the outside garden was the limit of their play area when no adults were there to watch over them. She and Bobby scrambled to their feet and she lifted Armand from his highchair, eager to be free of the constraints of grownups and the supervision of mealtime.

Once they were outside, Robert watched them attentively for a moment through the window. Then he turned to Zabette and began hesitantly.

"Zabette . . . , when Belton returns to Connecticut next week, I'm going to send Mary Elizabeth with him."

"What?" Zabette felt the blood drain from her face. She couldn't have heard him correctly.

"I'm going to send Mary Elizabeth north with Belton Copp. She can get an education in Connecticut. Belton has agreed to let her live with him and his wife. They both like children and have several of their own. They'll see that she goes to school."

"Oh, Robert, you can't. What will we do here without her?"

"It's for her own good. If she stays here, anything can happen to her. She's an undeclared mulatto, not slave, not free, but under Georgia law, as your daughter she's technically a slave. It's just too risky to let her stay here."

"What do you mean? She's not a slave any more than I am. Who's going to treat her like a slave? Who would report her to any authorities?"

Robert looked at her oddly, as though she had said something strange, as though he were biting back words he wanted to say. Then he replied, "Phineas Nightingale, for one. He'd do anything to get back at me."

"Robert, Mr. Nightingale is just not like that. He wouldn't do anything to hurt Mary Elizabeth. I know you don't like him, but he's not a cruel man."

Robert snorted. "You're a fool, Zabette, and you don't know anything about the Nightingales. They're about the meanest people on earth."

She was stung by his words. He had never called her a fool before, though she often heard him use the term toward others. She believed he was wrong about Phineas Nightingale, that he saw the other man's every move through the distorted lens of the hatred he had conceived as a young man so many years ago. Unlike Robert, she had felt sympathy for the Nightingales when they lost their land and were forced to move to the mainland. She believed that Mr. Nightingale loved Cumberland as much as she did. It had been his home since he was born, and she knew how painful leaving it would be to her. It must be the same for him. He too had feelings. She was sure of it.

"Robert, please don't do this," Zabette pleaded, blinking to keep back tears. She knew the anguish of losing one's mother at such a young age, of being torn from the life she'd always known. At least when her own mother had been banished from her life, she still had her father and grandmother, but Mary Elizabeth's entire world would vanish. She would live with strangers in a cold, unwelcoming climate. Robert himself had described its frigid winters and unfriendliness to outsiders. How could he do this to her? How could she live in such a place without her family?

"I've already made arrangements with Belton. He'll take her with him on one of his father's ships, where no one will ask any questions. He's doing me a big favor, Zabette, because you know what he risks if he's found to be transporting what some might consider a fugitive slave. He's doing it for my sake and for Mary Elizabeth's."

"Please, Robert, don't send her away." Tears were streaming down her face now, and through the double distortion of tears and the windowpane she could see Mary Elizabeth laughing as she chased her brothers in the garden. "Can't we at least talk about it?"

"There's nothing to discuss. It's already decided. They'll leave next week. Have her things packed and ready next Friday morning. You of all people should know that she can't have any kind of life here. I have no choice but to send her north."

Zabette rose from the table. She could see that nothing she said would move him from his purpose. He had not even consulted her about her own daughter. It was all happening again, just as her mother had been sold away from Darien, just as Zabette herself had been ripped away from her own mother. She had thought it could never happen to her.

ROBERT HAD KNOWN FOR A LONG TIME this time would come, that one day he would have to send his children away for their own good. Belton's arrival on Cumberland and his willingness to take Mary Elizabeth into his own home was like a gift from that God everybody talked about but in whom Robert didn't believe. He knew that sending her away would be the hardest thing he had ever done, but he also believed it was right, however painful. His children would never be slaves. Never—whatever it cost him. Not if he could help it.

ZABETTE WEPT FOR THE ENTIRE WEEK, if not with her eyes, then with her heart. She drank in the sight of Mary Elizabeth chasing butterflies in the garden or chiding her younger brothers about their table manners. She would slip into her room in the morning before the child awakened to watch her sleep. She memorized the sweet innocence of her face and the leap of joy in her eyes when she opened them to see her mother sitting beside her bed. Zabette held onto the precious scent of the child's warm body and the feel of the tight hug the little girl gave her when she sat up and said sleepily, "Morning, *Maman*." Mary Elizabeth did not yet know she was being sent away.

"When do you plan to tell her, Robert?" Zabette asked, her voice trembling, as they were preparing for bed on Tuesday night, only three days before her departure.

"Soon," was all he replied.

The next morning he took Mary Elizabeth into his study after breakfast. Zabette waited in the parlor, mending a wool sock salvaged from last year's clothing issue. She tried to focus on the acorn-colored sock, but it was impossible. From the first moment she heard her daughter's sharp cry, "No, Papa! No!" she could work no more. Her heart ached for her daughter.

She sat, expecting the door to open and Mary Elizabeth to fly into her arms. But the door did not open for a long time. When it did, Robert emerged, holding tightly to his daughter's hand. She was walking with the same upright stiffness as her father. Zabette could tell that she had been crying, but her tears were dried. She did not fly to Zabette's arms. She did not even look at her mother. Instead, without a word, she went upstairs to her room and closed the door.

FOR THE NEXT TWO DAYS, Mary Elizabeth said very little, as though she were detaching herself from her family. Robert noticed and felt a sense of pride in his daughter's stoic reaction. He had dreaded telling her she was to be sent away as much as he had dreaded telling her mother, but he had known he could put it off no longer.

When Zabette asked him what he had said to the child, he answered with as few words as possible. "I simply explained to her why she must go and the kind of life she could have there. She's a very reasonable girl. She's like me, you know."

He did not tell her that the child's cry of "No!" had pierced his heart and that he had wanted to take her in his arms and tell her she could stay with him forever on Cumberland Island. But he knew that he could not show such weakness and that he must teach her to be strong. It was best in the long run. He had explained to her that her mother was a slave and that, if she remained here, she too would be considered a slave.

The little girl had never heard such talk before, and she had not known that she was the daughter of a slave woman. He knew his words had frightened her and made her feel that her mother was different in ways she had never perceived. He had assured her that the Copps would treat her like their own daughter, that she would go to school in Connecticut and learn many things that would give her choices in life that her own mother never had. He helped her understand that the price she would have to pay in accepting his decision was her mother's warmth and love. But he could never explain all that to Zabette, for he knew that she would consider it the ultimate betrayal. *And perhaps*, he thought, *it was.*

THE DAYS UNTIL HER DAUGHTER'S DEPARTURE passed tensely. Zabette took the children to Plum Orchard so that Mary Elizabeth could say goodbye to her great-grandmother, who, she feared, might never see the child again. It was a raw parting, with Marguerite breaking down weeping and clinging to the child as Zabette had never seen her do before, and she worried for her grandmother's health and stability. Even Mary Elizabeth was in tears before they left, though she had let nothing else touch her emotions since her talk with her father the day before.

Robert saw to it as well that Mary Elizabeth spent some time during those final days with Belton Copp so that she could get to know him somewhat before he took her away. The evening before she was to leave, Belton took her for a stroll along the Main Road after supper in the general direction of Plum Orchard. Zabette watched them from the upstairs window as far as she could see. She knew that Belton was kind and gentle with the girl, for he was that sort of man. What they had talked about she would learn only later, when he described the stroll to Robert in the parlor, as she sat nearby embroidering a new smock for Mary Elizabeth to take with her. He had asked her about the things she liked to do and about her friends. She had none, he learned, except for her brothers. He told her how many young girls like herself she would meet in Connecticut, and he assured her that her father would come and visit from time to time.

Little by little, Mary Elizabeth grew accustomed to the idea of leaving Cumberland, and although she was apprehensive, she began to show a tinge of excitement about what her father had taken to calling her "adventure."

While they were out walking, Zabette finished her daughter's packing. Amid the few dresses, pinafores, and stockings, she lovingly tucked the much-mended rag doll made of multicolored cloth, which had been her own when she was a child, the one her mother had made. It would be Mary Elizabeth's one connection with her mother, she thought, her one comfort as she lay in strange beds, as it had been for Zabette when she was a frightened and lonely child. She remembered how she had clung to the soft doll, which smelled of her mother and the cabin they had shared together. It could comfort Mary Elizabeth as it had comforted her.

The porcelain dolls that Robert had bought for his daughter had been carefully packed in tissue paper and placed in boxes to be sent along with her luggage. There wasn't much else to pack. The child had relatively few belongings, for her life on the island was simple and they rarely had reason to dress up. Robert had given Belton Copp sixty dollars to buy her stylish clothes suitable for the northern climate. He was determined that his daughter should be well dressed for her new life.

ON THE DAY OF MARY ELIZABETH'S DEPARTURE, to Robert's obvious annoyance, Zabette insisted on taking the two little boys and walking with her daughter to the landing. From there, Mary Elizabeth and Belton would be rowed by Stafford boatmen into St. Marys to meet the ship that would take them to Savannah, where they would board the steamer to New London, Connecticut.

"You may go to the dock, Zabette," Robert said finally, "but you may not cry. Mary Elizabeth will have a dignified send-off." Zabette nodded, though she was not at all sure that she could trust herself to hold back her tears. She was willing to take the risk, for she was determined that Mary Elizabeth's last view of Cumberland Island would include her entire family.

Bobby and Armand scuffled along beside her, kicking at the oyster shells along the path. She held their hands tightly as she had wanted to hold Mary Elizabeth's, but the girl had pulled away to walk alone, carrying herself with that rigid bearing so like her father's. Water lapped along the shores of the river, the ripples ragged from the stiff wind. Fortunately it was blowing from east to west and would hasten their trip into St. Marys. But Zabette pitied the poor oarsmen having to row back against that breeze. At least they wouldn't have the weight of two passengers and their baggage in the sleek little boat, hewn like so many coastal vessels from a hollowed-out cypress log. It was one of the boats that Stafford raced occasionally in St. Marys, and it could cut the water like a knife.

Mary Elizabeth, sitting in the middle of the vessel, with a blue sunbonnet covering her unruly dark curls, looked small amid the men in their somber colors. Even Belton wore a brown coat and hat to block the sun. Zabette and the boys hugged the child before she entered the boat and stood on the shore waving and calling "*Au revoir*, Goodbye, Mary Elizabeth" until the small vessel made the first turn in the tidal creek and was completely hidden behind the tall spartina grass. Mindful of Robert's warnings, Zabette did not cry until the boat was out of sight. But as she and her two sons walked back toward Planters House, she could no longer hide her tears.

"What's the matter, *Maman*?" asked Armand.

She covered her mouth with her hand to stifle her sobs and made an effort to reply. "I'm just sad to see Mary Elizabeth go away."

"Don't be sad, *Maman*. It's a 'venture, Papa said." Armand tried to console her.

"It's a 'venture," echoed Bobby.

"Yes, my darlings," she said, kneeling to scoop them both into her arms, "I know. It's an adventure! I love you both so very much. You'll have to keep *Maman* company now. And never leave her. Promise?"

"We promise," they chorused together, squirming to get out of her arms. She put them down, and they ran as fast as their chubby legs could run toward the tabby wall that encircled their domain.

BACK IN THE HOUSE, Zabette, indulging her mother's heart, climbed the stairs to Mary Elizabeth's room. As she entered, she closed her eyes, smelling the sweetness of the child one more time, imagining her still there. When she opened her eyes again, they fell on the multicolored object lying beside the bed. There, crumpled on the floor was the rag doll she had so lovingly packed the night before. She picked it up, unbidden tears springing to her eyes, and pressed its mended, well-worn softness to her cheek. Now it smelled of her daughter who had last held it. Its fragrance bespoke her child's presence, her absence, her loss. This night, Zabette knew, like that night so many years ago, the little doll would absorb her grief and be her only comfort.

Chapter Twenty-Eight

PLANTERS HOUSE, CUMBERLAND ISLAND, NOVEMBER 11, 1848
"It's gone be another li'l girl," Amanda said, with certainty in her voice. "I can tell 'cause you's carryin' that baby real high." She nodded to give emphasis to her words.

"Oh, I hope so, Amanda." Zabette, pregnant again, still missed the sweet feminine presence of Mary Elizabeth, even though she had been gone for more than two years. Although Belton Copp wrote regularly to keep Robert informed of the girl's progress, it was hardly a substitute for the child herself. If his reports were accurate, she had adjusted easily to life in Connecticut, quickly made friends, and was doing well in school.

As her education progressed, Mary Elizabeth began to write herself. At first her letters were simple and rather crude. The first one read:

Dear Papa,

I am well. I hope you are well. I like Grotn. Skool is fun.

Your dawter, Mary

Belton Copp had explained in one of his early letters that she had taken to calling herself "Mary" rather than "Mary Elizabeth," which sounded better in Connecticut. He knew that the South had a penchant for double names, but in New England the shorter and the more clipped, the better. To the child, "Mary Stafford" seemed more dignified than "Mary Elizabeth Stafford," and it was more like the names her friends had.

Zabette wondered if she were being oversensitive in noticing that the part of the name she had chosen to eliminate was her mother's name and that her letters were always addressed only to "Dear Papa." She didn't understand the child's sudden distance toward her, but she had no choice but to accept it. Even though she wrote frequent letters to her daughter, Mary Elizabeth never answered, except indirectly through her correspondence with her father. Zabette felt almost as though she had lost a part of herself. She waited with anticipation for each one of the child's letters, which Robert always let her read only after he had examined the contents. She tried to love Bobby and Armand even more, if that were possible, and not to think about her daughter so much, but in spite of her efforts, not a single day passed that she did not recall some special moment with Mary Elizabeth—the times they walked together on the wide Cumberland beach, looking for new shells to add to their collection, their Sunday evenings listening to the singing outside the church, her ladylike correction of her little brothers at the breakfast table. Every memory was precious now.

But Zabette didn't spend all her time looking backward. She was also looking forward to the new baby that was due in February, fortunately one of the few months when she had a bit of leisure. The spring issue of garments for the plantation workers would be finished and almost ready for distribution, and it would be too early to begin planting the spring garden. The baby would be a welcome distraction at the perfect time. Zabette hoped that Amanda was right, that it would be a girl, but she knew that she would love it no matter what. She had once thought that having a daughter would guarantee that she would have one child who would not distance herself as she grew up. She expected that from the boys, who at four and five were already becoming little men.

Their father had begun to take them on some of his morning inspections of the plantation, with Bobby riding in front of him, while Armand rode with Peter, who always went along on these outings with the children. The boys loved it, at least for the first hour. When they grew tired and began to complain, Robert, compelled to cut short his rides and bring them home, was annoyed that they didn't have the same stamina as he. Little by little, they were learning not to make their discomforts known to their father.

Zabette was not surprised that the boys sought to please Robert. But a daughter, she had always believed, would grow closer to her mother in time. A daughter would be someone who would confide in her, who could sew beside her on winter evenings, and who would come to her for advice as she grew older. She realized it had not been like that with her own mother, but that, of course, was a different set of circumstances altogether. Yet even now she knew that Marie-Jeanne longed to have her come for visits, but Robert permitted these visits even less often than her grandmother had. Perhaps children were just God's instruments to break your heart and teach you patience.

The boys were still affectionate toward their mother, but she knew that, as they grew older, their sweet hugs, their joint efforts to find sharks' teeth, and their blackberry-picking days would likely come to an end. They would grow more manly, more like their father. She saw it already happening as a consequence of their rides together.

PLANTERS HOUSE, FEBRUARY 14, 1849

As time drew near for her baby's birth, Zabette invited Marguerite once more for an extended visit to Planters House. The old woman, who had to be helped up and down the stairs, complained that she was more trouble than help to Zabette. Her mind was not as sharp as it had once been. But she seemed happy to be included in events at the Stafford household. She spent less time now talking with Robert and more enjoying the company of Zabette and the children. She liked above all sitting with her granddaughter, as they had done in the old days, in the shade of the big magnolia tree and live oaks, embroidering or just watching the squirrels and grackles quarrel in the garden.

Bobby and Armand paid little attention to the two women. They played together in their own magical kingdom, where a green spike of a Spanish bayonet could serve as a wicked sword and a whelk shell became a bugle calling troops to battle. Sometimes they found arrowheads and old pieces of Indian pottery. The boys were now allowed to go outside the tabby wall to play, though if they wanted to fish in the river or the ocean shallows, Zabette always required Peter or one of the older slave children to go with them. She'd warned them to stay away from the wild animals, particularly the wild hogs if there were any piglets about, for they were dangerous and could attack without warning. She knew that she was probably overprotective, but anything could happen on the island, as her duties in the infirmary made clear.

Marguerite and Zabette were enjoying a quiet afternoon, darning the boys' socks, which were always full of holes, when suddenly Marguerite looked up and said, "Do you know where Pierre is? I need to send him on an errand."

Zabette looked up sharply at her grandmother. "Are you all right, *Grand'mère?*" she asked with concern, wondering what she should say. The truth always seemed best to her. "Do you mean your son, Pierre? My father? Don't you remember that he's gone to be with the Lord?"

Marguerite looked at her for a moment in disbelief and acute grief. Then the look faded, and she said, "Oh, I'm sorry. What am I thinking? For a minute I thought you were Catherine."

"No, *Grand'mère.* Remember? Catherine is married to William Laen now."

"Yes, of course. And their daughter is Margaret Elizabeth."

"She's Catherine's daughter, your granddaughter. The one she had with my father."

Marguerite looked confused for a moment, and then she smiled and said. "My granddaughter. That's right. I know that. Why are you telling me these things, Zabette?"

The two women sat in silence for a long time. Marguerite seemed fine for the rest of the day, but Zabette was shaken by the incident.

ZABETTE'S LABOR BEGAN AT DAWN two days later. Amanda ran for Maum Bella before she even started to cook breakfast for Robert and the children. Marguerite sat by her granddaughter's bed holding her hand during contractions, as she had held Marie-Jeanne's hand the day Zabette was born. But Zabette dared not squeeze her grandmother's hand because of Marguerite's arthritis.

Fortunately her labor was an easy one. The new baby, Ellen Stafford, was born before ten o'clock. When Robert came in to see his new daughter, he had Bobby and Armand in tow.

"They wanted to see their baby sister," he said to Zabette.

"Isn't she beautiful?" said Zabette, smiling at her sons. She had curly hair, a lighter shade than Mary Elizabeth's, dark eyes, and pale skin—the skin of a white child.

The boys grinned shyly. Armand reached out to touch the baby's cheek. "She sure is little," he said.

"But she'll grow. In fact, before we know it she'll be as big as you," teased Zabette.

"But I'll be even bigger then," he said uncertainly, seeking reassurance.

"Of course," said Robert. "You'll always be bigger and stronger than your sisters. They're girls."

"But we're boys, right Papa?" Bobby chimed in. "That's why we'll be bigger and stronger and better than girls."

"Well, we'll see about that," said Zabette teasingly. But she knew that was what Robert was teaching his sons. Like most men on the island, in coastal Georgia, and probably everywhere else in the world, he was impressing upon his sons that men were always better than women. She looked down at baby Ellen and thought, *Someday, my child, the world will learn what women are capable of.* "But you must always respect and protect women," was all she said aloud to both her sons. Marguerite nodded in agreement.

"*Oui, Maman*," Armand said, with Bobby echoing him. "Yes, *Maman*."

FREDERICK, PROMPT AS ALWAYS, ARRIVED THREE DAYS LATER with the Bernardey carriage to take Marguerite back to Plum Orchard. The new mother was already getting up a bit, though she had not yet gone downstairs. Zabette was worried to see her grandmother leave.

"Are you sure you don't want to stay here?" Zabette asked.

"Oh, goodness, no. I have too much to do at Plum Orchard," Marguerite answered.

Zabette was concerned nonetheless. She had told Robert about the incident on the veranda. "We'll just have to watch the situation," he said.

They saw no further lapses of memory during their next few trips to Plum Orchard or Marguerite's visits to Planters House, and Zabette relaxed a bit, thinking that perhaps the confusion of the afternoon was a one-time occurrence. She knew from encounters with elderly slaves that it was not uncommon for their minds to drift back to their younger days. She supposed it was part of the normal aging process—which she could understand—the desire to relive one's better and happier days. But she asked Robert to mention it at the earliest opportunity to Jamie Downes, who had finally persuaded Margaret Bernardey to marry him in July 1844. Now, four years later, the couple already had two children.

Since the marriage, Jamie and Robert had formed a friendly relationship. Robert had always liked the young man, but he saw a particular benefit in their friendship. Since Jamie's wife would one day inherit the other half of Mrs. Bernardey's land, they would have interests in common. It also couldn't hurt to be on hand should Margaret decide to sell, as her mother had done in 1842.

Margaret had grown into a pretty young woman with a cheerful disposition. With her light russet hair and her wide-spaced blue eyes, she bore such an uncanny resemblance to her husband that one might have taken them for brother and sister. Marguerite, no longer mindful or perhaps forgetful of Georgia social conventions, sometimes invited the two couples and their children to dinner. They never knew until they arrived who else might be there. Although Margaret had known Zabette distantly all her life, they had never been close. Zabette was six years older, and Margaret's mother, Catherine, had discouraged any kind of relationship between the two girls. After Pierre's death, Margaret and her mother had not stayed often at Plum Orchard, and once Catherine had married Captain Laen, Margaret almost never laid eyes on her half-sister.

At first Margaret and Jamie felt rather uncomfortable with Zabette. But little by little during their rare suppers at Marguerite's plantation, the two young women began to form a bond. Margaret and Jamie soon realized that Zabette was not really so different from them, even though her skin might be a slight shade darker. Margaret, who was pregnant again, began to ask Zabette's advice about tonics for the children or what to do for toothaches and rashes. Zabette, always generous with information, took Margaret for walks along the wagon road to show her where to find the prickly "toothache tree," the leaves of which would quickly deaden a sore gum and could be useful in small quantities during a baby's teething. Zabette taught her how to crush myrtle leaves to keep away mosquitoes and how to tell the difference between poison ivy and Virginia creeper, both of which grew in abundance on the island.

On one of these walks, Zabette confided her concerns about their grandmother, who was determined to live on at Plum Orchard instead of moving in with one of her granddaughters. It was good to have another woman—*a sister*—though they never spoke of their relationship, with whom to share these family matters.

Both couples enjoyed their visits to Plum Orchard. On such occasions Robert seemed to be in a rare good mood and regaled the younger people with stories about Cumberland, tales of the British invasion of the island in 1815, before any of them were born, and the Revolutionary General Lighthorse Harry Lee's stopping off at Dungeness to die. Jamie was particularly interested in the island's history and had gathered a collection of Indian pottery, as well as relics from the colonial period, buttons, clay pipes, and a few hand-blown bottles he'd found lying in the fields after plowing.

These afternoons were some of the best times Zabette would later remember. The children played along the riverbank after supper as the four of them watched from the wide porch, listening to Marguerite, who rocked Ellen and sang French folk songs. Reluctantly, before dark, they would gather up the little ones, kiss Marguerite goodbye, and have their buggies brought around for the ride home. Jamie and Margaret lived on the north end of the island, while Robert and Zabette headed south. As they crossed the little bridge over White Branch, they sometimes paused to watch the sunset. Zabette wondered if Mary Elizabeth ever saw such magnificent sunsets in Connecticut, where even in March and April, it could still snow.

THE WEATHER WAS STIFLING HOT and the air was still—one of those August days in coastal Georgia when all anyone wanted to do was sit in the shade and drink cold lemonade. Zabette helped Amanda squeeze the lemons as a special treat for the children. Amanda, over forty now, was pregnant again, and Zabette worried that she and Robert might be overworking her.

"Shucks, honey, I'se fine," Amanda assured her, clearly enjoying the attention. They were practically living outside these days, even though late summer insects could be a nuisance. Ocean breezes helped most of the time, but today the heat settled on them like a blanket. All Zabette wanted to do was sit on the porch and fan herself, but she knew that Amanda in her kitchen suffered far more than she did.

Robert had been sternly locked in his solitude of late, and Zabette never knew why. She was apprehensive. His dark moods always brought tension to the household, though she dared not ask the reasons behind them. He did not like such intrusions into his personal world, and she was not sure she really wanted to know the reason. These moods were often a foreboding of something ill to come. Instead, she tried to keep the children away from their father as much as possible at such times, fearful that he might visit on them the desolation he nurtured in his heart.

She would discover the reason all too soon. After supper, when the children had been tucked into bed, Robert poured himself a brandy. He'd been unusually restless the entire evening. He was carefully measuring out his jigger as Zabette entered the room, where darkness gathered.

"Shall I light the lamp?" she asked.

"No," he said. "Not yet." He turned to face her, taking a large swig from his glass. His face looked like a thundercloud.

"Sit down, Zabette," he said ominously. "I have something to tell you. Something I know you're not going to like."

Chapter Twenty-Nine

PLANTERS HOUSE, AUGUST 18, 1850

Robert's face reflected the parlor's gloom.

"Is something wrong, Robert? Have I offended you in some way?" She almost hoped that he would say "yes," for, if not, she feared what was to come. She suspected that Robert did not want her to light the lamp because he did not want to see her face when he told her what he was about to say. She held her breath.

"Zabette," Robert said slowly. "Belton Copp is going to be back in St. Marys sometime between now and the first of September," he said.

Her heart lurched.

"I'm going to send Bobby and Armand back to Groton with him to go to school."

A sob rose in her throat. "No," she said, not breathing. "No, Robert, I won't allow you to take away any more of my children!" she said again, trying to control the panic that was rising within her.

Robert looked at her ironically. "You won't allow it?" He laughed. "Zabette, you are forgetting who you are. You have no choice in the matter, my dear."

"Robert, they're just little boys. Bobby won't do well away from Cumberland, up north where people won't understand him."

"That's why I'm sending Armand as well. Bobby depends on his brother, and Armand will help him in his studies."

"Please, Robert. My children are all I have."

"It seems to me that you have rather more than most women in your position. You have a good home, nice clothes, another daughter to look after, and if I'm not mistaken, another child on the way. And you have plenty of duties to keep you occupied."

She had not told either him or Amanda about the new baby, for she wanted to be absolutely sure. But he had learned the symptoms as well as she had over the years—the morning sickness, the swollen breasts, and the slight irritability when he wanted to make love—all of which had begun almost two months ago. She could not deny it.

"Robert, so help me, if you send away Bobby and Armand, I'm going back to live with grandmother. She needs me anyhow."

"Are you threatening me, Zabette? If so, I wouldn't recommend it. You're not exactly at liberty to make these decisions, you know."

"I don't belong to you, Robert, and neither do my children. *Grand'mère* has always promised me that if I am unhappy with you I could come back to Plum Orchard. And that's exactly what I'll do." She knew she was taunting him in ways she had never done before, and she was keenly aware of testing the limits of her influence over him, which had diminished considerably in recent years. He no longer seemed to desire her as he had at the beginning of their time together, but it had not stopped him from demanding her body whenever he chose.

"Do whatever you want for now, Zabette." Robert said menacingly. "But in the final analysis you do belong to me—quite legally—and I have the bill of sale from your grandmother to prove it."

Zabette sucked in her breath, unable to believe his words. Her grandmother had sold her to Robert? If so, she had never been told of the transaction. It had always been her understanding that she was living with him at Planters House of her own volition and that she could go home to Plum Orchard whenever she chose.

"What do you mean?" He had confirmed her worst fear.

Robert looked incredulous. "Zabette, don't you realize that you were born a slave? Your mother was a slave, and that makes you a slave. You can be bought and sold. That's precisely what I am trying to save my children from. If you're a slave, then they can be considered slaves as well. I won't risk that. Can't you understand?"

Zabette felt her face grow hot at his words. "Even if what you say is true, the children are in no danger here with us."

"Trust me, my dear. The danger is very real. Suppose something should happen to me? My sons *will* go north, and they will grow up free men."

"You keep saying that one day all the slaves will be free. If that's so, what does it matter?"

"Yes, but who knows when that might happen? The South relies too heavily on its labor force to give up its slaves without a struggle. I think it will come, but it may not come in my lifetime, and I *will* protect my sons. I'm sorry, my dear. But you have no say in the matter."

"But the Copps have children of their own. How many more of our children can they care for?" She tried to reason with him.

"Mary will no longer be living with the Copps come fall. I have already paid her tuition to Bacon Academy in Colchester, where she'll board with a family named Sparrow. And I've arranged for the boys to be tutored by one of Belton's acquaintances, a retired schoolteacher named Samuel Lamb. I thought that might be better for Bobby than being in public school, at least for a while. They'll board with Lamb as well, so the Copps will not in any way be burdened with them."

"You've obviously thought of everything and, as usual, without letting me know anything about it," she said. Once again her daughter was to be uprooted and sent to a new town and school to live with strangers. And now her sons were to be snatched from her life, as well.

"I'm telling you now, Zabette." As far as he was concerned, the conversation was ended.

ZABETTE WOULD NEVER FORGET THE EARLY SEPTEMBER DAY when Belton Copp arrived on the island and, with Robert's blessing, tore her sons away from their mother's arms. She watched in shock as the boat skimmed away from the island bearing the tiny forms of her two little boys, Armand crying and Bobby looking bewildered. As soon as they were out of sight, she turned on her heel to return to Planters House, pack her few belongings, as well as clouts and little dresses for Ellen, say goodbye to Amanda, who wrung her hands and wiped her eyes with her apron, and set out to walk the three miles to Plum Orchard. She had strapped Ellen to her back, the way the slave women did when they worked in the fields while they were still nursing. In her left hand, she carried the carpetbag she had brought with her when she came from her grandmother's house and in the right a cloth sack with the child's things inside.

She had almost reached White Branch, where she planned to sit on the bridge, nurse her daughter, and rest for a while, when suddenly she heard a carriage approaching from behind. It was Robert, driving himself, his face red with fury.

"Just where do you think you're going?" he yelled down from the high carriage seat.

"I'm taking Ellen for a visit to *Grand'mère*," she answered. "We haven't seen her for almost a month," she said. Even though she was angry and upset with her grandmother over the news that she had sold Zabette to Robert, she would rather be with her than stay at Planters House, which now seemed so empty.

Robert had refused to let her take Bobby and Armand to Plum Orchard to say goodbye since Mary Elizabeth had returned so emotionally overwrought from such a visit just prior to her departure. "I need to tell her about the boys' leaving," she told him.

"Zabette, you're asking for trouble in more ways than you can possibly imagine," he said menacingly, "But goddamit, if you're so determined to go, I'll drive you. You can stay as long as you like, at least until you get over this little snit."

She hesitated, concerned that he might turn the carriage around and take her back to Planters House, but the road was too narrow at this point, and she knew that if he tried, the wheels would bog down in the sand. She put her carpetbag and sack into the back of the carriage, unstrapped Ellen so that she could hold her in her arms, and climbed up to sit stiffly on the seat beside him.

"Zabette," he said, in an almost conciliatory voice, "someday you'll understand. I miss the children too." Zabette remembered Armand's sobbing as the boat pulled away from the dock. He was only six years old, and he needed his mother. And little Bobby, how would he ever fare without her? No, she would never understand. She said nothing but stared straight ahead down the long road that wound through the green tangle of pines, oaks, and shadows. Robert drove in silence.

When they reached Plum Orchard, Daisy was sweeping the front steps. "Why, Lawd, ha' mercy, look who's here," she said in a welcoming voice.

Robert helped Zabette down from the carriage, and Daisy reached out to take little Ellen, who was sound asleep, from her mother's arms. Zabette gratefully relinquished her. "Where's my grandmother?" she asked.

Daisy looked at her sadly, "She's inside, lying down. Her arthritis is botherin' her somethin' awful, Zabette. She jes' ain't been herself of late."

"I've come to stay a spell, Daisy. I hope you can put up with two more mouths to feed."

"You always welcome. We sho' do miss you 'round here, Zabette," she said as the two women mounted the steps.

Then Daisy turned back to the carriage, "You gone come in, Mas' Robert?" she asked. "I got some blackberry cobbler in the stove," she said in an effort to tempt him.

"No thank you, Daisy, I'll be gettin' on back to Planters House. Amanda's expectin' me for dinner."

Zabette did not turn around, but she heard him flick the reins and trot away. This was the most daring thing she had ever done in her life, but she no longer cared. Her children, her only joy, were being systematically ripped from her life. He could beat her or even kill her if he was a mind to, but he could not hurt her worse than he had done already.

Zabette's stay at Plum Orchard stretched into late spring, and it gave her ample opportunities to visit her mother and Jack, for her grandmother no longer forbade it. In fact she no longer seemed to know who they were. Marie-Jeanne understood better than anyone her daughter's grief at having her sons sent away, but she didn't know her grandchildren very well, for as soon as they turned three years old, Robert had no longer permitted Zabette to bring them to her cabin. Sometimes she saw them playing in the yard on the other side of the orchard, but it hardly substituted for holding them in her arms. For the first time, she and Zabette talked openly about the pain of their separation that dreadful night so long ago. And they wept together as Zabette described her own children's departure. How Armand had to be forcibly put in the boat as he cried for his mother, and how Bobby had tried to console him with the idea of a *'venture*.

BUT THE TWO WOMEN SHARED NOT ONLY SORROW, but also the joy of Zabette's new baby, born at Plum Orchard in March. For the first time, Marie-Jeanne was able to be present at the birth and hold the newborn in her arms. Zabette named her new daughter Adelaide Clarice, though everyone called her Addie. Like Ellen, she had chestnut hair that curled softly.

When Zabette took the children for the first time to her mother's cabin, she nursed Addie, while Marie-Jeanne helped little Ellen set the table with sweetgrass plates she had woven for her to play with.

"I needs to make her a rag doll to cuddle," Marie-Jeanne said, kissing Ellen on the top of her head.

"No need," said Zabette, as she pulled her own doll from her pocket.

"You done kep' it all these years?" Marie-Jeanne could hardly believe it.

"Don't know what I would have done without it. My daughters have played with it, and I still love it. It's my most prized possession."

Marie-Jeanne gave her a hug. "But you got two li'l girls here now. I reckon I better still make another one or two." Zabette smiled in acquiescence.

Jack had grown taller and become a strikingly handsome young man, who had in recent years learned the skills of a house servant from his training in Marguerite's household, but now he went there no more.

"She done gone senile, Zabette," he said to his sister. "She can't teach me nothin' no more." But Zabette urged him to come to the Big House anyhow where they could see each other, though Marguerite always took him for Pierre.

Zabette loved the fact that her mother and brother had finally learned to relax around her, but she was disturbed to see her grandmother's rapid decline. Marguerite lived alternately in the present and the past. Sometimes she no longer recognized Zabette. And more and more frequently she appeared to forget all the English she had ever learned and spoke only French, especially to the children. Ellen was already chattering in French like a little magpie.

It broke Zabette's heart when, one afternoon as she was reading aloud some of her grandmother's beloved poems of Lamartine, Marguerite touched her arm. "You're so nice," she said sweetly. "What is your name?" Any anger she had once felt toward her grandmother had long since vanished as she felt her slipping away.

It was all Zabette could do to control her voice when she replied, "My name is Zabette. It's short for Elisabeth. I'm your granddaughter."

"*Vraiment*? Are you really?" asked Marguerite with pleasure in her voice. "How delightful!"

Sometimes when her grandmother spoke French, Zabette realized that she was not talking to her at all, but to her long-dead sister, and she replied accordingly. It confused Marguerite too much for Zabette to try to explain it all again, and she knew that her grandmother would not remember.

Marguerite and Ellen got along famously playing patty-cake. Marguerite sang to her the old songs she had known as a little girl back in France, songs she used to sing to Zabette. She was teaching Ellen to sing "*Frère Jacques*." And when the two of them sang it together, Zabette felt her heart swell with a bittersweet combination of pride and pain.

Sometimes Zabette wondered how Robert and the plantation were doing without her. She worried most about the sick people in the infirmary, but over the years she had taught any nursing skills she knew to several women in the quarters. She hoped they would be able to handle any task that might arise. But all the other duties, getting the clothing allotment ready, the spring planting and cleaning, she wondered if they were being done at all.

ONE AFTERNOON TOWARD THE END OF MAY, Robert showed up unexpectedly on his dappled horse, as Zabette and her grandmother sat with the children on the veranda. Addie slept in the cradle at her mother's feet, and Marguerite was holding Ellen and teaching her to count on her fingers: "*Un, deux, trois, quatre, cinq. Un deux, trois, quatre, cinq.*" Zabette wasn't sure whether that was all Marguerite could remember or whether the old woman thought it was the limit of Ellen's two-year-old capacity, but that was as far as they ever got.

Robert sat like a statue, taking in the scene on the porch. Zabette thought he looked old, tired, and stiff, perched like that in his saddle. He was sixty-nine now and looked every day of it. But he was still a strong and determined man with upright bearing and a stern, domineering face.

"All right, Zabette," he called in a loud voice. "You win. I won't let our children stay here, but I can send you to be with them. You've made it obvious that you no longer want to be with me."

"Hello, young man," called Marguerite gaily. "Do come in for tea."

Robert looked at her, startled. He dismounted, climbed the steps, and took a rocking chair beside Zabette.

"Howdy, Marguerite," he said, taking her hand. "I hope you're feelin' well."

"I'm fit as a fiddle for an old lady," she replied. "And who might you be?"

Robert looked at Zabette in disbelief. She nodded sadly. "I'm Robert Stafford, ma'am, from down at Planters House."

"I think I've heard your name somewhere before. Welcome to Bois Doucet," she said, naming her childhood home in France. Then she went back to counting with Ellen.

"Is she always like this?" he asked quietly.

"Most of the time now," Zabette replied. "How do you like your new daughter?" She gestured toward Addie, rosy cheeked, sleeping peacefully, her cradle gently rocking in the afternoon breeze.

"She's beautiful, Zabette. I came the day she was born, but Daisy told me you didn't want to see me."

"I'm sorry. That was unkind of me. But I was still angry and hurt about the boys. You were the last person I wanted to see."

"It's time for you to come home now, Zabette."

"For what? You don't need me. You don't need anyone. Besides, I can't leave *Grand'mère* here alone."

"She has Daisy, and I can arrange for someone to come and look after her. You also forget that you're not her only granddaughter."

Zabette had not forgotten, and she knew that Margaret and Jamie Downes were willing to take Marguerite into their own home or even move themselves to Plum Orchard to help care for her. But she had felt it was somehow her responsibility.

"Why did you come here, Robert?"

"I've already told you. I've come to take you home and to tell you that I'm making arrangements to send you to Groton to be with the children."

Her heart leapt at the prospect of seeing her children again, but she wasn't sure she could trust Robert anymore. Why should she go back to Planters House with him?

"You're always making arrangements for other people's lives. Don't you think you should at least ask?"

"I'm an old fool, I guess. More than you know. But this time I'm asking. Won't you come back and stay with me until I can get things ready for you in Connecticut?"

"How can I leave *Grand'mère*?"

"We'll find a way, Zabette. And I assure you, she won't know you're gone."

"But she enjoys the children so."

"The Downes have children too," he reminded her.

"Just give me another week with her, Robert, time to say goodbye and make arrangements. Then I'll come with you. I promise."

ROBERT RODE ALONE BACK TO PLANTERS HOUSE, with shame in his heart at the way he'd betrayed Zabette, not once but many times. As he rode, he hardened his heart in preparation to send his new mistress back to her cabin in the quarters at Rayfield. At the same time it was filled with joy at the thought of the return of Zabette and his two small daughters. His life wasn't over yet.

Chapter Thirty

PLANTERS HOUSE, SEPTEMBER 5, 1852

It seemed strange to be back at Planters House and even stranger to Zabette that she was packing for a real voyage. As excited as she was about seeing her older children again, she was uneasy about leaving Cumberland. She would miss it terribly. In all her thirty-two years, she had never been off the island except for the brief time she had lived on Jekyl as a young child.

Robert had kept his promise to try to reunite her with the children, but her departure would not be easy. Although she longed to see her children, she worried about her grandmother, whose condition continued to deteriorate until she now needed full-time care. Zabette hated to leave her, but Margaret encouraged her to go.

"I can look after Grandmother. She has no idea who either of us is anymore, Zabette. Go and be with your children. They need you."

Both Margaret and Jamie had been sworn to secrecy. If word got out that Robert Stafford was taking some of his slaves north to freedom, it could have serious repercussions. But they all agreed that it was in the best interest of everyone concerned. Even Margaret would be relieved not to have a mulatto half-sister on the island.

Zabette returned to Plum Orchard in mid-August to spend time with her grandmother before she left. She could do little for her except fan away the flies, hold her hand, and read stories that her grandmother had read to her when she was a child. Sometimes Marguerite laughed gleefully and at other times she fell into a morose silence. She slept most of the time now and ate less and less. She was frail as a sparrow, and it broke Zabette's heart to leave her, but she knew that Margaret would care for her with kindness and love.

Zabette spent a few final days with her mother and brother on the edge of the orchard but always returned to Plum Orchard to spend the nights with her grandmother.

Although the sun was still high, Marguerite was asleep when Zabette crept into her room for the last time to hold the small gnarled hand that had guided her own as she learned to sew and write. She straightened the gold locket around her grandmother's neck and caressed her forehead, which had furrowed in worry over her so many times through the years.

"*Adieu, Grand'mère,*" she whispered softly. "You have been good to me, and I will always love you and pray for you."

She kissed the wrinkled cheek and then slipped quietly out of her grandmother's life.

ROBERT WAS NOT HAPPY ABOUT ZABETTE'S IMPENDING DEPARTURE, but he saw no alternative. He knew how unhappy she was without the children, and he had watched her mope about the plantation without energy or interest. She would still succumb to his nocturnal demands, but without enthusiasm or warmth. It was simply not enough for an old man.

He also felt it necessary to send the other children north to protect them from the turbulence he feared was coming, and Ellen and Addie, with their chubby cheeks and soft brown hair, were both too young to go without their mother.

The South had grown increasingly intolerant of the rhetoric of northern abolitionists, more strident since "that Connecticut woman," Harriet Beecher Stowe, had published what southerners called her "inflammatory" novel, *Uncle Tom's Cabin*, in 1850. Threats of secession were already sounding in Savannah and elsewhere. In an effort to mollify the South, that same year Congress passed a Fugitive Slave Law that made it easier for Robert to travel north with his slaves, since it guaranteed that northern states would honor southerners' claims on runaways. But its passage only hardened regional positions toward slavery.

Robert had chosen Connecticut as the place to send his family not only because he knew it from his own boyhood and because Belton was there, but also because Connecticut had passed a bill for the "Defense of Liberty," which proclaimed the state's refusal to honor the Fugitive Slave Act. Zabette and the children would be safe there from any claims of ownership by any member of the Bernardey family. He could not imagine such a thing, since Jamie and Margaret were so supportive of her getting away, but one never knew when some distant relative might present a case, however remote the possibility.

He planned to accompany Zabette and the children on the trip north, to see them settled and to attend to business matters in Connecticut. Even before he sent Mary Elizabeth there, he had begun to acquire property in New London and Groton. Recognizing the political fragility of the southern plantation system, he was reluctant to keep all his eggs in his planter's basket. Southerners liked to tell themselves how happy their slaves were, but he knew better. As a young man, he'd watched slaves abandon the island in droves in 1815 when the British offered them a chance for freedom. He also understood the uncertainty of plantation economics and had lived through enough hurricanes and freezes to know how they could devastate a crop. Fluctuations in cotton prices sometimes threatened to bankrupt even the wealthiest planters.

Unlike Phineas Nightingale, Robert had been fairly lucky. By 1850 his slave population had grown to 348, while Phineas's had decreased to only eight. Phineas finally gave up on oranges and cotton altogether and moved away from Cumberland to buy a rice plantation on Camber's Island in McIntosh County and a small house on Richmond Street in Brunswick. Robert suspected that once again Phineas was going into debt beyond his means and that he wanted desperately to buy Dungeness back from his cousin Margaret Greene. If he did, Robert was sure it would become vulnerable once more to his creditors, one of whom was now Robert himself. When Phineas first declared bankruptcy, he encountered difficulty getting credit and had been forced to come to Robert, who was happy to see his adversary begging for money. He was sure that Phineas would always be on uncertain ground, and Robert was patient. He knew that he would collect what was owed to him in one form or another. He was willing to wait.

Meanwhile, he was looking toward better prospects in the North. He didn't know when slavery would be abolished in the South, though he had long predicted that someday it would be. But he also knew that local planters wouldn't give it up without a struggle. If by some chance his slaves were lost to him, he fully intended to have resources elsewhere. Having Zabette and the children in Connecticut would give him greater incentive to refocus his fortune there, though he had no intention of ever giving up his land on Cumberland Island or his dream of owning Dungeness.

As he prepared for Zabette and their young daughters to join the other children in Connecticut, he bought a small farm, sight unseen, but at a bargain price at Shennecossett Neck on the Thames River just south of Groton. With the help of Belton Copp, he purchased the main house fully furnished from a New England farmer in financial distress. While it was not suitable as a permanent residence, it would do until he could arrange for something more appropriate. He had talked with Belton about buying some land from the Copp farm in Groton farther up the Thames. If they could agree on the land and price, he planned to build a house there for his family.

ROBERT BOOKED PASSAGE FOR FOUR—himself, his two small "nieces," and their "nursemaid"—on a ship sailing to New London on the 15th. They would take a small vessel from St. Marys to Savannah where they would board a ship of the Collins Line for their voyage north. Robert was apprehensive about steamships because he remembered the sinking of the *Pulaski* in June 1838, when the boilers exploded in the middle of the night and so many Georgians lost their lives. Mary King Nightingale, Phineas's wife, had been aboard, but she was one of the lucky survivors. One family, he knew—the Lamars from Savannah—had lost eight members in the tragedy. But they had better regulations now, he reminded himself. And he preferred steamboats to sailing vessels, for they were usually faster and more reliable.

WHEN ZABETTE EXPRESSED QUALMS ABOUT LEAVING Cumberland, Amanda sympathized.

"Lawd, ha' mercy, better you than me, chile. I jes' ain't made for them northern climes. I hear it snow all the time up there."

"I'll miss you so much, Amanda," Zabette hugged her friend. "I wish you could come too. And little Cumsie," she said, touching the cheek of Amanda's new baby, who lay on a pallet on the floor. There was so much she would miss.

"Naw, I couldn't do that. I got my chillun here, Zabette, not like you, where they be gone. You gots to go, I reckon, but we'll sho' miss you 'round here." Zabette put her arms one more time around her friend, breathing in her welcome smell of biscuits and affection.

Saying goodbye to her grandmother, Daisy, and Amanda, to her own mother and brother, and to the people who worked with her in the infirmary and the cotton house, all trusted to keep her voyage secret, was heart-wrenching for Zabette. The women in the cotton house made her a special sweater, with yarn died red with walnut and elm leaves and knit in secret, each of them having some part in its making—whether spinning the thread, weaving or dying the cloth, or the actual knitting.

"You gone need this up north, Miss Zabette," said Nelly, the oldest among them who was the spokesperson for the group. Zabette accepted the sweater and their warm smiles with gratitude and misty eyes. She would miss them too, she knew.

Although they were sorry to see her go, many of them knew what it was like to have their children sent away to some other place. They wondered what Robert Stafford would do without her, but the months she had been away at her grandmother's had given them an inkling. It was a sure sign of the slaves' respect for Zabette that none of them ever told her what had happened during her absence. Robert had brought in from Rayfield Plantation a woman named Judy, about Zabette's age, to take care of her "duties." She had not filled in too well at the cotton house because she knew so little about the process, but she evidently did well enough in the Stafford bed, for when she was sent back to her cabin at Rayfield, she was pregnant with Robert Stafford's child.

Zabette would not only miss the people, but the island itself. She found an afternoon to walk alone one last time on the beach where her children used to romp, chasing gulls and terns. The sun reflected golden off the dunes and calm water. Shells littered the beach, like small treasures from God, so magnificently formed with their whorling shapes and intricate details. The largest lettered olive shell she had ever seen lay at her feet. She picked it up to carry it back to Planters House, where she would wrap its shiny surface in a soft cloth and pack it carefully in a box with the other shells she had collected to take to the children—channeled whelks, sand dollars, angel wings, even a few sharks' teeth for Armand and Bobby.

She would miss the beaches, the ever-changing marshes, the egrets, the gulls, the smell of the pine trees, the live oaks and palmettos, the deer and the wild horses, even the noisy grackles and wild turkeys that invaded her garden every morning. She tried to store them all into her memory, even making crude sketches to take with her. But the anguish she felt in leaving the island was offset by the expected joy at seeing her three older children at the other end of the voyage—pretty Mary, as she would make every effort to call her now, cheerful Bobby, and sweet Armand. Her heart sang at the prospect.

St. Marys, Georgia, Saturday, September 18, 1852

As their tiny boat sliced its way through the tidal creeks, Zabette's eyes filled with tears at watching the island recede in the distance, but as they approached the mainland, they sparkled with anticipation. She sat up straight, mouth agape, at her first sight of St. Marys, burnished in the morning sun. It was only a sleepy village, but to her it seemed a metropolis with people and activity everywhere, steel-banded barrels lined up along the wharf, loaded wagons rattling down the streets, children dangling their legs off the back. Women walked about jauntily, carrying bundles or holding the hands of small children, white women in calico sunbonnets and black women wearing bright-colored bandanas on their heads, like the ones Cumberland women saved for their Sunday best. Stores lined the waterfront, and from the dock she could see two churches along Osborne Street, the town's main "thoroughfare." A few clapboard houses with balconies on the second floor rose up from dusty streets, and children played under live oak trees that shaded the wide dirt road.

ROBERT, ZABETTE, AND THEIR LITTLE DAUGHTERS BOARDED the small packet *Palatka*, which took them from St. Marys and deposited them at the dock in Savannah by mid-afternoon. At 7 p.m. they were to depart for New York on a side-wheel steamer, the *Bridgeton*. Zabette welcomed the respite ashore, away from the rolling decks of the vessel. Although the voyage had only begun, she was already seasick from the incessant motion of the waves. Ellen had cried and vomited into the chamber pot during their first hour at sea. Little Addie had slept in Zabette's arms, apparently soothed by the rocking so like her own cradle. Thus far, the ocean had been calm, and Zabette dreaded the thought that they might encounter a storm somewhere en route.

They had several hours before boarding the ship, and Robert suggested a walk around the city. He took the lead, with Zabette trailing behind, carrying Addie in her arms, and holding Ellen's hand, as a good "nursemaid" would do. From the wharf they climbed the steps to the bluff that led to Factors Walk, then crossed Bay Street and ambled down the wide thoroughfare known as Bull Street. Zabette was overwhelmed by the city's size. It had been laid out, Robert told her, by General Oglethorpe more than a hundred years ago around a series of charming squares. They crossed Johnson Square, where a monument honored the former owner of Cumberland, General Nathanael Greene, Phineas Nightingale's grandfather. On that same square stood the imposing façade of Christ Episcopal Church with six majestic columns. Zabette had never seen such churches before built of marble and granite, with steeples that rose up seventy or eighty feet and led her eyes to the heavens.

When they reached Broughton Street, it was lined as far as the eye could see with beautiful homes, its broad expanse shaded by magnificent trees older than the houses themselves. Zabette had always thought Planters House rather grand until she saw Broughton Street.

As they approached the City Market, a cacophony of sounds greeted them. Wild birds attached to perches squawked at passersby, chickens cackled in cages, and vendors loudly hawked their wares. The covered marketplace in the center of the square displayed what Zabette believed must be every kind of food known to man, fish of all sizes and varieties—shellfish, flounder, grouper, trout, even fish Zabette didn't recognize—and bright-colored produce in season—squash, tomatoes, cucumbers, and corn, all arranged neatly in wooden boxes. The vendors were mostly black, many of them women in bright-colored kerchiefs folded like turbans around their heads, their cheerful voices calling out their wares in various pitches as though everyone were singing different, yet almost harmonious, songs.

They rested briefly in a nearby square before heading back to the waterfront, with Robert leading the way. He had booked a steamer that would leave in the evening to avoid the awkwardness of having to find a hotel in Savannah. It would be difficult to explain to Ellen why her mother had to be separated from the rest of the family. Knowing that it would be impossible for the four of them to eat together in the local inns or taverns, Amanda had packed a generous picnic basket, which Robert carried on his arm. Retracing their steps back to the bluff, they found a quiet place overlooking the Savannah River, and Zabette spread out the fried chicken, deviled eggs, and cucumber sandwiches. She sat under a tree to nurse Addie while Robert and Ellen took their meal.

As a "nursemaid," Zabette had her meal only after the others had finished. Robert told her that the rules would not be so strict once they reached the North. There, blacks and whites mingled more freely, he said, and Zabette, particularly with her light-colored skin, would not likely raise any eyebrows. The fact that Robert was so much older than she easily allowed people to accept him as the children's uncle, as he was pretending to be.

Once they were at sea again, Zabette was sorry that she had eaten anything at all, for once more both she and Ellen were seasick. Zabette lay in her bunk wishing she could die. Ellen lay beside her moaning for the first few hours, but she soon fell asleep, and by morning she was fine and ready to eat again.

Robert, with the help of two matrons from Savannah, watched over the children while Zabette was unable to do so. He explained that it was the first time the children's nursemaid had ever been at sea. The ladies "tsked tsked" over the situation and pitched in to assist the gentleman.

By midday Zabette had recovered enough to eat some bread and honey and swallow a bit of black coffee. She sat on a small barrel on deck, where she found the breeze refreshing. Far to the west she could see the Carolina coast sliding by. It looked inviting, and she wished she were there on dry land, but Addie and Ellen needed her, and she made an effort to spend most of the day upright and trying to amuse them. It took the better part of three days to reach their destination. At least, as Robert put it, she had her sea legs now, and she was able to eat sparingly.

"I'm glad to see you finally up and around," one of the Savannah matrons said when she saw Zabette walking Addie and Ellen around the deck. "Your master has needed you. These two little girls are just too much for him to manage."

"Yes, ma'am, I reckon so. You sho' is right. They can be a handful," Zabette replied, trying to nod affably.

"Why are you talkin' like that, *Maman*?" Ellen asked, when the Savannah woman had passed on by. "You sound like Amanda."

"I know, darling," she replied, "Amanda's the one who taught me what I should say. Don't you worry about it. I'll explain to you one day, but we're just pretending now. By the way," she added, "you shouldn't call me '*Maman*' when such ladies are around."

"Why not?"

"They think I'm just your nursemaid, and we want to let them think that, at least until we get to Connecticut."

"Why?"

"Why? Why not? Why?" She laughed, stooped down beside her children, and gathered them both in her arms. "You're just full of questions today, my precious girl." She pointed to the water. "Oh, look, I think I see a porpoise out there. And I bet I can spot the next lighthouse before you do." Ellen, her curls blowing in the wind, ran over to the rail and peered eagerly toward the shoreline. *Children are so easily distracted*, Zabette thought gratefully. *At least for now.*

THE DAYS PASSED SLOWLY AT SEA. They made a few brief stops along the way at Charleston, Wilmington, and Norfolk to unload passengers or take on more. When they finally reached New York, they debarked to take another steamer, the *Worcester*, through the Long Island Sound to New London. Groton, their destination, lay just on the other side of the Thames River, a short ride on the ferry *Mohegan*, Robert said. It would take them across the river to the home of Belton and Betsey Copp. And there, Zabette knew, her other children would be waiting.

GROTON, CONNECTICUT, SEPTEMBER 22, 1852

When the shiny black carriage Robert hired at the Groton ferry dock pulled up outside the Copp home, the front door flew open, and Armand, who looked as though he had grown a foot, bounded out and flung himself in his mother's arms, while Robert lifted Ellen and Addie down from the carriage seat.

"*Maman, Maman*, I've missed you so!" Armand cried. Zabette's heart melted to see her beautiful son, his hair so like her father's used to be, the color of wet sand.

"These are your new sisters—Ellen and Addie," she said, watching a shy smile play around his lips. Robert stood stiffly beside her, waiting his turn for the child's affection. Finally Armand looked up at his father and held out his hand in a manly way, "It's good to see you, sir." Robert shook his small hand and then turned to Bobby, who had lumbered awkwardly down the steps in pursuit of Armand. He too held out his hand to his father in imitation of his younger brother and hugged his mother.

Mary stood in the doorway, waiting for them to reach her. How she had grown! At almost thirteen she had become a young woman with a tall, pubescent body and pouting lips. She tilted her head for her father to kiss her cheek and permitted her mother to embrace her, though her greeting lacked the enthusiasm of the boys'. But Mary warmed quickly to the two little girls who stood shyly beside their parents staring in wonder at their older sister. Taking them each by the hand, she led them like a proud young mother up the steps and into the house.

Belton and Betsey Copp waited in the foyer of their home, giving their guests time to greet their children before they offered their own welcome. Zabette stood awkwardly beside Robert, who, after a cordial handshake, was engrossed in conversation with Belton.

When Robert showed no sign of introducing her, Betsey Copp took Zabette by the arm and said: "I assume that you're Elisabeth. I've heard so much about you from the children. We're so happy that you were able to come. Your two little girls are as charming as their brothers and seem to be much quieter." She chuckled as Zabette nodded in agreement. "And we have loved having their big sister in our home."

"Thank you," Zabette replied. "It's good of you to have looked after my children. I've missed them so much."

"I'm sure you have. I can't imagine what it must be like to be separated from them like that. It's kind of Robert to bring you to Groton."

"Yes, I suppose so," answered Zabette, who was charmed by Betsey's grace. She was an attractive woman, not beautiful, and appeared to be a decade younger than her husband. Her perky demeanor overcame whatever she may have lacked in comeliness. Her best feature was her wide smile, which embraced Zabette with kindness. She spoke with a clipped New England accent that lacked the slow rhythms of Cumberland. Yet it was a lovely, lilting voice, Zabette thought, wondering what she must sound like to Betsey Copp. Robert, who could talk just like the New Englanders, would blend better into their world than she.

"You must be exhausted after that long trip. Please come in. Have a cup of tea, and sit by the fire for a while," said Betsey. Zabette followed her into a cozy parlor, where a cheery blaze danced in the grate. The fire was welcome, for she had been chilled ever since she stepped on deck to see New London and Groton for the first time.

The sights and sounds distracted her from her discomfort. Never had she seen so many boats in one place in her life. Sailing ships, schooners, steamers, small vessels of every type cluttered the waters at the dock. New London was a whaling town, and rough-looking sailors filled the streets. The sea air felt different here—not like the gentle, balmy breezes that blew at Cumberland—but rather, stiff fresh winds that took her breath away. The trees on the distant hillside showed unfamiliar tinges of red and yellow leaves. There were no palms or palmettos, no sparkleberry bushes, but rather sturdy, upright, multihued trees, majestic in their way, that she would later learn were white oaks, walnuts, maples, and hemlocks. Here was an unfamiliar world, beautiful perhaps, but so very different from her island.

Zabette felt a sudden wave of homesickness for the mornings when live oaks filtered the sunlight, and Spanish moss festooned the branches and cast dappled shadows on the grass. She missed the marsh grasses waving in the wind, the plaintive sounds of mourning doves, the cheerful calls of Carolina wrens, and even the turkeys that minced about her yard looking for food. She missed the wide porch of Planters House, where yellow-throated warblers sometimes landed on the railing and hummingbirds fluttered about the red salvia in her flower beds. But at least the sea held waters that connected her to Cumberland. And best of all, her children were here.

Chapter Thirty-One

GROTON, CONNECTICUT, SEPTEMBER 22, 1852

Before nightfall Robert, Zabette, and the children said goodbye to the Copps and drove the short distance to their new cottage at Shennecossett Neck. The farm overlooked the Thames River. Behind the house Zabette could see apple trees with fruit hanging from the branches and rotting apples lying on the ground. The house, its white paint beginning to peel around the window frames, was simple, without the sprawling verandas of their Georgia home. Robert had arranged to have it thoroughly cleaned and aired, new linens brought in for the beds, and the pantry stocked. The overall effect was cozy and almost homelike.

"It's very nice, Robert," she assured him. The younger children were exploring the cottage and staking their claim to the bedrooms. Only Mary affected complete indifference and settled in a chair beside the window to read *Sonnets From the Portuguese,* a gift from Betsey. Zabette smiled to see them all together again and looked forward to a noisy family dinner for the first time in ages. With Bobby and Armand there, she knew she could count on the noisy part. She explored the pantry with anticipation, grateful for her days in the kitchens with Daisy and Amanda, which had prepared her for this moment. She was thinking about trying her hand at apple cobbler for dessert.

Once he saw them settled in, Robert announced that he would be spending the night in a hotel in downtown Groton.

"Oh, Robert, not tonight," Zabette protested. "We've just arrived." But he stood firm. To make the arrangement work, he had decided that since he would not live there, he should be viewed not as the children's father but instead as their benevolent uncle, while Zabette would continue in the role of nursemaid. They decided during the voyage that the children could continue to call her *Maman*. When they slipped up and called her *Maman* on the ship, even the ladies from Savannah did not seem to think it odd. After all, they themselves had called their nursemaids "Mammy." To them it was merely a term of endearment.

Zabette was relieved, but Robert was still adamant that they call him "Uncle Robert." If the Stafford children were to go to school here and mingle with the offspring of the predominantly white society, it would not do, he told Zabette, for it to be known that they were illegitimate and that their mother was a slave. Zabette hated the pretense. All her life she had been forced to pretend to be something she wasn't. She'd thought that here in the North such subterfuge would not be necessary, but Robert disagreed.

"Yankees are just as set in their ways as southerners, and family is important to them. Trust me. This is the only way." They spoke freely about the situation in front of the children, who for the most part paid little attention, but they too needed to understand to the best of their ability the arrangement they must all abide by. Robert was immovable on the issue, and Zabette made no further protest. She was simply happy to be with her children again, to have Armand clinging to her skirts and Bobby sitting on his father's knee playing with the handkerchief in his breast pocket.

Ellen huddled beside Mary, asking her a million questions about the book she was reading, and Addie climbed into her lap. Even Mary's determined indifference could not resist their sweetness, and she let them settle into the chair on either side of her while she read to them the evocative rhythms of Elizabeth Barrett Browning.

Zabette wouldn't have minded so much Robert's leaving for the night if everything hadn't been so new and strange. She had to build a fire to cast the chill from the house, which seemed odd for September, always such a delightful month at Cumberland, provided there were no storms. Fortunately, a rick of wood waited under the lean-to beside the house, and soon she had a crackling fire blazing in the grate.

None of the children, except Bobby, appeared particularly upset to see their father depart for the night. But the boy begged to go with him until finally Robert acquiesced. Why not, after all? A doting uncle could take his nephew for the night. Thus, before supper the two of them rigged up the horse and rented carriage and set out for a hotel, leaving Zabette and the other children behind in an unfamiliar world.

SHENNECOSSETT NECK, GROTON, CONNECTICUT, SEPTEMBER 1852

Zabette darted to the window when she heard the rattle of the approaching carriage the following morning. To her relief it was Robert and Bobby. For some unfathomable reason, she'd feared that Robert would send Belton Copp back with Bobby and return to Cumberland without even saying goodbye. She met them at the door.

"You've come back!" she said.

"Of course I've come back. I've made arrangements to stay at the City Hotel indefinitely."

"Really?" she said in disbelief.

"Really."

"But what about the cotton crop?" She knew that fall was a critical time. There was the picking still to do, the ginning and baling, and the shipping of the Sea Island cotton to Savannah.

"That's what I pay an overseer for. This year Dilworth gets to earn his keep. I wrote him last night and mailed the letter this morning. It's all settled." He had hired an overseer several years ago, but most of the time complained about having to pay him wages he didn't feel the man earned.

"How long will you stay?" she asked.

"As long as I need to. Until you're settled in at least." It was unlike him. He always assumed that everyone was as strong and resourceful as he was, but Zabette was unsure of her status in this new environment. She was grateful for his decision to remain, at least for a while.

THE FOLLOWING MORNING, WHEN HE ARRIVED, he announced to Zabette that he had hired a cook named Maureen.

"Should I take that as a comment on my cooking?" she asked with a laugh.

"Not at all," he told her. "But it's not your job."

My job? Zabette thought. She hadn't really thought of her role as nursemaid as a job. She was the children's mother in truth, if not in the eyes of the Connecticut world. It was her responsibility of course, but she did not consider it her "job." Still, she was not sorry that someone else would take charge of preparing meals. Maureen was a ruddy Irish woman, who set before them at every single meal some type of potato dish. In addition to cooking, she cleaned the small cottage, leaving Zabette, the "nursemaid," free to supervise the children.

AS THE UNFAMILIAR WINTER SETTLED IN, Zabette was comforted by Robert's presence, even though he didn't warm her bed on those chilly nights. At first the colorful fall and the coming of winter were like magic. Seeing them for the first time, she took in every detail. The trees turned all shades of dazzling red and gold. And in early November, she was delighted by the first snowfall. By morning the entire farm was dusted in what looked like powdered sugar. After the older children left for school, Zabette, Ellen, and Addie watched as the snow continued to fall, blanketing the landscape.

"I want to go play in the snow!" Ellen announced as soon as lunch was over.

"It's very cold," said her mother.

"I don't care. I want to go outside."

Zabette bundled the girls in the warmest clothes they owned, and hand-in-hand they ventured out for the first time into the snowy landscape.

"Ooh, it's cold!" Ellen said, with a giggle, trying to catch the large snowflakes on her tongue.

Addie too laughed with glee and said, "Col'," opening her mouth to the heavens, like her sister, to try to catch the falling flakes.

Together they learned to build a snowman, using sticks for his nose and mouth, and poking holes in the snow for his eyes. The effort was crude, for they had never seen snow before, but they were beginning to get the idea. When the children's teeth began to chatter and they looked nearly frozen,

Zabette scooted them back inside, where Maureen made them hot chocolate while Zabette rubbed their icy fingers to warm them up.

When the novelty wore off and once the older children were home to pull the younger ones on their sleds, Zabette found it more comfortable to stay inside and watch them play through the window, as she sewed or helped Maureen prepare meals. Mornings were hardest. The three older children went to school every day. Ellen mourned their absence and said she wanted to go home, back to Cumberland where it was warm. She was more whiney than usual, and two-year-old Addie imitated her sister. Zabette read them stories, helped them have tea parties, and took walks with them on the snowy bluff when it wasn't too cold. Winter was long here—*too long*—she concluded. Like Ellen, she pined for Cumberland. Even the sea was different here, not calm and gentle as it was on her island, but cold and rough.

She expressed her longing for the South during one of Betsey Copp's afternoon visits. "Summer will be better," Betsey assured her. "You'll like it here in the summer. No gnats or flies." Oh, but they must get through this endless winter first.

Little by little, the family settled into something of a routine. Robert picked the children up for school early in the day, then spent the morning in town looking at property or talking to businessmen about various financial possibilities. One of the opportunities that looked promising was the City Hotel where he was staying in New London. He told Zabette about its potential as a good investment if he could talk the owner into selling.

The owner was immediately acquiescent. The hotel had not done well in recent years, and he was eager to unload it to this man whom he took at first for a backwater southerner, a cracker without sophistication. He soon learned differently, as Robert shrewdly negotiated his price and conditions. Buying the hotel was one less worry for him, and Zabette could see that he was pleased with his purchase. He could stay there at length and at will now, whenever he wanted to come and go. It was inconvenient being on the New London side of the river, but that was where the whaling ships came in and where it was likely to do the most business, and the *Mohegan* ferry ran on a regular basis between the two towns. Robert was certain that the hotel could turn a profit with proper management.

Robert was also talking with Belton Copp about buying property, perhaps a portion of Copp's own land, to build a new house for the children and Zabette. At midday, Robert would come to the cottage for dinner and stay until the children came home from school, but he would leave before suppertime to return to his hotel.

SHENNECOSSETT NECK, FEBRUARY 14, 1852

In mid-February news arrived that Zabette hoped would never come. "Marguerite Bernardey passed away on January 26," Jamie Downes wrote to Robert. "I have seen to all arrangements. She was buried as she wanted, beside her son, Margaret's father, in the little plot behind Plum Orchard. Come when you can," he urged Robert. "As you know, you're named as administrator of the estate, and we need to take care of some business."

When Robert showed her the letter after the noonday dinner, Zabette took it and walked out in the snow to the slope that overlooked the river. There she read it once more and let her tears flow freely. She had so wanted to be with her grandmother to the end, but she knew that Margaret had taken good care of her and that she was now at rest. Jamie's letter did not mention that Pierre was Zabette's father as well as Margaret's. Perhaps he didn't want to acknowledge it in any written record, though he knew it to be true.

Zabette was sure that Marguerite would not have wanted to live longer in her failing body and especially without her sharp mind. Still, the thought that she would not be there if or when Zabette returned to Cumberland left an empty place in her heart. The chill wind cut through the thin shawl she had wrapped around her as she rushed outside. She could hear Maureen calling from the house, "Zabette? Are you out there? Come on in now or you'll catch your death." When she finally returned to the house, shivering, red-cheeked and red-eyed, Maureen chided her. "You shouldn't be out there like that. You have these children to look after, and you can't afford to get sick."

"I know, Maureen," she answered. "It's just that my grandmother died, and I wasn't there with her."

"Blimey, I know that's a hard one. I lost me own grandmum when I was a

child, before I ever came to America. 'Tis a sad loss indeed," she said in her Irish
lilt that Zabette sometimes had trouble understanding.

Even with the servants Zabette felt that her identity was a tightrope walk.
As far as Maureen knew, she was Zabette Bernardey, the Stafford children's
nursemaid, not their mother. She and Robert always talked in formal ways when
she was about. Although he still called her "Zabette," she referred to him as "Mr.
Stafford." She was always afraid that she would slip and say "Robert."

They arranged to have Maureen clean up the dinner dishes and prepare
supper so that she could leave for her own home about the time the children
came home from school. That way they could have a bit of family time every day
without anyone else around. Zabette was glad that the children called her *Maman*
instead of "Mama." Maureen, who didn't know a word of French, assumed, like
the southern matrons had, that it was just a pet name.

Zabette waited until Maureen left for the day to tell the children about their
great-grandmother. She planned to tell them at suppertime, though she doubted
that the little ones would even remember her. Mary would, no doubt, and
perhaps Armand, *but the others forget so fast,* she thought. She wasn't sure whether
Bobby would remember. His mind was not keen. He learned slowly and forgot
much of what he had learned. It became more obvious every year, as Armand
advanced rapidly in his studies, that he was leaving Bobby far behind. Armand
was protective of his brother and tried to help him as much as he could, but even
he realized that Bobby was not like most children his age. Zabette thought about
keeping Bobby home to protect him from the taunts of other boys, but she was
afraid that it would only make matters worse. He tried so hard to keep up, and the
boys provided a challenge. She could only admire his courage and tenacity.

At supper, as they asked the blessing over Maureen's pork chops and boiled
potatoes, Zabette added, "And God bless the soul of Marguerite Bernardey, my
beloved grandmother." The children looked at her with curiosity. Finally Armand
asked, "Was that *Grand'mère* you were praying about, *Maman*?" he asked in
English, spicing it with the two terms of affection he used for his mother and
great-grandmother.

"Yes, my darling. *Grand'mère* passed away the day after Christmas. I'm very
sad about it."

"What does that mean, *passed away*?" Bobby asked.

Zabette hesitated. How to explain in a way he would understand? "It means that she died, my darling. Do you remember the time at Planters House when the little kitten wandered away from its mama and fell into the river and drowned? It's like that."

"*Grand'mère* drowned?" he asked incredulously.

"No, but remember how the kitten didn't breathe anymore? How it couldn't run and play? And we had to bury it under the persimmon tree? That's what it means to die."

"Did they bury *Grand'mère* like that?" he asked, wanting to understand all the implications.

"Well, not exactly like that," she replied. "They made a coffin for her, a kind of wooden box, and buried her in that. Do you remember the little place behind her house where I always told you my papa was buried?"

Mary and Armand nodded. Bobby, seeing them, nodded as well.

"Well, that's where they laid her to rest."

"I'm sorry, *Maman*. I know you loved her," Armand said.

"We all did, *chéri*. We will all miss her. But she's in God's hands now." The children nodded solemnly.

Marguerite's death marked for Zabette the end of an important chapter in her life. She knew that she was wholly dependent on Robert now, that she could never again go home to her grandmother as she did before Addie was born. Now she belonged to Robert without recourse.

Chapter Thirty-Two

SHENNECOSSETT NECK, GROTON, CONNECTICUT, March 15, 1853 Zabette realized that she was pregnant again within a month after Robert's departure for Cumberland Island. There had been so few opportunities, and she knew it must have happened during the younger children's afternoon nap the week that Maureen had the grippe and did not come to work. Zabette was concerned because she was afraid that this new child would upset Robert's plans. How would anyone believe that she was merely the nursemaid now? When Zabette confided to Betsey that she was pregnant again, her new friend was supportive and assured her that everything would be all right.

"Nobody knows anything about you except Belton and me and, of course, Maureen. I guess you'll soon need to find a new cook."

"I hate to let her go for something that's not her fault."

"With a good recommendation from Robert and Belton, she can find another job quite easily, I think . . . . Have you written to Robert?" she asked.

"Not yet," Zabette answered. "But I will this week."

Betsey gave her a hug of reassurance and said, "Don't worry. It'll all work out."

ZABETTE WAS TRUE TO HER WORD and sent Robert a letter, the longest she had ever written, for her writing was poor, telling him about the children's progress in school, the endless potato dishes of Maureen, and her longing for Cumberland. She hoped he was well and that he would visit in the summer. "And I should also let you know that I am expecting another child, probably in November."

Although Robert did not reply directly to the letter, he sent Belton Copp precise instruction about when to dismiss Maureen, after carefully calculating when Zabette's pregnancy would begin to show. He thought they could wait perhaps only until the end of June. He would arrive sometime in July, he announced, to determine what should be done at that point.

Occasionally he sent Zabette short notes, inquiries about the children's health, and all too rarely a tidbit of news from Cumberland. "Amanda says to tell you that she'll send Maureen some recipes if I'll write them down for her. She also tells me that your old friend from Plum Orchard, Adeline, had another baby." He did not mention their own new baby directly, though he would say things like "I hope you're getting plenty of rest and taking care of yourself."

Zabette dreaded the day when Mr. Copp would have to fire Maureen. It seemed so unfair. But she underestimated his diplomatic skills. When the time came, he took Maureen aside one morning to inform her that a Mr. O'Neal in New London had made inquiries about finding an excellent cook, preferably Irish, like himself, and that he was willing to pay a considerably higher wage than Mr. Stafford was paying her. He suggested that he would recommend her for the position if she was interested. She was indeed and felt no compunction about leaving Zabette and the children to cross the river to New London for her new job.

"Well," Zabette said to Betsey, when she heard the news. "So much for my conscience. But what do I do now until Robert gets here?"

"Don't worry," Betsey, ever optimistic, reassured her. "It will only be a month or so, and it will all work out. I'll send over my Bridgit once a week to clean. She won't ask questions. And you're a better cook than Maureen ever was."

In fact, it was easier than she expected, and rather pleasant not to have Maureen always about. Bridgit proved to be a thorough housekeeper, going after every speck of dust and dirt as though it were her mortal enemy. A washerwoman in Groton picked up their laundry every Saturday and returned it the following week, clean and ironed. Belton Copp, as a director at the Whaling Bank of New London, took care of all the bills from Robert's account. Without such worries, Zabette had an opportunity to try out every single one of the recipes that Amanda sent. In fact, she was rather proud of her new cooking skills.

Now that the weather was warmer and all danger of snow long past, the children played outside most of the day. Zabette didn't worry about them, for she knew they would not stray, and they had been cautioned since childhood not to play near the riverbank. The drowned kitten had been a good lesson for them and taught them a healthy respect for the dangers of the flowing water. When the little ones went down for a nap in the afternoon, Zabette rested as well.

This pregnancy had tired her more than the others. She supposed it was because there were so many other worries and perhaps because she was growing older. But then she would think of the women in the cotton fields at Cumberland and how they had to work at least into their eighth month and still do the cooking and cleaning and laundry for their families. And Amanda had birthed Cumsie in her forties, while Zabette was still in her early thirties. What right did she have to complain? Those were women of courage, she thought, feeling ashamed of herself for letting a little weariness, the care of her five children, and a little cooking get her down.

She wondered how they were all doing, the women in the cotton house and the ones she had trained to nurse the sick at the infirmary, and she felt a wave of homesickness. She thought of Adeline and her new baby, and of Daisy. What was Daisy doing now that Marguerite was gone? She supposed that Margaret had taken her into her own household, for she was one of the better cooks on the island. They were not likely to waste her talent by putting her in the fields. She felt sure that neither Robert nor Jamie would ever sell her, for she had taken such good care of Marguerite until her death.

ROBERT'S RETURN IN LATE JULY answered many of Zabette's questions. He reported that the settlement of Marguerite's estate according to the terms of her 1842 will had been orderly and peaceable, and he thought Marguerite would have approved. She had bequeathed the five acres around the home place at Plum Orchard, as well as Marie-Jeanne and Jack and half her property, to Robert. Long before her death, Marguerite had discussed with Robert her expectation that the five acres were to be used as needed by Zabette, her mother and brother, though of course she could not leave such a bequest directly to slaves. She had no choice but to trust Robert to carry out her wishes. She had also left him all her money for their benefit, which by the time of her death amounted to virtually nothing. Except for a small bequest to a distant niece, the rest went to Margaret.

"I would have returned sooner," Robert told Zabette, "but I needed to take care of some matters concerning your grandmother's estate." There was the question of a tax lien against Plum Orchard to be dealt with, and on July 12 Robert had been compelled to hold a public sale of 300 acres of Plum Orchard land before he could make any final distribution of the estate. Robert wanted to add those acres to his own, but he thought it would look like a conflict of interest for him to bid on them himself.

"Jamie Downes offered to be my surrogate bidder at the auction," Robert told her. "And he bought all three hundred acres for $250."

Zabette nodded with appreciation, well aware that less than a dollar an acre was a bargain for good cotton land on Cumberland.

"Jamie was such a help with everything. He's a good man, and Margaret is lucky to have him for a husband."

Zabette agreed. He was not much to look at, lanky and awkward as he was, but she knew that he had a good heart.

"And Margaret sent you this." He pulled from his pocket a small leather pouch. Inside was the gold locket that Marguerite Bernardey had always worn around her neck. "She thought that you would like to have it."

Tears sprung to Zabette's eyes as she felt in her outstretched hand the weight of the heart-shaped object engraved with a scrollwork of leaves and flowers.

"Grandmother's locket! She wore it every single day!" It was the greatest treasure she had ever been given. "Oh, thank you, Robert. Dear Margaret. How generous of her to give it to me." *Yes,* she thought, *Margaret and Jamie were indeed a well-matched pair.*

Robert looked embarrassed by her show of emotion. "Well now," he said, quickly changing the subject, "we've got to make arrangements for the next few months until the baby comes."

She was relieved that he agreed to stay until their child was born, once more leaving his land in the hands of John Dilsworth, who had apparently done an acceptable job the year before.

Zabette sensed that Robert was beginning to shift the focus of his interests away from Cumberland and toward Connecticut. But she also knew that he had unfinished business at Cumberland, business she wished he would just forget.

He had not yet acquired Dungeness, which continued to gnaw at him. She knew that he would never rest until he had it in his grasp and saw Phineas Nightingale crushed underfoot. But from what Robert told her, Phineas was making a new life for himself on Camber's Island and in Brunswick and paying little attention to Robert Stafford, a fact that, in itself, Robert found irritating.

It was good for him, she thought, to be away from Cumberland for a while and take a greater interest in Connecticut, where he seemed infused with new vigor and where every waking moment was not marred by his hatred of Phineas, which could burst forth over the least reminder. His arrivals in the mornings to pick up the children were always brisk and positive. He talked during dinner about the possibilities that had arisen during his morning hours in Groton or New London. And he was as delighted as a child when, on August 15, he finally closed a deal with Belton Copp to buy thirty-three acres of his land on a high bluff overlooking the Thames River north of Groton.

That very afternoon he drove Zabette and the children out to see the land. The view took Zabette's breath away. It provided a spectacular panorama of the Connecticut countryside and the river and made the sloping fields of the farm at Shennecossett Neck look tame by comparison. She felt as one must feel in a hot-air balloon high above the earth, with a perspective over miles and miles of rolling hills and waterways. She could see all the way to Long Island Sound, and, she thought wistfully, if she looked far enough, she could perhaps see all the way to Cumberland.

"My children will have the best house in Groton to grow up in," he boasted to Zabette, as they all sat in his brand-new Landau carriage, overlooking his new domain. The Landau, shinier and more spacious than the dilapidated Phaeton that had come with the Shennecossett farm, allowed all seven of them to ride more comfortably. Zabette sat beside Robert on the driver's seat with Addie on her lap, though she would clearly not be able to hold her like that very much longer as the child in her womb grew larger. The other four children sat in the two back seats facing each other. Mary raised her chin to peer out over the vacant land, then turned to ask her father, "Will we have lots of servants?"

"As many as you need, my pet," he laughed, a rare sound that Zabette welcomed with all her heart.

"I want a house with twenty rooms and twenty servants," she announced.

"Good heavens!" said Zabette. "That sounds more like a hotel. What would they all do?"

"That many might stumble over each other, don't you think?" Robert asked, turning around to ruffle her hair. "But you'll have as many as you need," he promised.

Mary grimaced at her mother and smiled sweetly at her father. Nine-year-old Armand, noticing her disrespectful expression toward Zabette, stood up, turned around to kneel on the carriage seat and give his mother a hug. "I don't think we'll need so many, *Maman*," he whispered in her ear.

Zabette was overwhelmed at the prospect of overseeing such a household, but Robert and the children were so excited about it that she too began to enjoy their planning sessions.

"We'll need a room for each of the children and one for their 'nursemaid,'" he said gruffly but with a brief smile at Zabette, "in addition to servants' rooms, two parlors, a dining room, a butler's pantry, and a good kitchen," Robert suggested.

Zabette had noticed that the kitchens in the north were not separated from the rest of the house like they were on Cumberland Island. There, plantation owners wanted to separate the kitchen's heat from the main house, and they were always afraid of fires. But in Groton they had a fire department that would rush to the rescue when they heard firebells ringing, and heat was hardly ever a problem. On the contrary, the rooms nearest the kitchen were often the most comfortable in winter.

"Oh, Papa, can we have a widow's walk?" asked Mary. She had seen the small elegant structures perched atop some of the best houses in town, built in the new Italianate style. "Then our house will be higher than any other house in the county."

"Please, Papa," echoed Bobby.

"Then a widow's walk you shall have."

"And indoor plumbing!" shouted Armand. "And a bathroom!"

"And gas lights everywhere!" added Mary. They were all enthusiastically endorsing all the modern conveniences they had discovered only since coming to Connecticut.

Robert enjoyed their enthusiasm. But Zabette was thinking that such a house would cost a fortune. She remembered the simplicity of Plum Orchard and Planters House. And even simpler was her mother's cabin where there were only two real rooms—a sleeping room with a loft where Jack slept and a living room with a fireplace, where Marie-Jeanne could cook and weave and make her baskets. And that cabin was bigger than most of the slave cabins in the quarters, which were often just one room. On the island so much of the living was done outside, but that was impossible in Connecticut with its cold winters. This new house would no doubt be grand, but she knew that she could never love it as she had those simple structures at Cumberland.

As the weather cooled in September, Robert began to look for a contractor. He found a man named Ralph Arthur, a master carpenter and a well-known builder in the area. Together they pored over the plans for hours at a time, discussing the building materials, "which must be the very best," Robert reminded him. They considered how the house might best be oriented to take advantage of the view and the winter sun, contemplated the size of the bedrooms, and calculated the width of the porch that would wrap around the house. That had been Zabette's only request.

By the end of October, Robert and Mr. Arthur had come to an agreement on what needed to be done and settled on a price. When the winter snows and Zabette's labor pangs began, Arthur's men had already dug the cellar for the new structure.

Shennecossett Neck, November 20, 1853

Zabette's burst of energy on a late November day was, to her, a clear indication that she was about to give birth. It always happened like that, when she felt a sudden desire to clean out wardrobes or rearrange furniture. She begged Robert to spend the night at the cottage. He was reluctant, but he was even more reluctant to leave her alone, with only the children, who were much too young, he thought, to saddle a horse to summon him in the middle of the night. Besides, the ferry didn't run after dark.

Her water broke about 11 p.m. Against her protests, Robert woke up fourteen-year-old Mary to sit with her mother while he went to fetch Dr. Durfrey, the physician who had agreed to deliver the baby. Zabette listened anxiously to the rapid clopping of the horse as Robert left the house for the town of Groton.

Zabette did not like the idea of a white doctor attending her childbirth. She had little trust in males at such a time. The black midwives from her past birthings had always been so gentle and reassuring, tending to her emotional as well as her physical needs. She felt frightened at not having Maum Bella with her, and she missed the comforting presence of her grandmother, who always sat beside her bed and let Zabette hold her hand during her labor pains. Mary, fidgeting incessantly, showed clear signs of relief when, after about an hour, the hoofbeats of her father's returning horse could be heard on the cobblestones in front of the cottage.

Dr. Durfey arrived in his carriage almost forty-five minutes later, his black medical bag in hand. Robert was angrily pacing the floor at the doctor's failure to arrive promptly, when he finally heard his knock on the door. By then Zabette's pains had calmed a bit, and the doctor spent the first hour or two dozing beside her bed. By dawn the pains were back in earnest. As contractions grew more intense, she no longer cared who delivered the baby as long as he did so quickly.

The child was small, only six pounds, but she clearly had healthy lungs. Robert had long since learned that, at the mere cry of a baby, one did not burst into the birthing room without being summoned. But it would hardly have mattered to Dr. Durfey, who was less concerned about the aesthetics of childbirth than the Cumberland midwife had been. He made sure the mother was comfortable and sponged the baby a bit, but it was up to Zabette to see to any other details. Fortunately she had been through the process five times before and had laid out a clean gown, coverlet, and the same blue receiving blanket that had swaddled all her previous babies, as well as herself.

Dr. Durfey was still wiping his hands when he opened the door and invited Robert into the room. "You have another daughter, Mr. Stafford," he said warmly. "Just let the mother rest for a while. I don't think there will be any complications. But call me if you need me." He seemed eager to get away and even turned down Robert's offer of fresh, hot coffee, which he had made himself, probably for the first time in his life.

Before engaging Dr. Durfey, Robert had made inquiries about the town. He'd looked for a doctor whose discretion could be trusted and learned that Dr. Durfrey was not the sort to gossip about his patients. But the doctor had assured him that the one thing he would not do was falsify the record. He would register the birth accurately, with one mulatto parent and one white, and he assumed they were both named Stafford. Robert made no effort to correct his assumptions.

The new baby, whom they named Medora, but called "Dora" for short, was like her sisters, delicate, with dark curly hair and dark eyes. Mary was the first, aside from the parents, to hold the newborn. Zabette could see her instant bonding with the baby. Mary could be so distant, so cold sometimes, but she smiled tenderly at little Dora and cooed over her tiny hands and counted her toes. Armand was next, as he looked sleepily into the innocent dark eyes of his new sister. "Another girl," was all he said. And when Bobby's turn came, he agreed, trying to muster up the same annoyance as his brother, "Another girl." Four-year-old Ellen and two-year-old Addie, too small to hold their new sister, merely gazed at her in awe. This was what had so recently been in their mother's tummy. It seemed like a miracle to them both.

Zabette knew that the birth of this child would change her life more than any of the others. It would break apart her family as she had known it in recent months. Robert would go back to Cumberland and leave them all here to fend for themselves. And Zabette would once again be compelled to become the Stafford children's "nursemaid" and, she supposed, Dora's "wet nurse" in the eyes of the world.

But she also knew that the construction of the new house would bring Robert back as soon as possible. He and the children talked about it endlessly throughout the late summer and early fall. Construction had stopped for the winter when the snows began, but it would resume as soon as they ended.

ROBERT STAYED IN GROTON through the Christmas holiday before a break in the weather allowed him to make the trip back to Georgia. This time he was more reluctant to leave and promised to return as soon as spring planting was done. He was as eager as the children to see the house finished.

Before he booked his passage on the steamer *Rapidan*, he hired a new cook—a young woman named Hannah Gearm—and a man, John Meagher, a general handyman who would also tend to the horses and serve as carriage driver to Zabette and the children. He felt that they had imposed long enough on Belton Copp's generosity. John had recently arrived from his home on the Antrim coast of Ireland and seemed to feel quite at home on the brisk banks of the Thames River in Connecticut. As far as the workers knew, the new baby's widowed mother had died in childbirth, and Zabette had taken over the task of wet nurse and rearing the children for their grief-stricken uncle, Mr. Stafford. Robert, in his role as guardian, was leaving them all in the care of these two young Irish immigrants, both in their twenties, to tend to his lands in the South. They accepted the story without question, and Zabette as head of household in Mr. Stafford's absence.

This time when Robert left to return to Georgia, Zabette and the children accompanied him as far as the ferry dock, all crowding into the carriage driven by John. Seated on one side of her father with Bobby on the other, Mary, who loved to cuddle the baby, held Dora warmly in her arms, while Addie sat on her mother's lap between Armand and Ellen. It was quite a squeeze, with all of them bundled up against the winter cold.

"We'll miss you, Mr. Stafford," Zabette said, as Robert was about to board the ferry. She was well aware that John was within hearing range. "Please let us know of your safe arrival."

He nodded. "Take good care of the children."

"Of course I will," she smiled up at him.

He hugged each of the children in turn, with a special kiss for Dora, barely a month old.

The ferry was pulling away from the dock as Zabette called out, "Say hello to Miz Margaret and Mr. Jamie!"

Robert, wrapped in a gray wool overcoat and muffler, held his hat high in agreement and farewell. The children all waved with vigor. Snow was beginning to fall, and Zabette hurried them into the carriage for the cold ride back to the farm. Once settled in the carriage, she prayed for stormless seas for Robert and a safe journey back to her beloved Cumberland. Her second winter in Connecticut had begun.

Chapter Thirty-Three

SHENNECOSSETT NECK, CONNECTICUT, MAY 8, 1854
"Uncle Robert comes today!" Bobby shouted to no one in particular as he climbed into the driver's seat of the shiny Landau beside John, who had taken the boy under his wing during the winter months. Zabette frequently reminded the children that they must always call their father "Uncle Robert," when any of the servants were close by. She was relieved that Bobby remembered.

Zabette decided not to try to crowd all the children into the carriage to go to the dock to meet Robert, but Bobby insisted on going. Mary and Armand also begged to go. Hannah agreed to look after the younger children.

The day was warm and sunny, fragrant with new growth. Wild red columbine and blue phlox lined the roadway as the horses trotted smartly along. The horizon was alive with the tender green of young maple leaves and blooming tulip trees here and there. The children were in a festive mood, and Zabette found herself smiling at their high spirits.

Their household had fared well during the winter months with the help of Hannah and John. But they were all looking forward to Robert's arrival, which would spur on the building of the new house. Only now that the spring planting was done on Cumberland and the snows had finally stopped blanketing Connecticut was he able to make the trip.

Zabette and the children took the ferry to New London to meet Robert's ship, while John waited on the Groton side of the river with the horses. Bobby and Armand squealed with delight as they saw their father coming down the gangway. Mary waved with somewhat more decorum. And Zabette smiled in welcome, though she was shocked to see how Robert's hair had grayed during the winter months. He raised his arms in greeting, and the children gathered around him to help carry his luggage to the ferry. "Welcome back, Mr. Stafford," Zabette greeted him as she always did in public and picked up one of the small bundles.

The very first thing Robert wanted to do upon his arrival back at the Shennecossett Neck farm was to take the entire family out to the construction site where the new house was already taking shape. He preferred to drive the rig himself, leaving John behind, which gave them privacy and more room for all the children.

As the carriage approached the site, they could see the framework of the new house looming on the brow of the hill. It would not be as tall as Dungeness to be sure, but it would definitely qualify as a mansion, and it would certainly be the grandest house they had ever owned and one of the finest in Groton. The panoramic view from the bluff always took Zabette's breath away, and she could see all the way to the mouth of the Thames River where it emptied seamlessly into Long Island Sound. Blue forget-me-nots and yellow dog-toothed violets grew in profusion against the early green of the hillside, along with other wildflowers whose name Zabette did not know.

Robert seemed pleased with the progress at the worksite. The contractor had followed his plans and specifications with great care, and Belton Copp had overseen the quality of the materials.

The children climbed like delighted monkeys through the uprights and peered through imaginary windows, already framed into their locations. Mary sat on the framed window in her chosen room overlooking the river.

"I'll put my bed here," Armand indicated a spot beside the window of another second-story room where he could see the river.

"And mine will be here," shouted Bobby, pointing to the center of his room. Ellen and Addie, who wanted to share a room, laid claim to one across the hall. Zabette held little Dora in a seated position so that she could watch her brothers and sisters and chortle with pleasure at their shenanigans.

ROBERT DROVE OUT TO THE SITE DAILY throughout the summer, sometimes alone, sometimes with the family in tow, reviewing what had been done during the past twenty-four hours and demanding any modifications his racing imagination had conceived. Once he even brought John and Hannah out to take a look at the arrangement of the kitchen area, with servants' quarters on the floor above. Hannah would live there, along with any other female servants, he told them. John would have a room above the stable.

THE SUMMER PASSED QUICKLY, and by early August the outside of the house was complete. Even the square widow's walk Mary had requested perched like a bird house above the structure's low-pitched roof with overhanging eaves that shaded tiny round windows just below. Thin double columns supported the roof of the wide porch, which wrapped around three sides of the house, providing the perfect spot for Zabette to hang ferns in summer. Standing grandly on the highest point of the bluff overlooking the river, the house stood tall and naked without the trees, bushes, and grass that were to come, but one could already imagine its future splendor.

Crews of carpenters hammered and sanded the stairwell and moldings; plasterers were smoothing wall surfaces as stonemasons put finishing touches on the magnificent fireplaces. Mr. Arthur promised that the house would be ready for occupancy before September when Robert planned to return to Cumberland for the cotton harvest.

STAFFORD HOUSE, GROTON, CONNECTICUT, Saturday, March 8, 1856
Even living in the new house did not make the winters pleasant for Zabette.

"Not another weekend with snow," she moaned, when she came down to breakfast and looked past the lace curtains of the elegant dining room at the six inches of snow that had piled up on the bluff during the night.

"You are always complaining about the snow here," sixteen-year-old Mary, home for the weekend from school, chided her mother. "Can't you ever get used to it?" she asked with annoyance.

"I don't know," Zabette replied. "It seems as though it will never end. I so miss the Cumberland springtime." She sighed at the thought of the sweet early spring when watermelon-colored azaleas burst into bloom and gardenias scented the garden. She missed the brisk winters and even the autumn storms.

"Cumberland again? Mosquitoes, gnats, heat, and humidity. That's all I remember. Maybe the winters were pleasant, but summers were awful," Mary said, an edge of sarcasm in her voice.

Zabette was used to it. As Mary reached adolescence, she had become increasingly intolerant of her mother. She did not have the impertinence or the nerve to call her "Zabette," at least not to her face, but she rarely called her "*Maman*" anymore. And she never introduced her to her friends, if she could help it, except to say, should they inquire, "That's my brothers' and sisters' nursemaid." Never her own.

Mary's body had developed small breasts and curved hips, and her raised eyebrows and haughty tilted chin seemed to have become a permanent affectation, mirroring the proud airs of her affluent friends. Throughout the winter she had written to her father begging him to let her go to Wheaton Female Seminary in Norton, Massachusetts, in the fall. Some of her best friends were going there, she told him, which was enough to make Wheaton the most desirable place on earth.

"I agree with *Maman*," announced Armand. "I'd like to go back to Cumberland too." He had grown taller and more gangly as he approached his thirteenth birthday, but Zabette could already see, in spite of his awkwardness, that he was going to be a handsome man when he grew up. He reminded her a little of her brother Jack.

"Oh, Armand, you always agree with her. Can't you learn to be more independent?" asked Mary.

"Like you, you mean? You're not independent. You're just a copy-cat of all those silly girls you like so much."

"And you're impossible," Mary loftily chided her younger brother. "May I be excused?" she asked. "I've already had breakfast with Addie and Ellen." Zabette, who had come down later than usual, sensed an unspoken rebuke on her daughter's part. She had been up much of the night with little Dora, who had the croup, and she had overslept this morning.

"You may," she sighed. It was good having the children home from school during the weekend, but Mary's presence of late had increased tensions in the household. Robert had already confided to Zabette that he was strongly disposed to let Mary go to Wheaton in the fall, but he wanted to be the one to tell her when he came for the summer.

THEIR LIVES HAD CHANGED CONSIDERABLY since they'd moved into Stafford House. The townspeople in Groton now viewed the children as wealthy southerners with their own mansion and resident nursemaid. Whenever Zabette placed an order with local merchants, deliveries were always prompt, as were the payments made by Belton Copp. The children, at least those old enough to understand the changes, had become quite comfortable with their new station in life—especially Mary, who loved to invite her northern friends for visits. The young people who arrived in droves were impressed with the staff of Irish servants that Robert kept at Stafford House—not just Hannah and John, but also the recently hired Caitlin, the perky laundress and upstairs maid, and quiet Bernadette, the downstairs maid. The women all lived in servants' rooms above the kitchen, and John enjoyed his room over the stable. Zabette's "duties" as nursemaid required her to have a room on the second floor of the house near the children.

Robert had decided not to cultivate the land with any type of crop, with the exception of two small orchards, one apple and the other planted, at Zabette's request, with plum trees. It was the one thing that each spring reminded her of home. The sweet fragrance of their blossoms brought back the most joyous memories of her childhood and especially of her mother.

ZABETTE MADE AN EFFORT TO TEACH ALL HER CHILDREN as much French as they were willing to learn. She knew that here in the north it was considered quite an accomplishment for young ladies to speak French. Addie and Ellen, in particular, who had heard the language at their great-grandmother's house, were like little sponges and repeated everything she said to perfection. They thought it a delightful game, and Mary understood that at least a smattering of French was an expected social grace. Zabette's French was not as cultured as her grandmother's had been, and she had little understanding of grammar. But she spoke fluently, if not always perfectly.

Betsey Copp, during one of her occasional winter visits, told Zabette in confidence over tea that the mother of one of Mary's friends had contacted her "to inquire about Mary's 'nursemaid,' the pretty one from France," she said with a chuckle.

"She was hoping to find an acceptable wage that might attract you away from the Stafford household. So their daughters could learn French."

"What did you tell her?"

"Oh," she laughed again. "I told her that I doubted there was a wage high enough to take you away from the Stafford children . . . that you had been with them since birth and loved them as your own."

"Betsey, how naughty you are!" But she could not help laughing at the cleverness of her friend's truthful response. "Does no one suspect that I am really their mother?" Zabette asked earnestly.

"No one so far as I know. They just think that Robert Stafford is very lucky to have you looking after the children. They know that he's a southern slave owner, but I don't think anyone even connects you with that awful system of slavery."

"Do you think it will ever end, Betsey? Robert thinks so. In fact, it seems that he's already begun to transfer some of his assets up north."

"That's probably smart, but who knows? It could go on forever." Betsey frowned thoughtfully. "Zabette," she asked. "I hope you won't think me rude or impertinent, but we've never talked about your past before. What was it like there?"

Zabette was silent for a long time before she answered. "So much depended on the master," she said, a distant look in her eye as she remembered. "I've been luckier than most."

"Have you ever seen a slave whipped? I've heard so many abolitionists talk about brutality on the plantations."

"Once," Zabette responded truthfully, "when I was a little girl. It was terrible."

"I've heard that slave owners sometimes separate families and even sell children away from their parents. How could anyone be so cruel?"

"So cruel as to separate parents from children?" Zabette asked dryly.

"Oh, Zabette, I'm sorry. I'd forgotten how painful it had been for you when Robert sent Mary and the boys to Connecticut." Betsey touched her hand in sympathy. Zabette was grateful for the gesture and for Betsey's friendship.

Betsey was eleven years older than Zabette and had taken the younger woman under her wing and treated her almost like a daughter or a sister. Zabette had never had an adult friend like her before, with whom she felt so free to talk about her feelings and her thoughts. There had been Amanda, of course, whom she loved dearly, but even between the two of them, there were things she felt she could never openly discuss.

"At least I knew I might see them again someday," she said quietly. "But my own mother, when she was in her teens, was sold away from her mother. And I was separated from my mother when I was four."

"How terrible!" Betsey said, touching her arm. "I just can't understand how anyone can presume to own another person."

"You mean like me?" Zabette asked.

"You don't seem like a slave. You live in a mansion and run the household. Robert loves you and would have married you if it hadn't been against the laws of Georgia. I'm sure of it. And you come and go at will."

"Do I?"

"Well, I suppose you do need Robert's permission. But then, most wives also need their husband's permission to do much of anything at all. Most of us don't own property, at least not while our husbands are alive. We're kept in virtual ignorance of men's financial affairs. Our bodies are at their command, and a lot of men even beat their wives . . . not mine, thank God," she hastened to add. "But I know of some who do, and there's not much the women can do about it. Being a wife is in itself a type of bondage," she paused to think about what she had just said. "Good heavens," she laughed. "I wonder why any of us ever get married."

"Perhaps it's because women are powerless otherwise, with many responsibilities, but few rights," Zabette suggested. "At least with a husband you know you'll be taken care of."

"At least you hope so," Betsey added. She had always been impressed with Zabette's intelligence. "Don't misunderstand me. I'm very happy with Belton, and he treats me well. But all women aren't so lucky."

Zabette nodded, thinking of her own situation.

"Have you ever read the writings of Margaret Fuller?" Zabette had never heard of her, but Betsey continued. "She has written things that make so much sense. I have one sentence I copied and keep with me all the time."

She opened her little drawstring purse and pulled out a piece of paper from an inside pocket. "Listen to what she says about a woman thinking of marriage:

'In order that she may be able to give her hand with dignity, she must be able to stand alone.' She believed in the equality of men and women. And she hated slavery too, like all the Transcendentalists."

"What are Transcendentalists?" asked Zabette.

Betsey was disconcerted by her question, "I think it has something to do with their ideas about religion. But the most interesting thing about them, I think, is their social ideal. They are a group of people from New England, mostly abolitionists and enthusiasts for women's rights. They believe that men and women are equal and should have equal rights. I'm not sure Belton approves of their writings, but I read them anyway. It's my little rebellion. Shall I lend you some of my books?"

"I would love to read them," Zabette answered. She loved the fact that Betsey shared her thoughts, which Zabette thought quite profound. She had never had a female friend who talked with her about such ideas before. She was certain that such notions as equality between men and women would not be well received in Georgia, but the very idea excited her. Perhaps Mary would be exposed to these same ideas at Wheaton. It might give them something to talk about.

Throughout the rest of the winter Zabette pored over Betsey's books, which contained the writings of people like Margaret Fuller and Julia Ward Howe. She read slowly at first, trying to absorb the new ideas. Betsey helped her to understand the passages that were too difficult for her, and she felt her mind opening to a new world. She had no idea that people thought like that, especially women. When Robert returned in the summer, she put the books away, hoping to savor them again after he went back to Cumberland. In the meantime, it was exciting to know that life could hold other possibilities.

Chapter Thirty-Four

SEPTEMBER 1856

The house was calm after Mary left for Wheaton in September. Zabette missed her, even though they had not gotten along well since Mary turned fourteen, but it was little Dora who suffered most from her absence, asking for her a dozen times a day. When she finally came home for Christmas, the child was elated, though Mary, now eighteen, was so busy with her friends that she had little time for her baby sister.

Mary brought home with her from Wheaton not so much the new ideas Zabette was exploring but rather the latest notions about how people of their social station should entertain, and she was determined to try them all. As usual when Mary was home, a parade of visitors passed through the house, college students who arrived with their musical instruments, their card games of Whist and Bezique, and their board games of Backgammon and the Mansion of Happiness. Their laughter echoed through the large rooms of the house during the afternoons and well into the evenings. They had long debates about poetry and art, and prided themselves on being up-to-date on the most recent trends and movements. Ellen and Addie, old enough to observe but not participate, were dazzled by the older girls in taffeta and silk dresses, a few in ordinary skirts, but others already wearing the new cage crinolines, called hoop skirts in the South. Mary's dresses were still for the most part tight-sleeved and somber-colored, as her father thought fit, but she coveted the newer fashions the other girls wore, dresses in bright colors like magenta and mauveine, with puffed sleeves and necklines that could be pulled to the very edge of the shoulders. The young people talked of everything from the current fashions in Paris to the romantic poets of England and the symbolists in France. They were certain they must be the most daring generation that ever lived.

Zabette chaperoned, listened, and even learned from these lively conversations, though she never joined in. Her role consisted in making sure the visitors were well fed and provided with cider and hot tea at given hours. Mary did not ask her permission or apologize for any of the inconvenience she and her new friends caused. But Zabette was pleased to see her enjoying herself.

Armand and Robert, now fourteen and fifteen, were intrigued by these young people who had been away from home and believed themselves so knowledgeable. Sometimes Mary allowed the boys to hang around. At other times she found them a nuisance and told them to go to their rooms. More often than not, they went only as far as the top of the stairs, where they peered through the banister and listened.

DESPITE MARY'S OBVIOUS ENJOYMENT of Wheaton and her friends there, Robert decided after two years that he would not send her back the following fall. He didn't like some of the ideas she was being exposed to, and he thought that she already had quite enough education. Mary took her resentment out on Zabette, but she was determined, nonetheless, to keep up with her social life. She began to pay regular visits to one of her friends in East Haddam, a town about thirty miles away on the Connecticut River. Zabette suspected that the real attraction in East Haddam was a young man she'd met during one of her visits there, but she did not worry, for she made certain that her daughter was well chaperoned. And, she even found Mary's frequent absences rather restful.

AFTERNOON LIGHT FILTERED THROUGH THE LACE CURTAINS and fell across the parlor rug as Zabette read aloud to Dora and Addie, who were settled on either side of her. A sharp tap on the front door interrupted her story. Caitlin rushed to answer it, and Zabette heard the familiar voice of Betsey Copp's coachman, Philip, speaking in low tones. Then a moan from Caitlin, "Oh, no," she said. "Best y' tell her yerself."

Zabette slipped out from between the children and went to the door.

"Hello, Philip, is Mrs. Copp with you?" she asked.

"No," he replied, his broad face reddened by the sun and the wind, holding his hat in his hand. "She sent me to tell you the sad news."

"What sad news?" she asked, her brow furrowed.

"About Mr. Copp," he said reluctantly, as though not to say it would make it not true.

"What's wrong, Philip, is he ill?"

"He passed away last night, Miss Zabette."

"Good heavens." Zabette could not have been more shocked by his words. The last time she had seen Belton Copp he appeared to be in perfect health. "Please, Philip, come inside and tell me what in the world happened."

The heavy man stepped across the threshold, but refused to go any farther.

"Heart attack, we think. He came home from the bank earlier than usual, said he didn't feel well. Mrs. Copp put him to bed and called the doctor, but there wasn't anything he could do. By the time he got there, Mr. Copp, well . . . he was gone."

"Oh, how dreadful," Zabette said, wringing her hands. "And how is Mrs. Copp holding up?"

"She's been very strong. But I know she's quite upset."

"I should go to her right away."

"Miss Zabette, she wanted you to know, but she said to tell you not to come. Not yet. There are already lots of people there, family mostly, and she said she would need you more later. She thought you needed to stay here with the children."

"Tell her I'll come anytime she needs me. Anytime at all. Do you have time to wait for me to write her a little note?"

"Yes, of course. I'll wait."

"Caitlin, take Philip back to the kitchen and ask Hannah to fix him a cup of tea. I won't be long."

As she wrote Betsey a brief note of sympathy, she was acutely conscious of her poor spelling and her crude handwriting. She'd never had any formal education, only what she had learned from her grandmother. Betsey would understand, of course. But nonetheless, she wished she could express herself with greater accuracy, especially on such an occasion.

After Philip had left, her brief note of sympathy in hand, she sat down to write once more:

> *Dear Robert:*
>
> *Your good friend here in Groton, Belton Copp, died yesterday afternoon of a sudden hart attack. His wife Betsey is hartbroken, but holding up well, I am told. I wish you could be here to comfort her. I do not know how any of us will manage without him. The children are well, except for Armand, who catches every cold and coff that comes his way. I remain,*
>
> > *Your faithful,*
> > *Elisabeth Bernardey*

What would happen now? It was Belton who paid the wages of the servants and who settled all the accounts. She wished Robert were here to advise her or that she were free to make the decisions, but of course she had no money. Her heart went out to Betsey and her children. She knew they were grief-stricken. And by her own admission, Betsey had not much more knowledge of the financial world than Zabette. Perhaps they would both have to learn. It suddenly dawned on her that she had not even asked Philip about funeral arrangements. She would have to send John to town to inquire. How would any of them manage?

Chapter Thirty-Five

NEW LONDON, CONNECTICUT, JUNE 27, 1858
"Uncle Robert," called Bobby, as he spotted his father on the gangway. He had almost called him "Papa" but had caught himself just in time.

Robert gave a quick wave to his son and to John, who were waiting on the docks. It was Sunday, and the New London wharf appeared quieter than usual, with only a few dockworkers, deck hands, and passengers scurrying about. He handed his valise to John and shook hands with Bobby, putting his arm briefly around the young man's shoulder in what for Robert passed as an affectionate embrace.

"You look fine, boy," he said. Robert beamed at his father's approval.

Robert had arrived earlier than usual, for much needed to be done in the wake of Belton Copp's death. He expected to spend several months in Connecticut taking care of business matters and looking for a new trustworthy and discreet attorney to handle his interests in Groton and New London. The man who replaced Belton as director at the bank was a lawyer named Augustus Brandegee, a Yale graduate and a legal partner in a firm called Lippitt and Brandegee. He had a good reputation, Stafford knew, and had been elected to the state's House of Representatives. But was he trustworthy and discreet enough for Stafford's purposes? That remained to be seen.

ROBERT SET UP A MEETING AT BRANDEGEE'S LAW OFFICE in New London on Wednesday morning at nine o'clock. A secretary ushered him into a well-appointed, wood-paneled office with large windows. Behind the desk sat a dapper-looking man in his early thirties, with frank gray-blue eyes, a neatly trimmed beard, and hair cut short and combed straight back from his high forehead. In a charcoal-colored three-piece suit, white shirt with a high collar, and necktie neatly knotted at his throat, he stood up and held out his hand in welcome.

"Augustus Brandegee, Mr. Stafford," he said. "Please have a seat." He gestured toward a tweed-upholstered Queen Anne chair that faced his desk.

Robert liked him instinctively. He was younger than Belton, less experienced obviously, but he looked solid. Robert prided himself on his good instinct for character.

"I appreciate your seeing me on such short notice," said Robert, "but I have business that won't wait."

"I'm delighted you're here," responded Brandegee smoothly. "I know you by reputation. Belton Copp thought highly of you."

"Not everyone shared his opinion," Robert said dryly. "Belton and I had been friends for a long time. We knew each other as boys. He handled a lot of rather sensitive matters for me, and I'm looking for someone I can trust as I trusted him."

"No one can replace one's lifelong friends, Mr. Stafford, but I can guarantee you my integrity to handle any matters you may have with discretion and honesty."

"Of course. Your honesty is a given or I wouldn't be here. It's mainly the discretion I'm looking for," Robert said candidly. "How much do you know about me?"

Brandegee looked at him steadily. "I know that you're from the South, that you own slaves, and that you have a household of nieces and nephews here in Connecticut that is overseen primarily by their governess, a mulatto woman, if my facts are correct."

"Your facts are absolutely all I would expect you to know at this juncture. But if we can do business together, you will eventually need to understand my situation in much greater depth. What are your feelings about slavery, Mr. Brandegee?"

"I must confess that I am deeply opposed to the owning of slaves, Mr. Stafford, and I would be unable to handle any business for you that involved buying or selling slaves. I would be willing, on the other hand, to help you free any slaves that you might own. But somehow I don't think you're here for that reason."

"I appreciate your candor." said Robert. "I wouldn't think of asking you to handle any matters that might compromise your stand on slavery. And to be perfectly frank, I think the whole institution would come to an end if we in the South didn't rely so much on crops like cotton and rice. I don't like owning slaves. They're a damned nuisance, and I would be perfectly happy to free them all if there were any other way to handle my crops."

"Well, be that as it may," Brandegee leaned forward, "that isn't what you've come here to discuss with me, is it?"

Robert leaned forward as well. He liked the young man's straightforward manner, but Robert was a cautious man, not yet fully ready to trust his affairs to the lawyer facing him across the desk. There were things he needed to know before he made a final judgment. "I must have your word that anything we discuss will not leave this office."

"You have my word, Mr. Stafford," Brandegee answered.

"The woman you called the 'governess' of my children is really their mother. Legally she is my slave, but she has never been treated as one. Her father was a white man, a planter at Cumberland Island in Georgia, and she was raised by her grandmother, a fine woman from France. She's dead now."

"I see," said Brandegee.

"And the next and most important thing for you to know is that I am the father of the children."

Brandegee said nothing and showed no surprise. He waited for Robert to go on.

"I set up trusts for each of them with Belton Copp, who was the administrator. I never want my children to return to the South, where their legal status because of their mother would make them slaves. I want them to live well here in Connecticut. You might say that I am freeing them under the table."

"And their mother?"

"I would like her to live with me, but I won't force her, and at the present time she has chosen the children over me. I visit for as long as I can during the months when I am able to leave Georgia, but I always stay at my City Hotel here in New London. It's damned inconvenient, but it's necessary for the reputation and welfare of the children. In the eyes of the world, I am their uncle, and they are orphans."

"I see."

"And that's how I want to keep it. You need to know the truth, of course, so that you can understand the legal implications. I thought of you as the next administrator because you took over Belton's position as director at the Bank where the trust funds are kept. Given my conditions for secrecy, are you willing to take on the administration of the trusts?"

"May I ask a question or two before I answer, Mr. Stafford?"

"Of course."

"Do you have a wife in Georgia?"

Robert looked Brandegee directly in the eye. "I have no legal wife."

"Good, because I don't handle cases where adultery is involved."

Robert nodded. "I understand."

"And why did you not marry the children's mother?"

"Because it is against the laws of Georgia. I would have if I could have done so legally, even though I'm thirty years older than she is."

"Why have you not married her here?"

"That's a fair question. But I think you already know the answer. How can I when we already have six children together? It would raise too many questions. Zabette and I are satisfied with the relationship as it stands."

"Are you sure?" asked Brandegee.

Again Robert paused. To be perfectly frank, he had never thought to wonder whether Zabette might be satisfied or not. But it was too late to worry about that now. He was too old at almost sixty-eight to begin thinking about such a tomfool thing as marriage. "I'm sure enough," he answered.

"Mr. Stafford, is there a trust fund for the woman in question or just for the children?"

Robert had never thought about setting up a trust fund for Zabette. He assumed that when he died she would live with the children. But what if that didn't work out?

"That's a matter we may need to consider at some future date, Mr. Brandegee, after we've worked together for a while. At the present time, the answer is no."

"My final question is this: Are you fully satisfied that you want to move the trusts into my care?" Brandegee asked frankly.

"I'm satisfied."

"Well, then," said Augustus Brandegee, pulling out a ledger and raising his pen from its holder on his desk, "Let's get down to business."

STAFFORD HOUSE, GROTON, CONNECTICUT, JULY 5, 1858

Summer was passing all too quickly. One Saturday afternoon in July, a carriage appeared unexpectedly in the driveway of Stafford House. It was a small rig pulled by two horses that looked thirsty and tired. Robert and Zabette were sitting on the front porch of the house, while the children played a noisy game of croquet. The older children were managing quite well, and Mary was helping Dora handle her mallet. Robert sat in a rocking chair on the porch, sipping lemonade and peering through his new gold-rimmed spectacles, attached to his vest by a heavy gold chain, reading the New London *Daily Chronicle*, while Zabette mended the children's socks, which were always full of holes.

When the carriage stopped, Robert stood up to greet the driver—a young nervous-looking man whom Robert had never seen before.

"Good afternoon, young fellow, what can we do for you?" he said affably, as the young man jumped down from the carriage seat and strode toward the front steps. Although he was at least six feet tall, Robert was taller by several inches. He always stood erect, believing his posture to convey an attitude of firmness and authority, which it inevitably did.

Mary recognized the carriage in the driveway and abandoned Dora to greet her friend. Zabette got up and moved to the yard to help her youngest with the mallet, which was much too big for her to manage alone.

The visitor couldn't have been more than twenty years old. He was thin and blond, with shy-looking blue eyes, and he held out his hand awkwardly to Robert. "How do you do, sir, I'm Frederick Palmer. My family lives in Norwich, though they're originally from East Haddam. I'm a friend of Mary.

We met when she was a student at Wheaton." The words came pouring out, and they sounded rehearsed.

By this time Mary was beside her father, smiling down from the porch at the young man standing on the front steps. John had come from the stable to take charge of the horses.

"I trust you'll be staying for tea," Mr. Stafford said.

"Thank you, sir, I'd like that."

"John," Robert said to his stable man, "take Mr. Palmer's horses for some water and hay, and tell Hannah that we'll be having a guest for tea."

Robert gestured for Frederick Palmer to sit down in the chair Zabette had vacated. Mary moved to the porch swing and perched nervously on the front edge.

"Well, now, it's nice to meet a friend of Mary's," Robert said. The name of Frederick Palmer was already familiar to him, thanks to Mary's constant chatter about her friends, and he recalled having heard this name a bit more than some of the others. Zabette recognized him as one of the young men at the young people's Christmas celebration. She had thought him nice enough and quite animated, particularly when he talked with Mary.

The three chatted for a while, as Zabette and the children finished the game of croquet. Hannah brought out the tea tray, and Mary took over the role of hostess to pour tea and pass out the cucumber sandwiches and lemon cookies Hannah had made. Zabette settled at the other end of the porch to assist the three youngest girls with their plates and saucers. Mary seemed to be managing well enough, with hardly a clink of the teacups. The boys took their tea standing, leaning against the porch banister, trying to look manly.

Frederick made an effort to be sociable with the two boys, asking them about school and their friends. But they had little to say in response. Trying to be a good hostess and divert attention away from her boorish brothers, Mary began to chat about their mutual friends in Groton and New London. After they were done with their tea and Hannah had cleared the table, the young man, elbows braced on the arms of the chair, leaned toward Robert and said, "Sir, if I might, I'd like to have a word with you alone."

Robert nodded, and Zabette began to herd the children inside. Mary hesitated, then followed them in through the front entrance.

Urging the children to go upstairs, Mary paused behind the lace curtain of the parlor, where she could hear what was being said through the open window without being seen. Once the younger children were settled in their rooms, Zabette went back downstairs and stood behind Mary to listen.

"I have a good job, sir, and I can support her. I come from a good family. And I thought that I should talk with you first, as Mary's guardian," young Palmer was saying.

Mary was waiting tensely for her father's reply and had evidently known in advance the purpose of Frederick's trip. Robert didn't say anything for a very long time. Through the screen of lace, the two women could see him staring off into the distance. Palmer shifted uncomfortably in his chair. "Sir?" he reminded Robert of his presence.

Finally Robert turned to him and said, "Son, I have no objection to your asking my niece for her hand. If she's willing, there's something you must know. I don't want your marriage to begin without complete candor between you."

Mary stiffened visibly, and Zabette heard her whisper, "Oh, no," ever so softly. Tears were welling up in her daughter's eyes, and she laid her hand on Mary's shoulder.

"Yes sir?" the young man waited expectantly.

"Son, Mary has Creole blood. Her mother was a quadroon." It was the closest he could come to the full truth without humiliating his daughter, should the young man change his mind. If he didn't, Robert would tell him later the full truth about her parentage. But not yet. Not until he had a chance to judge the young man's character and disposition.

Mary waited, breathless, for Frederick's reply. He laughed lightly, "Sir, I think in my family that would be viewed as rather exotic. My father's always saying we need some new blood in the Palmer veins."

"I'm not sure that's what he has in mind, young man."

"My family already loves Mary, sir. They know why I'm here today."

"Well, I'll leave it up to you to tell them or not, as you see fit. But I wanted you to know so that nothing is secret between the two of you."

"May I . . . may I ask Mary for her hand then?"

"Why do I get the feeling that you have already taken that step, provided I give my permission?" he asked. "Of course you may. I'll get her. I doubt that she's gone far."

Mary met her father in the doorway to the parlor and hugged her thanks. She turned quickly and without a backward glance at her mother, rushed out onto the porch where her husband-to-be waited.

THE YOUNG COUPLE DECIDED TO DELAY THEIR WEDDING until the following June, when Robert Stafford would return to Groton after the spring planting. The prospect of marriage seemed to Zabette to have improved her oldest daughter's disposition immensely. She appeared more eager to hear the domestic suggestions Zabette had to offer and to ask questions about children and the household. Mary had also paid more attention to the Thanksgiving menu and place settings than she had ever done before. In fact, for Zabette, she was a joy for the first time in many years.

Betsey Copp throughout the fall made weekly trips to Stafford House, and Zabette always welcomed her with warmth and sympathy. Betsey had told her after the first visit how much she appreciated Zabette's letting her talk about Belton.

"So many people are embarrassed when I speak of him," she said to Zabette. "But I so want to talk about him and about our life together. I find it a great comfort."

"People are often uncomfortable with the grief of others," said Zabette.

"But not you. You let me talk. You let me cry. You help me to get it all outside somehow where I can deal with it. Thank you for being such a special friend, Zabette."

"You would do the same for me, Betsey," she said, hugging her friend.

"I hope so."

They sipped their tea and toasted their feet before the fire in the parlor grate as Betsey talked about her early days with Belton before the children came, and how things changed once the little ones began to arrive.

"But I guess they always do. I hope you're preparing Mary for all she has in store."

"I try, Betsey, as much as she'll let me."

"Oh, by the way, I brought some recent copies of the *New York Times*. Belton subscribed to it, and I'm still getting it. One of those Georgia islands of yours is much in the news." She opened a little sack and pulled out copies of newspapers for the last several days. "Have you heard of Jekyl Island?"

"I was born there," Zabette answered.

"Well, it seems that some of your Georgians have broken the law and brought in a shipload of more than four hundred Africans on a yacht called the *Wanderer*. It landed in late November on Jekyl Island."

"Oh good heavens," said Zabette, taking the paper she held out. "I hope this doesn't do anything to worsen northerners' feelings toward the South. There's already so much tension."

"It's certainly not going to help. People in the North are pretty upset about it. There's an arrogant Mr. Lamar involved, who contends that the law prohibiting importing Africans is unconstitutional."

"Oh, dear, why did it have to be in Georgia? And so close to Cumberland." Zabette thought about Robert and all her friends there. Although she knew they would not be involved in anything like this, she felt it brought shame to the South. "You'd think they already had enough slaves without bringing in more."

"And do you know how they justify it?" Betsey lifted her chin in indignation. "They say the Africans are savages, that they're bringing them to a Christian nation where they can be saved." The two women looked at each other in dismay, both fearful, from their very different perspectives, of the consequences.

ZABETTE THRIVED ON BETSEY'S VISITS. They filled the void that followed the excitement of Mary's wedding on the following June 23 during Robert's summer visit. Zabette had not been asked to attend the wedding, which was a quiet ceremony before a justice of the peace in the parlor of the groom's parents' home in Norwich. Now Mary was expecting her first child in late March.

When Zabette heard the carriage coming, she stepped outside. Betsey's Phaeton pulled up in a cloud of dust.

"I'm so glad you're here," Zabette greeted her. "I was just about to have tea all alone." Dora, at almost six, had started to school and the house was so empty with all the children gone. The two women went arm-in-arm into the parlor, where

Hannah had already laid out the tea, adding a second teacup for Mrs. Copp. There were always enough sandwiches and cakes for an extra guest or two. If they weren't eaten, Hannah, Caitlin, and Bernadette would enjoy them later in the kitchen.

"What do you hear from the little mother-to-be?" asked Betsey, as she took off her bonnet and cape.

"Not very much, I'm afraid. I assume Mary is doing well and she looks happy."

"But a first child can be a rather daunting experience," Betsey said.

Zabette urged her toward one of the two chairs in front of the fire, their favorite spot on cooler days. Between them sat the silver teapot, with two china teacups and saucers, an assortment of cakes, and both chicken curry and ground walnut sandwiches.

"Tell me all the news," Zabette said, as she poured the first cup. When Robert was not there, the newspaper did not come, and Zabette had come to depend on Betsey's weekly visits for news of the world outside.

"Not very good, I fear. Oh, Zabette, I'm so worried that we are coming closer and closer to war over this slavery business."

"Robert thinks so too. He has started to sell some of the slaves at Cumberland, he tells me. But he's promised to try to keep them on the island and not to split up families."

"I wish everyone would just free them and be done with it."

"It's not that simple, I'm afraid. Free people of color in Georgia have a hard time, I'm told. But tell me, what's happened?"

"You've heard of that abolitionist, John Brown? The one who started all that killing over slavery out in Kansas a few years ago?"

"I've heard of him," Zabette said. "Robert called him a 'damn fool' at the time it happened." She blushed at saying the word 'damn.' out loud. "Of course, to him anybody he doesn't happen to agree with is a 'damn fool.'"

"Well, a few nights ago he led a raid on a federal arsenal in Harper's Ferry in Virginia. Apparently he was trying to capture all the weapons and start a slave uprising."

"Good heavens," said Zabette. "I don't think that would help the slaves in the long run. Some whites in the South can be brutal." She thought of Amanda and all her friends back at Cumberland. Of the people who toiled in the fields from sun-up to dusk until they were too old and broken to do any work at all. She thought of her mother and brother Jack. What would happen to them in a war? She shuddered to imagine.

"What finally happened at . . . Harper's Ferry?" she asked Betsey.

"Well, the troops captured Brown and the other men, and it looks like they're going to be hanged."

"Do you think it can ever be settled peaceably?"

"A lot will depend on politics, I guess. We'll have a new president next year. Maybe he'll be someone who can help the country come together."

BUT THE COUNTRY DIDN'T COME TOGETHER. Zabette and Betsey followed the news anxiously. Lincoln's election in 1860 drove an even deeper wedge between the North and the South. Before the end of the year, South Carolina seceded from the Union, followed in quick succession in early 1861 by Mississippi, Florida, Alabama, Georgia, Louisiana, and Texas. Before dawn on April 12, Zabette learned from Betsey, troops of the newly formed Confederacy had fired on the federal Fort Sumter in Charleston. The war they feared had begun.

In retaliation for the attack on Fort Sumter, President Lincoln on April 19 ordered a naval blockade of the southern coast. It was an effort to strangle southern shipping, to keep Confederates from selling their cotton, and to prevent supplies from getting through.

When she learned of the blockade, Zabette sent word to Mr. Brandegee that she would like to have a daily newspaper sent to Stafford House. Except for Betsey's visits, she was cut off from all outside information, and events were happening so fast she didn't want to wait. He obliged promptly.

When the newspapers reported the evacuation of the coastal islands along South Carolina and Georgia, Zabette assumed that Robert had evacuated with everyone else and was safe somewhere in the interior of Georgia. She wondered about her mother and Jack. Mail from the South was not getting through on a regular basis, and she heard nothing from Robert. She worried about all those she knew at Cumberland—Margaret and Jamie, Daisy, Amanda, the women from the cotton house, and Adeline and her family Where were they? How were they living? Would she ever see them again?

The newspaper reported that there might be a conscription—a draft requiring young men to serve in the Union army. Her two sons were now seventeen and eighteen. What would happen to them? She worried less about Bobby because his slow ways might keep him out of service, but Armand? He would be eighteen in December, and he was eager to rid the world of slavery. He would want to serve, she knew, but would he have to? She hoped not, for he caught cold so easily, and she couldn't imagine him sleeping night after night in a tent on the damp ground.

Oh God, she thought, *war is so dreadful.* Yet as she sat in the parlor of Robert's Groton mansion, she doubted that she would experience the horrors of war to the extent of those on Cumberland. Of course anything could happen. If only there were news from Georgia.

Chapter Thirty-Six

CUMBERLAND ISLAND, PLANTERS HOUSE. MARCH 1862

Robert sat on the front porch at Planters House, watching five mounted Union troops, sun glinting off the metal of their rifles, ride up his driveway. Scouts, he surmised, sent by Admiral DuPont, who had set up headquarters at Dungeness. Robert had no doubt that the admiral chose it, as the British had in 1815, because it was the most comfortable place on the island.

Phineas Nightingale had finally managed to borrow sufficient funds to persuade his cousin Margaret to deed Dungeness back to him in return for his promise to provide her annuity on a regular basis. But he had not been staying there with his family at the outbreak of the war. Like most other Cumberland planters, he had fled inland at the first sign of conflict and the moment Lincoln had ordered the blockade. But Robert refused to run. Why should he? He had no fear of Union troops. He had as much interest in the North as in the South. And he had long expected this war was coming.

As tensions increased, he had begun to sell his slaves little by little. Where he had owned 348 men, women and children in 1850, by the time the war came, their number had been reduced to 110. Robert congratulated himself on his foresight. Nightingale on the other hand, Robert chuckled to remember, had gone the other direction. The thought of Nightingale's increased numbers of slaves being freed as contraband gave him particular satisfaction, especially since he still refused, even though he was living on borrowed money, to sell him Dungeness.

No doubt Admiral DuPont found it quite satisfactory as a headquarters. At this time of year, the gardens were lush with lilies, tea roses, and heliotropes. Stafford had heard that DuPont's men were astounded at such a place of grace and beauty in the South. Then one of officers explained: "Why, sir, the lady is a northern woman." *Fools,* he thought. Robert never ceased to be surprised how the North and the South misjudged each other. He had decided long ago not to choose between them, but to profit from both.

"Afternoon, sir." The Union officer in charge touched the bill of his cap in greeting.

"Afternoon, Lieutenant." Stafford stood at the top of the stone steps to greet his visitors. "What can I do for you?"

"We're reconnoitering the entire island to see how many residents are still here. Quite frankly, we're surprised to find you on the premises."

"Far as I know, I'm the only white person left on the island. Plenty of slaves still here, I reckon."

"They're no longer slaves, sir," said the young man, uncomfortably. "They're free now. Most of your fellow planters have moved inland, we understand."

"That's right," said Stafford, "but I'm a Union man. I have nothing to fear from you folks. In fact, I'm from New London, Connecticut, major stockholder in the Whaling Bank of New London."

"Is that right? I'm from Maine myself," said the lieutenant without a spark of interest, though Robert was speaking with his best Connecticut accent.

The lieutenant went on, "Do you think you're safe here from the people still roaming the island? I know some have fled to Fernandina, but a lot of them are still here."

"I'm quite safe. They won't harm me. I've always been a good master. You're probably in as much danger from them as I am," Stafford said with assurance.

"I don't know, sir."

At that moment, Amanda appeared with a pitcher of lemonade and enough glasses for all the soldiers in the small group. She refused to leave the island, preferring to remain in her own cook's cottage than to live in God-knows-what in Fernandina. But she had made it clear to Robert that, like the others, she figured that she could leave at any time. For now, however, she was used to Planters House, and she had decided to stay put.

"As you can see, gentlemen, I have the loyalty of my people. Won't you join me in a glass of lemonade on this warm afternoon?"

With a nod from the lieutenant, the soldiers dismounted and each in turn climbed up to the veranda to accept a glass of the lemonade Amanda was pouring.

"How is it that your people haven't run off like all the others?" asked the lieutenant, who was so young that Robert peered at him through his glasses, trying to determine whether the bare-faced young man had ever had any need to shave.

"Oh," said Robert. "A lot of them have. Some of the young bucks in particular. They've been slipping away a few at a time. I've made no effort to stop them. But some of them stayed on to help me bring in the cotton crop. I guess they just didn't have any place to go. Or maybe it was the tales coming back from Fernandina of how your troops were treating them."

The lieutenant ignored his remark. "We have orders to escort any people who want to leave the island to Fernandina—black and white alike. I'm not sure you should stay here, sir. You're at their mercy, you know. And a lot of rough characters are roaming about."

"I've always treated my people well. They've had plenty to eat, plenty to wear, and freedom to move about the island as they needed to. I even built them a church and a hospital. Why would they want to turn on me now? We never whipped the slaves. Not unless one got completely out of control. No, lieutenant, I've been a pretty good master, all things considered." Amanda tensed her jaw at his words but continued to pour the lemonade.

"That's what I've heard a lot of southern slave-owners say, sir, but their former slaves don't always agree."

"Well, mine do," said Robert firmly. "What else are you men looking for?"

"Our orders are to find food supplies on the island."

"Well, I have plenty of cattle and hogs to sell if you're looking for meat." Robert had ordered the slaves who remained in the quarters to round up the stray cattle and pigs left behind when other planters went inland. He figured they were his now, since they were confined in his pastures and pens. If he could sell some of them for food to the Union army, he could recoup some of the losses on his runaway slaves and have fewer livestock to care for.

"I can requisition them and give you a receipt, but I have no funds for actual payment. You'll be reimbursed by the federal treasury."

"Indeed? Don't guess I have much choice in the matter, do I?"

"No sir, I guess not," replied the young lieutenant.

"Well, then, get your troops to round up whatever you need. I guess I'll just have to trust the government, which is more than most do around here."

"Yes sir," said the officer.

In the end the Union troops rounded up a good many of Robert's cattle, horses, and hogs, along with some of the corn and potatoes he had stored. They left him with a requisition and a receipt, but who knew whether he'd ever collect? It was, in fact, a relief to get rid of some of the animals, and he didn't need as much corn and potatoes now that so many of the mouths he had to feed had run away. He would have done the same for any Confederate troops who showed up at his door. He intended to survive this war any way he could, but he would never give up his land and he had no intention of leaving.

CUMBERLAND ISLAND, PLANTERS HOUSE, AUGUST 31, 1862

At the end of August, Robert's world changed again. This time from the parlor window he saw coming down his driveway not Union troops, but armed black men, eleven of them, yelling at each other and waving guns about. He took a pistol from his desk drawer and stuffed it into his waistband before stepping out onto the veranda.

Drawing himself up to what remained of his six feet and three inches in an effort to intimidate them, he asked gruffly, "What are you boys doing here?"

It was the first time field hands, as these rough men appeared to be, had ever come in such a way to his front door.

"We got permission from that Yankee colonel over in Fernandina, Colonel Rich, he call hisself, to hunt on this island, and we needs a place to stay while we here," said the man in front, a tall, husky dark-skinned man in his forties. He too was standing as tall as he could, well over six feet, though he was compelled to look up at Robert who stood at the top of the steps.

It seemed to Robert a reasonable request under the circumstances, and he began to relax. "Well, there are some abandoned cabins in the quarters you could use. Just don't bother the folks who still live out there."

"Yeh," the man said. "We done look at them cabins. But they kind of small. We like this house better." The man turned back to grin at the others, and the group of men all nodded and said things like "Yessuh, tha's right. We like yo' place. It's plenty big."

"This is my home," said Robert firmly. "You can't stay here."

"Well, now, Massa, what you gone do 'bout it if'n we don't agree?" the man asked, with an unpleasant edge to his voice. "Seems like we be the massas now, don't it?" The man moved menacingly up the steps, his gun pointed at Robert, "Now let's go inside and look around."

Robert reached for his pistol, but the younger and quicker man, who had reached the top of the steps, grabbed his arm, twisted it behind him, and took the pistol from his waistband.

"Well, looky here. You wadn't gone shoot us now, was you, Massa?" the man said, tightening his hold on the old man's arm.

For the first time in his life, at seventy-two, Robert felt completely helpless. At least six guns were pointed at him, and he had no idea who the men were or what they were capable of. There was no way he could overcome the group's leader physically, and even if he could, there were all the others backing him up. He had no choice but to allow the men to push their way into the front parlor.

Amanda met them, coming from the direction of the dining room, a heavy wooden spoon in her hand, which she waved about like a weapon. "What y'all doin' here. Git on outta here. Go on now," she tried to shoo the men back out the door. But they weren't budging.

"You a sassy thing," one of the men said, "and I'm shore scairt by that big old wood spoon." The men all laughed.

Suddenly, the laughter ceased as they sensed a movement on the stairs. There stood an attractive, well-dressed black woman in her early forties, her arms outstretched to protect two lighter skinned girls, about eight and ten years old, hiding behind her back.

"Well now," said the man in charge. "What we got here?" He looked at Stafford with false admiration. "Ole boy still got a little get up 'n go, I reckon."

The other men were guffawing in the background. One of them teased, "C'mon down here, girl, and gi' me some sugar."

The woman took one step backward.

"Judy, take the girls upstairs," said Robert in a voice as commanding as he could muster.

"Yo' name Judy?" asked one of the men. "And what these girls here called?"

"You leave them alone," said Stafford.

"Yeh, I know Judy," another man said. "I seen 'er up there at Rayfield. These gals her daughters, I reckon. They be Cornelia and Nannie. And from the looks of 'em, I'd say they pappy be Massa Stafford here."

Robert stood rigid, despite his humiliation, as the men slapped him jovially on the back, grinning suggestively. "Yep," one of them joked, "The ole boy still got it, I reckon."

"You men get on out of here. You can stay in the quarters," Robert tried again.

"Well now," said the tallest of the group, "I don't reckon you is the one who give the orders 'round here no more." He waved Robert's own gun deliberately in his face.

Robert recognized none of the men. They were not from his plantations, but from their comments, he gathered that at least some of them had lived on Cumberland.

By this time several of the men were sprawled on the sofa and in the chairs of the parlor. The leader of the group said, "Wha's yo' name, gal?" He was looking at Amanda.

She clamped her mouth shut, shrugged a haughty shoulder, and turned to go back toward the kitchen.

"Cat got yo' tongue?" he asked, grabbing her arm and lifting the hem of her skirt with the end of his rifle.

"You don't scare me none, you trashy men. You git on outta here. Didn't yo' mamas teach you no manners?" Amanda said angrily, snatching her skirt from the barrel of the gun.

"Now listen here, gal," the man said, "We in charge here, and we hungry. You git on out to that kitchen and make us some food. George," he gestured to a younger man plopped down in one of the parlor chairs. "You go out an' keep her comp'ny."

"I don't reckon I needs yo' comp'ny," she fumed.

"Well, you got it anyway, honey," the younger man said as he pushed her through the dining room door toward the kitchen.

"Now we ain't gone hurt y'all none, if you does like we say," the leader said to Judy and the two girls on the stairwell. "Y'all hear me," he said over his shoulder to the men. "Ain't nobody here gone hurt these gals. Now, I mean it."

He turned to Stafford, "Now what you got to drink here, man?" He was eyeing the liquor cabinet beside the fireplace. Another of the men got up and opened the cabinet, took out a bottle, uncorked it, and drank a slug of the brandy inside.

"Whooeee," he said, rubbing his mouth with the back of his hand. "Don't know what this is, but it sho' taste good." He passed the bottle on to the next man.

Within an hour the men had polished off two bottles of brandy and a bottle of sherry that Robert had in the cabinet. The men were clearly enjoying their position of superiority over the former slave master. Robert had no idea what to expect from them, but the fear within him grew with every swallow of liquor the men drank.

THE MEN TOOK OVER ALL THE BEDROOMS in the house and the parlor sofa, leaving Robert, the women, and the children to sleep on the floor or share Amanda's cabin, which Judy and her daughters chose to do. When the men were finally all asleep, even the one they had left to guard him, Robert sat at the dining room table to write a letter to Colonel Rich, the commander of the Union troops at Fort Clinch at Fernandina, pleading for help. Whether he could get anyone to deliver it was another matter.

He slipped out the back door to the cabin to entrust the letter to Amanda, who set out for the quarters to see if she could find someone willing to take it to the mainland. Judy, Nanette, and Cornelia, frightened of the drunken men in the house and feeling vulnerable without Amanda there to protect them, went with her. Perhaps they could even find help in the quarters or at least another place to sleep where they might feel safer. Robert was tempted to join them, even to try to hide in the woods, but he had never run from anything in his life, and his pride held him in place. He would not abandon his property to these hooligans.

By the next morning, he ached all over from sleeping on the hard floor of the dining room. He hoped, however, that by the time the men awoke they would realize the danger they put themselves in by terrorizing him and the women and go away. If not, he was hopeful that help would come from the quarters or from the troops in Fernandina.

By ten o'clock all the men were awake, demanding food. But Amanda was gone, and they were forced to fend for themselves in the kitchen, which didn't put them in a cheerful mood. Later in the day three more men arrived. These Robert did recognize. They were his former slaves—Ansel, George, and Warren. They came in response to Amanda and Judy's appeals, but as it turned out, not to help Robert but to join the others in plundering Planters House.

Stafford could only watch as they turned the house inside out, looking for valuables, stuffing silver candlesticks and riding boots alike into the croker sacks they had found in one of the sheds. One of them even put Robert's reading glasses into his pocket. When Robert protested, he suddenly found several guns pointed sharply at his head. Three of the men had gone across the road to the field and begun to shoot the few cattle the Union soldiers had left behind, presumably for food, though Robert could not imagine how they would get the meat back to Fernandina.

Robert had not eaten since the day before, and he felt weak and sick to his stomach. What was he to do, but watch and wait and hope that someone would come to his aid? Never before had he felt so helpless, like such an old man, as he did now. But perhaps, he thought, Amanda and Judy and the two girls would find help somewhere. Or perhaps they too had abandoned him. He lay most of the day, feeling sorry for himself, on the makeshift pallet he had put together out of the tablecloths and napkins he had found in drawers of a chest in the dining room. He felt too sick to do anything else.

By the following morning, Robert was unable to rise. One of the black men brought him a couple of hard biscuits, which he ate gratefully lying on his side.

"Don't you go die on us now, you ole buckra. We'd rather kill you ourselves than have you starve to death," said the man who seemed still in charge of the group.

ABOUT NOON, A COMPANY OF UNION MARINES under the command of a young officer named Louis West rode up to the front of Planters House to confront Stafford's captors, who scattered to hide. The soldiers had been summoned thanks to a middle-aged man from the quarters by the name of Prince. With the help of several other former slaves, he had rowed to Fernandina the preceding afternoon to take Robert's message to Colonel Rich. The colonel in turn had sent troops to protect the old man who had earlier proclaimed his loyalty to the Union.

Robert would later learn that the slaves who helped him did not do so out of affection. As Amanda would point out to him, "they was decent, God-fearin' men," who, though they despised slavery and everything that made it work, realized that Robert Stafford was now "a pathetic ole man" who needed help. Though she stressed that they certainly felt no loyalty to him personally, they feared that he might be killed by the renegades who had invaded his home, and they didn't want his blood on their hands. Whatever their reasons, Robert, despite his flicker of annoyance at being called a pathetic old man to his face, expressed only gratitude.

THE UNION TROOPS, WHO WERE BETTER EQUIPPED and greater in number than the renegades, quickly rounded up the black men from their hiding places and took them into custody. They had brought a ship's doctor with them who, at once, began to feel Robert's pulse, listen to his heart, and then ordered one of the marines to give him water from his canteen.

"I don't think we can take them all back to Fernandina, sir, at least not all at once, but can you point out the ones you think might be most dangerous?" the officer asked.

Robert, who was sitting up on his pallet now, pointed first to the three men who had been his own slaves. He didn't want them going back to the quarters to brag about what they had done. Then he identified the group's leader, another man they called George, and four of the larger and older men. Those remaining looked sheepish and embarrassed at not being considered particularly dangerous, but they were grateful not to be arrested.

"Wha's gone happen to us?" asked one of the men in custody, his hands tied behind his back.

"That's for Mr. Stafford to decide," the officer replied, pushing him out the front door and down the steps toward the hitching post, where they tethered all the men together, leaving them under armed guard, while the rest of the marines searched the house and quarters for weapons. Some of the guns found were those the renegades had brought with them, but others were rifles the slaves had always used to hunt in the forests of Cumberland and which Robert himself had provided. Nevertheless, these too were confiscated, over the protests of the peaceable blacks still living in the quarters—even those who had gone for help.

Robert, still lying on his pallet in the house, tears of shame and indignation running down his cheeks, was begging Lieutenant West to leave a guard. His ill health left him feeling vulnerable and feeble. "Please," he begged, "leave us some armed troops or else take me some place safe."

The lieutenant briefly consulted with the doctor, who indicated that he didn't think Stafford should be moved just yet. As a result, Lieutenant West ordered six marines to remain at Planters House to guard Robert and all his remaining valuables.

"We'll be back in a few days when you're able to travel."

"I'd rather just keep the guards here," he said weakly, remembering how Dungeness was plundered as soon as the Union troops left.

"That's out of the question, I'm afraid, sir. We don't have troops to spare for guarding private citizens on a permanent basis."

Lieutenant West ordered his men to help Robert to his bedroom, where the doctor checked him over one last time and left instructions for his care. Robert was asleep before the front door closed behind the departing men.

TWO DAYS LATER, THE MARINES ON GUARD at Planters House received orders to transport Stafford to Fernandina as soon as he was feeling up to it. By this time, Robert had eaten well, slept soundly in his own bed, and was already feeling stronger. Judy and the girls did not return while the troops were in the house, but Amanda came back as soon as the intruders had been taken away. She preferred her own cabin, which was significantly larger than those in the quarters, and she missed her privacy. As long as she stayed there, she felt a sense of obligation to cook for Mr. Stafford. She was by nature a neat, industrious woman with a good heart and a sense of propriety, and Robert relied on her more than he had ever realized. He had always taken her for granted before, but now he took nothing for granted. When she brought a bowl of hot soup and bread and a cup of good strong tea to his bedroom to help him regain his strength, he thanked her for coming back.

"I ain't sayin' I'se here to stay," she told him, "but I reckon I'm here for now till we see how this war is comin' out." It still didn't occur to Robert to offer to pay her for her services, and it didn't occur to her to ask, but he did for once express sincere gratitude for all she did for him, recognizing the fact that he would be not only helpless but also hungry without her. He had never been in a kitchen before in his life except to bark orders and had not the slightest idea what to do to prepare food. He was completely at her mercy.

When he felt like coming downstairs again, the commander of the six marines judged that he was also able to travel. By this time, however, Robert had changed his mind about leaving.

"Our orders are to bring you to Fernandina, Mr. Stafford," the lieutenant said, irritated by Robert's unwillingness to go. "And I'm afraid that you no longer have a choice in the matter since you called for our help."

Although Robert grumbled that he was a free citizen and ought to be able to do whatever he wanted, he packed a few things in a small grip and grudgingly followed the men to the wharf, where they used one of his boats to row to Fort Clinch on the outskirts of Fernandina at the north end of Amelia Island. The fort, built in the 1840s and occupied briefly by Confederates, had been seized by Union troops earlier that year. Robert sat stiffly in the small wooden boat, remembering the evacuation by the Confederates. Robert E. Lee had wanted to concentrate his troop strength farther north at Savannah and had ordered the withdrawal of all troops not only from Forth Clinch, but also from Jekyl Island and Saint Simons, leaving the planters at Cumberland completely exposed to the Yankees. Those who had not already left the island did so immediately, with the exception of Robert Stafford. Little good it had done him, he thought, feeling like a fool sitting in this boat as it slid through the water toward Amelia Island.

ONCE THEY HAD DEBARKED AT FERNANDINA, a Union officer returned Robert's glasses, which had been found in the pocket of one of the prisoners, and offered to escort him to a hotel in town. Robert couldn't believe the change in Fernandina. Virtually all the Southern whites had evacuated and moved inland. The small, once-quiet village was noisy, littered with uncollected trash, and crowded. The streets bustled with Union sailors, some of whom were obviously inebriated, and with former slaves, more than six hundred in all, the

officer told him, who had been released from their bondage by Union troops.
They stood or squatted in small groups up and down the streets, some of them
families with young children and nowhere to live.

It was a Saturday, and all types of people moved about the streets to take
advantage of whatever opportunities, legal or illegal, arose. Fancy women stood
in doorways displaying their wares to passing sailors. Men were gambling and
drinking in the streets and alleys, and even in the hotel lobby. Robert looked
around in disgust, made up his mind that he could not stay here, and demanded
that the officer take him back to Fort Clinch to speak with Colonel Rich.

THE COLONEL SAT BEHIND HIS DESK and glowered up at the tall old man
who stood stubbornly before him, demanding to be returned to Cumberland.

"Mr. Stafford, we have better things to do than shuffle you back and
forth from Cumberland to Fernandina, whenever you get scared or it suits
your fancy."

Stafford's lips narrowed in anger, and his steely eyes, red now from trying to
manage so many days without his spectacles, bore down on the man behind the
desk, who didn't even have the courtesy to offer him a chair.

"And what do you want us to do with those nine blacks we arrested at your
house? They're now in irons on the *Alabama*." Robert knew that the U.S.S.
Alabama was one of the Union ships anchored off the coast of Fernandina. "Do
you want to press charges and take up the time of a military tribunal? Or can you
suggest some other course of action?"

"I really don't care what you do with them," he said, "as long as they're never
allowed back on Cumberland."

"Not much we can do if you don't press charges. We can't keep them forever
in chains without some kind of trial. And they really didn't hurt you, did they?"

"Can't you just hold them until this damned war ends?"

"Certainly not. Unless we enlist them in the Navy and put them to work on
one of our ships. That's what they want. But they're contraband—and we have no
legal right to hold them captive unless you press charges."

"I don't ever want to see them again, much less testify in some court. I don't
give a damn what you do with them. Just don't let them back on Stafford land.

"Would you sign a paper giving up any claim to them as your slave property, and let us enlist them officially and put them on the *Alabama*'s roster as members of her crew?"

"As far as I'm concerned, I don't own slaves anymore. Anybody who stays on my property works for his keep. As for these nine, you're welcome to them, provided you can find someone to take me back to Cumberland. I have no money with me to pay and no way to get back, unless your men will escort me." The vandals had taken all his cash when they looted his house and stuffed it in their pockets. None of the money had been returned to him.

"I'll have you taken back this afternoon. But Mr. Stafford, if this sort of thing ever happens again, do *not* feel free to contact the U.S. Navy. We are in no position to come at your beck and call. We did so this time because of your cooperation and your willingness to provide us with supplies, but we can't come repeatedly. We suggest that you evacuate the island to a safer place."

"I understand," said Robert, lifting his chin and straightening his back even more. "And I'll remember that the next time you need cattle to feed your men."

"If we can perform any other service for you," Colonel Rich said in a conciliatory tone, "please don't hesitate to ask."

"Can you see that a letter gets to my business manager in New London, Connecticut?" he asked. Robert wanted Zabette and the children to know he was safe, to give them some idea what was going on at Cumberland, and since the mail packet no longer ran to Cumberland, he'd had no opportunity to write them. He felt it might be safer to send them word through Augustus Brandegee rather than risk all the questions he might encounter if he wrote directly to Zabette.

"No problem at all. Do you have it with you?"

"I would need stationery and a place where I might write for a brief time."

"I'll have my adjutant fix you right up."

ROBERT SAT AT A SMALL TABLE IN THE ANTEROOM of the colonel's office and wrote a crisp message to Brandegee, asking him to inform Zabette and the children that he was safe and still on Cumberland, but that he might not be able to communicate regularly or visit Connecticut for the duration of the war. He dared not leave Planters House, for fear that it would be pillaged and vandalized, as Dungeness had been. He asked Brandegee to look after his family and told him that he would communicate as often as possible.

He sealed the letter and handed it over to Colonel Rich's secretary, knowing that it might be his last opportunity to write for a long time. Perhaps ever. Then he returned to the colonel's office.

"I'm ready to go, Colonel, whenever your men can take me," said Robert. He knew he had to go back. He could not sit here in Fernandina wondering what might be happening at Planters House. But he had no idea what awaited him at Cumberland Island and even less what the rest of the war might bring.

Chapter Thirty-Seven

GROTON, CONNECTICUT, STAFFORD HOUSE, JUNE 8, 1862
Zabette stood with her back to the front door after Augustus
Brandegee had left. She was relieved to know that Robert was
safe at Cumberland, but she longed for more details. Where was Amanda?
Where were her mother and Jack? What was happening on the island? All she
knew was in the brief letter Mr. Brandegee had shown her, saying that Robert
was all right but that he might not be able to write or come to Connecticut any
time soon, maybe for the duration of this horrible war. And who knew how long
that might continue? The letter was written on United States Navy stationery.
Under what circumstances? It raised more questions than it answered.

Mr. Brandegee had assured her that Robert's assets and the children's
trust funds were more than adequate to cover household expenses during the
war, barring some unexpected and absurd inflation. But Zabette hated the
uncertainty.

Already, her worst fears had been realized; just days earlier, six months after
his seventeenth birthday, Armand had sat down to talk with her.

"I've heard that Jed Randall and Jabez Smith are thinking of organizing
a company of volunteers from Groton to join the Connecticut Twenty-Sixth
Regiment," he told his mother excitedly. "I'm thinking of joining up."

Zabette was horrified. "But, Armand, you're much too young. We need you
here, and there are plenty of older boys who will join the company, I'm sure."

"*Maman*," he said insistently, "a lot of boys my age are planning to sign up.

You wouldn't want me to go against my conscience, would you? And if I do anything to help end slavery in the South, just think, you would be free."

Zabette was touched by his comment. She knew that her status bothered her children—those who were old enough to understand—though it was something they almost never mentioned.

"My freedom is not worth your life," she said softly. "Please think about it carefully. Whatever you do, Bobby will want to do as well, and you know how difficult and dangerous the army would be for him."

"I know," Armand sighed. She knew that he had already given up a great deal for his brother. He refused to consider college because he knew that Bobby could not go. He loved his brother without question. But she was not sure how this war might affect that relationship.

"Just think on it awhile. The children and I need you here. You're the man of the house now, you know," she reminded him.

"Well," he said thoughtfully. "They haven't started really recruiting yet and it may never materialize. But *Maman*," he added, "I can't let all my friends go to fight this war while I sit at home with Bobby."

TWO MONTHS LATER, ON AUGUST 10, a notice appeared in the Groton newspaper that Jedediah Randall and Jabez Smith were now accepting volunteers for their new Company K. All interested men must sign up before September 10, when the company would leave for training at Camp Russell in Norwich. At the beginning of the month, Armand sheepishly informed her that he had added his name to the roster.

"But we're only going to Norwich, *Maman*. I won't be so very far away, and I'm sure I can come home for weekends," he told her, "and perhaps Bobby can come for visits."

It would be hard to let Armand go. She knew that mothers should never have favorites, and she loved all her children. But she and Armand had always had a special attachment. Even as a little boy, he was protective of her, and she loved him fiercely. The thought of his carrying a gun or being shot at by people she might have known in Georgia was a dreadful thought. Though she knew that mothers in both the North and the South were already carrying this heavy burden, she was afraid it was more than she could bear.

When the time finally came on September 11 for the men to depart for Norwich, Zabette could only hug Armand, help him pack, and wish him farewell. She made sure that he had plenty of warm underwear and socks. And she asked Hannah to wrap up some of his favorite foods to take with him, for she had heard that food in military camps was not, as the soldiers put it, "fit to eat" and some of them had taken to calling it "grub."

When all preparations were made and it came time for him to leave, the children stood on the veranda to say goodbye. Armand hugged them all in turn, and picked little Dora up to hold her in his arms. She was seven and a half now, and her legs dangled almost to his knees, "Now you take care of everyone for me while I'm gone," he told her.

"I will, Armand," Dora answered solemnly, planting a wet kiss on his cheek.

He bent down to kiss Ellen and Addie, who hugged him as hard as they could. Then he stood up to say goodbye to his brother. Tears were streaming down Bobby's cheeks. He wanted to go as well, but as Zabette predicted, Jed Randall had turned him down. She knew it was the right thing for him to do, for Bobby would never be useful as a soldier. He needed to learn to cope as best he could by himself, for Armand wouldn't always be with him. Someday, Zabette thought, Bobby's younger brother would marry and leave home for good.

Armand saved his hug for his mother until last. He took her in his arms and held her close for a long time. "I'll miss you, *Maman*," he said softly. "You take care of yourself. And don't worry. I'll be home before you know it."

"Try to stay dry and warm," she whispered to him one last time. Quickly she unhooked her grandmother's locket. "Take this with you to protect you," she said, slipping it into his hand at the very last minute.

"But *Maman*," he protested. "You always wear this."

"I'll be closer to it if it's with you," she said. "*Je t'aime, mon fils.* I love you, my son." She said it in French, in case any of the Irish servants were listening.

He smiled and waved as he mounted his horse. They watched as he trotted toward the road and waved vigorously until he was completely out of sight. As she had learned to do when the children first left Cumberland for Groton, Zabette reserved her tears until he was gone. Then she excused herself, went to her room, and let herself weep freely. *God protect him*, she prayed, *and bring him safely home.*

EVERYONE IN THE FAMILY READ THE NEWSPAPERS more closely now, hoping the war would end before Armand's unit was sent to fight. The most exciting piece of news appeared in the newspaper on September 22, less than two weeks after Armand left. The proclamation from President Lincoln made Zabette's heart race. He had declared that as of January 1, 1863, "all persons held as slaves within any State or designated part of a State the people whereof shall then be in rebellion against the United States shall be then thenceforward, and forever free."

Free. The word jumped out at her. *Free. Freedom.* She said it aloud. It felt good on her tongue. On January 1 she would no longer belong to Robert Stafford. Her mother and Jack, Amanda, Daisy, Adeline and her family, the women in the cotton house—they would all be free. She could hardly believe it. She would no longer be at Robert's beck and call. He could never force her to do anything again because she was his property. On January 1, her children would never have to think of their mother as a slave again. The question of whether she or they were slaves because of their birth would no longer exist. They would all be free to choose their own lives.

A letter from Armand came the same day and reported a rumor that when his training ended, his regiment was being sent to Louisiana, where, thus far, thank God, there was no serious fighting. The battles recently fought in Tennessee and Virginia had been horrible. At Shiloh back in April, almost twenty-four thousand men had been killed. In August the newspapers reported another terrible battle at Manassas, Virginia, calling it "the second battle of Bull Run," where another twenty-two thousand young men had been slaughtered. Then the battle of Fredericksburg had come in mid-December. Robert E. Lee and his Army of Northern Virginia seemed to triumph at every turn. If the South won, what value would Lincoln's proclamation have?

When Zabette and the children received word that the Connecticut Twenty-Sixth Regiment had left Norwich and gone to a place called Port Hudson, Louisiana, they were still worried by the string of Confederate victories. Port Hudson was on the Mississippi River, and from what Zabette heard, the Union army was making a determined effort to gain control of the entire Mississippi. They already occupied New Orleans and Memphis, but Port Hudson was another story.

Union troops had attacked Port Hudson on May 27, but the fort there had not fallen. John and Bobby went into town every day to see what news might be arriving by telegraph. Finally on the third day of June, a list of the dead and wounded arrived in Groton. The carriage raced into the yard just after noon, and Bobby jumped out before the wheels stopped turning. He was weeping and yelling, "Armand's wounded!"

Zabette reached the front door just as he called out again, "Armand's wounded!"

Her heart was racing. *Wounded. Oh, God, no!* But then she thought with relief, *That means he's still alive.* "How? Where?"

"It was in that attack on Port Hudson," he told her. "I don't know anything else."

It was difficult to get news, but Armand had not been sent home, *so it must be a wound they can treat on the battlefield,* Zabette reasoned. At least there was no new fighting in the area, just an endless siege that kept the Confederates pinned down inside the fort. Every day they waited for further word. How bad was his wound? Was he getting proper medical care? The silence from the front was torture. "No news is good news," Hannah reminded Zabette.

Finally, the last week in June the postman delivered a letter. The handwriting was Armand's. Zabette did not trust herself to read the letter aloud, and she handed it to Ellen, who was standing beside her. Zabette held her breath as Ellen read aloud:

> *Dear family,*
> *I didn't want you to hear this from anybody but me. That way you will know I'm all right. I was wounded in the shoulder during the attack on Port Hudson, but I am recovering very well. It was not too serious, and I'm grateful my life was spared. I'm back in the unit now, with my shoulder all patched up. All I have now is a bad cold. I know you don't like to hear about my being hurt, but I'm better off than a lot of men. James Tinker, I'm sorry to say, was killed by a sniper's bullet on April 17. We all miss his cheerful spirit here in the company.*

Zabette did not know the young man, but it was clear from Bobby's "Oh no!" that he did. Ellen read on:

> *The men in my company are all fine fellows. Till I was wounded, I shared a tent with Patrick Martley, Moses Latham, and Ezra Roath. You may know them, as their families are all from Groton. I send my love to all and hope to see you before too much longer. Your brother and fils,*
> *Armand*

The siege continued, the newspaper reported, as the outnumbered Confederates refused to surrender. One article said that they were becoming so desperate for food that they were taking to eating their mules and dogs to stay alive. Zabette hoped it was not so, for no human should have to do such things. *Southern stubbornness,* she thought. She had seen it in men like Robert and Phineas Nightingale. They would probably eat each other before they would surrender. She prayed for her son every night but tried not to show her fears in front of the children. All they could do was wait.

The week after they received the letter, things began to turn around for the Union forces, and on July 4, newspapers were full of the northern victory at Gettysburg. The children, elated, marched around the house singing "Yankee Doodle," even enlisting Hannah, Caitlin, and shy Bernadette into their victory march. But Zabette could think only of the twenty-three thousand boys and men, Union and Confederate alike, who had died at Gettysburg.

When they read the following day of the Confederates' surrender at Vicksburg, again the household cheered. The war seemed suddenly to be turning their way. The news from Vicksburg was especially welcomed because it lay on the Mississippi to the north of Port Hudson.

THAT EVENING AFTER SUPPER Zabette gathered in the kitchen with the Irish servants. She knew that they often sat there to talk about the war after the children were in bed. And tonight she felt the need to join them. Hannah welcomed her with a cup of tea.

"I know you're still worried about Armand," she said, "as we all are."

"He's just a boy," said Zabette, "and his health has always been fragile."

"But he's a soldier now. You're so good to those children, Zabette. They're lucky to have you," said Caitlin.

Zabette smiled. "We've had good news this week," she said.

"Aye," John agreed, "Surely with the Union holding Memphis, Vicksburg, and New Orleans, the Confederates at Port Hudson can't hold out much longer."

They all nodded thoughtfully, afraid to trust his words, and Zabette noticed Caitlin knocking softly on the table with her knuckles. "Knock on wood for good luck," she said, smiling at Zabette. "Old Irish custom," she explained. They all nodded and rapped the table gently.

FIVE DAYS LATER, THE NEWSPAPERS AT LAST REPORTED the surrender of Port Hudson. It had been inevitable with thirty thousand Union troops surrounding the little town and only sixty-eight hundred brave, stubborn Confederates trying to hold on. Surely now, Zabette thought, the men of the Twenty-Sixth would be coming home.

The family sat on the front porch talking of the news. John, pruning shrubbery nearby, joined in the conversation, "They were a feisty bunch—those Rebs. Held us off for forty-eight days—and outnumbered four to one, they were."

"So many deaths," said Zabette, "and for what?"

"I've heard they were eating rats before they finally surrendered," John said.

"Eeeuuuwww." Addie, Ellen, and Dora grimaced in simultaneous horror. "I'd rather starve," said Addie.

"More than twelve thousand casualties in all, they say." Zabette murmured, praying that Armand was safe and healthy again.

"Some of the soldiers there were Negroes, I'm told—called Louisiana Native Guards, but fightin' for the Union. People say they fought really well and showed lots of courage," John said as he snipped at the boxwood. Zabette nodded, not surprised by their courage, but that they were allowed to fight. Even in the North she knew there were suspicions that colored soldiers could not be trusted. She was glad they had proved them wrong.

"Some of the soldiers were from Connecticut," Bobby added, proudly, "and *my* brother was one of them."

Within two weeks another letter from Armand arrived at Stafford House. His company was being sent home. His shoulder was almost healed, and all he suffered from now was a bad cold. It was the best news they had received in weeks. The children all cheered when they heard it, none more loudly than Bobby.

AUGUST 17, 1863

With Armand's anticipated homecoming, the house filled with the aromas of his favorite foods, which Hannah was preparing—pork tenderloin with sautéed mushrooms, mashed potatoes, green beans, and apple pie. The children made a big banner saying "Welcome home, Armand" from cut-out letters of old newspapers and any other paper they could get their hands on and hung it across the archway that led from the foyer into the parlor. Mary and Frederick and their three-year-old daughter, Roberta, had arrived for the festivities. Armand was mustering out of his unit in Norwich on that day, but no one had any idea when he might arrive. Bobby kept watch all morning on the front porch.

"Here they are!" he called at long last.

Zabette, the children, and the servants rushed out to the porch to welcome their young soldier home. Armand's uniform was dusty from the wagon ride he had hitched from the dock. He leapt out of the carriage, wincing only a bit when he hit the ground, and ran toward the children.

Scooping Dora up with his right arm, he asked, "Did you take care of everyone while I was away?"

"Yes, I did, Armand," she answered solemnly, hugging his neck.

He was compelled to put her down before embracing all the others; his left arm just didn't seem to perform as well as his right, and his mother could tell that he was carrying it at an odd angle. She noticed that he winced again when Bobby hugged his left shoulder too tight.

He leaned forward to embrace little blonde-haired Roberta, who squirmed in Mary's arms, kissed his older sister on her proffered cheek, and shook his brother-in-law's outstretched hand.

Armand had grown and matured in his year away from home. He looked more manly and sported a small moustache.

"Oooh, that tickles," squealed Addie when he kissed her.

Zabette stood back until he had greeted all the others, even the servants. But then Armand found her. "*Bienvenu, mon fils,*" she said in welcome, taking him in her arms.

"*J'ai un cadeau pour toi, Maman.* I have a gift for you," he said. From his pocket he pulled a small carved wooden case. He opened it and held it out to her. It was an ambrotype of himself in uniform. He looked splendid but solemn, as he gazed at the photographer. It was the first photograph of any member of her family Zabette had ever seen, and she knew that she would cherish it always.

"Oh, Armand, it's beautiful, but not as beautiful as the real thing," she said softly, hugging him, careful to avoid his shoulder.

At the same time he gave her the picture, he held out his hand and said, "I have one more thing for you." And into her palm he placed the gold locket she had given him when he departed. "It kept me safe, *Maman*, and I want it to always keep you safe, now that you're free." He smiled down into her soft brown eyes. "I want you to know that's what I was fighting for. And I would enlist again to keep you free. *Je t'aime, Maman.*"

Zabette hugged him, blinking back tears of joy. Arm-in-arm, they went from the sunlight into the cool interior of the foyer, the children trailing behind, all eager to enjoy Hannah's sumptuous meal.

ALTHOUGH ARMAND'S SHOULDER WAS HEALING WELL, his hacking cough would not go away. Despite everything Zabette did, spooning into his mouth each evening her remedy of lemon, honey, and whiskey, as well as a few less agreeable concoctions that Hannah recommended, Armand was unable to shake it off. The damp Mississippi air of Port Hudson had not been good for him. He and his unit had been cut off from the river, which they'd sought to control, for more than a month, and sometimes the only water they had to drink was what had collected in the trenches after a rain. Several of the men were sick as a consequence.

Armand's cough became progressively worse. His face grew pallid, and his eyes took on a hollow look. Sometimes he had night sweats and bad dreams, crying out as though minié balls were flying all around him. Some days he felt perfectly fine, and other days he could hardly get out of bed. Zabette nursed him with constant care, brought him hot soups and teas, and sat beside his bed holding cool damp cloths to his forehead on days when he burned with fever.

Betsey Copp sent out a tonic of her own that she thought might help, along with books of inspiration and support. But in spite of all their efforts, he grew thinner and thinner. Zabette tried to chase from her mind the memory of Robert's mother and sister. He seemed to be slipping from her grasp just as they had.

She summoned Dr. Durfey many times. Each time he examined Armand, he listened to his breathing with growing concern. Lung sickness was not uncommon among the war veterans, he told her, especially for those who had had to drink bad water. Armand needed to be sent to a warm, dry climate and rest for a good long while, he said. But where could anyone go while this wretched war dragged on? If it weren't for the war, she would take him to Cumberland. There at least the climate was warm, not this cold, damp, endless winter. Zabette kept the fire constantly built and stoked in Armand's room, and she made sure he got plenty of rest. But despite all her efforts, he grew weaker.

DECEMBER 24, 1863

On Christmas Eve Armand came downstairs and sat by the fire in the parlor watching the children trim the tree John had cut down in the woods. Addie and Dora looped strings of cranberries and glass beads around the tree, while Ellen fastened to its branches her own creations of gay-colored ribbons and little bouquets of paper flowers. Zabette tied lace bags filled with colored candies that the children would be allowed to eat on Christmas day. When it was all done, Bobby stood on a kitchen chair to reach the top branch and fasten there the glittering star of gilt paper the children had made. Addie and Ellen attached wire holders with small candles, sixteen in all, at various spots on the tree, and lit the candles.

"Dora," said Zabette, "Go ask Hannah and the others if they'd like to come see the tree."

Dora skipped off to the kitchen where the servants were gathered around the table enjoying their own Christmas Eve toddy. Zabette turned the lamps down low, and they all stood around admiring their handiwork glowing warmly in the darkened room.

Armand, who had contributed nothing, sat silently and watched. Then softly, he began to sing "Silent Night." When his song dissolved into coughing, Zabette put her hand on his shoulder and picked up the carol in her high, clear voice. The servants joined in, as did the children. Armand held his handkerchief to his lips as he listened. When the song ended, everyone stood silent for a moment, lost in thoughts and memories before they blew out the candles.

IN FEBRUARY, DURING THE WORST SNOW OF THE SEASON, Armand gasped for breath most of the night. Zabette sent for Dr. Durfey before midnight, but the snow was piled so high along the roadways that his sleigh couldn't get through the drifts. Toward dawn Armand died in his mother's arms. Bobby sat beside him on the bed sobbing without restraint. Their sisters crouched, holding each other, in the hallway outside the bedroom.

All night the terrible sounds of Armand's labored breathing had filled the house. Now there was only silence. Zabette held her son's limp body, so thin and frail, close to her breast, unable to let him go. Little by little his body cooled, though still she held him, her warm tears falling onto his cheek. Finally, Bernadette crept into the room and whispered to Zabette, who looked up at her in dazed confusion. She let Bernadette help her to lay Armand back onto the bed. But still she sat beside him, holding his hand, while Bernadette fetched a basin of warm water. Together they washed the body.

"He was your favorite, wasn't he?" asked Bernadette after Bobby finally went downstairs at Hannah's encouragement for a bite of breakfast.

"They are all my favorites," Zabette said, "but Armand *was* special." She said no more, for she did not trust her voice. Once she had thought that nothing could be worse than having her children sent north while she had been forced to remain at Cumberland. She knew now that there was loss far more incalculable.

ZABETTE HAD NEVER KNOWN THAT GRIEF COULD BE SO PHYSICAL, so debilitating. She continued to go about her daily tasks, but the ache in her breast would not go away. When winter finally gave way to spring and the plum trees budded, she remembered Armand as a child bringing her a bouquet of pink blossoms from the orchard behind his great-grandmother's house at Cumberland. He had been only four years old at the time.

"Here, *Maman*, I brought you a present," he'd said, holding out the five small branches, smashed at the bottom from the heat of his eager little hand. She'd gathered him and the flowers into her arms before putting the tiny branches in a vase on the parlor windowsill. He knew even as a child how much she loved the orchard, its color and fragrance. Now, as she walked in the barren Connecticut orchard, her heart ached for that tiny vase of flowers and the son she had lost.

She wrote to Robert of Armand's death, but he did not respond.

May 18, 1864

As the war continued, the South suffered defeat after defeat, yet Confederate president Jefferson Davis refused to concede. As long as Robert E. Lee commanded his army, he appeared confident of victory. But the situation was growing desperate. Zabette read with horror of the Battle of New Market on May 15, 1864, when cadets from the Virginia Military Institute, sixteen years old or even younger, marched out to face seasoned Union troops in the Shenandoah Valley. The reporter noted that they performed well under fire, but Zabette grieved over the loss of so many young lives. Why didn't the South surrender? How many more boys would have to die before it was all over?

Union troops had begun to mass outside of Atlanta, and in September, General William Tecumseh Sherman began his savage march to the sea, to Savannah, to her beloved Georgia coast. The soldiers burned and pillaged every step of the way, leaving behind only scorched earth and hunger. It was said that Sherman even sent a cable to President Lincoln on Christmas Eve, offering him the gift of Savannah.

This Christmas at Stafford House was nothing like the previous one, for they all still mourned for Armand. Bobby wept even in his sleep and wandered the house during the day like a lost puppy. Once again John cut a fir tree for the parlor, but this year the children used the leftover ornaments from the year before rather than make new ones. Instead of Bobby's placing the gilt star at the top of the tree, Dora put it in the window in memory of Armand. War hung over the house like a pall, and the household took no joy in the string of Union victories.

In April, news came finally that Lee had surrendered at Appomattox Court House. The North celebrated briefly, but the victory was almost forgotten at the terrible news of the death of President Lincoln from an assassin's bullet just over a week later. It was over, but at what cost and with what a dreadful end?

Then the orchard bloomed again. Spring turned to summer, blossoms fell, and fresh young fruit began to appear on the plum trees. Even Zabette felt her heart lift a bit. Perhaps now news would arrive from Cumberland. Perhaps the days of anxiety and death and suffering were over. Perhaps now they could all go home and enjoy their freedom.

Chapter Thirty-Eight

P LANTERS HOUSE, CUMBERLAND ISLAND, JUNE 1867
Robert was angry. He was often angry these days. The war was over,
and his plantation, like most others in Georgia, lay in shambles.
Little good it had done him to be a Union man. It had made his southern
neighbors hate him more and won him few favors with northern troops. But what
did he care?

He had finally gotten his land back, *after that fool Sherman had issued that
damned field order giving all the Sea Islands to the slaves.* The one good thing that
came from the Lincoln assassination, he thought, was that when the southerner
Andrew Johnson became president, he abolished Sherman's field order and
restored the land to its rightful owners. But during that interim, even Robert had
been compelled to evacuate briefly to the mainland, despite his Union sympathies.
He'd left Cumberland under protest and military escort, and had then spent six
weeks in the godforsaken town of Waycross. *A damned inconvenience.*

Just as he'd feared, when he returned he found his house a wreck and,
although no one had the audacity to still be living in it when he arrived, the slave
cabins to the east were full of former slaves, some of them his own, but mostly
people he had never seen before. When he asked them if they were here to work,
they scoffed at him. Finally, he hired some men from Fernandina to help him
clear them out, driving them from the cabins at rifle point.

"I'll burn these damned cabins before any of you will live on my place without
working," he shouted. The freedmen, intimidated by the guns, gathered up their

few belongings and headed reluctantly for the landing or other parts of the island. He didn't care that they were homeless. If they wanted work, they could come back one at a time and apply for it like any white man would have to do. It never occurred to him that they had never before had an opportunity to apply for work to support their families and that they might not know how.

A few did come back. But it was not the same. He could no longer force them to work if they were sick or needed time off for some reason. *They have some tomfool idea that freedom means not having to work if you don't want to. But by gum, they're always in line on payday,* he thought, infuriated by his lack of control.

All this recordkeeping about work hours and pay that the Freedmen's Bureau required was a *damned nuisance,* in his opinion. And in the end it amounted to much the same thing. Only now they had to pay rent and buy their own clothes and food. In exchange they could walk away whenever they chose. For the freedmen it was a good exchange. For Robert it was just an inconvenience. He was seventy-seven years old and tired of having to reinvent his life.

But he was better off than most of the planters he knew. He had hedged his bets before and during the war, selling off many of his slaves and investing in northern banks and properties. To his regret, he had left some assets in southern banks, all lost now, of course, but mostly he still had his land and, unlike many others in the area, could afford to hire workers and pay his taxes.

When the war ended, Judy stayed on just long enough to make sure her children were provided for. Robert sent them north and set up trust funds for them, just as he had for his children with Zabette. Once that was done, Judy called him a "cranky old man" to his face and set out for the mainland. He didn't much care. He was tired of her anyhow. He missed Zabette and her gentle ways. He had managed to hire a woman named Catherine Williams as a housekeeper to take care of the Big House. And Amanda's daughter, Cumsie, agreed to come cook for him. She was only in her teens and not much of a cook, but Amanda refused to come back, and Cumsie was the best he could do. Amanda helped her sometimes and was teaching her what she needed to know. *But tarnation,* he thought, *she has a long way to go before she can cook like her mama.* Their presence in the household helped, but he needed a woman in his bed—even at his age he needed a woman. *It's time,* he thought, *for Zabette to come home.*

He had received her letter about Armand's death, but not until six months after it was written. He had not replied. He was sorry to lose his son, but what good would writing do, especially after all that time? It had been so long since he had seen his sons and daughters. In his mind they were frozen in their childhood selves of six years ago. It was impossible to imagine Armand as a soldier, wounded in battle. Although he was sorry over his son's death, it seemed that of a stranger, someone he had never really known.

When he could get things settled at Cumberland, he was going to Groton to bring Zabette home. But could he make her come? She was free now, just like all the others. He had never cared much for slavery, but now that it was ended, he began to see just how convenient it had been for him—when he could compel her to do whatever he wanted, when workers were at his beck and call, and when he had never had to worry about whether or not they would show up for work on a given morning. He'd tried to hire a new overseer. Dilworth had abandoned his post to go join the army, *like most of the other hotheaded fools in Georgia,* thought Robert. And half of them had come back with one leg or half an arm or not at all. It was hard to find anyone he could trust who had the stomach to oversee the plantation now, and he had already been compelled to cut back on what he planted. He would have to wait and see the fall crops harvested before he could go north. He dreaded the trip. He was tired, and sometimes all he wanted to do was lie down and rest. But he was determined to bring Zabette back—if she would come.

Most Cumberland planters had returned to the island, but not Phineas Nightingale, who was living instead at his plantation on Cambers Island. His confiscated Cumberland lands had been restored to him in 1866, but Dungeness stood empty and abandoned. Occupied by Union troops early in the war and later by freed slaves, it now sat deserted and deteriorating. *Why should I even want it in its present condition?* Robert wondered. But he knew that his own desire for Dungeness had nothing to do with its monetary value. It stood as a symbol of Nightingale's supposed superiority, of his snobbery, and of Robert's need for revenge.

At last Dungeness appeared to be within his reach, and Robert had no intention of letting it slip away again. Nightingale owed him money for loans he had not repaid. As always, Phineas needed money and could not afford to pay the taxes on Dungeness. It looked like the perfect opportunity for Robert to seize the property he had always coveted.

He sat down at his desk and carefully composed his offer to Phineas. Determined to get it at a good price, Robert phrased the letter so as to make it appear that he was doing Phineas a favor by taking the property off his hands, property on which Stafford placed a value of $6,000 when it had been in good condition:

> The place has been occupied by Negroes & headquarters for others, both black and white, coming over from Fernandina, stealing my cattle, hogs and nearly everything else they can lay their hands on, even my dogs. I think it would be best for me to purchase it, & put some clever man there in charge, to keep them off, if you will sell at a fair price. Please let me know the lowest price you will take for it. The house can never be repaired again & will cost considerable to remove the old walls & rubbish off the grounds and out of the way.

Convinced that his proposal provided the only logical path for Phineas to get out from under his burden, Robert waited impatiently for his response. He wanted the matter settled before he headed north. The reply was not long in coming. It arrived by mail packet two weeks later. Robert tore open the letter at the dock, eager to read Phineas's concession and already exulting in his triumph and vindication.

The words were like a slap in the face. They made clear that in spite of Nightingale's need for money and whatever logic Stafford might see in the sale, Phineas had no intention of ever letting Robert Stafford have his land and his Dungeness home. Instead, he announced, he had mortgaged it to a Savannah man named Edmund Molyneux in order to repay Robert and prevent his foreclosure on his loans, but the letter also stated that he considered the $6,000 value an insult in light of the fact that he already had an offer of $80,000 for the property from a Rhode Island man named William Sprague.

Anyone watching the old man as he read the letter would have seen his spine stiffen and his face redden in fury. He wadded up the letter, and thrust it in his pocket. Stung, frustrated, and consumed by anger, he struggled to get on his horse. He jabbed the horse's sides with his heels and rode furiously away, his mount's hooves kicking up shells and clumps of sand in his wake.

It was well into January before Robert felt he could sail for Groton. The harvest, such as it was, was in, and spring planting would not begin until March. He hated the roiling winter seas, but they couldn't be helped. The railroads were still not fully repaired since the war, and sea travel was more reliable.

He booked passage to New London, remembering the first time he had made this trip with Zabette, how seasick she was, but how her eyes had sparkled to discover the bustling world outside of Cumberland. It had been an adventure then, but now the four-day trip from Savannah to New York was only exhausting and unpleasant.

When the seas were calm, he wrapped himself in his coat and blankets and sat on deck, watching the gray floes rush by. He had sent a telegram to say that he was coming, but he never trusted these newfangled ways of communication. He wouldn't be surprised if no one were there to meet him. Not surprised at all. Perhaps they wouldn't even care that he was coming.

New London, Connecticut, dockside, January 18, 1868

As he descended the gangplank, Robert saw Bobby waiting on the dock, stamping his feet to keep warm. He hardly recognized the boy whom he had not seen for more than seven years. Bobby was now twenty-one, tall and thin like his father. He had grown a rather scraggly moustache, but his eyes still had that shy immaturity that marked his uncertainty in a complicated world.

"Papa," the young man called out to him, rushing forward to hug him.

"Not here, Bobby," Robert said in irritation. "I'm your uncle, remember?"

"Yes, sir," Bobby said sheepishly. It had been Bobby who had always loved his father most, and Robert's brusque words appeared to wound him deeply.

Regretting the harshness of his words, Robert held his son at a distance and looked him over. "You've grown at least a foot since I saw you last. It's good to see you, boy." He slapped him on the shoulder with what he hoped passed for affection. "What time's the ferry to Groton?"

"Three o'clock, sir. We can just make it if we hurry."

New London had changed very little since Robert's last visit, and the old ferryboat was still the same. As they crossed the Thames River, Robert could just make out Stafford Place on the brow of the bluff north of Groton.

"How are your . . . sisters?" Robert asked, once they had settled onto the boat for the brief crossing. He had almost asked "How are your brother and sisters?" but at the last moment remembered and caught himself. Apparently Bobby did not notice.

"They're fine, sir. Mary has two children now, both girls, and my sisters are all nearly grown. It's been a long time since we've seen you, sir." The boy could apparently think of nothing else to call him but "sir."

"I was sorry to hear about Armand," Robert said. Bobby nodded but could make no reply.

Neither of them said anything more until they reached the Groton shore, debarked, and climbed into the waiting carriage. John had trotted the horses about the town to keep them warm while Bobby went to meet his father. But as the ferry approached, he pulled the carriage up to the dock and had plenty of blankets ready behind the rear seats should the old man need them.

"Welcome back, Mr. Stafford. It's good to see you again," said John.

"It's good to be back, John."

They drove in silence back to Stafford House.

The girls all rushed out to meet the carriage as it pulled up in front of the steps. Zabette had reminded them that they were not to call him "Papa," so they called him nothing. Just spoke their greetings, a bit intimidated by the stiff, hoary man whom they hardly recognized. He had grown old during the war, he had no doubt of that, but he too had to look them over carefully to decide who was who. It had been such a long time.

"Please, sir, can't you stay at the house tonight?" asked Bobby. "You can sleep in Armand's room. We have too much space now," he finished lamely.

"We'll see, Bobby," Robert said. He was waiting above all to speak to Zabette and see how she might greet him. Standing in the doorway, she was smiling but formal. He wasn't sure what to expect. It had been so long, and freedom shone in her eyes.

He was shocked to see Ellen and Addie, both grown women now. Even Dora, at thirteen, had tiny budding breasts that strained against her smock. Zabette had changed too, grown into a mature woman. Her hair was still dark though it showed a light salting of gray. Her body was more rounded and her breasts fuller, though she was still the same beautiful woman he had taken to his bed as a teenage girl. If anything, she was more beautiful. But there was a new look about her as well, a self-assurance he did not remember being there before. A womanliness in command of itself. She was almost intimidating, for Robert knew that he did not own her anymore, not legally and not emotionally. The control was no longer his—if it ever had been, he thought wryly. But he knew that it had once been his to use, to squander, to throw away.

"Hello, Zabette," he said. "You're looking well."

"And you, sir," she replied, though he could see in her eyes the shock of his physical changes. He had no illusions. He knew he was thinner, slower in his movements. His hair was stark white, and his eyes had sunk deeper into their sockets as the flesh around them lost its firmness. He knew what she saw. He was no longer the six-foot-three man she had known before. Although he had not measured himself, he knew that he had shrunk by several inches in recent years. But he still carried himself as rigidly upright as his bones would allow.

He took her hand and held it for a moment, looking down at its smoky softness. She had such beautiful hands, such gentle eyes that now gazed on him as on a stranger.

Zabette had notified Hannah that Mr. Stafford would be staying for supper and perhaps they could persuade him to stay overnight. There was no need for him to go back to the New London hotel when they had plenty of room at Stafford Place, especially on such an evening, when snow was already beginning to fall. It was his house, after all. And what difference did it make now, he thought. No one would suspect this doddering old uncle to be up to any shenanigans with the children's nursemaid. The thought of going back out into the icy January wind after dark had little appeal to him, and they had already made up Armand's old room, just in case he decided to stay.

For supper, Hannah served an Irish stew, ballymaloe as she called it—her specialty, filled with lamb, onions, potatoes, carrots, and parsnips, with parsley and secret herbs she would not reveal thrown into the pot. It was delicious and especially welcome on such a cold evening. The smell of it cooking had given Robert an enormous appetite, which he welcomed, for these days he seldom had any.

It was the brightest and most cheerful scene he had witnessed since the war ended—his children, with their smiling faces gathered around the table and Zabette at the other end, acting as hostess. Mary and her family were invited for Sunday dinner the following week, Zabette told him, so he would soon get to meet his "great-nieces." Suddenly, even for him, all this pretense seemed foolish. But it was too late to change any of it now. The cities of Groton and New London would think him daft to suddenly claim these children and grandchildren as his own.

"I must call on Betsey Copp tomorrow," he announced abruptly. "How is she doing?"

"Well, I think," replied Zabette. "Her children are still with her or close by. One boy, John I believe, has become a lawyer. Daniel has taken over his father's agricultural interests. And the youngest, Belton, and his brother Billy, are both still living at home. She's very proud of them all."

He noticed her animation when she spoke of Betsey Copp. He was pleased that the two women got along well, though he knew almost nothing of their relationship and would have been very surprised at the matters they discussed.

Around the table the children shared their accomplishments one by one. Addie had taken first place in French at school, she announced proudly. Ellen had learned to knit and had made him a scarf, she told him, smiling shyly. And Dora could ride a horse sidesaddle. Bobby, unable to think of anything else, added eagerly, "I can ride too. Real good."

"That's fine, children. I'm proud of you all," said Robert. Then he turned to Zabette. "I received your letter about Armand," he said. "It arrived six months after his . . . the event. I should have written, but it seemed so long ago, so pointless after so much time."

"We still miss him very much," said Zabette, a catch in her throat in spite of herself. The children nodded. "He was discharged from the army with a distinguished service record. You would have been very proud of him."

"I wish I could have seen him in his uniform."

"He left a picture," shouted Bobby. He leapt up from the table to fetch the ambrotype from the parlor mantle.

"Here he is, sir! Don't he look fine?" he asked with pride.

"He does indeed, Bobby. A very handsome soldier," Robert said softly. Could this really be little Armand? This austere-looking private in a Union uniform? He thought of all the young soldiers who had swarmed over Cumberland at various times during the war, even some from Connecticut, and the picture made him wish he had been kinder to them.

"I wanted to join up too, sir, but one of us needed to stay home to look after the family," Bobby announced.

"You're quite right, Bobby. I thank you for doing that."

Zabette leaned forward to squeeze Bobby's hand and smile at him.

"We hope you will stay for the night, Mr. Stafford," she said. "As we indicated earlier, the room is ready for you, if you choose to stay. I'm sure John will welcome not having to get the horses out again tonight."

"I thank you all," said Robert, "and I accept. In fact, I've already had John take my bags up to the room." It would be the first night he and Zabette had spent under the same roof in a decade, the first time he would see her face over breakfast in as long a time. Yes, he would indeed stay for the night.

THE CHILDREN WENT TO BED ONE BY ONE. "*Bonne nuit, maman*," each one said to Zabette in turn, and then to their father, "Good night, sir." The servants had long since disappeared, and suddenly Robert and Zabette found themselves alone in the flickering gaslight.

Robert could think of nothing to say in the parlor. Although the others were not present, one never knew when someone might be listening from the shadows. How he wanted to take her to his bed, to feel her body warming his old bones. It had been so long, but he felt a flicker of desire, something he had not experienced for some time now, though he was not sure he could sustain it. But he would be satisfied just to feel her body close against him.

"Shall we go up?" he asked.

She lit a kerosene lamp and turned off the gaslights. Together they made their way upstairs.

"You remember where Armand's room is?" she asked, gesturing to the closed door at the end of the hall.

"Yes," he answered. "Good night, Zabette." He took her hand and squeezed it.

"Good night, sir," she replied, withdrawing her hand and turning to her own room.

He supposed that when the children were all asleep, she would come to him. He lay, waiting and listening, for more than an hour. The house was still, no welcome creaks of the floorboards, no subtle hinge noises that indicated a door being opened. They needed to talk, *damn it,* and this was the best possible time. He supposed he would have to demean himself and go to her. He hated the idea of creeping into the cold hallway, groping in the dark for her door, and then finding her perhaps sound asleep with no thought of him. But he had no other choice.

Her door was closed but not locked, thank God, and his hopes stirred. She was lying snugly in bed, the covers pulled up to her chin. He could see the moonlight from the window reflected on her hair, splayed out across her pillow.

He sat on the edge of the bed and whispered, "Zabette."

She opened her eyes and said sleepily, "Robert?"

She had not been expecting him. That was clear.

"Zabette, we need to talk." He pulled back the covers and crawled in beside her.

"The children . . . they'll hear."

"I don't think so. We'll talk softly, and they're all asleep."

"Ellen is a light sleeper," she said, remembering the times when her eighteen-year-old daughter had suffered a sleepless night worrying over some wayward beau.

"She's at the other end of the hall," he replied. In any case, what difference did it make? It was not as though the children didn't already know they had slept together.

Robert reached out to pull her toward him, but she did not acquiesce. It had been so long that both of them perhaps had lost the instinct, the urge to come together. There would be time enough later, he supposed. Tonight he would be satisfied with just her warmth and her agreement.

"Zabette," he whispered into the darkness. "I want you to come home."

"Home?" she echoed.

"Back to Cumberland. I need you there with me. Everyone has deserted me, and you've been here with the children for more than fifteen years now. They're all grown up and are capable of taking care of themselves. I want you to come home with me."

"What about Dora? She's only thirteen, still a child."

"She can come with us. The older children can make their own choice. I'll provide for them. You know that."

He sensed her hesitation. He'd thought about it. There was no way they could live together in Groton. And he still had not accomplished all he intended at Cumberland. He still did not own Dungeness. And his mother and sister were buried on Cumberland. How could he come here now, after all the pretense, and live any kind of normal life? It was impossible.

"I need you at Cumberland, Zabette." He felt the heat from her body and longed to pull her closer. But she lay stiffly, unresponsive, beside him. Reluctantly, he sat up and put on his slippers. He might as well go back to his own, to Armand's, room.

"Think about it, and we'll talk more tomorrow," he said. She murmured something he couldn't quite make out, though it might have been "good night," and then turned her back to him. He made his way quietly down the dark empty hallway to return to his own cold bed.

AFTER HE HAD LEFT, ZABETTE FELT A TWINGE of guilt about her coldness to Robert. He had grown old, but that wasn't it. His old sense of power was gone, but that wasn't it either. Why had she reacted as she did? She didn't know. She only knew that the thought of lying in Robert's arms held no appeal for her, only revulsion.

The thought of going back to Cumberland excited her. She longed to go back. It was her home. She had never liked Connecticut or this false life she was forced to live here. She wanted to see her mother again, and Jack. Questions about Cumberland kept her awake much of the rest of the night. Was Amanda still at Planters House? What had happened to Daisy after her grandmother's death? What had become of Plum Orchard during the war? How were all the people living now that they were free to do whatever they chose? So many questions.

But there were the children to consider, as well. She knew in her heart that she wanted to go back to the island, but feared her children would not want to return. They had grown up in Groton. It was their home in ways it could never be hers. Their friends were here. And they had so many plans for the future. Her only real friend here was Betsey Copp, but Betsey focused her life now on her children and grandchildren, and Zabette saw her rarely. Still Betsey was the only person in Groton with whom she had been able to be completely honest, and she would miss their friendship. It had stretched her mind and made her realize that even as a woman, she did not have to accept a subservient role, especially now that she was no longer a slave.

This was the first decision of any real importance she would have to make about her own life. She knew that Mary, with her young family, would never go back to Cumberland, but perhaps the other children would at least consider the possibility. She lay sleepless much of the night, considering her options. For the first time in her life, she was free to choose. The decision was hers, hers alone, to make. She prayed that she would make the right one.

Chapter Thirty-Nine

MARY AND FREDERICK PALMER and their two little girls arrived at Stafford House in a flurry of snow and sunshine. When he heard their carriage in the driveway, Robert stepped onto the front porch to greet them, the rest of the family trailing behind. Zabette watched Robert's reaction as he saw Mary for the first time since before the war. She had become more and more like him every year—tall and dignified, somewhat reticent except with her daughters, whom she adored. Her eyes were sharp and her dark hair swept back into a bun, which made her tight curls less obvious. Amber earrings dangled from the lobes of her ears. She stretched out her long neck to allow her father to kiss her cheek, and then she introduced the two grandchildren he had never seen.

"This is Roberta," she said, shoving her oldest daughter forward to give her grandfather a reluctant hug. "She's named for you."

At almost eight Roberta was the image of her mother. She could have been Mary as a child—the Mary he no doubt remembered best. Robert beamed his approval.

"And this one?" he asked, gesturing toward the smaller girl, her head surrounded by a halo of blond curls, holding her father's hand and looking up at Robert with mistrust. "This must be Mary Ellen."

"We call her Mellie," said her father. "She's two and a half now."

"Mellie, what a pretty name," he said, tousling her hair. She drew back, to hide behind her father's trouser leg.

"She's a little shy with strangers," said Mary. Zabette noticed Robert wince at the word. And yet to Mary's children he *was* a stranger. Neither of them had ever seen him before, and Robert's appearance was hardly the sort to instill confidence in youngsters. His hollow cheeks and untamed white hair, his bony hands, and even the way his mouth turned down most of the time now gave him a rather menacing demeanor. But although they held back from their grandfather, both little girls rushed forward voluntarily to give a hug to Zabette, whose open arms gathered them in.

"Do come in and wash up. Dinner will be ready soon." Soon might mean as much as two hours from now, but it would give them plenty of time to visit.

Dora took the little girls by the hand and led them up to her room. Zabette knew that soon they would all be clambering up the steep stairs to the widow's walk to peer out at the passing ships on the river. There were not many vessels this time of year, as the river's ice made passage more difficult and dangerous. But looking down on the river and New London in the distance made the children feel that it was a toy town they were viewing. Zabette also knew they would not stay long in the widow's walk, for there was no heat except for what drifted up from the floor below. Even so, it was always the place they liked to begin their visits. In the summer they would have tea parties there, but not in January.

Robert seemed enjoy getting to know his children again. Bobby followed his father about like a puppy. It was the first male companionship he had known since his brother died—except for the few times that John made a special effort to take him riding. Zabette wondered, now that Robert had seen the children again, whether he might change his mind and want to stay in Groton. She knew that she could not return without him, for, slave or free, she was still financially dependent.

THE QUESTION OF RETURNING TO CUMBERLAND did not arise until after the sumptuous dinner that Hannah had prepared to welcome Mary and Frederick and their children back "home," as Hannah always called it. She had prepared a pot roast, surrounded by whatever vegetables were still available in the root cellar in January. When they had all finished eating and smacking their lips over Hannah's spice cake, Robert pushed back from the table and announced:

"I'm hoping to take Zabette with me back to Cumberland this time."

The children reacted visibly, their mouths dropping open. They could not imagine their mother wanting to return to the life she had led there where she had been a slave. But then they did not understand what the island meant to her. None of them preserved any special fondness for it or any exceptional recollections, except for Bobby, whose memory of Cumberland centered around his brother. But he couldn't conceive of what it would be like there without Armand.

To Robert's surprise, Zabette followed his announcement with one of her own. "And I have decided to go," she said with conviction, underscoring the word *decided*. "I hope that you, some of you at least, will choose to come with me."

"But why, *Maman*?" asked Addie. "We have such a good life here. Why would we want to go back to that old plantation?"

"And why would *you* want to go back, *Maman*? There must not be many good memories there," said Ellen. She herself could not really remember it, but she knew that the gay social life they enjoyed in Groton would not exist on Cumberland.

"Oh, but there are. So many memories and people I haven't seen for such a long time."

Robert, elated by Zabette's unexpected announcement, said, "You can make up your own minds about going. You're all old enough to take care of yourselves now—except Dora."

"But I don't want to leave Groton either," whined Dora.

"The choice is not yours to make, my dear," said her father. She might be free but she was still a child.

"Frederick and I could move into Stafford Place to look after the younger ones," Mary said quickly. Zabette sensed a relief in her voice, almost a pleading. She knew that since their marriage Mary and Frederick had moved about a good deal, and she had the impression that Frederick was having difficulty settling down into a solid job and family life. She knew that for them finances were a problem. Perhaps this was just what they needed. A home they did not have to pay for.

"What about you, Bobby?" she asked. "Wouldn't you like to come?"

He hesitated, looking from Robert to her, then one by one at his sisters. "I don't know," he said finally.

"Perhaps it would be best if you went with them, Bobby," said Mary. Zabette suspected that she did not want the responsibility of looking after her brother, who would never be independent.

"But I could help here," he said stubbornly. "I'd be the man of the house."

"No," Mary said emphatically. "Frederick would be the man of the house."

"I could help John in the stables," he insisted.

"No doubt you could, Bobby. But we'd love to have you come to Cumberland with us," Robert said with as much warmth as he could muster.

"No," Bobby said firmly. "I'm a man now. I'll stay here and help take care of my sisters."

Mary sighed, knowing that if she had agreed to look after one, she had agreed to look after all.

Zabette sat quietly, watching and listening as the implications of her decision sank in. Perhaps they were right to want to stay. Who knew what things were like at Cumberland now? They were old enough to decide for themselves. And Mary would take care of them. Whatever she might be, Mary was a responsible woman, strong, reliable, and clearly the rock in her marriage to Frederick.

In any case, Zabette thought, her departure did not have to be forever. She could come for visits with or without Robert. She could travel as a free woman, if Robert would pay her passage. She longed to see her mother again and her brother, and Amanda and so many others. She had tried to ask Robert questions about them all, but his answers were vague and unsatisfactory. She needed to go to Cumberland to find out for herself what had happened to her island home, to Plum Orchard, and to all those she loved there.

AFTER MARY AND FREDERICK HAD BUNDLED up their little girls to head back to Norwich the next morning and the household had settled into a quiet afternoon as everyone rested in their rooms, Zabette picked up her mending and motioned for Robert to sit with her before the fire in the parlor. He was happy to toast his feet beside the grate.

"Robert," she began, "I've been thinking."

"Thinking? What about?"

"I'm willing to go back to Cumberland with you, but I want some assurances that I can come back to Groton from time to time to visit the children."

"Assurances? Of course you can."

"No, I don't mean just your word. Suppose something happened to you. How could I ever afford to travel? To live? Neither of us is getting younger." Robert was well aware of his age although since the war he had regained at least a modicum of his old vigor. But Zabette wanted assurance. From her conversations with Betsey Copp, she had come to fully understand the importance of economic independence for a woman.

"As a matter of fact, I've already talked to Mr. Brandegee about a trust fund for you," he said. It wasn't exactly a lie, for Brandegee had hinted at such an arrangement during their first meeting. No doubt it would be the right thing to do.

"Really?" she said. "I had no idea."

"I'm hoping to get all the details worked out during this trip." He had already arranged for a meeting with Brandegee to review the children's financial situation, and perhaps they would discuss it again.

Zabette felt reassured by his promises, and it made her even more eager to go home. She would miss the children, she knew, but they were so involved in their own lives, and emotionally, they had already asserted their independence. It would not be so painful as the separation when they were small and had needed her. But they no longer depended on her to dry their tears or bandage their wounds. They did not want her to cuddle them after a bad dream or sing them lullabies when they couldn't go to sleep. *God tells us when it's time to let them go*, she thought, *when it's time for them to fly on their own*. They would have better schooling in the North, she knew, and she wouldn't deprive them of that opportunity. When Medora was older, perhaps she would want to return to Connecticut as well. *Oh God*, she prayed, *let this be the right decision*.

New London, Connecticut, February 3, 1868

Augustus Brandegee stretched out his hand to greet Robert and gestured toward the chair in front of his desk. "It's good to see you again, Mr. Stafford. I hope things did not go too badly for you at Cumberland Island during the war."

"We survived," Robert said tersely. "But much has changed, as you might imagine."

Brandegee nodded. "You were very wise to move so many of your assets north before the war began. It was a terrible time."

"Indeed." Robert's mouth felt dry, as his eyes darted around the room at the fine appointments and dark oak paneling of Brandegee's law office. The man sitting on the other side of the desk smiled affably.

"I suppose you're here to check on the state of everything you left in my care. I'm happy to say that your assets are intact and have gained considerably in value over the last eight years."

"I certainly hope so because I can't say the same for my properties and assets in the South. Fortunately, I never invested in Confederate bonds and I kept relatively small amounts of cash in Confederate dollars. All that was lost, of course."

"I understand. What can I help you with today?" asked Brandegee, flipping open the folder marked "Stafford, R." that lay before him on his desk.

"I wanted to make certain that the assets in the children's trust funds were sound and that I have no reason to worry about their solvency when I return to Georgia."

"You plan to return? I had thought that perhaps you might make your home in Connecticut now that things were in such disarray in the South," said Brandegee.

"My presence is needed there more than ever, and I'm taking the children's mother and our youngest daughter with me. The other children will be on their own for the first time, and I'm hoping that you will be willing to advise them on their investments as needed. Mary, who's the oldest and who is married, will look after the younger children, including her brother Bobby, who . . . has difficulty understanding such things. Her husband is Frederick Palmer, and he too will no doubt help."

"I see," said Brandegee, nodding his understanding. Bobby Stafford's slowness was well known in Groton and New London, and Brandegee looked relieved to know that his sister and her husband would serve as guardians. He hesitated a moment. "I wonder if you have thought any more about the matter of a trust fund for their mother."

"I've thought about it, but I haven't fully decided what to do about it," Robert snapped. He was annoyed that Brandegee had raised the question again. It was true he had thought about it, but he knew that the only control he now had over

Zabette and her movements was money. She could go nowhere, do nothing, without his help. For the moment he wanted to keep it that way. Perhaps later, once they were back in Georgia and he had tested her loyalty, he would be willing to trust her with funds of her own. But not yet. He needed to be sure that she wouldn't up and leave him, as Judy had done, whenever he had one of his fits of temper.

He knew that he was misleading Zabette, who thought he was here today to take care of precisely that matter. But there was no need for her ever to know that it wasn't a *fait accompli*. He had even decided what he would tell her when he returned to Stafford House. *If anything ever happens to me,* he would say, *just contact Augustus Brandegee. He will know what arrangements have been made.* That was perfectly true, and before his death, Robert assured himself, he would make certain that Zabette was provided for. *If she proves loyal,* he thought, *which remains to be seen.*

New London Harbor, March 1, 1868

Zabette dabbed at her eyes with her handkerchief as the steamer, its horn sounding a deafening blast, pulled away from the dock, separating her from her children, who stood on shore waving their farewells. They were all there, even Mary and Frederick and their two children. They had arrived two days earlier to move into the spare bedroom at Stafford House, which had been a merry place indeed for the past two days. Zabette had instructed Mary on the various duties of the servants, as well as the lessons and needs of the younger children. Mary listened patiently, but Zabette could tell that she was growing weary of her mother's instructions.

Dora, who had moped about the house all week, refused to pack. "I won't leave all my friends. I won't. I don't want to go to Georgia," she sobbed. She had been born in Groton and had no concept of what the island was like.

"Let her stay, *Maman*. I'll take care of her." It was the first time Mary had called Zabette *maman* in years.

"I can't leave her, Mary. She's much too young."

"But she knows nothing of Cumberland. She'll be much better off here."

Mary was persuasive, easily convincing Robert, who was already tired of Dora's whining. It was harder for Zabette, but in the end she relented. Dora squealed with delight and rushed into her mother's arms. Zabette held her close as long as she could, until the child broke away and threw herself into Mary's arms. Zabetter shed her tears later, alone in her room as she packed, so that no one could see her disappointment.

Zabette's emotional goodbyes to Hannah, Bernadette, Caitlin, and John had also taken place out of the family's sight. The servants promised to write to her and she to them just to keep in touch. And they assured her they would look after the children to see they were properly fed and cared for. She knew that it was Mary's responsibility, but she also knew that the servants were fond of the children.

"Don't worry about Bobby," John said. "I'll take special care of him," he assured her. All they knew was that she was returning to Cumberland to be with her mother and brother, whom she had not seen since before the war. Whether they ever understood her relationship with Robert, Zabette was not sure, but they never mentioned it and never asked questions. They were good people, she believed. And she cared about them as though they were family. "I'll feed them like they were me own," whispered Hannah when the two had hugged for the last time.

At the dock, Robert frowned his disapproval at Zabette's tearful goodbyes with the children. But she didn't care. She hugged them all, not knowing when she might see them again. And she looked deeply into their faces to memorize every feature.

"We'll miss you, *Maman*," Dora whispered. "But I know you need to go back to see your own *maman* again. We'll all come and visit, I promise."

Would they, Zabette wondered? *Would they ever come to Cumberland?* She doubted it. The trip was long, and their lives here in Connecticut were full. They would grow up and marry and raise their own families. But she would be able to come back to visit them. Robert had promised.

The ship's horn sounded for the second time. Water swirled behind them, and the vessel moved farther away from the crowded dock and turned south toward Long Island Sound. Zabette watched until the waving figures on the dock grew small and turned back toward the ferry that would return them to Groton.

THIS TIME ZABETTE HAD HER OWN STATEROOM, where she could withdraw from the cold sea winds and reflect on all that had happened to her since she had come to Connecticut. It had changed her life, she knew. She had learned so much from Betsey Copp and her books, from the Irish servants, and from life in the North. She knew she could never go back to life at Cumberland as she had known it before, for that life had been swept away by the war. But Cumberland was her home, with all its wonders and even its flaws, and she needed to return.

She wondered what Robert expected of her now. Their relationship had been more formal in Groton than it had ever been at Cumberland. Her role in Groton had been clearly defined. She had been the nursemaid in charge of the children. But without the children, who was she? Why did Robert want her to come back? Surely not to be his mistress again. All that was in the past. He was nearly eighty now, and Zabette herself almost fifty—forty-seven to be exact—and a grandmother. Inside she didn't feel any older than the day she'd first left Cumberland, yet so much had changed.

Finally, on the morning of the fourth day, Zabette stood with the other passengers on deck to watch the steamer sidle up to Savannah harbor. She was surprised that the city seemed unaltered. It had no doubt been cleaned up from its Union occupation of two years earlier, and most of the buildings along the waterfront, where the cotton factors had their offices, were intact. *It's so different from New London,* she thought, remembering how in Connecticut everyone seemed to rush about, always in a hurry. Here rhythms were slower, gentler, and figures sat on the dock watching the ships come and go. She was impressed by the large live oaks in the old squares, the barrels and bales of cotton that sat on the wharf. A little boy of maybe seven or eight dangled his feet over the edge of one of the bales, his dark face a striking contrast to the whiteness of the cotton that showed through the burlap and the metal bands that held it together. *What a beautiful child,* she thought. She was amazed by the number of black faces, which she had not seen for more than a decade. Although an occasional black man or woman passed through Groton, they were few and far between. The beauty of their faces, some with skin as dark as mahogany, some like coffee with cream, some as light as her own, and with all shades in between, struck her with force. She realized how much she had missed them. Even though they flowed through her dreams and memories, their actual presence warmed her spirits. This was her place and these were her people—all of them, black and white—and she had missed them.

She sat on deck as much as possible for the rest of the journey back to St. Marys, her eyes bright with wonder at the distant islands and glimpses of marshlands. She could make out palm trees, live oaks, and tabby ruins that occasionally rose up on the shoreline. She could smell the sea as she watched the gulls and brown pelicans soaring behind the vessel. Once a pair of porpoises raced alongside the boat. She was delighted by their leaps and antics, remembering how she used to sit on the porch of Plum Orchard with her grandmother and watch them playing in the river. *Oh, God, she had missed it all so much.* The marshes still displayed much of their winter brown, but she knew that it would not be long before they greened again, sheltering and nurturing the tiny and fragile sea creatures that were born there.

The icy March wind of the north had given way to warmer breezes now, and she had long since taken off her heavy coat to let the southern air caress her body. She breathed deeply, feeling the salty air brushing her cheeks and the gentle weight of the sun on her back.

The vessel stayed in deep waters until it reached the lower tip of Cumberland Island, where it veered right into the river toward St. Marys. As they rounded the southernmost point, she was shocked to see the charred chimneys of Dungeness looming over the island.

Robert was staring at it, too. She looked at him and saw the stubborn set of his jaw as he answered her unasked question. "They say drunken soldiers burned it down." But the hungry look in his eye told her that he desired the land no less. He could do without the house.

Her heart raced as they approached the St. Marys dock and she began to recognize familiar sights. Although she had been there only once before, it was imbedded in her memory. Stores, churches, and houses still lined Osborne Street. People still ambled about the dusty streets, not paved like those in Groton and New London, but sand and shell to ease the horses' hooves. The town looked, if anything, poorer than when she'd left. Some of the buildings needed coats of paint, and a broken-down wagon stood abandoned to the right of the dock. Otherwise it had changed very little. She peered intently at the people to see if she could recognize any of the faces, but though some looked familiar, she could not say for sure whether she knew them.

Once they had debarked, Robert approached a group of freedmen gathered on the dock to see if they would row them to Cumberland. Zabette found it strange to watch him negotiate the price with the cluster of black men, who were dressed in poor garments, almost colorless from many washings, men he had once ordered about imperiously.

"Any of you fellows have a boat?"

"I'se got one, boss," replied one of the men, sitting on a low barrel and mending a fishing net. Three others surrounded him, one leaning against a piling, and the other two squatting on the dock, their arms resting on their knees. They gazed with curiosity at the white man and the mulatto woman standing behind him.

"How'd you boys like to earn a little money?" Robert asked.

Zabette saw the man clench his jaw just for a moment at the word "boys," but he replied amicably enough, "We'd sho' like that, boss." He glanced around at the other men who nodded. "What we got to do?"

"Row us out to Cumberland," Robert said.

"Whooee, tha's a long way. How much you gone pay?" the man asked.

"Four dollars—a dollar each," Robert offered.

"Well, I reckon tha's a mighty long way for such a little bit. Don't know if we can do that. I reckon we needs a little mo'."

"Tha's right," said the man leaning against the piling.

Zabette could see Robert's face turning red at being refused. "All right. Six dollars, then, but that's my final offer!"

The men, who obviously needed the money, talked among themselves for a moment, then nodded in acquiescence. "Tha's fine, boss. You wants to leave now?"

The deal struck, Robert and Zabette stepped into the boat, hollowed out from an ancient cypress tree like those she had known on the plantation. The boatmen loaded their valises.

As in the days before the war, the men chanted as they rowed, the slender vessel cutting through the water. It seemed to make their job easier, and it certainly made the trip more pleasant to listen to their deep voices echoing over the tidal stream.

Zabette could see egrets among the marsh grass, every now and then lifting a leg to stand on only one. Their whiteness looked pink as it reflected the rosy light of the sun sinking lower in the sky, promising a magnificent sunset. The soft warmth of the breeze brushed her skin. For the first time since she left Groton, she relaxed completely and let the sweetness of the Georgia coast wash over her in all its beauty. She realized how deeply she had missed the island, but she was almost home.

She could see it now. From a distance across the marshes it looked uninhabited, except for two wild horses grazing along the riverbank. As magnificent as the green expanse of island was, she could not quite dispel a sense of unease at what she might find there.

Chapter Forty

CUMBERLAND ISLAND, GEORGIA, MARCH 6, 1868
Fifteen-year-old Henry Commodore was waiting with a buggy at the dock. He sat hunched over, half asleep on the driver's seat, as the impatient horse stamped its feet. Robert had notified his housekeeper that they would be arriving today, and she had sent Henry, whom Robert had hired to do odd jobs around the plantation, to meet them. The vehicle had not been cleaned. Henry didn't consider that one of his duties. He'd been hired mostly to look after the horses and dogs, but he seemed to enjoy his role as driver.

He jumped down when he saw the small boat approaching. And once he helped Robert, Zabette, and their belongings into the buggy, he flicked the whip smartly against the horse's flank.

SIGNS OF HUMAN NEGLECT AND THRIVING NATURE greeted Zabette at every turn. Wildflowers were profuse, but most of the fields were overgrown and did not appear to have been worked for several years. Fences were rotting and barns collapsing in upon themselves as morning glory vines consumed them. She saw few indications of people. As they drove down the Main Road toward Planters House, they passed only one elderly black man walking along the road, a hoe over his right shoulder as he led a mule with lumpy sacks slung across its back. Robert nodded at the man as they passed, and the man nodded back, his eyes widening as he saw Zabette sitting on the buggy seat beside the white-haired man.

Zabette caught her breath as they approached Planters House. She had never seen it so unkempt before. The walls looked like they hadn't been whitewashed since before the war, and sections were crumbling from the tabby wall Robert had built to keep the deer and horses out of her flowerbeds and to prevent the children from wandering away when they were small. A rusty harrow lay in the front yard, and the gardens were grown up in weeds. One scraggly camellia bush defiantly displayed its bright-pink flowers, even as a wild blackberry vine climbed the stems.

At their approach, a pack of hound dogs penned up behind the house—there must have been twenty-five or thirty of them—began to bay and bark all at once. Robert had always kept a few sleek well-trained hunting dogs on the place, but never anything like this. They were dirty and thin and had apparently been allowed to breed indiscriminately. The hounds kept up their noise until the buggy had pulled up in front of the stone steps. Henry lifted down the valises and carried them into the house.

"Shut up," Robert called loudly to the dogs, which yipped a few times more and then skulked to shady places in the pen to lie down. They knew their master's voice and seemed to understand the consequences of disobedience.

Clearly, thought Zabette, *there is a lot of work to be done to make this place livable again.* As she climbed the front stone steps, she saw two unfamiliar girls in their teens peering at her from behind the curtains of the open window of the parlor and giggling behind their hands.

"You two get back to work," Robert shouted. "Pay them no mind, Zabette. They're the housekeeper's daughters. I hire them to help their mama. She wouldn't work unless I hired them too. They're a damned nuisance most of the time. But it's right hard to get people to work anymore."

Zabette said nothing as she reached the porch, wondering what she would find inside. The parlor was dark, and some of the furniture was missing. But overall the house was clean and orderly. She recognized its familiar woody smell. As Robert busied himself with instructions to Henry, she took a deep breath, turned into the dining room, and walked out the back door of the house that led to the kitchen, searching for the familiar face of Amanda. The two girls had skedaddled from the parlor at Robert's orders and were huddled on the back steps. Zabette smiled at them and asked, "Is Amanda in the kitchen?"

"No'm," said the oldest of the two. "Amanda ain't here. Jes' us and our mama."

"An' Cumsie," the other girl reminded her. "She Amanda's girl."

"An' Cumsie," the older girl added. "An' Henry," she remembered.

"And what are your names?" asked Zabette.

"I'm Christie," the older girl said. "Really Christiana, but ever'body call me Christie, and this here's Adeline."

"Really?" said Zabette. "I once had a friend at Plum Orchard named Adeline."

"She be our granny, I reckon," said Christie.

"You're Adeline's granddaughters? How wonderful," said Zabette. "And how is she? I haven't seen her for many years."

"She doin' right poorly. Don't get around too much no mo'," Christie replied solemnly.

Suddenly the back door opened, and an aging woman with a clear sense of authority on her round, unsmiling face said sharply, "What you girls doin' out here? You need to get yo'selves back to work," she said. "Now go on."

She turned to Zabette as the girls dashed off toward the kitchen, "I'm Catherine Williams," she said, "Mr. Robert's housekeeper. I hope them girls wasn't botherin' you."

"Oh, no, not at all. They told me that their grandmother was Adeline from Plum Orchard. Are you their mother?"

"Tha's right," she said.

"Are you Adeline's daughter?"

"No'm. My husban' was her son."

"Was? Where is he now?"

"Dead," said Catherine, "two years ago." She supplied no more details.

"And where is Adeline?"

"She live over in Fernandina wit' one o' her daughters who look after her."

"Is she not well?" asked Zabette.

"She done grieved herself half to death after her husband Solomon died a few years back. Jes' worked hisself to death. And then she lost her oldes' boy, my man Frederick. She jes' cain't seem to get over it. And she cain't walk no mo'. She be in right bad shape."

"Oh," Zabette said, remembering the sprightly girl who had been her best friend at Plum Orchard. It was hard to imagine Adeline as a helpless old woman, yet younger than herself. All those years working in the fields, she thought. Zabette wrinkled her forehead, "I'm so sorry to hear that. I would love to see her again."

"I 'spect she wouldn't know you," said Catherine. "She don't hardly recognize me no mo.'"

"What about Amanda who used to be the cook here? Is she still around?"

"Amanda Cooper? She live over in the settlement," Catherine gestured vaguely in no particular direction. "Her daughter Cumsie has done started cookin' here now, but she mighty young and ain't too good at it yet," the older woman laughed good-heartedly. "But she sho' do try, and her mama help her when she can."

It sounded strange to Zabette to hear all the former slaves identified with a last name. But she had heard they had been required by the Freedman's Bureau to take one. "I'm glad to know she's still here, still alive. I haven't seen her since before the war," said Zabette.

"ZABETTE," ROBERT CALLED from inside the house. "Are you comin'?"

"Yes, I'm comin'," she replied. Then, turning to Catherine, she said, "I hope we can be friends. I'm very glad to meet you. And I want to hear all about Adeline."

Catherine made no reply, but she nodded. Zabette smiled and went back into the house.

Robert waited beside the banister to lead her upstairs.

"Robert, I want to go and see Amanda and Mama before I settle in. Catherine said that Amanda lives over in the settlement. Do you know where she means?"

"Well, there's a couple of settlements, but Amanda and her husband moved in near the old Downes place on the Brickhill River. I let them live in the house for a while after Marguerite died."

"You mean Plum Orchard?" she asked. "And what became of Jamie and Margaret?"

"Well, Jamie died in 1859, a while after you left, I guess. I thought I wrote you about it. And Margaret moved to Florida to a place called Woodstock Mills during the war. I think she's livin' over in St. Marys now, or maybe Fernandina, but she still owns the place. I'm sure I wrote you about all that."

"If you did, the letters never arrived," said Zabette. But she knew that during the war letters often went astray. She didn't doubt his word.

"And Mama? What do you know about her?"

"Last I heard she and Jack were still livin' in their old cabin that your grandmother built for them."

"Can I get Henry to drive me up there, do you reckon?"

Robert hesitated, but he finally said, "The team is still hitched up. I'll have him take you, but be home before supper."

Zabette looked at him but did not reply. It was obvious that Robert still wanted to be in control like the old plantation master he used to be. But it was also obvious he was not. He had the money to pay his servants, but they also had the freedom to walk away at any time, as did she, if his demands were unreasonable, and he knew it. It didn't stop him from barking orders at them, but Zabette knew that his harsh tone covered his inner fears of being left alone.

HENRY COMMODORE SEEMED DELIGHTED to drive Zabette to the Brickhill settlement, for as she would learn, he had many friends there, and he was eager to make a good impression on Cumsie's mother in hopes that one day he could get permission to marry her daughter.

Zabette drank in the sights and sounds of the island, delighted as a child to see the shy, soft-faced deer that peered out from behind palmetto foliage and lizards scurrying up the tree trunks. It was all new to her again, almost as though she had never seen it before. It was like Eden before the fall, she thought. Resurrection ferns unfurled in greenness told her that it had rained during the night, and invisible mockingbirds called to her from the oak branches.

It was good to be alone, away from Robert's watchful eye. She had grown so accustomed to her relative independence in Connecticut that it was hard for her to be at his beck and call again. She could feel her spirit resisting his domination, and even a hint of defiance on her part made him more stubborn than ever that she abide by his wishes.

As they approached Plum Orchard, she could see that her grandmother's old tabby house stood in an even greater state of neglect than Planters House. No one had lived there, she surmised, since the beginning of the war, maybe even since Jamie's death. Vines crawled up the walls and threatened to overtake the porch.

And there were holes in the roof where rain could pour through. Behind the house she saw two graves, her father's and what she presumed was her grandmother's, but no tombstone covered the second grave or bore her grandmother's name.

"Henry," she asked, climbing down from the buggy, "do you know why there's no tombstone here? Was one never put up?"

"No'm. I don't rightly know. They used to be one, but them Yankee soldiers broke up lotsa stuff, and maybe they busted it up."

The contrast between man's work, which was everywhere in a state of decay and in constant need of tending, and God's, which seemed only more beautiful from man's neglect, impressed itself upon her. *If I ever have money of my own,* thought Zabette, *I'll replace Grand'mère's stone.* She leaned down to pull away a briar creeping over the grave.

As she bent down, her eye was drawn through openings in the trees by a distant splash of pink. The plum trees were in full bloom. She climbed back into the buggy as she gazed at the orchard. Some of the limbs were dying and broken, and weeds had grown up around the trees, but she thought, *I can tend them and make them healthy again.*

"Henry," she called out to the young driver. "What do you know about plum trees?" Given the state of the Planters House garden, the care of which was one of his duties, she wasn't too impressed with his horticultural skills, but he was young. He could learn.

"Not much, Miss Zabette. But I can ask about and see what need to be done if you wants to work on that orchard."

"Please, just call me 'Zabette,'" she told him. "And do ask about the orchard. I don't know much about it either." She knew that tending the plum orchard wasn't something she could pay him to do, but maybe he would help her anyhow, or if not maybe Jack would help. She just wanted to see it one more time the way it used to be.

THE ONLY WAGON ROAD THAT LED to her mother's house passed hrough the old slave quarters. As they approached she could see that the community had changed. Some of the cabins had been torn down. Others had been built in their place, most with at least two rooms opening toward the river. The sandy yards were swept clean, and in little fenced garden plots beside the houses she could see squash, corn, melons, and beans all planted in neat rows. The fences were made of whatever the people could find—old fence posts, split cedar logs, and baling wire, for the most part—an effort to keep out rabbits, deer, and wild horses.

Zabette could feel the excitement rise within her as they approached, and she saw dark faces appearing at the windows and figures standing in the doorways. At first she recognized no one. Then she heard a voice.

"Lawd, ha' mercy, it's Zabette," said the unmistakable voice of Amanda. By now a dozen or so people had come out of their houses and were standing there to greet her. She recognized one or two of the women from the cotton house, but many of the others were strangers to her. She waved at them all and the ones who knew her waved back, their faces opening with welcoming smiles. "Howdy, Miss Zabette," they called stepping outside their houses to wave. Children were running behind the buggy as it slowed. When Henry reined in the horses, Zabette jumped from the carriage, greeting the women who gathered around her with hugs and smiles. Then she raced in the direction of the first voice.

"Amanda," she called out to the dark face still hidden by shadows. "Is that you?"

The old woman stepped into the sunlight, which burnished her brown arms as she held them open in welcome. Zabette rushed into them. "It's so good to see you. I've missed you so much," she said.

"I missed you too, chile. Welcome home," Amanda said warmly, pushing her back to get a good look at her. "You looks mighty fine, a sight for sore eyes, I reckon."

"So do you. I can't wait to hear all the news, but first, I want to run over to *Maman*'s cabin and see her and Jack. Robert tells me they're still living in the old cabin on this side of the orchard."

Amanda frowned and wrung her hands. "Oh Zabette," she said, the words sounding almost like a low wail. "I reckon Mr. Robert don't know. Or else he didn't want to tell you."

"Tell me what?" asked Zabette. She didn't like the dark expression on the older woman's face.

"Yo' mama done took ill, but I don't reckon he heard about it up there at Planters House. I don't reckon Cumsie mentioned it 'fore he left."

"What is it, Amanda? Is something wrong?"

Amanda put her arm around Zabette's shoulder, "Yo' mama—Marie-Jeanne. She done passed on, chile, while he was gone. We buried her in the orchard not too far from her cabin. Tha's what she wanted."

"Oh, no," cried Zabette. "I didn't get to tell her . . . " She felt tears springing to her eyes. There was so much she wanted to say. How much she regretted that they had not had more time to spend together. How much she had learned about being a mother that she hadn't known before. How much she loved her.

Amanda put her arms around Zabette. "I 'spect she know ever'thing you need to tell her."

"What about Jack?" she asked when she felt in control of herself again.

"He still here, and he gone be glad to see you, but he ain't here right now. He work over in Fernandina and come home on the weekend. He married now and have two chillun—Marie and James. I reckon you can meet 'em later, 'cause I 'spect Jack would want to be here when you meet 'em for the first time."

Zabette nodded in agreement.

"Now why don't you come on in and set a spell?" asked Amanda.

Zabette allowed herself to be led up onto the little cabin's front porch, where two benches provided ample sitting room. But Amanda ushered her on inside the house.

It was small, but it had two rooms, a bedroom and a sitting room with a fireplace. Amanda gestured Zabette toward the rocking chair beside the hearth, a chair softened by a blue handmade cushion, while she took the straight chair beside it. Zabette hesitated, but she understood Amanda's gesture of generosity and hospitality and sat down. The house smelled of baking bread and woodsmoke. The darkness of the walls was brightened by a patchwork quilt that covered the bed Zabette could see in the next room, and a large sweetgrass basket held a few sticks of firewood on the hearth. A cheery fire was blazing in the grate beneath a covered iron pot, steam rising from the edges around the lid. Amanda swung the pot out from over the fire, as Zabette sank into the rocker and wiped tears from her eyes.

"Tell me about *Maman*," she said finally. "How did she . . . die?"

"It were right peaceful," Amanda said. "That ol' hoot owl started up durin' the night, and we was afeared it might be the end, but she was ready, I reckon. An' the good Lord took her wit'out no sufferin.'"

The two women sat quietly, staring into the fireplace for a long time.

"I miss her, Amanda," said Zabette. "Even though I didn't live with her and hadn't seen her for a long time, I miss her."

"I know, chile," said Amanda. "I know."

They sat in silence again, the only sound the creaking of the rocker.

Finally Zabette said, "I hear Cumsie took your place cooking at Planters House."

"Well, she givin' it a try," Amanda chuckled. "Want the truth, I 'spect she mo' interested in that Henry Commodore than she be in cookin'."

Zabette laughed. "Well, you look like you're in good health. Why did you give up cooking for Mr. Stafford?"

"I jes' couldn't stand it no mo'," said Amanda. "That Judy and her chillun jes' 'bout drive me crazy."

"Judy?" asked Zabette. "Who's Judy?"

"Lawd, ha' mercy, you mean you don't know 'bout that? He brung you back here and you don't know. That man's meaner'n a snake."

"Are you talking about Robert?" asked Zabette.

"Honey, the whole time you gone, he have this woman from Rayfield livin' at Planters House. Her name be Judy, and they done had two daughters."

"Two daughters?" asked Zabette. "I don't understand. Where are they now?"

"Judy . . . she done gone to St. Marys. They live there for a while, and I hear that them girls . . . Cornelia and Nanette be they names. I hear they gone north like your chillun, but I don' rightly know."

"He had children by another woman?" Zabette asked in disbelief.

"I shouldn'a told you 'bout them, I reckon," said Amanda, stirring the contents of the pot before swinging it back over the fire. "But that Judy, she be jes' what he deserve. She could sho' give him what for." Amanda cackled at the memory.

"How old are the girls?" asked Zabette.

"I don' rightly know. The oldest, I reckon she be 'bout eighteen or nineteen by now."

"That old? That much older than my youngest daughter?" *Then before I left he had already . . .* Zabette did not want to believe what she knew in her heart to be true. Amanda would never lie to her. "Amanda, did you know before I left Cumberland?"

"We knowed. All us knowed, but nobody want to tell you, Zabette, 'cause don't nobody want to hurt you. It all started when you was at yo' grandmammy's plantation, 'bout the time li'l Addie was born. Or not long after. I reckon he was jes' mad you left him by hisself."

"And why did she leave?"

"I don't rightly know. Mebbe that Judy jes' got tired of him complainin' or maybe he sent 'er away so he could bring you back. But I think he got jes' what he deserved. That Judy, she could be right spiteful. An' them girls 'bout drive me crazy."

"Thank you for telling me, Amanda." Zabette didn't say anything for a long time, and the shadows were growing long.

"I reckon I shouldn'a told you, but I figured you already knowed by now," Amanda said.

"I'm glad you did. I needed to know."

The two women sat silently for a while. Finally Zabette said, "I reckon I best be gettin' on back to Planters House. But before I go, can you show me *Maman*'s grave?"

Amanda nodded and rose. Zabette followed her out the door and toward the orchard.

A plain wooden cross marked the grave between the last two trees where a small mound of dirt was still visible. The blooming trees were fragrant. Zabette broke a small branch of blossoms from each of the trees at the foot and head of her mother's grave and laid them like an X in front of the cross.

"I love you, *Maman*," she whispered, remembering the day so long ago when she and her mother had raced among the trees, the blossoms falling like snow. Kneeling beside the grave, she bowed her head to say goodbye. "I miss you. Forgive me my neglect."

WHAT SHOULD SHE DO NOW that she knew the truth, she wondered, as Henry drove her back to Planters House. Zabette recalled how she had worried about Robert while all along he had a woman—this Judy—in his bed. She remembered the night she had come with him from her grandmother's house, their first night together when she was only sixteen, how he had taken her to his bed and the words he had spoken, words that had lifted her heart. "I take thee, Zabette, to be my wedded wife . . . Till death do us part . . . . If not before a man of God, then before God himself," he had said. She knew now that his vow had been given lightly, that it had meant nothing to him.

But in her heart Zabette knew that his betrayal was not the only point. She, too, had whispered, "Till death do us part." And whatever commitment she had made to Robert had been hers alone. The fact that he had broken his promise to her changed nothing. She would not break her vow. She would stay with him and take care of him. But she would not sleep in his bed. Never again. She was free now, and not his slave. His power over her had ended.

TELLING HIM WAS THE HARDEST PART. When she returned, he was waiting for her in the parlor, sipping a glass of sherry and peering over his spectacles at a newspaper that had arrived during his absence. Cumsie, or Zabette supposed it was Cumsie, was already setting the table for supper.

Maybe I should wait until after supper? Zabette thought. *Maybe even until tomorrow?* No, she knew it must be now. She must not let him harbor any false expectations of her. "Robert," she said. "Can we talk, perhaps upstairs?"

He arose at once to follow her eagerly to the second floor. As soon as they reached his bedroom, where Henry had left her valise, Robert pushed the door shut with his foot and reached out for her. She pushed him away gently, though he tried to pull her back again. "No, Robert, let me speak."

The puzzled expression on his face was not something she had often seen before. Robert was always a man of certainty, a man without doubts. But this time he let her go and looked down at her with questions in his eyes. For a moment he said nothing. Then she saw a brief flash of anger cross his face, then only resentment. Zabette was searching for the words to begin, when finally he broke the silence and said, "You've talked with Amanda, haven't you? She told you."

"Yes, Robert, she told me. About Judy. About the two girls, one almost the same age as Addie."

"But Zabette, you were gone. I needed a woman, godammit. Don't you see?"

"No, Robert, I don't," she replied honestly. "I don't see or understand."

"You left me for your children."

"*Our* children, Robert," she reminded him.

"You're angry with me."

"Not really. Anger is not the word. I feel numb, beyond anger. Disappointed perhaps. But I do know that things between us can't ever again be the way they were before."

"Zabette, for God's sake. You can't mean that. I came all the way to Connecticut to bring you home. You can't leave me. I won't let you."

"Robert," she reminded him, "You came only after Judy left. And you must remember I don't belong to you anymore. I'm free. It's not up to you to say what I can and cannot do."

His eyes flashed in fury, and she thought for a moment that he was going to strike her. Then she watched him regain control of himself and his anger subside to impotent frustration. "I would miss you, Zabette," he said finally.

"I'm not going to leave you, Robert," she said softly, hoping to make him understand.

The furrow between his eyes shifted to a question once more.

"But I'm not going to share your bed any longer. I will stay at Planters House for as long as you live, for as long as you need me. I will look after you, help with the work, and make certain that you are never left alone."

She could see shadows around his eyes, as he blinked hard in disbelief.

"If you'll let me, I'll live in the cook's cabin. No one lives there now that all the servants go back to their own homes and families at night. It will be my home. If that's all right with you."

"What's wrong with you, woman?" he began. But it was obvious almost at once that his bullying would get him nowhere.

She just looked at him steadily, not allowing her eyes to waver.

"Zabette, can't I change your mind?" he pleaded. "Stay here. Please. It won't happen again."

"No, it won't, Robert." She smiled sadly. She felt foolish standing in front of this pathetic old man. They were not young lovers after a silly quarrel.

"Robert, we are too old to pretend, too old to start over again. Maybe it *would* be easier for us both if I just went away," she said, though she didn't have any idea where she might go. She could live with Jack perhaps and his family.

"No, don't leave," he said quickly. "Live in the cabin if you want to. Maybe in time, you'll . . . "

She shook her head. "No, Robert. I don't want you to have false hopes." She hesitated. How could she tell him that something within her, whatever affections she may once have had for him, had vanished with Amanda's revelation? Perhaps, in truth, they had vanished even before, when those wonderful early days of their relationship had ended so many years ago. Whatever bond she had felt with him had been broken by his obsession with Phineas Nightingale, with Dungeness, with his own determined resentment. But she had always counted on his fidelity. And given him hers.

"I don't know how to make you understand," she went on. "Whatever was between us is over. I won't pretend. But I will be here as long as you need me. I will even take my meals with you, if you like. You won't be alone. But I won't sleep in your bed. Not ever again."

A helpless, bewildered look settled on his face. She had never seen him like that before, but she stood before him with firmness. She knew that she would not change her mind, and it would be cruel to let him think she might.

He nodded curtly, but with apparent resignation. "I'll take your valise to the cabin myself, after the servants leave for the night, if that's all right with you."

She understood. He did not want to face their questioning looks. Not tonight. If it happened after they left, perhaps they would think he had sent her away, banished her to the cabin, and never know that the choice was hers. She was willing to let him keep that dignity.

"That will be fine. Thank you, Robert."

He said nothing, turned on his heel, and went downstairs to take his supper alone.

Chapter Forty-One

NEW LONDON, CONNECTICUT, AUGUST 18, 1872

At eighty, Robert knew that he was too old to have made this trip. It seemed only yesterday that he had been leaving New London to take Zabette back to Cumberland, and yet it had been four years already. His back ached from the days of forced confinement on the steamer, and he leaned on his cane as he waited on the dock. Henry had helped him ashore and carried all the bags and parcels. Robert paid him well to accompany him on the voyage, for he could never manage the trip alone. Even with Henry at his side, it was a difficult journey. This would be his last trip to Connecticut. Of that he was certain. Only this sad duty compelled him to make this voyage one last time.

Zabette had begged to come with him, but he had refused to pay her passage partly out of lingering annoyance that she still refused to live with him as his wife, but out of a greater fear that this time she might decide not to return to Cumberland. He was well aware that she could never pay for her own passage. Free or not, she still lived on his charity, he thought with a sense of satisfaction, and she needed to know that.

In any case, there was nothing she could have done. Bobby was gone. She had mourned Armand alone; now she needed to let him bear the grief for Bobby. He had thought about his son a great deal on the steamer, remembering how as a child Bobby had preferred his father to anyone else on earth. He may have been the only person in Robert's life to feel that way. Now, he knew, everyone thought him a crotchety old man without feelings. *I have feelings,* he thought. *I just don't see any reason in tarnation to spread them out for display. It's nobody's business but mine.* He remembered hoisting Bobby up in front of him on his saddle as a little boy and how the child had squealed with delight during the early morning rides they had taken together. Bobby's had been the purest love Robert had ever known in his life. He wished he had spent more time with the boy and not given over so much of the responsibility to his younger brother.

They had received word of Bobby's illness in late July, and then on August 8, word had come that he had died—of pneumonia, the telegram said, at age thirty. That was all they knew.

"Uncle Robert!" Mary and Addie suddenly extricated themselves from the hordes of people that milled around on the dock. "I'm sorry we're late, but the ferry doesn't always run on schedule as you know."

Addie hugged her father with enthusiasm, but Mary hung back, waiting her turn with decorum. "We're so pleased you could come," she said, offering him her cheek to kiss. "*Maman* didn't come with you?" she asked.

"No," was his terse reply. He chose not to explain. "Only Henry." He gestured to the young black man who was walking down the gangplank, his arms laden with the last of the parcels. Wide-eyed at the bustling seaport of New London, with its tall whaling vessels crowding so close to one another, Henry gazed about the busy dock with uncertainty.

"Can we get a porter?" asked Robert. "I don't think Henry can manage all this by himself all the way to the ferry." Mary waved her handkerchief for one of the Irish porters loitering about the dock. He brought over a cart, and together he and Henry loaded the bags onto it.

"Why did *Maman* not come with you?" Addie asked.

"She had things to do," he said noncommittally.

Addie looked disappointed. "I wanted to show her how well I can speak French."

"I'll tell her for you," was all he answered.

The shiny Palmer Landau waited on the Groton side of the ferry. Robert, assisted by Henry, settled into the carriage facing his two daughters. Henry climbed onto the seat beside the driver John, who nodded at him curtly. Robert had bought Henry new clothes when they stopped over in Savannah, and he looked rather splendid and proud of himself sitting high on the carriage seat.

Groton had changed little since Robert's last visit. A new building here or there, perhaps, but overall the same quiet New England town it had been for years. His daughters, on the other hand, had changed a great deal. They were not only older but looked more sophisticated. Mary, with her haughty expression and upswept hair looked very fashionable in her black dress and bonnet, worn, he supposed, in mourning for her brother. Addie too was dressed in black. She was probably the prettiest of the lot, thought Robert. She had an almost Mediterranean look about her with her olive skin. Her hair was nearly as dark as Mary's, but without those tight curls Mary worked so hard to control. They were both far too young to be wearing those dark, dreary dresses, he thought. It just didn't seem right that his daughters should have to wear mourning for their thirty-year-old brother who had been healthy as a horse the last time he saw him.

As they turned into the driveway at Stafford Place, Robert looked about with satisfaction. It was a fine-looking house, very stylish and well kept. John had done a good job on the shrubs around the house and the trees in the orchards. Everything looked neat and trimmed and healthy. So much better than Planters House, he thought, where he couldn't find enough workers to keep things shipshape, much less try to work the fields and grow cotton. He had almost given up on the cotton crop, which had done so poorly the year before. And keeping the accounts was more than he could handle anymore. He had even had to ask Zabette to read him the figures because his eyes had gotten so bad.

HE WAITED UNTIL THEY WERE INSIDE Stafford House, out of earshot of John and Henry before he asked about Bobby. Once in the parlor, he turned to Mary and said finally, "Now tell me what happened."

Mary looked at Addie for support, but Addie stood silent, staring at the floor. Mary wrung her handkerchief trying to find the right words. "Papa, he was never the same after Armand died and *Maman* went back to Cumberland. John tried to teach him about training horses, but he showed no interest in anything. He would sit on the verandah for hours staring out at the orchards. It was almost like he was willing himself to join Armand."

"And what did you and the other children do to help?" asked Robert.

Mary and Addie exchanged looks he could not read. Mary said nothing.

Addie finally ended the silence. "I guess we didn't do enough, Papa," she said. "We were all so intent on our own lives that we just didn't realize . . . " her voice trailed off.

"And then he got sick and took to his bed. It was like he didn't want to get up anymore . . . " Mary added.

Robert frowned, understanding the situation more clearly than either of the two women could realize. He remembered his mother and how little he had done to make her want to live anymore. He could hardly blame his daughters when he had been no more thoughtful toward his own mother, until Zabette had prodded him, and then it had been too late.

But he could also understand Bobby's despair. He remembered himself as a lonely boy in New England, mocked by his peers. He had had no family there for support. And evidently, he thought with bitterness, neither did Bobby. The young man was too slow to interest the eligible women in Groton, though that would not have prevented his having feelings and being attracted to them. Perhaps Bobby, like his father, had even fallen in love with a young woman who had laughed at him and at his slow, stammering ways. *I survived that mockery*, thought Robert. But Bobby was not strong like his father had been. Armand had been his only true friend, and without him he was lost.

"I should have insisted on taking him back to Cumberland," Robert said with a pang of guilt, something he rarely felt. He had taken Bobby's mother, the one support he had left, back to Planters House for his own selfish reasons, reasons which now mocked him, for in the long run they had amounted to nothing. He and Zabette lived separate lives for the most part, though she would sit with him whenever he asked. She helped Cumsie in the kitchen and sometimes took her meals with him in the dining room when he invited her. If he was sick, she was always there to tend him. But she had kept her vow not to come to his bed again. He had grown used to it by now. Although her presence at Planters House was a comfort to him, it was not all he wanted. But it was all he would ever have.

If he had left her here, she could have been a comfort to Bobby, nursed him back to health. But *dammit, it was Bobby's choice. He wanted to stay. And Zabette wanted to go back to Cumberland.* It was not his fault, he reasoned, but theirs.

In any case, Robert refused to dwell on it. His son was gone. That was that. Now he had only daughters. "And where are Ellen and Dora?"

"They should be home shortly. Both of them were invited to an afternoon tea at the Brandegee home."

"Were you not invited?" he asked.

"Oh yes, of course we were," said Addie, "but I didn't want to miss your arrival for anything. There are plenty of teas to go to. But how often do we get to see you? They wanted to meet you too, but we didn't think there would be room for everyone in the carriage. We didn't know *Maman* wouldn't be with you."

The mention of Zabette and the Brandegees' tea reminded Robert of the other reason for his visit. He had finally decided that Augustus Brandegee was right and that he would be remiss not to leave Zabette some means of support after his death. He needed to make some adjustments in his will anyhow since Bobby had died, and he might as well establish an annuity for the children's mother.

He had thought about it a great deal. At first he had been so angry at her decision to live in the cook's cottage instead of with him that he had decided it was another betrayal, just like that of Judy. In such moments, he thought, *she can fend for herself. I owe her nothing.* Then he thought of how she was always there when he needed her, when he was sick, when he just needed company, and he realized that she hadn't abandoned him like Judy at all. She was always with him, understanding him better than anyone else.

She could, after all, have stayed in Groton and refused even to come back to Cumberland. Sometimes, when he remembered their life together, it crossed his mind to write her into his will, for now that she was a free woman, she could inherit. He even thought of leaving her what he owned of Plum Orchard, her grandmother's house where she had grown up and which he knew she loved. At such moments he recalled the depth of her eyes, the softness of her hands, and the sweetness of her voice. But then he would consider all the questions and embarrassment such a legacy might cause his nieces and nephews in Georgia who would inherit the rest of his land on Cumberland. It just would not do.

The only control he had left over Zabette was his money, and whatever he did he would never tell her. That he knew. He recalled his vow to leave her an annuity only if she remained faithful to him and didn't desert him like that Judy, of whom he had seen neither hide nor hair since he set her daughters up for life. He felt well rid of Judy and had no intention of leaving her a penny, but he had been fond of the girls, he had to admit. Nanette was the bright one. She wanted to go to college, even be a doctor. Robert had laughed at that. *Whoever heard of a colored woman doctor?* he thought. But he was glad she had ambition.

In the end Robert realized that Zabette *had* in her own way remained faithful—to him and to the children. She had lived up to all his expectations but one, and to a man in his eighties, that one should perhaps no longer be the most important consideration. He had not made the final decision until he was forced into so much contemplation during the recent sea voyage to New London. He *would* provide something for Zabette, he had concluded, and he planned to meet with Augustus Brandegee as soon as possible.

MARY HAD MADE A NUMBER OF CHANGES in the house. The furniture was more elegant now, all expensive mahogany or walnut, polished within an inch of its life. She had replaced the old upright piano with a grand piano imported from Germany, so that little Mellie could practice her scales. And the comfortable old sofa that had sat in front of the fireplace had been discarded. On either side of the chimney stood horsehair-stuffed love seats with button backs, scrolled rosewood, and tufted arms. They didn't look a bit comfy to Robert, who elected to sit in one of the side chairs, where he could prop his cane against the arm and wait for the return of his other two daughters.

PLANTERS HOUSE, CUMBERLAND ISLAND, AUGUST 18, 1872

"Zabette," said Cumsie, looking up from the dough she was kneading. "Can I get you somethin'? I'se worried that you look so sad."

"I'm fine, Cumsie. But I am sad, I guess. I keep thinking about poor Bobby and wonderin' about his last days. I'm sad that I didn't get to go to Connecticut with Robert at least to put flowers on Bobby's grave. You don't remember him, I'm sure. You were just a baby when he left Cumberland."

"I used to hear Mama talk about Bobby all right. She say he was a sweet, gentle chile and always kind to ever'body."

"Both my boys are dead now, Cumsie," said Zabette.

"But you still got daughters. Some people don't have nobody," Cumsie said.

"Yes, I do, but I don't know whether I'll ever see them again. Your mother has you with her here at Cumberland."

"Tha's right," Cumsie said. "I reckon we's right lucky."

"I think you are," said Zabette. "No, I'm sure you are. You have a wonderful mother, you know."

"I do know," Cumsie said proudly. "My maum's somethin' special."

"Yes, she is. She's been like a mother to me, as well."

Pinching off a piece of the dough Cumsie had set aside while she greased the bread pan, Zabette put it in her mouth, letting it take her back to her own childhood. She had done the same thing when she had been a little girl at Plum Orchard, sneaking pieces of dough from Daisy's unbaked bread. Now its yeasty taste called up so many of those memories.

"Why didn't you go to Connecticut with Mr. Robert?" asked Cumsie as she nestled the loaf of bread she had shaped into the tin pan and put it in the oven.

"He refused to take me. I guess he's still a bit angry with me for things not being like they used to be."

"He be angry 'most all the time, 'bout most ever'thing," Cumsie said.

"You're right," Zabette nodded sadly. "I think he's been angry most of his life. But it's only because he was hurt at such a young age."

"Hurt?" asked Cumsie. "How come?"

"Well, from what he told me, when he was just a young man, he was in love with a pretty young woman named Caty Nightingale."

"Yeh," said Cumsie. "I know 'bout them. Miss Caty was Mr. Phineas's big sister."

"That's right, and from what Robert told me, he went to court her, but she turned him away and laughed right in his face. He was humiliated, and she broke his heart. I hear she went on to marry a cousin. It affected Robert for the rest of his life, and I think it's the reason for so much of his anger."

Cumsie had been listening intently, "Tha's some story!" she said. "But it sho' ain't the way I heared it," Cumsie said.

"What do you mean?" asked Zabette. "What did you hear? And where did you hear it?"

"The cook what used to work over at Dungeness—Abigail—she tell me that Mr. Robert done broke Miss Caty's heart."

"What?" asked Zabette in disbelief.

"Abigail say Miss Caty was real sweet on Mr. Robert. He was tall and han'some, and they wasn't many young men on the island. She was really sweet on him. Tha's what I heared."

"But what happened?"

"Well, Abigail tell me that one day Miss Caty come runnin' down to the kitchen boo-hooin' and carryin' on somethin' awful. She was real mad at her brother Phineas. And she just pour out the whole story. Her mama wouldn't listen, so Miss Caty come to Abigail."

"What had happened?"

"Well, Master Phineas, he used to always make fun of Miss Caty and her crush. You know how tall Mr. Robert was—way over six feet. And that Miss Caty, she was jes' a little bitty thing—not much more'n five feet tall. Mas' Phineas . . . Mr. Phineas," Cumsie corrected herself, "he used to call 'em 'the long and the short of it.' I'm sure he didn't mean no harm, but it got to be a joke in the fam'ly. And Miss Caty's mama and her Aunt Louisa, they never did like Mr. Robert."

"So I've heard," Zabette said.

"Well, one day Mr. Phineas and Miss Caty was sittin' on the front porch, him on the banister and her in the swing. And Mr. Phineas, he musta been 'bout fourteen years old, he caught sight of Mr. Robert ridin' up the driveway of Dungeness to court Miss Caty."

So far it sounded like the same story Zabette had heard from Robert, except for the part about Caty Nightingale being fond of him.

"And then what?" she asked eagerly.

"Well," said Cumsie, "Mr. Phineas he say to Miss Caty, 'Well looky here, here come the long of it,' and Miss Caty, in spite of herself, she bust out laughin'. When Mr. Robert rode up and saw 'em laughin', he must think they be laughin' at him, an', the way Abigail tell it, he turn his horse right aroun' and started to ride away."

"Oh, no," said Zabette.

"Miss Caty, she jump up and start to run after him, but he is gallopin' by now and don't look back, and he be gone fore she hardly get out o' that swing."

"Oh, how terrible," said Zabette. "You mean she didn't mean to send him away?"

"Oh, no," Cumsie said. "From what I hear, she was real sweet on Mr. Robert."

"Then what happened?" Zabette asked.

"Miss Caty, she run down to the kitchen where Abigail be gettin' ready for supper, and she cryin' like her life be over. She tell Abigail what happen, and she was mad as a hornet wit' her brother."

"Why didn't someone go after Robert and tell him that it was just Phineas teasing Caty?"

"Mr. Phineas was just a boy, but he try. But Mr. Robert, he was long gone, and he wouldn't talk to nobody for days after that," Cumsie said.

"What finally happened?" Zabette asked.

"Well, Miss Caty, her heart was broke in two. And Mr. Robert, he never would listen. You know he be a stubborn man. An' like you say, she fin'ly marry her cousin—John Littlefield—but from what I hear, they never was too happy. Lived up in Tennessee, I hear. And then Miss Caty, well, she died about ten years after her marriage. I don't think they ever had no children."

Tears had sprung to Zabette's eyes. She could hardly understand how such a small incident had ruined Robert's life, and yet she believed the story. It was unlikely that the Nightingale's cook would have made up such a story. Robert hadn't been rejected by Caty. On the contrary, she felt rejected by him. And on this fiction he had built all his lifelong anger. She was amazed how such a misunderstanding could have affected his life—and hers—in such a way. Had Caty Nighingale not laughed at her brother's silly joke, Robert and Caty might have married. And if they had married, Mary, Bobby, Armand, Addie, Ellen, and Dora might never have existed! How strangely life works out.

"Oh, Cumsie, thank you for telling me all this," Zabette said. "But poor Robert. He built his whole life around something that was never true."

"I reckon lots of people does foolish things wit' their lives," said Cumsie.

Cumsie's words struck Zabette full force, and for a moment she was once again a little girl, with her face pressed against the window glass, watching her father strike her mother. That dreadful night, she later learned from her grandmother, that awful night too was the result of such a misunderstanding. *Why oh why*, she thought, *can't people learn to talk with one another? Why don't they try to communicate?* But she knew the answer. She knew the painful ways of the obstinate heart.

THE QUESTION THAT PLAGUED ZABETTE now was what should she do? Should she tell Robert? Or keep the information to herself? She knew that she had weeks to decide, for Robert would not return for at least ten days or perhaps more. It was not an easy decision, and finally she went to the Plum Orchard settlement to talk it over with Amanda, who, next to her, knew Robert as well as anyone did.

The two women sat on the front porch of Amanda's little house, fanning away the heat and August flies. "What do you think, Amanda?" Zabette asked, "Should I tell him what really happened?"

Amanda thought for a long time, staring off into space. Then, after several minutes had passed, she replied, "Zabette, I think you ought to jes' let it be."

"You don't think I should tell him the truth?"

"Zabette, he done built his whole life around the story—thinkin' Miss Caty made fun of him. Ever'thing he done since then be settled 'round that moment, from what you say. You tell him now, ever'thing he ever believe come a-crumblin' down. Ever'thing he ever done will be full of regret. Wit'out that story, he jes' don't exist and his life ain't got no meanin'. Ain't no need to stir it all up again."

"Perhaps you're right," Zabette said, taking a sip of the sweet tea Amanda had made. She would have to think about it. But what Amanda said made sense. She knew the old woman had gained a lot of wisdom over the years.

What good would it do now to tell him the truth? To tell him that his life had been wasted, based on a silly misunderstanding. But had his life been wasted? He might think so if he knew, but he had fathered eight children—two of whom were now dead, it was true, but six young women, her beautiful daughters and Judy's, whose lives might in fact be fruitful. Wasn't that worth something, after all? Why, at this point, should he be made to regret the only things that had made his life worthwhile? He had helped her grandmother and done what he thought was right. He had no doubt done many regrettable things, foreclosed on mortgages of people who lost everything. But in Robert's mind, even those acts were in the end for the benefit of his family. Why cause him unnecessary regrets?

It was not an easy decision, and she was not even sure it was the right one, but in the end, Zabette decided to say nothing, to keep the Cumberland secret that had remained dormant for so long. To let Robert live the rest of his life in peace, at least in as much peace as he was capable of finding.

GROTON, CONNECTICUT, AUGUST 19, 1872

On the morning after his arrival in Groton, Robert had an early breakfast before anyone else in the family had arisen. He sat alone at the large mahogany table in the dining room, as Hannah served him hashbrown potatoes and scrambled eggs, toasted bread, and coffee. He missed Cumsie's biscuits and country ham and knew that he preferred southern cooking to Hannah's. But he ate with relish nonetheless.

"Hannah," he said, "ask John to come inside? I've got something I want him to do."

"Yes, Mr. Stafford," she said, scurrying back to the kitchen and out the back door to the kitchen garden, where John was pulling weeds from around the tomato plants.

"JOHN, I WANT YOU TO PICK ME A FRESH BOUQUET for Bobby's grave."

"Wouldn't you like to select the flowers yourself, sir?"

"No, no. Whatever you choose will be fine. And when you're done, hitch up the horses. I'd like to drive over to the cemetery this morning. And tell Henry I want him to come along."

In truth, Robert would have preferred to have Henry alone drive him, but John knew the way, and Henry was not familiar with the horses, which tended to be more high spirited than the ones he was used to handling on Cumberland. But Robert still needed Henry to help him in and out of the carriage. He just felt better when Henry was with him because the younger man had learned to anticipate his needs and knew his weaknesses. They weren't something that had to be explained. It always galled Robert to have to ask for help, but he just couldn't get in and out of these high carriages anymore without a boost.

THE CEMETERY WAS COOL AND QUIET this morning. Only one other carriage was parked eight or ten rows away from Bobby's grave, beside that of his brother. A woman dressed in black knelt beside a new tombstone, while a bored-looking driver slouched beside the carriage, holding the horses' reins.

Robert looked with satisfaction at Armand's upright stone. He had not seen it before; as a rule he hated cemeteries. Mary had selected it, he suspected. The stone was shaped with a pointed Gothic arch at the top. Engraved at the top of the stone was an S for Stafford, with three vertical lines running through it. To Robert it looked rather like a dollar sign with an extra line, but he dismissed the thought. It was a handsome stone that gave Armand's name, the dates of his birth and of his death. Nothing more. Simple, classic. He would have an identical stone carved for Bobby, and the two would lie side-by-side, with Bobby and his brother together again.

Robert ran his hands over Armand's stone. Bobby's grave was now only a mound of dirt, with faded flowers lying on top.

"Get rid of those dead flowers," Robert ordered, and Henry began to gather them up.

"What do I do with 'em, Mr. Robert?" asked Henry.

"Just put them up over there," he pointed to an empty plot, "I'm sure someone will dispose of them later."

When Henry returned from piling the brown flowers one on top of the other in the vacant plot, Robert took the roses and asters John had chosen and divided them into two smaller bouquets, laying one on Bobby's grave and one on Armand's. He should have asked for more flowers, he realized, but these would have to do. He stood silent for a moment before the grave. *Goodbye, my sons,* he thought. He could think of nothing else to say, refusing himself any emotions, as he turned and said to John in his most officious-sounding voice, "Now, I'd like you to drive me to Augustus Brandegee's office. I have important business there."

Chapter Forty-Two

PLANTERS HOUSE, CUMBERLAND ISLAND, AUGUST 1, 1877
A wave of hot, humid air greeted Zabette as she emerged from her cabin, which still held some of the coolness of the night. It was very early in the morning for such heat, even in August. The air barely stirred as she made her way toward the kitchen, where she knew Cumsie would have Robert's breakfast tray waiting. It was always Zabette who took it up to his bedroom and who fed him his breakfast.

Ever since his trip to Groton five years earlier, he had grown weaker. The trip, even with Henry's help, had been hard on him. After his return, he stopped riding his horse altogether. It was too humiliating for him to have Henry help him into the saddle. Instead, he spent his mornings on the front porch gazing at the river or contemplating his overgrown cotton fields. Since his stroke in December, he had hardly left his bed and seemed to have given up on life.

The stroke had affected his ability to hold a book and read. It didn't matter much because his eyesight was so bad that he could no longer read anyhow. Zabette read him the newspapers or the Bible as she sat beside his bed on days he did not feel like getting up. He liked the Old Testament stories best—the stories of David and Goliath, of blind Samson pulling down the pillars to collapse the roof and destroy the Philistines, of Joseph rising in Egypt to lord it over his treacherous brothers. He drank in her words like the brandy he could no longer have. He always liked stories about the underdog, the younger son, the one who always triumphed over those who thought themselves superior. The Bible was full of them. He would growl his approval. These were the closest moments the two of them shared now.

"MORNIN', CUMSIE," SAID ZABETTE. "Looks like it's gone be mighty hot today."

"Sho' do," Cumsie said, leaning over her churn, as she worked the plunger up and down to make new butter to stock the well house. Zabette wondered how she could still work as much as she did, for she was well along in her second pregnancy. Since her marriage to Henry Commodore four years earlier, Cumsie had blossomed with maternal sweetness. And she had her mother's strength.

"You feelin' all right today?" Zabette asked with concern.

"Right as rain," said Cumsie. "You jes' worry too much, Zabette. Women's been workin' and havin' babies out here for a long time." Cumsie paused and chuckled.

Zabette envied her happiness. She and Henry obviously loved each other, and they were a team at Planters House, always working hard and doing whatever needed to be done around the place, helping each other if one's work was done but the other's wasn't, but always returning to Brickhill in the evening to enjoy their family.

As she watched Cumsie's vigorous churning, Zabette remembered their wedding. It had not been a broom-jumping ceremony like Adeline's. After freedom, when their marriages could be legally registered, most island blacks chose to marry instead in traditional ceremonies more like those of the island whites. Henry and Cumsie had said their vows in the whitewashed church Robert had built north of Planters House.

Members of the community had decorated it with a profusion of Cherokee roses and palmetto fronds, and the pews were crowded with as many people as they could hold. Those who couldn't get inside stood under the trees to listen. All the people from Brickhill and the Settlement just south of Half Moon Bluff came for the wedding. Families with chosen names like Mitchell, Alberty, and Merrow celebrated with the Commodores and Coopers the union of their families.

Zabette was one of the lucky ones who had found a seat inside, and she had wept at the beauty and simplicity of the service as Cumsie and Henry were joined in holy matrimony. She had long since begun to feel accepted as one of them, especially in the little church she now attended, and Amanda and Cumsie treated her just like they treated all their other friends. She was no longer the "massa's gal." Even though she still lived at Planters House, Amanda made sure everyone knew that she was living on her own in "Zabette's cottage," as everyone called it now, and not sleeping in Robert Stafford's bed. Somehow it gave her a greater place of acceptance into the community.

"She cain't help what she is," Amanda had explained to everyone, while Cumsie would say "Uh huh," in agreement. "She be born and raised by white folks, but her mama was one o' us and she be one of us now."

"Tha's right," said Cumsie. "Tha's right."

AFTER THE WEDDING ENDED, people poured out of the church onto the wide sandy space under the trees where the congregation was accustomed to gather after Sunday service. The women had all brought food to spread out on makeshift tables of sawhorses and planks, covered by colorful tablecloths. Just as had happened at Adeline's and Solomon's wedding, a child, a boy this time, stood at the end of the table to fan away the flies with a large palmetto leaf once the food was uncovered and while people filled their plates and congregated in shady spots to eat and talk.

Zabette helped herself like everyone else to the roasted raccoon and the fried chicken. Amanda had made hoppin' john, a tasty concoction of rice and red beans, and Henry's mama had made a huge bowl of sweet potato poon. Casseroles of every variety—squash, potato, and green bean—decked the table. Smoked mullet and roasted oysters added to the tantalizing combination of smells. A two-tiered wedding cake, decorated with white icing, was the centerpiece as far as every child was concerned, and a bowl of the fragrant lilies that still bloomed in Marguerite Bernardey's overgrown garden at Plum Orchard, a gift from Zabette, graced the table.

As she was tasting her last bite of potato poon, Zabette looked up to see an attractive man about her age, maybe a little older, under an oak tree on the other side of the church yard watching her intensely. He seemed vaguely familiar, but she could not remember where she had seen him before. He had on a dark suit, well worn along the cuffs, but he looked quite distinguished since some of the men were there in overalls, probably the only clothes they owned. When he caught her eye, he sauntered over to the tree under which she was sitting.

"How ya doin'?" he asked.

"I'm doin' just fine," she answered with a smile. "How're you?"

"Fine. Jes' fine," he said. "I don't reckon you recollect meetin' me a long time ago?" It was a question.

"Well . . ." she hesitated. "You look sort of familiar, but I don't . . . "

"Seem like we meets only at weddin's," he grinned.

Suddenly she did remember. He was the attractive man at Adeline's wedding who had approached her and even touched her briefly before Daisy had shooed him away so unceremoniously. She remembered his name, the indelible impression he had made on her at the time, and even the warmth of his hand.

"You're Ben?"

"I'se Ben. Ben Freeman," he said, holding out his hand to shake hers. "I'se su'prised you recollect. We jes' met that one time."

She'd quickly wiped her hands on the napkin to rid them of the grease from the fried chicken she had eaten and held out her right hand to shake his.

"You're hard to forget," she'd said with a smile. "It's good to see you again."

"It's good to see you too," he'd replied awkwardly. Then he'd stood silent for a few moments. "I hear you livin' in the cook's old cottage down at old man Stafford's place," he said.

"That's right. I help around the house and take care of Mr. Stafford best I can."

"How you do that?" he asked, genuinely interested in what her duties might be.

"Well, mostly I read to him and help him with his meals, give him his medicines, things like that. I'm kind of like a nurse."

"You reckon I could come down there sometime and pay you a visit?"

"Well, maybe," she said coyly, but with an even broader smile. "Do you live here on the island?" she asked.

"I lives over in Fernandina right now, but I rents a barn from Mr. Clubb up at High Point. I got a blacksmith shop up there, an' I'se tryin' to get him to sell me a li'l piece of land out here to build me a house," he explained. Zabette knew that the Clubb family had opened a small hotel at the north end, and they needed a blacksmith for the horses they made available to their guests.

"Well, Ben Freeman," she said, "I wish you luck, and if Mr. Stafford needs any smithin' done, I'll surely recommend you."

"I rightly 'preciate that," he said.

He was no longer the young man she remembered, but he was still handsome, with broad shoulders and strong hands and a touch of gray in his dark hair that set off his coffee-colored skin. His eyes were lively, and his smile was infectious. Zabette had never felt more drawn to anyone so spontaneously. *Yes,* she thought, *this is a man I would like to know better.* She hoped against hope he would follow through with his intent to pay her a visit. She would be waiting.

SINCE THE WEDDING she and Ben had spent occasional afternoons together when he wasn't busy shoeing other people's horses. They felt comfortable with each other. He had lost his wife not many years before, and he had three grown children who no longer lived with him. She and Ben found much to talk about. She had asked him if he knew about her children.

"I knows all 'bout that," he said.

"Does it bother you?" she asked.

"Only thing bother me is that you didn't have no choice 'bout none of it, but I'se right happy that you's back on Cumberland and didn't stay up north with yo' chillun. Or with old man Stafford."

"So am I, Ben. I missed Cumberland so much. And my children grew up and didn't want to come back." He nodded.

"I reckon you miss 'em though," he said. Of course she missed them, but their lives had diverged, and she wondered if she would ever see them again, despite their promises to visit her, and especially since Robert had not kept his promise to pay her passage back to Connecticut to visit them.

She was glad that Ben was in her life. He was like her in so many ways. He loved life and this island. He loved being free to make his own way in the world. They could be together for hours talking, listening to the mockingbird calls, or just sitting in silence, holding hands, comfortable in their thoughts. She thought of the time she had asked Ben about his chosen name.

"It wasn't too hard to figure out. I'se a free man now . . . an' I wasn't about to take any old massa's name. I'se free and tellin' the world," he said, with one of his contagious smiles.

Yes, she liked this man and the way he thought. She liked him a lot. His presence filled an emptiness in her life.

ZABETTE LOOKED OVER THE TRAY that Cumsie had prepared for Robert's breakfast. Soft scrambled eggs just the way he liked them. Ground up country ham. He couldn't chew meat any more since he had lost most of his back teeth, so Cumsie put it through the grinder ahead of time. A napkin and a spoon. Zabette no longer tried to feed Robert with a fork. It was like caring for a baby, soft food, spoons, and other ways that she didn't like to think about. She picked up an extra napkin to use as a bib and pushed open the door with her hip to carry the tray from the kitchen into the Big House.

It was cooler inside. Catherine was busy in the parlor dusting furniture that already gleamed under her care. "Mornin'," she said to Zabette.

"How're you this mornin', Catherine, and how're Christie and Adeline?"

"Meaner'n ever," Catherine teased, affection obvious in her voice. The girls had both found work and husbands and no longer came to Planters House on a regular basis. Catherine did Robert's laundry and ironing and kept the unused house clean. Sometimes she worked in the flower garden with Zabette, and together they had revived some of the roses and lilies that had grown almost wild from their years without tending

"Has Mr. Robert been hollerin' for his breakfast already?" asked Zabette with a smile.

"Naw, he been quiet this mornin'. I don' know if he even wake up yet."

Zabette mounted the staircase, trying to make as much noise as she could. Robert didn't like her to wake him up, but he wanted attention the moment he was wide awake. By this time he was usually shouting, "Zabette! Zabette! Where's my breakfast," his booming voice still strong enough to roar commands. It frightened Catherine and Cumsie, and as a consequence, Zabette was inevitably the first person to see him in the morning.

Before she fed him, she would wash his face and hands, comb his hair, and plump up his pillows. But this morning, as she opened the door, she saw him still lying on his side, his back to the door. He hadn't stirred, even though light was pouring into the room through the east window.

She set the tray on the bedside table and reached over to give his shoulder a gentle shake. "Robert," she said softly, "Robert, wake up. I have your breakfast here."

He did not move.

She tried again, a bit louder, "Robert, Cumsie's fixed you some country ham."

Still he did not move. Zabette reached out to touch his face. It was cold, and, leaning over him, she saw that his eyes were open, staring sightless into space.

Oh God, no! she thought. *Robert.* She felt for his pulse, as her father had taught her to do when she was a little girl. She rolled him gently onto his back and closed his eyes with her fingertips. Then she pulled a chair up beside the bed and sat down, reaching out to take his cold hand for a moment. He had been dead for several hours, she guessed from the temperature of the body. She hated that he had died alone there in the dark room.

But Robert was always alone, she thought, except for that brief period early in their relationship when he had reached out to her and shared his innermost feelings. Those were such good days, if only they could have lasted. She gazed at his still form. *All those ambitions for land, all that anger and energy, when you could have had so much. We could have been happy, Robert. We could have loved our children, lived with them, and played with our grandchildren. But you threw it all away. For what? Your lust for Dungeness? Just a ruin now. What good would it be?* But it seemed to have been Robert's nature to shut out the world and count success only in terms of possessions. In the end, she felt that's what she had been to him—a possession. The brief tenderness they had shared was so fragile that it had taken only one more snub from Phineas Nightingale to undo it—to cause Robert to revert back to the hard man he had been before he took her to live with him.

When Phineas had died four years earlier, Robert fumed all day that he was unable to go to the funeral in Brunswick. He wanted to see his old enemy buried and in his grave. And he wanted to gloat that Nightingale had died penniless, in debt to people from Savannah to New York, though not, he'd grumbled bitterly, to Robert himself. Phineas needed money so much at the end that he'd even mortgaged his plantation at Cambers Island—Honeygall, he called it—to several people at once. He tried desperately in those final years to sell Dungeness, or what was left of it, to anyone but Robert Stafford. Though he'd claimed he had a good offer from a Rhode Island senator named William Sprague Jr., the deal fell through, and Edmund Molyneux's widow, who held the Dungeness mortgage, took over the Cumberland property in July 1870 when he couldn't make payment.

Nightingale also lost his plantation at Cambers Island two years later when creditors foreclosed on those mortgages. Discouraged and still up to his ears in debt, he died in Brunswick the following April. Robert was gleeful over every one of Phineas's misfortunes.

Dungeness. Zabette wished she had never heard of it. Her eyes were dry as she said a final prayer for Robert. *May God give you peace at last.* Then she went downstairs to tell Catherine and Cumsie. Death was so final. She had devoted forty years of her life to this man, whose only hope of peace lay in death. It would take her a long time to sort out the meaning of it all, if there were a meaning. Only God could be the judge of that.

THE AUGUST HEAT MADE A RAPID BURIAL ESSENTIAL. Zabette asked Henry to carry the news to St. Marys, where most of Robert's family lived. By late afternoon Thomas Hawkins, the son of Robert's sister Susannah, and John and Robert Tomkins, sons of his sister Mary, nieces and nephews who had never visited him, were on the island barking orders to the servants in imitation of their uncle. The funeral was to be held the very next day.

They sent Henry up to the Settlement to find an island carpenter to make the coffin. And Robert Tomkins volunteered to find a preacher who would come to the island and say a few words over the grave. Zabette busied herself in the steamy kitchen with Cumsie, mixing dough, cutting biscuits, and frying chicken, helping prepare food for the mourners. She took little time to consider what Robert's death might mean in her own life. She did not know what would become of his property or of her. But there was time enough later

340 JUNE HALL McCASH

to think about all that. For now, she wanted to do her part to see that Robert had a decent burial.

FEW MOURNERS SHOWED UP at the funeral. They all fit easily inside the tabby walls of the small cemetery Robert had built so many years before. Beside the graves of his mother and sister, covered by identical slabs of marble, a deep hole in the earth stood ready to receive Robert's body. Stafford nieces and nephews and their children stood around the grave with various members of the Clubb and Bunkley families, who had come to pay respects. Amanda, who had worked in his kitchen for so many years, stood behind them with Cumsie and Henry. Zabette held the hand of her brother Jack, and Catherine Williams stood a few feet away.

The face of the young preacher from St. Marys glistened with sweat throughout the service. He did not know Robert Stafford and, thus, said only the most general things one says at a funeral. Without fanfare, beneath the live oak tree in the corner of the graveyard, Robert's hastily made casket was lowered into the ground. No one sang. The preacher prayed, asked the people to join him in reciting the twenty-third psalm, and it was over. Eighty-seven years of Robert Stafford's life ended with inelegant simplicity and without love.

THE NIECES AND NEPHEWS SHOOK HANDS with the Clubbs and Bunkleys and consumed the food Cumsie and Zabette had prepared. After the women washed and put away all the dishes, John Tomkins assembled the servants in the parlor.

"My brother and cousins have talked about what we want to do with Mr. Stafford's property out here," he began. "We understand that we're his heirs, but none of us want to live on Cumberland, so we're probably goin' to sell his property out here." It sounded as though they had all discussed the matter long before Robert's death. The parlor shadows were growing longer as the sun began to sink lower in the sky. Zabette watched, distracted, as dust moats floated on the sun rays that still penetrated the room.

"I know y'all have served my uncle faithfully in recent years, and we want to do what's right by you. First of all, we're goin' to give each of you twenty dollars," he said with what he thought was magnanimity. The little group gathered in the parlor listened and said nothing, though some of them nodded.

"Cumsie," he began again, "I know you're a right good cook, and if you'd like to move over to St. Marys and cook for my wife and me, we'd be proud to have you. There's not much work here on the island, I hear."

Cumsie looked at Henry and he at her. "I'll think on it, and I 'preciate the offer," she said politely but without warmth.

"Catherine," he said, "I know you have people in St. Marys, so I don't expect you'll have any problem finding work over there, maybe even cleanin' for my brother or my cousins' families. Lots of people need housekeepers."

She pressed her lips together and nodded.

"Henry, we need somebody out here to oversee the place until we find a buyer, so if you're willin'... we'd like to keep you on at whatever Mr. Stafford was payin' you. Would you be willin' to do that?" asked Tomkins.

"I reckon," he answered obligingly.

"And finally, Zabette," said Tomkins. "I know your situation was a little... " he hesitated, "special. And I know you took good care of my uncle till he died. You can stay on here, in the cook's cabin, without payin' rent, of course, till we sell the property. After that I can't promise anything, but I'm hopin' my uncle may have made some provision for you. I just don't know right now."

Zabette nodded like the others. She remembered Robert's promises to leave her an annuity, but whether he had done so, she could only wait and see.

"Now once more, I want to say thank you for all you folks did for Uncle Robert over the years, and if you ever need references, you can count on our family to provide 'em. Now, Cumsie, you jus' let me know what you decide."

"Aw right," she replied noncommittally.

The awkward scene ended, and the servants were dismissed. Zabette knew that Cumsie, who had become a fine cook over the years, would never leave Henry to work for the Tomkins, not at any price. But she wouldn't talk about it in front of the others.

Zabette was relieved to know she would not have to leave her cottage just yet. She looked around the parlor one last time. It was spotless except for the sand on the rug that had been tracked in from the graveyard on the feet of the bereaved. She wondered who would clean the rug now. She wondered, in fact, what would become of the rug and all the furniture. The round table at the end of the sofa had a few scratches on the legs where Armand and Bobby had played. She remembered tea parties with Mary Elizabeth on the coffee table. This had been her home once. But it no longer was. She had said goodbye to the Big House—long before and without regret.

"Zabette," called Jack, who had been chatting with some field hands passing by on the road, while he waited for his sister. He walked over to the cabin door, where she waited for him.

"I don' know what you gone have to do now," he said, "but I want you to know that you can come live wit' me and my fam'ly as long as you want."

"Thank you, Jack," she said, giving him a hug. "I really 'preciate that, but Mr. Tomkins said I can stay on here for a while."

"Well, you jes' know that if you needs a place to go, you got one."

Her heart filled with love for this brother she had hardly known growing up. He looked so much like their father that it was uncanny. But he sounded like their mother, with the rhythms of her voice and her generosity.

"I'm sure I'll be fine, but y'all come see me when you can," she said. "I mean that."

"We will, Zabette, and I want you to come up an' see us at Brickhill. We always got plenty o' room." Only two rooms, she knew, but they were her people and would make room for anyone who needed a place. She remembered how, when her mother was sent to a one-room cabin in the quarters, the family somehow found room for her and for little Jack when he arrived. Their cabins were like their hearts. There was always room for one more.

News of Stafford's death took its time to reach Connecticut. All of Zabette's daughters wrote letters of condolence after several weeks. They were clearly pleased at their inheritance, which included all of Robert Stafford's considerable property in Connecticut and elsewhere in New England.

Mary wrote the longest letter. Her father's estate in Connecticut, she boasted, amounted to more than four hundred thousand dollars. "The younger girls plan to travel," she wrote, "but I haven't been feeling too well of late and I also have a small son, so I shall probably not accompany them." Zabette knew that she had divorced Frederick Palmer in 1874, the year after little Roberta died of scarlet fever, and that five months later she had remarried a Yale-educated doctor. This letter was the first Zabette had learned of her new grandson. "He was born seventeen months ago and is a precious little child with blond curls. I'm sorry Papa never got to see him." Mary had changed little over the years.

Nine weeks passed before Zabette finally received a letter from Augustus Brandegee, explaining to her the terms of the annuity Robert had left her. She would receive $300 a year for the rest of her life, he informed her. "I hope that this small annuity will help to make your life easier. You have my sincere sympathy in your loss," he wrote. It was not a princely sum, by any means, but if she were frugal, grew most of her own food, and bought only the essentials, she could scrape by. At least it would relieve her of the worry of utter poverty in her old age.

Zabette was fifty-seven years old now, and while she could no doubt find a job cleaning or cooking for someone, few people on the island needed such services, except perhaps for the Clubbs' hotel at the north end. She was determined not to leave Cumberland. Ever again. She would find some way to survive. That is, after all, what life had taught her to do best.

Chapter Forty-Three

APRIL 4, 1885

Supper was over. Ben and Zabette moved the rocking chairs out onto the tiny front porch and then rubbed their arms and necks with the myrtle leaves Zabette crushed to keep away mosquitoes and no-see-ums.

"That was a mighty good supper, Zabette." Ben patted his stomach in satisfaction. She had fixed all his favorites—fried chicken, rice and gravy, turnip greens, and stewed tomatoes.

She thanked him and smiled into the darkness. She didn't light the kerosene lamp because she knew it would attract insects. But the moon was bright enough to make out Ben's face and to see the silhouettes of Spanish moss that swayed in the trees.

It was always good to have Ben across the table. He complemented the coziness of the little house. She had moved into her mother's old cabin on the edge of the orchard earlier that year when the Carnegies bought all the Stafford lands. They had built a brand-new and even larger mansion on the site of the Dungeness ruins, but kept the old name. When they had asked Zabette to vacate the cook's cottage at Planters House, her mother's cabin was the only place she could go and have her own home. Jack had long since vacated it and moved his family up to the Settlement farther north where so many freedmen had bought an acre or two of land and were building houses. People in the community were even collecting money to build a new church. For now, though, Sunday services were still held in the modest church Robert had built so many years ago or sometimes under the live oak trees at the site proposed for the new place of worship.

She supposed one day the Carnegies, as their family grew, might build another fancy mansion near her grandmother's old house, for the location of the rundown tabby house was one of the most beautiful on the island. Then she might have to move again. But for now, they didn't seem to mind her living in the cabin as long as she didn't bother anybody and occasionally sent them a jar of plum jelly, a dozen or so of the brown eggs her chickens laid, or one of the sweetgrass baskets she wove to occupy her time. Cumsie, who now cooked for the Carnegie family, carried these offerings for her to Dungeness. Zabette had become quite accomplished at basket-making, copying the old designs worked out long ago in some African village, passed down to her mother, and now to her. Her mother had tried to teach her, but more recently, Amanda had shown her how to start a basket and how to bind the sweetgrass with strips of saw palmetto just the right thickness to be pliable and yet strong enough to hold the strands intact.

BEN AND ZABETTE SAT FOR A LONG TIME side by side, saying nothing, just letting their minds drift as they listened to the night air filled with chirping crickets, croaking frogs, and the deep bellow of an alligator calling for a mate in a nearby pond. They watched the lightning bugs and stars move slowly, each at their own pace, through the openings between the branches of the live oak trees. One of the openings framed the Big Dipper—the drinking gourd, they'd called it in slavery times, when it had pointed the way north for anyone who had the courage to try to escape. Zabette rocked, enjoying the easy rhythm of the night and the comfortable presence of Ben beside her.

He came to supper at least once or twice a week, and on Sundays she sometimes went up to his house for dinner. He had finally talked James Clubb into selling him a half-acre plot not too far from the family's hotel, now called High Point House, so that he could be close by when the horses needed shoeing. With the help of friends, Jack included, he'd built a three-room house with a kitchen, a bedroom, and a sitting room. But so far, he had not been able to talk Zabette into marrying him and moving in.

As they sat together, she began to hum softly the simple melody of the hymn they had sung at Sunday worship, "Amazing Grace." She sang in the choir now and listened hungrily as Reverend Lockett told them with such passion and enthusiasm about the grace and love of God. She could see the preacher even now in his dark suit, his well-worn Bible in his hand, sweat dripping down his face. His voice grew louder and more rhythmic in response to the shouts of "Yes, Jesus," and "Praise the Lord" from members of the congregation giving assent and encouragement to his words. It was the focal point of her week, when the entire community came together to sing and pray and simply commune with one another.

Zabette was keenly aware that Ben's deep bass had joined in her humming and was following the rhythms she had learned so well from Sister Trimings and Cumsie—Sister Commodore as she was called at church—who stood beside her in the choir. Zabette had never known such peace as she felt here in her cabin on the edge of the plum orchard with Ben beside her, their wordless voices blending like two notes of the same chord, yet each going its own way in unexpected and inexplicable harmony. The final words of her favorite verse passed through her mind, "And grace will lead me home."

I am *home*, she thought, her gaze drifting out over the plum trees gone almost wild, their blossoms pale and fragrant in the moonlight. God's grace had protected her throughout her life's journey and brought her back here where she was meant to be. This corner of the world He had given into her care. She had done what she could to revive the orchard, pruning back dead branches and trying to keep the island's wild horses and deer from chewing on the lower branches, a task that proved almost impossible. But she still gathered enough fruit each spring to make her jams and jellies, and the flowers of her grandmother's garden thrived in her tending.

For Zabette it was a joy to depend on the land and in some small way to have it depend on her. The annuity Robert had left her was not much, but it was enough to sustain her with essentials. The money arrived promptly by mail packet each January, and she was able to buy supplies—rice, coffee, bolts of cloth to make her clothes, not very different from the sturdy clothing she used to help make for the slaves at Planters House. Sometimes she even splurged on flowered calico to make herself a Sunday dress or on a bonnet to keep the sun out of her eyes. Everything else she needed came from her own garden's neat rows of sweet corn, beans, and squash, from the henhouse out back, or from the island waterways' abundant supply of oysters and fish.

The melody ended. They sat quietly again, unspeaking, just listening to the sounds of the spring night. Suddenly Ben broke the silence, "Zabette, when you gone marry me? We ain't gettin' no younger, y' know. And I'm tired of livin' by myself." Ben's wife had died more than a decade earlier, and his two sons and daughter had long since married and started raising their own families.

"I loves you, Zabette, an' we ain't got a lotta time left. I needs you, and I wants you to b'long to me, as my wife."

"Now, Ben," she replied quickly. "We done talked 'bout all this lots of times. I just ain't sure I ever want to belong to anybody again." Over the years she had adapted her speech to the special cadence and flow of the island dialect she had heard as a child. There was a music in it that wrapped around her and drew her into the community and closer to Ben.

"Yeh, I been thinkin' 'bout what you said 'bout belongin'. I been studyin' on it, and I'm thinkin' that they's different ways to belong. Belongin' to a church or to people, where ever'body love you and take you in, tha's a good thing, a good kind of belongin'. That ain't the same as belongin' to somebody like a slave. I jes' wants to take you in and love you. I wants us to belong to each other. You to me and me to you."

"Oh, Ben," she said, leaning forward to put her arms around him. He always knew just what to say. And he was right, of course. What concerned Zabette was the matter of belonging by legal contract, which marriage implied. She had often thought about the words that her friend Betsy Copp had carried about in her drawstring purse: "In order that she may be able to give her hand with dignity, she must be able to stand alone." Before she felt worthy of marriage, Zabette wanted to be sure that she *could* stand alone and that she would be giving herself to Ben and becoming his wife for all the right reasons. She knew she was close now, independent, free in every sense of the word. She felt she *had* learned over these recent years to stand alone. But marriage, she believed, had to be a union of two equals, and she wanted to be sure she was prepared.

Belonging. It was complicated and simple at the same time. She belonged to Cumberland, to Plum Orchard, and it belonged to her—not legally as it did to the Carnegies. It might never belong to them as it did to her. They came and went, spending part of their time in Pittsburgh and part of it on the island. They'd bought not only Robert Stafford's old lands, but Phineas Nightingale's as well. They owned the title to Dungeness. But they did not belong to Cumberland, not yet, any more than it belonged to them. Only time could make you belong to a place or a place to you—time and love. It was the same with people, she thought. Belonging—at least the right kind of belonging, the kind that Ben described— had nothing to do with legal papers.

Zabette knew that she would be buried here, that she would be absorbed into the very soil of the island, as her mother and grandmother had been. She had borne all but one of her children here. The sands of Cumberland had collected her tears, and the trees of the orchard still echoed on windy days with her mother's singing. The crumbling steps of the Plum Orchard Big House, where no one had lived for many years, were worn with her grandmother's footsteps. And she still tended the roses Marguerite had planted in the garden overlooking the river. She and Plum Orchard were so much a part of one another that she could no longer imagine her existence elsewhere. That's what belonging meant. She knew that she and Ben loved each other. She was closer to him than she had ever been to anyone else. But the belonging he described could come only with time, shared memories, and a mutual sense of having no existence one apart from the other. A piece of paper would not ensure it. That was an act of faith.

"Promise me that you'll think on it, Zabette," he whispered, pulling her closer.

"I promise, Ben. I truly promise," she said, returning his embrace.

She enjoyed her freedom to wake up in the morning to the bright call of the lark, to stretch her body, aging though it was, and know that the day was hers. She would sit on her front porch with her cup of coffee feeling the sun on her face and watching the wild turkeys forage in the grass. Sometimes she would walk over to the beach and wade in the warm surf, laughing at the sanderlings scurrying along the water's edge and remembering how she and Mary Elizabeth used to chase them, though they could never be caught. Sometimes she would go to Brickhill and spend an afternoon quilting with Amanda, who was teaching her the art. One of the quilts they made together, each patch of cloth holding a special memory, now covered her bed. She spent an occasional afternoon visiting the graves of her mother, her father, and her grandmother whose bodies were now part of the earth of Cumberland. And sometimes she just wandered in the orchard or through her grandmother's garden, breathing in the heady scent of the plum blossoms or roses and thinking about her children.

She still heard from them once in a while, and she still grieved for Armand, whose ambrotype sat on the table by her bed, for Bobby, and most recently for Mary, who had died of tuberculosis five years ago now. She wondered what had become of the children Mary had left behind, precious Mellie and the tiny son with the impressive sounding name of Robert Horace Gaylord, the grandson Zabette had never met. Mary sent her a picture of him when he was only three years old, a solemn-faced child with light blond curls and the same sober look in his eyes as in his mother's. Zabette treasured the picture and had asked Jack, now making his living as an expert cobbler, to make a leather frame for it. It sat on the table next to the image of Armand. She had written to Mary's husband to offer her sympathies and ask about the children after Mr. Brandegee informed her of Mary's death, but he had not replied.

Zabette's children had belonged to her once, but now they were no longer hers—not in the way they once had been. Those who survived had created independent lives. Pretty Ellen now lived in New York and was married to a man named Benjamin Brady. Medora had moved to London, and Addie had accompanied Ellen to New York and then, after Ellen married, accomplished her lifelong dream of moving to Paris.

Zabette smiled to remember Addie's pride in her French medals and to see where they had led her. She would never forget the day she went to pick up her mail, which she did once or twice a month, and there was a large, fancy-looking envelope with an elegant crest on the back. It was from Addie, a formal printed notice announcing the "wedding of Adelaide Clarice Stafford, daughter of the late Robert Stafford," to the Count Charles Cybulski at the Cathedral of Notre Dame in Paris. Addie had also enclosed a newspaper clipping for her mother that described the bride as "tall, lithe, graceful, with olive-tinted skin and lustrous eyes" and her husband as a "Russian diplomat." But the little hand-written note that she found tucked inside the envelope meant more than anything to Zabette, and she kissed the piece of paper where it said, "I wish you could have been there. *Je t'aime, Maman,* Addie."

Tucking the note into her pocket, Zabette laughed to think how delighted the Carnegies would be to welcome the Count and Countess Cybulski into their drawing rooms, though they would never welcome the countess's mother, one of Robert Stafford's former slaves.

She raced back to Brickhill to show the announcement to Amanda.

"You'll never guess what's happened!" she exclaimed.

Amanda looked up from her sewing and asked "Wha's that?"

"Addie married a count!" Zabette told her.

"Lawd, ha' mercy. This be a crazy world, I reckon." Amanda chuckled.

The entire community embraced the news with light-hearted cheerfulness, and, once the news reached the Settlement, one of the younger men, Jesse Bailey, tapped a keg of home-brewed beer to help them all celebrate. It was no longer just Zabette's news. It was the community's news, the community's pride. The community to which she now belonged.

BEN'S VOICE BROKE INTO HER THOUGHTS. "I reckon it's gettin' late. I best be gettin' on home," he said.

It was dark, and Zabette hated the idea of his heading out onto the long, empty road with his wagon and team of mules and only a kerosene lantern to light the way. But the mules knew the route by heart. He'd be fine unless a raccoon or a bobcat startled them and caused them to bolt. Still, she always worried until she saw him again.

"Now you promise me you'll think on it, Zabette," he reminded her. "We ain't got forever, y' know. You gots to make up your mind."

"I know, Ben." He held her in his arms, kissed her lips gently at first, and then more urgently as her body responded. When he finally tore himself away, Zabette felt he'd ripped away a part of herself. They may not be young anymore, but the old urges were still intact for both of them. Her heart was full to overflowing. "You know I love you, Ben," she whispered.

"And I loves you, Zabette. And you know deep down we belong together," he said in a husky voice.

Yes. She did know. Yes. All at once, certainty bubbled up within her. After all these years, she couldn't bear the thought of his driving away tonight. She wanted to hold him close, to sleep in the warm curve of his arms and to awaken tomorrow morning and every morning for the rest of her life with him by her side. She knew he found her to be a beautiful woman despite her sixty-four years. He had told her so many times. But he had also made it clear that it was more than her physical beauty that attracted him. It was the same for her. He was still a good-looking man, but it was his spirit, his character, his inner fineness that she loved most.

They belonged together—the way a man and a woman could belong to each other for all eternity. Suddenly it was all so clear. Why had it taken her so long to decide? This was why she had come home—where God had sent her to rediscover the only place on earth she wanted to be and to find the only man she'd ever wanted to belong to. Their years would be few perhaps, but they would be rich in love.

"I reckon you just needs to love me more," Ben said, as he climbed onto the wagon seat without seeing Zabette's eyes now full with tears.

"You know what, Ben Freeman," she said, "It's just not possible that I could love you more. I'm so filled with it already. Now you get down from there and come on back inside. We got a lot of plans to make." Her arms were open.

A smile of understanding broke across his face. She didn't have to say it twice.

Epilogue

CUMBERLAND ISLAND, MAY 24, 1886

The boy tugged on the kitten's tail. It struggled to get away, but its small body was not strong enough to elude his grasp. Its claws were still too soft to scratch deep enough to cause him pain. He laughed, picking up the tiny animal, tawny and striped like a tiger. "That big wind is gonna blow you away," he said, turning round and round, faster and faster, swinging in a circle the kitten he still held by the tail and making the whooshing sound of the wind. He was thinking of a story he had heard from Cumsie about Brer Rabbit fooling Brer Tiger into letting him tie him to a tree so he wouldn't blow away. The terrified animal clawed frantically at the air and yowled in painful protest.

"Put that kitten down, little boy." He heard the command before he saw where it had come from. There was no room for negotiation in the voice approaching from the dock, where a supply boat from Fernandina had just arrived. Used to obeying stern commands from his father, the boy dropped the animal, which streaked off into the palmettos.

When he turned to face the voice, expecting punishment, he was surprised to see a woman, her long skirts brushing the sandy road. She was not young. Her hair showed streaks of gray. Her face was tanned, and he could see flecks of gold in her dark flashing eyes. She freed an arm by shifting the large bundle she was carrying to her side, crooked her elbow and set her hand with determination on her hip. She was tall and erect, vigorous for her age, and she looked as if she would brook no nonsense.

"What's your name?" she asked.

"Cole . . . Coleman Carnegie," the boy said reluctantly.

"How old you be?"

"Seven."

"You live down there at Dungeness, don't you?"

He nodded.

"Didn't your mama and daddy ever teach you not to hurt little critters that can't help themselves?"

"I guess so," he said, staring at the ground, afraid to look up at the accusing eyes. He didn't see the flash of anger soften and disappear as the woman sought a way to make the child understand.

"Tha's what I thought. And you old enough to remember. That kitten is just a baby," she said. "Its mama died and can't protect it no more. Now you think about that. What if your mama wasn't there to protect you? And don't you hurt that kitten no more, y' hear?"

He knew the truth of her words. The thin motherless cat had hung out at the dock for days, mewing and rubbing up against the legs of anyone who would give it a bite of food.

"Yes, ma'am," he replied. His parents had taught him to say "ma'am" when he was in the South. His first instinct had been to run away, back to safety behind the forbidding stone entrance to Dungeness. He knew he wasn't supposed to be out here all by himself without his older brother, Tommy. But now he felt rooted to the spot.

"You think about it. S'pose you was that kitten and lost your mama. How would you want to be treated?"

The boy hung his head and felt his bottom lip begin to quiver. "I'm sorry," he said, scuffing the toe of one shoe in the sand.

"Now you remember to be nice to critters that need your help. Don't you be mean no more." He sensed a sudden kindness in the voice.

"Yes, ma'am." The boy looked up now, cautiously, to gaze into a pair of warm brown eyes and at a face that was beginning to smile at him. She nodded and turned toward the Main Road that led to the north end of the island.

The boy watched for a moment as she shifted the bundle to her other hip and moved on with simple and natural grace. He saw, approaching from the opposite direction, a wagon pulled by two mules, with a black man driving. The wagon stopped when it reached the woman. The man got out, took the bundle from the woman's arms, and put it in the back of the wagon, while she climbed up onto the seat. He got up on the other side and leaned over to kiss her on the lips. She laid her head on his shoulder and slipped her hand through the crook of his arm as he turned the team around to head north again.

The boy wondered who she was. He couldn't remember ever seeing her before. No one had ever spoken to him like that except for his parents. As he watched the wagon move on in the distance, he was suddenly aware of a slight movement in the palmettos near his feet. A furry head looked out and mewed loudly. He squatted down on the edge of the road.

"Here, kitty, kitty. I didn't mean to hurt you." He held out his hand toward the kitten, which shied away in distrust—unlike the first time he had seen it when it wrapped itself around his ankles, purring.

The boy didn't move. Finally the cat stepped out from behind the palmetto fronds and approached his outstretched hand with cautious, forgiving curiosity. The boy let it lick his fingers with its rough tongue. Then he opened his hand slowly and gently scooped up the soft animal, cuddling it against his body and stroking its head. The kitten began to purr.

"Let's go see if we can find you some milk," he murmured to the cat as he turned in the opposite direction from the woman and man, who were already out of sight. With the kitten tucked safely in his arms, he hurried through the stately stone gateway toward Dungeness.

AUTHOR'S NOTE

The Plum Orchard of the title is not the sumptuous mansion of the same name that visitors see today on Cumberland Island. That structure was built in 1898 for George Lauder Carnegie. The modest ruins of the tabby house originally called Plum Orchard and owned by the Bernardeys lie just to the north on what today is private property not open to tourists. The original Dungeness, which suffered from fire and almost two decades of neglect after the Civil War, was demolished in early 1882 by the family of Thomas Carnegie. Two years later the Carnegies began construction of a sumptuous new mansion, also called Dungeness, the ruins of which are visible to tourists today. The church about to be built at the end of the book is the First African Baptist Church founded in 1893, where John Kennedy Jr. and Carolyn Bessette were married in 1996.

The story of Elisabeth Bernardey and Robert Stafford is in its essence true. Even the names of the enslaved characters come from the Cumberland Island slave lists of the era. This book, however, makes no claims to being history. It is historical fiction in which the spoken words, motivations, emotions, and personalities that propel the action and drive the characters are of my own invention. The first name of Pierre Bernardey's father is thus far unknown, though I have chosen to call him Jacques. The only purely fictional characters in the book are the Scarritts, who are modeled after far too many slave owners, and Ben Freeman, who allowed me to give Zabette a happy ending.

It is true that Robert Stafford sent his children north to be educated, permitted Zabette to join them, and built for them an Italianate mansion like the one I describe on the outskirts of Groton. Armand was indeed wounded in the battle of Port Hudson and died following the Civil War. Betsey and

Belton Copp were real people, as were Augustus Brandegee and Phineas Nightingale. Even some of the details of the story that may seem most unlikely are true. Zabette's daughter, Adelaide Clarice, did become a countess when she married Russian diplomat Count Cybulski at Notre-Dame Cathedral in Paris. And Nanette Stafford, despite my fictional Robert's skepticism, went on to Howard University and became a doctor, later practicing her profession at the University of Zurich in Switzerland. Even Zabette's reprimand of the Carnegie child at the end of the novel is based on an actual incident.

Although I have on very rare occasions altered the order of events for dramatic effect, I have made every effort not to falsify information that could be verified. The wording of Marguerite's will and her legal transfer of ownership of Zabette to Robert Stafford are taken from actual documents, as is the wording of Stafford's offer to buy Dungeness. Sometimes, however, even historical sources are unclear or contradictory. For example, significantly different dates are recorded for Armand's birth, one on his tombstone, others on military and census records. Census records themselves are contradictory. I have chosen the tombstone as most likely to be accurate. Another instance of uncertainty is the name of Robert's second mistress. Both Mary Bullard and Charles Seabrook have given her name in their printed works as Catherine Williams; however, later information contained on a web site established by Mary Bullard and based on information from Stafford descendents indicates that her name was, in fact, Judy, a name that indeed appears among Robert's Rayfield slaves. Thus, the latter version seems to me more probable, and Judy is the name I have chosen to use.

Like all historical novelists, I am deeply indebted to scholars and historians who have done so much excellent research in bringing to light the essential outline of the lives in question, of uncovering sources, found for the most part in public repositories or collections in various archives mostly in Georgia and Connecticut, that document these facts. At least three books of Cumberland history record the basic events of this story. The one that has been most helpful in setting forth the facts and revealing the documentary sources is that of Cumberland Island historian, Mary Bullard, *Robert Stafford of Cumberland Island: Growth of a Planter*, originally published by the author in 1986 and reprinted as a Brown Thrasher Book by the University of Georgia Press in

1995. Bullard also discusses the lives of Robert and Zabette in a somewhat briefer version in *Cumberland Island: A History* (University of Georgia Press, 2003), as does Charles Seabrook in his book entitled *Strong Women, Wild Horses: The Story of Cumberland Island* (John F. Blair Publisher, 2002). For readers who would like to know more about the actual history of the people in question, I urge them to consult these excellent sources.

I am also grateful to the late Patricia Jones-Jackson for her book *When Roots Die: Endangered Traditions on the Sea Islands* (University of Georgia Press, 1987), seeking to preserve the Gullah-Geechee folk tales, language, and social structure of coastal African Americans in South Carolina and Georgia. Although I have tried to give some flavor of island speech among the black characters of my book, I have modified it to make it easier for most twenty-first century readers, who would likely find the language a bit daunting. Cornelia Walker Bailey's book *God, Dr. Buzzard, and the Bolito Man* (Doubleday, 2000), which tells of the generations of her family's life on Sapelo Island, Georgia, just a few islands north of Cumberland, has also helped to enrich my work. The wonderful performances of the Sea Island Singers of Saint Simons Island, Georgia, influenced my description of Adeline's broom-jumping ceremony. I am also grateful to have attended the February 2008 conference in Savannah on "The Atlantic World and African American Life and Culture in the Georgia Lowcountry, 18th to the 20th Century," sponsored by the Ossabaw Island Foundation. It was an extraordinary opportunity to learn more about the Gullah-Geechee heritage in the area from both scholars and descendents. These are but a few of the ongoing efforts to preserve the rich traditions of a rapidly disappearing culture before they are lost to us forever.

I would especially like to thank Jamie Ferguson, a Carnegie descendent whose family still lives at Greyfield, now an inn, built in 1900 on the old Spring Plantation that once belonged to John Grey, for giving me a personal tour of parts of Cumberland Island not open to tourists. Among the many sites we visited on the north end of the island were the ruins of the original Plum Orchard, Planters House, and the surrounding plantation sites—including the remains of the slave quarters, the hospital, and the cemetery where Robert Stafford, his mother, and sister are buried, as well as the First African Baptist Church. Our excursion allowed me to visualize and describe with greater accuracy events and locations in the book. I am also grateful to Ron Messier, who accompanied us on the tour, for the wonderful photographs he took that day, one of which appears on the cover of this book.

The story of Zabette is quintessentially a story of the South. While it may reflect the ambivalence of biracial descendents about their ancestry and the place of their birth, it also suggests the complex relationships between the races in this geographical area. Zabette is above all a woman like all women, regardless of color, who must discover their identities in a world where nothing is simple, where loyalties are often divided, even fragmented, but where they seek among the fragments only unity, harmony, and love.

ACKNOWLEDGMENTS

I want to thank the following people for reading all or part of this manuscript at various points during its creation and for their valuable suggestions: Emily Messier, Mimi Thomas, Susan Ashley Michael, Debbie Conner, Kathleen Ferris, Margaret Ordoubadian, B.J. Chrisman, members of the Murfreesboro Writers Group, and especially my editor and friend, Michelle Adkerson. And, above all, to Dick Gleaves, my wonderful husband, who passed beyond this world shortly before the publication of this book, I would like to pay a special tribute for being my sounding board, for listening so patiently to versions of my chapters and never falling asleep, even on a third reading, and for loving me anyway. I will miss him.

QUESTIONS FOR BOOK GROUPS

1. How does the story of Marie-Jeanne's mother, whose name we never learn, replay itself for the next two generations?

2. Why does Pierre buy Marie-Jeanne? And why does he send her away? In the end, what do you think of Pierre? Do you consider him a "good" character or a "bad" character?

3. Why does Amanda resent Zabette when she first comes to Planters House? How does Zabette win her over? What do these situations tell us about human nature?

4. What events or factors in Robert's life make him into the man he becomes by the end of the book? Does he have choices?

5. Discuss Zabette's relationships with her children. Is Robert right or wrong to send them to Connecticut?

6. Discuss the changes in Mary Elizabeth that take place in the course of the book. Why do you think her choices are so different from those of her mother?

7. What does the role of misunderstanding play in the unfolding of this novel? Can such misunderstandings occur in real life? If so, what can we do to avoid them?

8. Critics have often identified a "sense of place" as a predominant characteristic of the southern novel. Does a sense of place play a role in *Plum Orchard*? How? Is a sense of place important to you as an individual? Do you think it is more important to a southerner than to any other American?

9. Can you think of any reason why the author would choose "Jacques" as the name (still unknown) of Pierre's father?

10. How does the role of the Irish servants in Connecticut differ from the role of the enslaved workers in Georgia? Think of the question from the point of view of the servant/slave and from that of the boss/master. How is Zabette's role ambivalent in both worlds?

11. In what ways does Betsey Copp compare slavery to a wife's role in 19th-century America? Do you agree or disagree that there are similarities? How do the two roles differ? What importance does economic independence have in any relationship?

12. Does Zabette's leaving her children in Connecticut to return to Cumberland surprise you? Would you have made that decision?

13. Do you understand Zabette's loyalty to Robert after she learns of his betrayal with Judy? On what is it based?

14. How does the concept of "belonging" shape Zabette's life? What must she learn in order to reinterpret that concept? What does the term mean to you?

15. What do you think the author seeks to convey by including the scene with the child Cole Carnegie and the kitten at the end of the book?

ABOUT THE AUTHOR

JUNE HALL McCASH was named Georgia Author of the Year in 2011 for her first novel, *Almost to Eden*. She is also the author of three nonfiction books about Jekyll Island, all published by the University of Georgia Press. In addition, she has published three books and numerous articles about the Middle Ages. She holds a doctorate in comparative literature from Emory University and has been a fellow of both the National Endowment for the Humanities and the American Council on Education, as well as a trustee of the Jekyll

Photo by Richard D. Gleaves

Island Foundation. She was the recipient of awards for teaching, research, and career achievement during her tenure as a professor at Middle Tennessee State University and of an Outstanding Alumna Award from Agnes Scott College. In addition she has won other awards for her fiction, nonfiction, and poetry. Now a full-time writer, she divides her time between homes in Murfreesboro, Tennessee, and Jekyll Island, Georgia. She is currently working on her next book, a nonfiction work entitled *A Titanic Love Story: Ida and Isidor Straus*, to be published by Mercer University Press.

CPSIA information can be obtained at www.ICGtesting.com
Printed in the USA
LVOW120255111012

302247LV00002B/24/P